LEX DE MORTUIS

DIVISION ZERO
BOOK TWO

MATTHEW S. COX

DIVISION ZERO PRESS

Lex De Mortuis

Book 2 of the Division Zero series.
Second Edition

Original © 2014 by Matthew S. Cox
Revised edition © 2018

ISBN: 978-1-949174-14-4 (Ebook)

ISBN: 978-1-949174-17-5 (Paperback)

CONTENTS

WRAITH

Ominous shadows hung in the windows of a freestanding house, squares of infinity amid flashing chaos. A vibrating nimbus of red and blue glowed upon the building's white face. Two Division 1 patrol craft and a MedVan sat at the edge of a cul-de-sac, invading the lawn in a district full of suburban houses that offered a glimpse of the pre-war world.

Kirsten steered in to land near the cluster of vehicles. The cobalt blue of her patrol craft's bar lights added to the veneer of color on the house, tinting it purple in snap flashes. A creaking groan came from the wheels absorbing the armored patrol craft's weight. She shoved the gull wing door up, allowing a blast of freezing air inside. As soon as she emerged from the car, a wave of oppressive dark energy coming from the house stunned her motionless, her breath frosting in small clouds.

Oh, shit. Something bad *is in there.*

Her Division 0 blacks didn't provide enough protection from the cold this near the northeastern edge of the sector map. Though the elevated city surface stopped twenty miles south, the political boundary of West City kept going for another ten sectors.

She glanced at her left armband display: thirty degrees Fahrenheit. Merely looking at the two innocuous digits made the wind on her thighs feel colder. She let go of the door, which sank closed, and took a step toward the house while surveying the scene.

Dorian coalesced at her side.

Normally, only the wealthy could afford to live in homes built upon the natural ground, but the paranoia of the Badlands made this area an exception. People who dwelled here expected the occasional bioengineered horror or rogue cyborg to wander in. However, what had befallen this house, few even believed real.

At least with the ever-present danger of Badlands wanderers, no street gangs came around here. Humanity's need for violence channeled itself into local militias, non-governmental groups who patrolled the border against whatever might wander in.

"Funny how that works," said Dorian.

Kirsten glanced at him.

"Out in the Badlands, armed people guard the walls with guns. We're not as far removed as we think. Civilization is an illusion."

She exhaled into her hands, trying to warm sensation back into her fingers. "Nice houses here, though—except for that one. Practically mansions."

"These would've been considered 'middle class' before the war. Normal homes are expensive because we now cram a hundred people into the same space. One little house takes up the same amount of land as a slice of high-rise."

The panicky wails of a small child came from the MedVan, mingling with the continuous soft howl of distant wind. Kirsten glared at the house, but the windows darkened as if something didn't want her to see inside.

For a moment, it seemed as if the house itself *stared* at her

One patrol officer stood near the front door beside a glowing apparition of a headless woman missing her arms below the elbows and her legs below the knees. Kirsten drew a breath to gasp, but didn't sense any paranormal energy from her. She blinked, took a step closer, and realized the officer spoke to a living woman in a plain white sleep suit that only appeared to glow in the glare from all the police vehicles colored lights. In contrast to the pure white fabric, her brown skin blended into the night. Kirsten exhaled in relief that the woman hadn't died.

A woman in a white medtech jumpsuit hurried over. Small flashlights mounted to her shoulders illuminated the woman's upper body, revealing jagged scratches on her cheek and small, bloody handprints on the shoulders of the sleep suit. The medtech pulled a silver wand-like device from her belt and held it to the scratches, sealing them one by one.

Kirsten approached with one hand on her stunrod to keep it from tapping her thigh. The woman pleaded in Spanish: with the police, with God, with nothing in particular, for an explanation of why her daughter went crazy. The patrol officer's confidence shrank as soon as he saw Kirsten's black uniform.

"What's the situation?" Kirsten asked the officer before switching to Spanish. "Calm down, ma'am. I am here to help."

"Got a juvenile female, age six, in the MedVan. The techs are checking her out now. Unprovoked psychotic episode. The girl went crazy and did a number on her mother's face."

"It wasn't unprovoked." Kirsten eyed the house.

The woman gathered herself, answering in English. "Something's gotten into my daughter, Maia. I don't think the police can help us. Are you a priest?"

Kirsten stifled her urge to roll her eyes. "Priests can't help. Can you tell me what happened?"

"We moved here a few weeks ago to get away from the city. Maia right away started fussing. Whenever we were inside the house, she was quiet, moody, and later, angry. Outside, she seemed happy, like she normally is. The bad dreams started the first night. These past weeks, she's become worse every night. Tonight, she woke screaming and ran out of the house." The woman pointed out of the cul-de-sac at the road. "She went down the street. I found her in a neighbor's yard. When I tried to take her inside, the crazy took her."

"Kid went ballistic, kicking and slapping. She scratched her mother's face bloody to get away. She did *not* want to go back in that house." The officer gestured with his head toward the MedVan. "The kid seems calm now. The medtechs were ready to sedate her, but as soon as they carried her away from the house she became completely docile. All the brain scans came back clean. Kid just keeps yelling '*El diablo está ahí.*' That's why we called you in."

Once she finished repairing the scratches on the woman's cheek, the medtech squeezed the handle of the toothbrush-sized wand and the green light at the narrow end went dark. She twirled it over her finger and stuffed it in its belt compartment. "That should do it, ma'am. Does anything else hurt?"

"No." The woman dabbed at her cheek with a small cloth, wiping away blood. "Thank you."

With a nod, the medtech walked off toward the MedVan.

"Officer, stay with her, don't let anyone go inside," said Kirsten. "I'm going to see what the child remembers."

She jogged after the medtech, rubbing her hands up and down her arms in a futile effort to warm up. The rear doors of the hover ambulance hung open, the interior awash with blinding white light so intense the mass of flashing red ones on the outside seemed dim.

Inside, another Division 1 officer and a medtech stood on either side of a thin girl seated on the edge of a stretcher, her legs dangling. Streaks of blood, grass, and dirt stained her pink nightgown. One bare shoulder peeked out from where the garment had ripped during her struggle to flee her mother's grasp. She swayed her feet idly while the medtech tended to her left hand.

The little girl glanced over as Kirsten climbed in, all innocence. Thick brown hair, long enough to touch the gurney, slipped off her shoulder. A rubberized thimble engulfed one of the girl's fingers, connected by thin tubes to a device mounted in the wall.

Kirsten stepped into the opening between the officer and the tech, standing right in front of the child. "Agent Wren, Division 0. Is she okay?"

Maia looked down, sniffling and trembling. Being stuck between a wall and three adults seemed to frighten her. The medtech, a short, stocky woman with a touch of grey in her hair, smiled as she continued to remove bits of skin and blood from under the child's fingernails.

"This lady will make the bad spirit go away. She's a special kind of cop." The tech spoke in soothing Spanish as she removed the finger shroud to examine a shiny new nail.

"Was she hurt?" Kirsten reached over and tugged the blanket tighter around the child.

"She detached two fingernails and broke a toe. Nothing I can't fix," said the tech, winking.

Dorian came out of the wall behind Kirsten. "There is definitely an entity in that house. As soon as I went in there, this external anger started making me want to kill someone."

She turned. "Think you can hold it together, or should I go in alone?"

"Well, if it's what I think it is, it turns inner darkness outward. I don't think it will do a damn thing to you." Dorian winked. "You're packed full of fluffy white bunnies."

Kirsten rolled her eyes.

"All you Zeroes talk to yourselves?" The Division 1 officer waved a hand over Kirsten's face.

"My partner's right there."

The patrolman chuckled. "Sure."

Kirsten squatted in front of the girl and took her hand, mimicking the medic's calming Spanish. "Hello, Maia. I'm Kirsten. I am going to get the bad thing out of your house. No one will make you go back inside until it's gone. Can you tell me what you saw?"

The child's shoulder slipped out as she shrugged it up to the side of her head. Her caramel-hued face hid behind a waterfall of black hair. When she figured the kid wasn't in a mood to talk, Kirsten adjusted the blanket snug once more and peeked into her surface thoughts. Maia feared how angry her mother would be with her so much that she couldn't talk.

"Honey, your mommy is *worried* about you. She is not angry."

Shivering, Maia looked up and whimpered in English. "I don't wanna 'member it."

The girl's thoughts leapt straight to what she tried to forget. She'd been lying in bed, head turned toward the left. Vaporous blackness exuded from under the door of a pink bedroom, gliding up along the wall and collecting at the corner of the ceiling. Malice, pure and hateful, rained down from the mass at a half-awake girl. Maia had lost control of herself to panic, certain the 'demon' wanted to kill her.

"Maia?" Kirsten patted her on the hand. "Do you see a man standing next to me, wearing the same black uniform?"

The patrol officer looked where Kirsten gestured, and crept backward.

"Umm." Maia scrunched her eyebrows together, calling Kirsten crazy with a stare.

Kirsten grinned. "Have you ever seen a ghost before?"

Maia shook her head back and forth in an exaggerated gesture, tossing her long hair around. "No, just the one in my room. He's mean."

Dorian waved a hand in front of the girl, eliciting no reaction. "The kid isn't seeing me. Whatever's in the house is visible to normal people, or at least showed itself to the girl."

Kirsten sighed. "Crap. It's a damn wraith."

Clank. The patrol officer knocked something off a table. "What, you Zeroes have categories for this bullshit?"

Sensing the look on Dorian's face, Kirsten shook her head. "Don't."

Her gaze switched to the man in blue armor. "Yeah, we do. There's simple haunts, latent apparitions, lost souls, poltergeists, phantoms, phantasms, standard ghosts, and about two dozen more. Please tell me no one went inside?"

"So, what's a wraith then?" asked the medtech, one eyebrow up. Her expression gave off genuine curiosity instead of mockery.

"Short answer? Pure malice. Usually, they're what happens when someone truly evil dies and winds up lingering. They radiate animosity and they hate anything noble or innocent," said Kirsten.

"It's going to *love* you." Dorian winked.

The Division 1 officer scratched his head. "Martinez and Long did a walk-through about ten minutes before you got here. They didn't find anything in there at all. Came out in the middle of a wicked argument about Gee-ball though... Looked like they were gonna get into a fistfight."

"They probably would have had they stayed inside that place much longer." Kirsten ruffled the girl's hair. "Give me a little while and I'll make the bad ghost go away. Can you be brave for a bit?"

The kid's flat affect didn't change.

"Aww. That usually gets me a smile."

Maia looked down at her lap, shivering.

"She's terrified," said Dorian. "If they try to take her back inside, she'll flip out again. She knows it wants to kill her."

Kirsten patted the girl's clasped hands, then stood facing the officer. "I don't want anyone attempting to take this girl inside until I declare the site clear. Maia can sense it. She will know when it's gone. I'll be the one to go back inside with her when it is safe."

Dorian flashed a crooked grin. "Wraiths often cause extreme terror in the minds of the innocent. Are you sure *you* want to go in there?"

"Very funny." She stepped to the rear doors and beckoned the mother over with a wave. "I already told you I'm not as innocent as I look." Kirsten helped the woman up into the MedVan. "Maia is worried you're angry with her. Please stay here with her while I handle this."

"All right."

Maia initially cringed from her mother's approach, but as soon as the woman scooped her into a hug and started crying, the girl burst into tears as well, clinging and apologizing.

Kirsten hopped out and nudged the doors closed so the girl and her mother didn't freeze, then fixed the house with a determined stare.

Okay. Time for you to go away.

The walls appeared to expand and contract as if the building breathed. She steeled her mind, raising a psionic defense against astral influence, and the illusion stopped.

"Going to take a little more than that to scare me off."

Kirsten frowned and held her left forearm guard up. Shimmering holographic light formed a square panel in midair above it. She accessed the police network, pulling up all records associated with this address. Over the past hundred years, the property had been involved with a large number of domestic violence calls and noise complaints, but surprisingly, no major crimes. Kirsten switched to municipal records and found the property had been listed for sale roughly every two years. Despite having a price well below market, it had gone long stints unoccupied.

"Wow," muttered Kirsten. "That woman bought this entire house for less than I pay in rent for eight months."

"You don't have Badlands combat mutants ringing your doorbell twice a month either," said Dorian.

"No." Kirsten smirked. "Just Theodore dropping by unannounced. Not sure which is more inconvenient."

He chuckled.

"This wraith is old. Possibly prewar. This house has only been here for about sixty years, but a residence had been here going back longer than our records."

Dorian rubbed a finger over his mouth. "If no major crimes happened here, either this thing is migratory or one bad dude died before the Corporate War."

"Ugh. That would make him almost four hun"—she shivered—"I don't want to think about it."

"It concerns me the mother didn't notice." Dorian advanced toward the door.

Kirsten let her arm fall. the holo-panel folded in on itself and vanished. "It may want her here, hoping to get into her head and make her..." She coughed, having choked up.

"You don't have to say it." Dorian patted her on the back.

With the image of Maia's delicate face and sad eyes fixed in her mind, Kirsten shoved the door aside. Black flames seethed at the walls in the living room, lapping at the ceiling and making the space feel many times colder. A powerful sense of evil soaked through the drywall, as obvious as water after a flood. Whispers came from beneath the floor, dread from above.

Dorian crossed the dining room area to the kitchen. Kirsten followed. Ethereal vapor spewed from spectral holes in the walls. She brushed her fingers over one, finding smooth wall.

She teased at the threads of vapor. "Bullets hit the wall here, after killing someone. But not in *this* house. In what stood here before."

He pointed at a flimsy white door past the fridge. "Sounds like they're still down there."

"Damn. I hate basements." She clasped the doorknob, gasping at the unexpected iciness in the metal, and yanked the door open. Wooden stairs led into darkness wavering with ghostly light from an unseen source.

"This house is old. Well, at least I know why they listed it so cheap."

"Yeah." Dorian touched the wall. "Paranormal discount. Her neighbors likely paid ten times the amount. And, if they extended the wall this far north, all this would become a playground for the super-rich."

Kirsten concentrated on her desire to see into the Astral realm, and her eyes lit up with white energy. Color drained out of the world, replaced by a shifting sepia-toned environment. Spectral copies of surfaces and objects wavered and flowed over reality. Division 0 called it Darksight. By opening her perception to the spirit realm, an astral sensitive could perceive the world's ethereal shadow. Mostly, it came in handy to 'see in the dark,' but it also revealed areas charged with spectral energy—like the bloody smears and handprints along the bare cinder block walls on either side of the stairwell.

Kirsten descended into the damp, musty confines of a frozen basement. A massive pool of blood covered the floor at the bottom, barely a patch or two of unpainted concrete left exposed. A man in a black windbreaker, emblazoned with DEA in large yellow letters, stood at the bottom of the stairs with his back to her. A two-inch wide hole straight through him cut out most of the E. He shook his head at a dozen Hispanic men writhing on the ground by the far wall. All had their hands bound behind their backs with plastic zip-ties, and a bullet wound in the head.

In various degrees of coherence, the men protested in Spanish about not being informants for the 'feds.'

"Well, I can take a guess what our wraith did for a living." Dorian chuckled.

Kirsten muttered, "Great. It's a four-hundred-year-old killer."

The DEA man turned, giving Kirsten a view of the entry wound responsible for the hole in his back. Blood, long ago gushed from his nose, blackened his mouth and chin. When Kirsten made eye contact, he jumped back.

"I'm sorry." She held a hand up.

"Sorry, toots. Restricted area. Crime scene," said the man.

She frowned. "My name isn't toots. It's Agent Wren. I'm with the National Police Force, Division 0."

"Huh..." He shrugged. "Never heard of it. I'm DEA Agent Fowler." He shook her hand. "Got these dozen Mexicans rounded up, but I'm not sure where Gonsalves got off to. Slippery son of a bitch. Stupid bastards think we're focusing on Mexico so much they can truck the junk in from Canada." He looked her up and down, raising an eyebrow at her clingy uniform. "Oh, wait a minute... Little early for the guys to send me a stripper. They could have waited for the after-party. The cop costume is cute, though." He winked, making a clicking noise.

Dorian turned, covering his face to hide his laughter.

"I'm not a stripper."

Agent Fowler appraised her again, brown caterpillar eyebrows creeping together. "Except for the boots, that getup of yours looks painted on. I don't recognize your insignia, and the blinking thing on your hip looks like a prop from *Star Trek*."

"I hate to break it to you, Agent Fowler, but you're not in command of this operation any more. You're dead." She pointed at his wound.

Dorian's eye appeared at the back of the tunnel in the man's chest.

Kirsten flinched away with a gasp. "Dammit, Dorian."

He chuckled. "That guy had some heavy artillery, maybe a .50 cal."

"Dead?" DEA Agent Fowler stuck a finger into his chest. "I can't be dead, I'm still here."

"Trust me, pal. You're as dead as I am," said Dorian, wandering around front. "Fowler, was this Gonsalves guy known to use a large weapon?"

"Yeah, the tool had a Desert Eagle. He loves his action movies. Thing's all nickeled up with mother-of-pearl grips, too, real pimp."

"Huh?" Kirsten tilted her head. "What does a gaudy handgun have to do with pimps?"

Fowler blinked at her. "Are you for real?"

Dorian chuckled. "If memory serves, that's a .50 caliber. Firearms used to have brass casings holding propellant, and physical triggers. They don't even manufacture those types of weapons anymore."

"What year do you think it is?" asked Kirsten.

"2022," said Fowler.

"You've been dead 396 years." Kirsten waved her arm through him. "See? It's 2418 now."

Fowler stumbled to the side, falling seated on the steps with a look of utter disappointment. He remained quiet for a minute or two, then deflated. "I guess that's why backup hasn't shown up. It did kind of feel like they were taking their damn sweet time."

"What happened here?" Dorian paced the line of executed men.

"We got a tip the cartels were using this house as a relay point to ship product into the States. Eduardo Gonsalves, a real piece of work. He went by the street name of *El Santo de Sangre.* We'd been giving them a big headache down south, so they tried to do an end run on moose back."

Kirsten glanced at the bloody walls. "Guess he lived up to his name. Fowler, you don't have to stay here. There's nothing else you can do."

"He won't let us leave," one of the executed men wailed, in Spanish.

Kirsten went over to them, switching to Spanish as well. "Who won't?"

A few seemed shocked she could see them.

"The Blood Saint. He thinks we ratted him," said another man.

The nearest spirit rasped, "It was his daughter, Dominique. He couldn't believe it, so he killed all of us trying to find the traitor."

"Yeah. Local police got a tip from a little girl." Fowler wandered over, speaking English, despite being apparently able to understand them. "The kid said her daddy did bad things and she was scared because people would hurt her." He laughed. "Who said DARE never did any good, huh? Kid heard drugs are bad in school, so she turned her old man in. We came in on a joint operation with the local PD, found a few million worth of coke down here."

Dorian and Kirsten exchanged a look.

"That's a lot of soda." Kirsten shook her head.

Fowler blinked at her. "Guess it's true what they say about blondes, eh?" He elbowed Dorian with a conspiratorial wink. "Cocaine, not soda."

"The hell is cocaine?" asked Kirsten.

"It was a plant derivative narcotic. Closest modern equivalent would be Zone4." Dorian gestured at the executed men. "The wraith is drawing power from them. I can feel him trying to snare me, too."

Kirsten closed her eyes and called out.

"You're wasting your time," said Dorian. "*They* can't get in here. Gonsalves, or what's left of him, is too strong. Why do you think these poor idiots are still stuck here? The Harbingers would have been all over cartel soldiers within minutes of their death. Something's keeping them out, and this doesn't strike me as holy ground."

"Holy ground?" She sighed. "Really? So if the wraith is blocking the Harbingers, we drag these men outside?"

Dorian eyed the row of dead men. "Gonsalves is binding them here, somehow. It almost feels as though he has some sort of connection to them. I doubt we'd be able to move them from where they're stuck."

A sudden sense of pervasive dread fell over the room. The executed ghosts all stopped muttering. Fowler gazed up at the ceiling, seeming paler. Every spirit in the basement turned to look at the same casement window an instant before a shadow crept by outside.

Dorian took a step back, closer to Kirsten. "Guess they're still listening to you."

She exhaled. "Yeah…"

"What was that thing?" Fowler pointed at the window.

"You were DEA?" Dorian asked with a wry half smile. "Someone who wants to have a word with you."

Fowler quirked an eyebrow at him. "What?"

Kirsten bit her lip. "Right, so, if we can't drag them outside…" *Damn, he's gonna be strong.*

"The focus of a wraith's dark deeds makes them more powerful." Dorian folded his arms. "You could destroy them to weaken the wraith, but…"

"They're not threatening anyone at the moment, and I'm no executioner."

She headed for the stairs.

"Hey wait," said Fowler. "What's that thing outside want with the DEA?"

"I know you too well." Dorian chuckled at her before he pointed at Fowler. "You stay here, don't do anything. You've been exposed to the wraith's energy for too long. He could drain you to boost himself. And that DEA thing was a joke, forget it."

Fowler set his hands on his hips and grumbled. "You can't take him on without backup. Aren't you at least going to call it in?"

Kirsten paused on the second step. "I'm the only one on the West Coast who can deal with this… at least that we know of."

Might as well start in that kid's room.

She rushed up to the kitchen, across the house, and to the second story, but stopped short at the top of the steps. The residual manifestations of long-ago screams, gunshots, and explosions broke the silence, sounding as though a small war went on in the back yard—though she hadn't heard any of it until entering the upstairs corridor. Billowy darkness shrouded the walls and ceiling. Dire energy charged the air, resisting her presence. Orange-pink light leaked from an open door catty-corner to the master bedroom. Kirsten focused her psionic energy against the gelatinous feeling in the air, pushing it aside and out of her way. The smoke clinging to the walls receded from her advance, as if afraid.

"Sounds like a damn war is going on out there."

Dorian chuckled. "Imprints from the DEA raid, I bet."

Kirsten leaned against the wall, edging up to the first door. "What is DEA?"

"Was. Special branch of law enforcement tasked with combatting illegal drugs." Dorian took a position in front of the door, as if to rush in the instant she opened it.

She scrunched her face. "Really? They actually cared enough about people getting high to have special cops specifically for drugs? Old government had too much money, I guess."

"Well, we still go after Lace labs."

"Good point, but that stuff is more poison than recreation."

She nudged the bedroom door open. Maia's bed lay open and abandoned, stuffed animals and datapads scattered about the floor. Dorian advanced to the outside window, squinting at the glare of emergency lights outside. Inspired by the child's memory, Kirsten started toward the closet, but a sudden roaring, like a waterfall, erupted behind her. She whirled around, raising her arm in defense.

Thick black vapor from the hallway billowed into the room and migrated to the corner near the ceiling on the left. The door slammed itself with a loud *bang*. Kirsten backpedaled, gaze locked on the cloud of darkness. Inky wisps of vapor built and rolled in on themselves, darkening into a thick mass from which extended a pair of phantasmal arms. Wisps of shadow burst from the ends, traced in the shape of claws. A flash of ice like a frozen hand clutching her heart, stabbed her in the chest. The closet door flew open; inside, her mother's visage appeared. The apparition screeched and flew at her, expanding, wailing. Kirsten tripped over a plush rabbit and landed seated on the bed. Dorian stooped forward, both hands clamped to the sides of his head. He glared at Kirsten with a look that said he wanted to harm her, but trembled from his effort to fight off the wraith.

Kirsten screamed like a terrified child, crossing her arms over her face as the huge, vaporous head of her dead mother washed over her. The woman passed through her, intangible.

A male voice rasped from the darkness within the closet. "Hey, kiddo, you still hungry?"

Heavy vapors tumbled from the closet, lapping at the rug like a lake of malice. A disheveled man in clothing made from pre-war scraps sewn together leaned out of the black, waving a dented octagonal can at her as if teasing a hungry dog. He flicked at the pull tab on the lid.

"Come on, sweetie. I know you want more. You can pay for it the same way you did the last time." He flashed a sinister smile.

Kirsten clutched at her chest, struggling to overpower the icy claw trying to freeze her heart. She remembered his face, she remembered his stink, and she remembered him being much larger. He didn't scare her. The sight of him brought only anger. She tapped that anger for strength, latching onto the sense of paranormal energy reaching inside her, and shoved it away. The cloud of darkness in the corner shrank in on itself, quivering. She rubbed the numb spot over her sternum, recognizing the piercing cold. Two ghosts had tried that trick on her in the past, attempting to scare her literally to death. Those, she'd blown off with ease.

Damn, he's strong.

Dorian fell to one knee, shaking his head while screaming. He looked as if he could kill someone without a care. Tendrils of shadow rose up from the floor like a mass of serpents, weaving back and forth before seeping into him. He lurched to his feet, incoherent rage boiling out in a howl as he plunged his hands into the side of a wardrobe cabinet, wrenched it into the air, and hurled it at Kirsten. An instant before his hands released it, a part of his true self came back to the surface. He twisted, pushing the flying cabinet enough that it missed her by inches. Kirsten rolled off the comforgel pad, skidding to the floor amid a rain of child's clothing. The cabinet smacked into the wall leaving a gouge.

With a tortured moan, Dorian fell against the wall where the dresser had been, punching at it, but his hand passed through without damaging it. "Get out of my head…"

Faint violet spots appeared at the top of the floating shadow like eyes. Kirsten stood, pulling a tiny dress off her head and flinging it to the side.

Scintillating white light formed around her hand and unfurled into her Astral Lash. The wraith surged left but didn't move fast enough. Kirsten leapt after it, rounding the energy whip and plunging it into the center of the inky cloud. Her psionic weapon flickered with a brilliant glow that made Dorian cringe back, shielding his eyes.

The holo-terminal on the desk exploded. Both lights in the ceiling sputtered and died.

Dorian lurched up, his expression once again normal—albeit furious. Kirsten coiled the lash around for a second swipe, but the wraith dashed into the wall beside the closet before she could attack again. Dorian ran and dove after it. She scowled at the spot of wall for a half second, then sprinted out the door and rushed toward the sound of a fight in the adjacent bedroom.

Police hand-to-hand combat techniques went only so far when employed against an amorphous mass of hatred. Whenever Dorian tried to pin the wraith, it flowed and stretched out of his grasp. Kirsten ran in the door, lash poised, but the two spirits had locked together so closely, she couldn't attack without hurting Dorian as well. The wraith emitted a low, growling snarl, threading around Dorian like a snake. It flowed behind him and raked wispy claws down his back. Dorian let off a loud groan. Faint white vapor spurted from the spectral wounds like blood.

Kirsten snapped the lash high on purpose intending to miss both of them. Her hope that the wraith would flee from the energy paid off. It detached itself from Dorian and fled across the room in a shadowy blur. Kirsten leapt through Dorian, swinging the astral whip down on top of the racing cloud. The energy tendril divided the mass like a blade, creating two smaller clouds that hung in space for a few seconds before combining. She swung sideways, but the creature dipped under the white cord and zipped toward the hallway.

A flying tackle from Dorian slowed stalled it at the door. The wraith clawed at the floor, its spectral talons finding no purchase. Dorian dragged the struggling wraith backward, closer to Kirsten. The wraith stretched and spun about, spearing one clawed hand through Dorian's chest and grabbing his neck from behind.

"Dorian, no!" she wailed.

Color drained from his apparition. He diminished into a transparent black-and-white image, then an indistinct blur of light in the general shape of a human. The wraith thickened and grew darker. Desperation surged down her arm; she coiled the lash around and spun it over her head.

Blue-white radiance flickered on the walls as she struck out, screaming, "Dorian!"

The luminous tendril seared the dark mass it in half once more. Loud static erupted from her earbud, and her armband terminal powered down on its own.

Dorian's amorphous light-cloud body quivered as if reacting to the hit. His moan came from somewhere far away. A second later, the luminous mist coalesced back into his usual ghostly self. He collapsed limp on the floor.

The wraith gathered itself into an orb no larger than a skull. The sight of Dorian so weak brought tears of rage. In anger, Kirsten attacked with reckless abandon. The wraith swam around the Lash and pounced on her chest, raking and shredding. A sensation like a rain of razor-sharp icicles tearing at her skin paralyzed her. Her concentration shattered, the energy whip faded out.

Her lungs stopped reacting; her heart pounded in her head. She fell over backward under the weight of ten men crushing her into the floor. Ice gnawed at her breasts, face, and gut. The wraith paused to glance over its shoulder, raising a shadowy clawed hand at something she could not see.

Dorian must be okay.

Exploiting the brief distraction, Kirsten infused her body with astral energy, making it solid to ghosts. Threads of frigid ice where its talons gripped her became sharp blades. Warm blood trickled over her ribs. She growled and wrapped her hands around the closest thing it had to a throat, her legs around its body, and called the lash.

It had nowhere to go.

With her hand pressed against its 'neck,' all ten feet of the Astral Lash unfurled inside it. She pictured the terrified little girl outside and tapped her emotional need to protect that child. A weak moan from Dorian added grief. That it had dared use Mother against her added rage.

Kirsten let out a primal scream and poured all her emotion into the attack.

The wraith exploded in a torrent of black slime that coated the entire room. Where once had been a creature of torment and darkness lay a drained and weary Hispanic man in his later thirties. She ignored the pain in her side and tackled the disoriented spirit to the ground. With one arm across his neck and a knee in his back, she held him down.

"Don't give me an excuse, *pendejo*."

In seconds, a familiar eerie feeling came over her from behind. She wrenched the spirit's body around to face the Harbinger hanging in the room, one of the shadows circling the house since she first wanted them to appear. The billowing mass of blackness with piercing, silver eyes drew nearer, reaching toward the Blood Saint. Six more Harbingers drifted in through the floor and walls, coming together into a curtain of night that engulfed her. She knew why they had come, but fear gripped her anyway. Cold unlike anything she had ever known washed over her. She closed her eyes, clenched her jaw, and held as still as possible.

The dead man's scream fell silent.

When light returned, El Santo de Sangre was gone.

Kirsten flopped on her side, shivering. *Compared to a swarm of Harbingers running me over, it feels like summer outside.* Her chest burned; blood seeped into the undamaged black cloth of her uniform and stained the rug. Wincing, she propped herself up to check on her partner. One remaining Harbinger hovered by Dorian's inert figure. He hadn't moved since he fell. She crawled toward him, gathering his motionless body into her lap. A Harbinger checking him out didn't bode well.

"Please, no." Kirsten cradled Dorian tight. Tears streamed down her cheeks. She sniffled and peered up at sparkling silver eyes. "Please... not him."

2

THE AMBUSH

Fatigue dragged Kirsten's run to a stagger, then to a halt. She leaned on the side of a building, gasping for breath. The psi-armor helmet enclosed her head in a claustrophobic cage. Though it weighed no more than plastic, it burdened her as if made of iron.

After running over a dozen city blocks, her breathing had fogged the visor into an opaque haze. Trickles of perspiration stung at her eyes, ran down her cheek, and tickled the back of her neck. Division 0 tactical armor was a new feeling, a new, *heavy* feeling, and she didn't much care for it at all. The extra weight and lack of ventilation ruined her.

Deserted, the street held a few abandoned cars as well as fragments fallen from crumbling buildings on either side. Up ahead, gunfire popped at random from alleys along with distant sounds of rioting, sometimes followed by the shriek someone taking a bullet. Paper trash skittered by in a faint breeze laced with the fragrance of chemicals and urban rot. A scream for help echoed. She spun around, unable to tell where it came from.

"Civil unrest in Sector 77. All personnel be prepared to encounter armed aggressors." The digital voice seemed so loud, her entire helmet vibrated with it.

The same scream repeated, drawing her attention to an alley half a block away. She couldn't tell by sound if a woman shrieked in terror or if a man had been stabbed with a red-hot vibro-blade.

After taking a couple more breaths, she forced herself up to a jog, E-90 in hand. The roar of fighting grew louder as she neared the alley. She ran against the wall at the corner, gathered her wits, and whirled around with her weapon raised. Four men, jackets emblazoned with gang markings—The Disowned—surrounded another man. Cowering in a ball, the object of the gangers' amusement begged for his life, oblivious to Kirsten's arrival.

"Police, against the wall, now!" she yelled.

The Disowned looked up at the diminutive shout. Outright laughter stalled at the sight of her laser pistol. Whimpering, the victim crawled away from his tormentors. The four thugs raised their hands, but continued to grin as if up to something. Kirsten wagged her weapon to the left.

"Over there, against the wall. Do it." A flick of her eyes at the helmet visor opened a comm channel. "Dispatch, need a suspect transport. Sector 77, track my signal."

"Copy that, en route." A brief static crunch preceded and followed the voice in her helmet.

She eased closer, gaze shifting among the men. "Move, now."

Kirsten almost shrieked as a boarded up window to her right burst open, spraying her with splinters and boards. A man grabbed her by the arm and threw her headfirst into another ply-board panel. It broke under her impact, sending her spilling into a face-first slide along the floor of a derelict building. The disorientation of the maneuver left her motionless for an instant, mystified by the echoing clatter of wood in the cavernous empty space.

She snapped out of the daze in time to notice a man about to drive a heavy armored boot into her side. A quick roll got her out of the way. The man put so much strength into the kick, he knocked stumbled, nearly falling when he made contact with nothing but air. Kirsten scooted back and scrambled upright before raising her... empty hands. She glanced around, but the E-90 appeared to have vanished.

The huge man also wore the colors of the Disowned. The top of her head barely reached his pectorals, and his arms made her thighs feel thin. After recovering his balance, he turned toward her, snarling. Something familiar in his green eyes caught her off guard and killed her fear of him.

For a second, she lost herself admiring his handsome face and perfect muscles.

A punch to the helmet knocked her back three steps.

This isn't fair.

She ducked a telegraphed kick, avoiding it in the exact way he expected her to—right into his waiting hands. He hauled her into the air and threw her chest-first into drywall. She bounced away, right back into his grip. His arms closed around her from behind, crushing her against his chest.

Reacting on instinct, she planted a foot on a nearby cart and shoved herself up, mashing the top of her helmet into his chin. He staggered back, losing his grip. Kirsten recovered her balance and spun around with a high kick, slapping him across the face with her boot. His head whipped to the side, but he smiled.

"Nice form, but you kick like a ten-year-old girl." He rubbed the spot. "Probably because you're the same size as one."

Kirsten growled, pulling the stunrod off her belt and lunging in with a wild overhead swing. He caught her wrist and flipped her over onto her back. A skillful twist sent a thread of agony up the nerve in her arm. Her hand snapped open as if of its own accord. The stunrod fell away.

A heavy gasp fogged the visor of her helmet.

"And, you're dead," he taunted before letting go of her and taking a step away. "Aren't you supposed to be a police officer?"

She rolled upright and backed off, favoring the arm. The urge to knock a few of his teeth out grew strong, but they were so perfect. His face entranced her again.

The cute ones are always so shallow. Plus, he is trying to kill me.

Adrenaline welled up as he came in with a series of rapid jabs. She blocked each in turn, backpedaling to make him advance. The gleam of a knife at his belt took her eyes off his perfect teeth.

A kick she didn't see coming crashed into her ribs. She staggered, spraying spittle onto her visor.

"You get angry too easy. Don't fixate on the weapon. Watch my entire body. Watch my eyes. You can't read where your opponent goes if you fixate. If you give in to rage, you lose your edge."

I am...

He faked another stab. This time, she blocked the kick. The knife came around the other way, but she got a forearm up to catch his wrist. Her body jerked from the impact of the block, but she kept her grip and wrenched him around by it, applying twisting pressure. He stumbled after his trapped limb, and lost his grip on the knife before slumping to one knee.

"Not bad, but a little more torque on the hand would have incapacitated me."

Letting his weight take him down, he pulled her into a stumble and kicked her legs out from under her. Kirsten landed flat on her front. They rolled away from each other and stood at the same time. He shook his almost-sprained wrist out while she tried to cradle her left breast despite having armor it the way. The spot the wraith had clawed open *still* hurt. Out of the corner of her eye, she spotted the stunrod a few feet away and went for it.

He leapt at her, distracting her from the weapon. No longer enamored by his looks, she ducked and spun under his arm, pulling it over her shoulder before flipping him with a hip thrust. He hit the floor on his back. She wrapped her entire body around his arm, bracing her heel against his throat. If she pulled just right, she could break his neck.

She chickened out.

The man howled under her attempt at a pain submission hold. She applied a little more pressure and he stopped fighting.

Stalemate.

"You're getting better," he croaked. "About time to call it for today, I think."

"Okay," said Kirsten, releasing her grip and simply lying there, too tired to get up.

Tingles spread down her body, riding the forefront of a wave of numbness that soon became total paralysis. Brightness intensified, washing out the details of the ceiling until she floated in a vast nothingness white light.

"Simulation end," chimed a pleasant, omnidirectional female voice.

The oppressive glow dimmed and shrank into several rows of bright parallel lines, LED tubes. A padded chair appeared beneath her. Sweat dripped down the sides of her head, though wonderful cool air lifted the sweat from her thin white bodysuit.

Kirsten started to sit up, but the helmet she forgot she had on jerked her back into the seat by the wires tethering it to the machinery.

"Ow." She undid the chinstrap for the senshelmet and pulled it off, leaving it hanging on the wire tethering it to the chair. "Why am I so damn sore?"

"It's your brain. Takes a few minutes for you to figure out it was all fake."

The same man she'd been fighting a moment ago—with much shorter hair—came around the side of a console of blinking lights in a blue-grey Division 2 jumpsuit. Kirsten's gaze went right to where the lowered zipper exposed some of his chest, left of the name 'Silva' on a tag. She whispered it in her mind, unable to suppress a wry grin at how he'd embellished his physique in the sim.

"You're improving." He extended a hand to help her off the big VR chair. "Starting to feel more like a sparring match now instead of just me stealing your lunch money."

She accepted his hand and slid off the thick, black cushions, winding up on her sock-covered feet mere inches from him. At least in the real world, he didn't tower over her so much. The scent of his exertion mixed with a hint of cologne, and she found herself in no major hurry to move away. Despite the fight happening within cyberspace, the training had worked them both to the point of needing a shower.

"Thanks for staying late. I really appreciate it."

He grinned while grabbing a towel from a nearby tray. "Your captain was concerned enough to make the request after the incident with the mercenaries."

Arms folded over her ribs, she cringed at the memory of clinging to an ad-bot. "I'm not sure hand-to-hand training would have helped. That bastard had vibro claws."

"They're not much different from a knife to be honest. Same reach considerations, but the major problem is you can't twist cybernetic claws out of someone's grip with a pain-compliance technique."

Kirsten took hold of his wrist, spinning with a slow-motion ju-jitsu maneuver that pressed her back to his chest. "So what's the best way to defend against them?"

"Shoot him before he gets close."

She poked a teasing elbow into his ribs.

"Oof." He took a step back and swiped his hand in a playful attempt to 'claw' her.

She caught his wrist the same way she'd defend against a knife—but he thrust his left hand 'claws' into her belly and tickled.

Peals of laughter came out of her as she leapt away, doubled over.

"Most mercs who install claws do both hands. The best you can do is stay away from them or use a weapon with better reach."

"Like a sword?" she rasped, trying to catch her breath.

"Yeah, that could work. Most police don't carry them, though."

The chair creaked as she leaned into it. "Some of ours do. They're easier to use on astrals. Bullets don't have much effect, not a lot of surface area to bind. How much reach do you get with a sword?" She blushed before he caught the innuendo.

"K, he's married." Dorian the Dream-Killer appeared out from the wall.

Picking at her ear with her middle finger, she sighed at her teacher.

Gabriel Silva, martial arts instructor for Division 1 training academy. Of course, you're married. You're too damn perfect.

"You okay? Looks as if you just got some bad news." He patted her on the shoulder.

His ring had been obvious the whole time.

"Nothing I'm not used to. I guess I'm just tired."

"Okay. I'll see you on Thursday, right? You're taking to the ju-jitsu pretty well so far. We can see how you handle some Wushu sword forms next week if you want."

"Sounds awesome," she muttered, trudging for the showers.

Dorian winced. "Sorry. I know how you are about getting things out of the way sooner rather than later."

She slammed the locker open. "He knows I'm psionic and doesn't care."

"You'll find someone."

Kirsten let her arm dangle on the tiny door. "I hope you're feeling better. I haven't seen you for two days… Was starting to worry."

He grinned, holding his arms out. "Like new. Just needed a long nap." His smile fell flat. "Thanks for… umm."

"I don't think they'd listen to me about that. Did you ever consider that you're not on their list after all?" She slipped her socks off and put them in the locker.

Dorian gave her his usual big-brother smile. "I find it more comforting to think they listened to you."

"Your soul isn't as dark as you're afraid it is." Kirsten pinched the nanomesh clasp at the neck of her white bodysuit, looking over her shoulder at him as she peeled it open from throat to hip. "Gonna watch me shower, too?"

He held his hands up, shook his head, and wandered off into the wall.

"Sorry!" she yelled. *Damn.* She let the wet garment hit the ground and stepped out of it. *Lonely* and *a bitch today.*

Dorian poked his head back out. "It's okay. We both had a rough day."

Kirsten smiled and slouched with relief. "See you upstairs in a few."

He nodded and pulled his head back into the wall.

After a peek over her shoulder to see if anyone happened to be watching her, she stripped despite there being three men and two other women in various stages of showering or changing. No one seemed to care, but she kept her back to the room as much as possible and crept to the nearest autoshower tube.

How do soldiers ever *get used to this?*

3

HOPE

Grimaldi's was the kind of place most people took a date to in order to make a good impression. Armando, or whatever his real name was, suggested the place after a brief chat in a virtual nightclub. In cyberspace, he'd looked more like a Latin movie star. Then again, she couldn't criticize too much. After all, her avatar mostly looked like her but she added five inches of height, mostly to protect herself from anyone who might mistake her for a teenager, and prefer that.

She sighed in her head at the pasty white guy across the table in an ill-fitting suit. While he certainly didn't have the smoldering hot looks of a holovid star like he did online, he still ranked far from ugly.

He doesn't look like an Armando.

Kirsten couldn't tell what to feel more foolish about: resorting to cyberspace dating, or spending C4,000 on a shimmering emerald gown. The expensive garment left her shoulders and most of her back bare. The right side hem stopped mere inches down her thigh, while the left extended it to mid-calf with some purposeless long trailing strip of fabric for decoration. While the menu absorbed his attention, she cradled her chest, trying to rub soreness away.

Damn, two days and my boob still hurts. I hate wraiths.

Awkwardness pervaded her being. A few strands of hair that escaped the clip tickled at the nape of her neck, every so often making her grab for a nonexistent insect. She fidgeted at the short right side of her dress the whole time she sat there. One slightly wrong move would give everyone on one side of the restaurant a look at her highly unsexy plain white panties. She couldn't remember the last time she had worn a dress, much less one so short. Most of her effort went toward keeping tabs of how she positioned herself.

Armando seemed nice enough, but she had yet to come clean with him. Every time she thought about it, the silver finish of her high-heeled shoes became quite fascinating. She smiled and nodded at his attempts at conversation. Fortunately, he didn't drone on and on about his success, or money, or other such trite things. He did mention he worked in technology, some manner of investor or engineer; she hadn't been paying enough attention when it came up. He had gone over it out front while they waited for a table while she'd been too distracted staring at the floor and worrying about people staring at her. Whether or not anyone had, she didn't know.

"… and that's when I told him we'd have to start over from scratch. The system infrastructure was too—are you all right? Is your foot bothering you?"

Her face grew warm, red. "I'm okay, I'm second-guessing this gown… It's a bit, umm…"

"Radiant. Matches the woman wearing it. The green sets off your hair."

More heat came to her cheeks. "The sides are too open, not my usual sort of thing…"

You'll have to show a living man the goods sooner or later. Theodore's voice mocked her from memory.

"It is fine, Kirsten. You should see some of the trash in Paris these days. They might as well not even bother wearing anything at all. Sometimes you wonder how it even stays on." He sipped his wine, leaning back. "Of course, it's cyclical. In two years, there won't be a scrap of skin showing and they'll have floppy bags on their heads or some such nonsense."

She laughed, though couldn't hide her nerves. A waiter arrived, setting a small bowl of shrimp cocktail in front of each of them, flecked with scallions and shaved cucumber. Kirsten fumbled to get a grip on her fork, again fascinated by the reflection on her shoes.

"You've the look of a guilty conscience. Don't tell me you're having doubts this early on?" His concern seemed genuine. "Was this an unfortunate choice of location?"

"It's…" She sighed, losing a staring contest with her shoes.

"Are you sick? Dying?"

"No… it's—"

He lowered his voice to a whisper. "You prefer women?"

She giggled, looking up. "No." Taking a bite of shrimp delayed her having to keep talking.

"Dangerous ex?" He followed suit, lifting an eyebrow. "Rather good food here. I hear they ship it in from a colony."

"Pointlessly expensive." She poked at the next shrimp. "It tastes the same as vat-grown."

He chuckled. "It tastes a lot better if you have it fresh, loses something in shipping. Have you ever been to a colony settlement? It's adventurous."

"No." Again she found her shoes fascinating. "I've enough adventure down here."

"So what's making you all mopey?"

She looked into his hazel eyes. "You don't give me the feeling you're just trying to get in my pants for a night."

He coughed, gathering a napkin over his reddening face.

"No… I'm not saying…" She blushed. "That's what I want. I'm looking for more than a one-nighter." She lowered her volume when a few people nearby glanced over. "I want something real, but…"

Armando swallowed, then sipped some water to clear his throat. "What's wrong? Can't have kids? Leaving the country soon?"

"Is your name really Armando?"

He laughed. "Is that all? It actually is… I changed it a few years ago. I was born Brian, if you want to know. Not very sexy."

"You're kind of pale for an Armando; Brian is cute."

He smirked, finding her assay of him as 'cute' a bit deflating.

"I like you, Brian, Armando, whatever. I've had a damnable time finding a guy I can trust." She stared deep into the woven tablecloth, as if some secret to love hid among the threads. "I have to tell you something."

He tensed. "All right."

"I have a son."

His cringe was nigh imperceptible.

"I didn't have him as a baby. I took him in, a special situation. I mean, technically he's not my son yet. Right now it's more of a foster situation."

Brian/Armando relaxed. "Oh, well, perhaps I should meet him soon. That isn't such a big issue."

"There's more." She picked at the shrimp. "I never did tell you about my job."

He squinted. "Something less than legal?"

Her sudden laugh startled the room silent. When the din returned to normal, and her cheeks to normal color, she gazed at him as her last threads of whimsy mixed with sadness. "I'm with the police."

"Oh." He bit his lip, shifting in the chair.

Two strikes. Kid, cop. Great. Dammit.

"Well, I suppose... You don't really seem to be the type of woman involved in that sort of thing."

So help me, if he says delicate flower... "I'm not a beat cop. I'm with investigations."

"Oh, well that's better, I think? Don't have people shooting at as much?" Armando/Brian took a sip of wine. "I'm not sure I would be able to cope with wondering *if* you came home each night."

She lifted her glass to her lip, enough to smell the wine, but hesitated. *No, I just get blown off the eleventh story of parking garages.* "Not so often. I usually deal with people after they're dead." *Damn it, K, just spit it out.*

Last shrimp gone, he had another sip of wine, and smiled while dabbing at his lip with the napkin. "So you're a homicide detective? You must have some stories."

Kirsten stared at her appetizer shrimp cocktail, compliments of the house. She took in a deep breath. *Better now than after I get attached.* "I'm with Division 0."

The expected cough, the chest patting, the usual lifted brow. "There's a zero?"

"Yeah, it's small. There's not many of us. I'm ps—" A well, or ill, as the case may be, timed shrimp muffled the last bit.

"Pardon?"

She chewed it like gum. The longer it took to swallow, the longer she could entertain the fantasy this man would be different. He wouldn't be the same as all others. *Adventurous.* "I'm psionic."

"I see." Color drained out of his face.

The lip bite, the shift in posture, interest became trepidation.

Figures. What would his family think if he brought a psionic girl home?

"I don't mess with people's heads. I just see ghosts and such." She flashed a hopeful smile, trying to look as innocent as she could. A cat hoping its owner adored a dead mouse.

His lips twisted into the bastard child of a grimace and a smile. He gazed off at the windows.

Great. Too innocent. Now he's looking at me like I'm underage. Cop, has a kid, psionic, three strikes.

"Do your parents know you're one of… those?" He slipped a hand into his suit jacket, trying to be subtle.

"Yeah. Dad's okay with it, Mom… not so much. She won't be a problem, but I have a feeling it's a bit late for worrying about how my parents would react to you." She gave up on her last shrimp. "You don't have to fake the emergency call. Go ahead and run away screaming now if you want." *Adventurous my ass.*

He withdrew his hand from his pocket. "Look, Kirsten, it's not…" He fidgeted. "You said you have a child to look after and that's important, and you're a cop… My dad's not big on government, the whole nanny state thing, you two wouldn't get along."

"You don't have to be afraid of me. We are not all dangerous… I mean—"

Armando/Brian/Douchebag stood. "I'm sorry, Kirsten. You are really very pretty but… I just don't see any kind of future mingling genes with a psionic. I'm sorry for wasting your night."

As if it's a damn choice… Go to hell, Armando/Brian/Asshole.

She watched his blur slide over the toe of her silver shoes as he hurried for the door without looking back. Blush saturated her face as she bristled with yet another rejection. *Why do people hate us so much? I didn't choose to be born this way.* She could pick into his brain, find some embarrassing tidbit and scream it at the room to get him back for how he made her feel. No, that would prove him right. That's what they all feared —not having secrets.

The host gave her departing date a strange frown, then looked in her direction. He appeared to be paying particular attention to Kirsten's half-empty wine glass. By the time he arrived at the side of the table, she had her ID out.

"I'm twenty-two, and a cop."

He bowed. "My apologies, miss. You—"

"Have a young face, tiny boobs, and I'm short. Yeah… I know. Is it too late to cancel one entrée?"

After checking his datapad, he grimaced. "I'm afraid your meals are already being plated."

Of course. Now I have two *dinners I don't want to eat.*

"Can you please just wrap it to go?"

The man drew a breath, shifting side to side. "Our presentation is exquisite, miss. Our food does not travel well and we would rather not sully our reputation with a substandard experience. We are not a *take-out* establishment. If—"

"Fine, whatever." Kirsten lacked the energy to become angry at his fluffed-up offense. "I need to use the bathroom."

He bowed, backing away as she stood. She wobbled halfway across the dining area, firm in her regret about wearing high-heeled shoes. Most of the room watched her rendition of an ostrich on ice as she tried to balance on the alien torture devices. Humiliation piled on top of indignation and depression, a three-way wrestling match to determine how she felt at being dumped again. The added weight proved too much for the ungainly footwear, and she wound up on the floor.

The dining public turned away, affording her a tiny bit of reclaimed dignity. Anger swirled. She tugged the straps off her ankles and stood, barefoot, with the damnable things tucked under her arm. The frosted glass door to the ladies' room slid out of her way. Once inside the protective shell of a private area, tears came out in force. Before anyone else could find her, she ducked into a stall, locked the door, and sat on a closed toilet.

A few minutes later, the sobbing passed. She looked up from mascara-covered hands at the impressionistic watercolor beach painted on the partition, wondering if anyone heard her. A few deep breaths helped regain her composure, and stood. The autoflush startled a shriek out of her. Once she re-composed herself, she stepped out of the stall and approached the sinks to wipe trails of mascara from her face. That done, she glared at herself in the mirror.

"Screw him. I don't need an idiot like that." A few passes of her fingers got her hair back to rights. No point redoing the eyeliner. "Someday I'll—"

A familiar smell came out of nowhere, flannel and cheap cologne.

"Dad?"

His face poked through the door with a tentative peek. Seeing no one else inside, and his daughter decent, he walked up to her and tried to put an intangible arm around her.

"Oh, dammit." She closed her eyes and made herself solid to ghosts. "You *are* still around..."

Her father rubbed her back. "Are you okay, hon?"

"Nothing I haven't dealt with before." She dabbed a towel at the corners of her eyes. "I don't give a crap about him. It's just…" Kirsten rested her weight on the counter with both hands and stared down at her toes. "…I'm so tired of being hated for what I am. Every time I try to go on a date, the same thing happens. I didn't ask to be different."

"You'll find someone, and I'll be here for you until you do."

She hugged him, letting his presence dispel her growing sense of worthlessness. For a few minutes, she lost herself in his company. *If I was normal, Dad wouldn't have run away from me, spent so much time traveling.* Kirsten started to slide down a spiral of self-pity, but jumped with a gasp at the faint chirp of the outer bathroom door opening, admitting two women in evening gowns.

Hoping they didn't notice her hugging thin air, Kirsten fumbled at the sink. The women paid her no attention and went toward the back stalls. She gathered her shoes, purse, and father, and padded out of the bathroom, back to her table.

The food had arrived in her absence. She fell into the round white cushion of her seat, dumped the shoes unceremoniously in a heap, and smirked at the orecchiette pasta dish she had, up until a few minutes ago, thought looked amazing. Her father sat in the abandoned chair on the other side, watching her pick at it.

"What the devil did that idiot order?"

She shrugged. "No idea, something with little squid. Sorry I gave you a hard time about the PubTran."

"It's all right. I'm not going anywhere until you don't need me anymore." He glanced at the door. "Why don't you call that Templeton fellow? He didn't seem very worried about your gift."

A few people turned to look at her sudden bout of coughing. Most attributed the redness on her face to issues involving lack of air. The host hurried over.

"Are you all right, miss?"

She nodded and waved him off. "Yes. I'm not choking."

The man bowed and walked away.

"Dad…" Kirsten sighed. "He's just…"

"What?"

She wiped her chin. "I dunno, a little… old. He's thirty-six."

Her father laughed. "You looked at his file?"

"No." Kirsten couldn't maintain eye contact. "Okay, fine. I did. But, he showed me his ID, I already knew." Her eyes lifted until she pouted at him. "You don't have to linger if you don't want to."

"Nonsense, hon. It's the least I can do." He reached across the table, squeezing her hand. "No guilt, Kirsten. You're not *keeping* me here. I want to be here for you."

"I should have tried to call you, but I was afraid of Mom."

"Shame about that Dorian fellow."

She stared at her toes, finding them far less mesmerizing than a silver shoe. "Yeah… I"—she waved at the waiter—"You just gave me an idea."

Her father tilted his head. "But he's a spirit."

The waiter arrived. "Yes? Oh, and for what it's worth, the man's an idiot."

She managed a weak smile. "Please, can I get these wrapped? I have to leave."

"Of course." The waiter picked up both plates and carried them off.

"No, not *with* Dorian. *About* him." She thumbed her NetMini and glared at the hateful shoes.

Ten minutes later, Kirsten waited at the curb with C1,702 credits worth of high-end Italian take-out under one arm and a C240 worth of cheap shoes below the other. Her father waited at her side until the PubTran cab squeaked to a halt. Standing barefoot on the sidewalk reminded her of the almost-two-years she'd spent as a street kid. Having her dad so close made her regret not trying harder to contact him after Mother had been arrested—but she'd been hurt and angry, and he never had gotten over his fear of ghosts.

Until he became one.

4

OLD WOUNDS

The driverless taxi rolled to a halt under a covered walkway at the main door of an apartment building identical to a thousand others around it in almost every way except for the people inside. Kirsten ducked out when the side hatch opened, and hurried across a sidewalk of cold plastisteel to the lobby.

Happy yelling from small children echoed from a hallway in the back. The sounds of play brought a smile to her face and made her forget all about what's-his-name. A Class 1 doll in the image of a twenty-something brunette in a neat uniform, jerked upright in the only chair behind the reception desk, ready to interact with Kirsten should she approach. Its rigid face was molded in a permanent smile, though its mechanical eyes whirred wider in an effort to appear welcoming. Traces of light from the AI core in its skull glowed from seams behind the ears and gaps around the mouth. The smoldering fragrance of dust baking off electrical contacts surrounded it.

Just human enough to be creepy.

Kirsten padded across a floor of resin tiles an off-putting shade of pale maroon verging on puke. At the elevator, she fumbled to keep her shoes under her arm as she hit the call button. The faint pat-pat-pat of her impatient foot tapping drew the attention of a brown-furred dog from the hallway where the kids continued laughing and shouting at each other.

Lime green numbers ticked down in front of her. A handful of people trickled in from the street, mostly commuters arriving home from work. The curious animal darted out of sight at the arrivals. She sighed at the hideous floor, feeling extra stupid for wasting a day off on Brian/Armando. The people walking in arranged themselves among the six elevators. When the doors at last opened, an older Chinese man, a woman who appeared to be his wife, and a young black man in an unassuming navy blue top and dark grey pants joined her in the cab.

The Asian couple offered her a pleasant nod and continued talking about their daughter's impending wedding. The young man checked Kirsten out with chivalrous subtlety, but she still noticed. She smiled at him, for a moment considering giving up on her intended destination to split the food with him instead.

The door chimed and closed, the cab shuddered into motion.

"Hi."

"Hello yourself." He offered a slight bow and made a humorous gesture of an impossible handshake, noticing her arms were full. "Lawrence."

Hmm. Surface thoughts check out, thinks I'm cute in a barefoot-waif kind of way. "Kirsten."

Lawrence leaned against the railing. "You live here?"

"No, visiting someone."

"You're gonna break my heart, aren't you?" He winked. "A guy?"

"No, my partner's ex-partner."

His face froze in a look of confusion for a moment. She couldn't help herself, still eavesdropping. "No, partner as in cops. I don't have a girlfriend." *Shit. Play it off his face.* "Couldn't help but notice that look." She loosed an impish giggle. *Dammit, don't lie.*

His cologne wrapped around as he leaned in. "Heh, so you're a cop? You don't look like one."

"I'm more of an investigator." *Get it over with.* "Division 0."

"You one of those psionics?"

"Uh-huh."

Lawrence edged to the corner, a wary look stiffening his features. She closed her eyes and sighed. The older couple glanced at him, at her, back to him, and then started chuckling. The cab stopped, the older couple got out. He eyed the hallway, debating.

"Just because I'm psionic doesn't mean I'm going to attack you." She looked up at him.

He cleared his throat and tried to act casual. Lawrence needed acting lessons.

Kirsten stepped out on the thirty-ninth floor, scowling at the sigh of relief behind her that fell short of being silent. *Not worth it to make a scene. Just let it go.* When she reached apartment 3918, she'd almost stopped grumbling. She waved her hand at the silver square on the wall beside the door, triggering a doorbell sound inside.

Within a moment, a tiny speck of chromatic light appeared at head level on the door.

"Umm… I think you have the wrong door," said a woman's voice from a speaker in the panel.

"Nila Assad?" asked Kirsten.

A transparent holographic bust with coffee-colored skin faded in above the glowing speck. "Yes, do I know you?"

"I'm Kirsten Wren, umm. Agent Kirsten Wren, Div 0 I-Ops."

The ethereal head looked her over. "Did they alter the uniform since I've been on leave? And are they seriously putting thirteen-year-olds out in the field now?"

"No." She sighed. "I'm not a kid. Just had a bad date. Can we talk?"

Nila's holographic face disappeared, darkening the hallway. With a pneumatic *puff*, the door slid sideways into the wall, opening. Kirsten hadn't expected Dorian's former partner to be quite as tall as she was, and tilted her head back to continue maintaining eye contact. Tank top with no bra, sweat pants, barefoot on thick carpeting—merely looking at the woman made her jealous of the comfort.

"Well, since you're here… may as well come in," said Nila, backing away.

Kirsten followed her inside, the door closing on its own behind her. The smell of child saturated the apartment, a presence in the air she found soothing. On the way to a plain white table in the kitchen, they shared complaints of high heels and wished ill fortune upon whoever had invented them.

Kirsten offered her the plastic carton containing Brian/Armando/Douchebag's order. A mass of red sauce, pasta, and squid sloshed to the side. "Do you like seafood? The idiot got this, but he left before they finished preparing it."

"I could 'sem something for Shani. She'll probably be mad at me, but this smells wonderful. Never had it before… Is it any good?" She sat at the table, then flipped the lid open, sniffing at it. "Wow, there's so much of it, I'll split it with her."

"It should be good. It was like C925."

Nila coughed. "Jerk."

Kirsten leaned on the table, propping her head on her arm. "Yeah. I'm getting used to it."

"So what brings you here with expensive charity seafood?" Nila chuckled, and hopped up to grab a couple of plates and some forks.

"It's about Dorian."

Smash.

One plate dead, one clamped in an awkward stance to her thigh. Forks bounced onto the rug. A little girl of about seven ran out from a back hallway, gaping at the broken plate. Silver sensgoggles clung to a thick mass of dark brown hair; the girl's cheeks glowed in light cast off from a paused video.

"I'm sorry." Kirsten rushed over and dropped to her knees, gathering bits of broken flatware.

"No, please… I'll get it. You're a guest."

Shaking, Nila set the remaining plate on the table, cleaned up the mess, and returned with new forks. The girl clung to the corner of the hallway, trying to bore a hole in Kirsten's chest with her eyes.

Nila sat. "Sorry. Not an easy subject for me. What about him?"

"I'm an astral sensate and—"

"Oh, God. Is he still here? Has he come to see me?"

Kirsten leaned against the chair. "Uhh. Okay, that was easier than I expected. Usually people don't believe me."

"I'm not a civilian." Nila tasted the food, curiosity became confusion, and then her eyes narrowed as she chewed.

She must like it. "Yeah, but even a lot of Zeroes seem to draw the line at ghosts." She ate a forkful of pasta. Without the emotion of Brian's rejection weighing her down, it tasted as good is it had looked when she picked it from the menu. "I doubt he's come *here*. He doesn't want to bother you. I don't want to upset you, but he's beating himself up because of guilt. He's taken the blame for what happened."

The child squinted at Kirsten, darting out of sight as soon as she tried to look at her. Nila pulled one foot underneath her on the chair and nudged closer to the table.

"Shani's afraid they'll send someone to make me go back to work and get killed." Nila doled some food onto a plate for her daughter. "Are you here to talk me into going back?"

"No. I'm not here in any official capacity at all. Only had this food and got the random idea to finally meet you. I wanted to see how you were doing. Dorian's kind of become my partner now in an odd sort of way. He's attached himself to the car."

"Shani, come, eat." Nila held the second plate out.

After a moment, a little face peered around the corner once again, staring in terror at Kirsten.

Unable to handle a child looking at her *that* way—afraid—Kirsten averted her eyes and poked at her pasta. The child's shadow crept across the floor. Shani risked getting close only long enough to grab the plate and run into the back hallway.

"It's not you personally. She knows you're with the department." Nila stuck her fork into the food twice, twirled, and then pulled it up an inch. A tiny C'thulu balanced atop linguini for an instant before slipping back to the plate. She impaled it. "I know I cheated death. I don't want to get killed. Something tells me it'll happen if I go back." Nila stared at her fork, mesmerized by tiny tentacles. "I should have died with him."

"He thinks it's his fault for pulling into the front lot so fast, as if it was an ordinary warrant run on some low-grade suggestive con man."

"Neither one of us expected laser rifles—or a handful of former ACC mercenaries from Mexico. Rene was up to his neck in some crap working for some heavy equipment corp. He turned his bodyguards into fanatic servants."

Kirsten held a hand up, trying to chew faster. "Mmf. No, it was organized. Exotech was a front. Rene had syndicate connections. He didn't work for them—he used them."

Nila blinked. "Do they know that?"

"Not as far as I could find out, but it probably wouldn't be too healthy for Rene if they did."

"Div 9 should already be looking for him. He killed a cop," said Nila.

"You sure you're okay? He's worried about you, even though he won't admit it."

Nila leaned her head back, stretched, and exhaled. "I don't want to die. I'm happy here at home with Shani, where we are safe."

Kirsten studied the remnants of her food. *Don't tell her he had feelings for her. That will hurt more.* "He thinks your nerve broke."

"I'm fine. I'm still on psych leave, still getting paid. I could do some consulting I guess, but I can't go back out there..." Nila gazed past the vertical blinds at a stream of hovercars. Passing headlights sent glowing bands scrolling across her face.

The thousand-mile stare.

Kirsten sulked at her lap. "I shouldn't have come here. This was a bad idea. I'm sorry if I've upset you."

Nila shook it off, flashing a nervous smile. "I'm not angry at Dorian. Like I said, we had no idea Rene had laser rifles, or soldiers. The armored windscreen didn't do a damn thing. All I remember was orange light, smoke, flying bits of glass... then I woke up in a gel tube."

"I'm not fond of those tubes. So embarrassing." Kirsten reached across the table to take Nila's hand. "Even if they are doctors."

"It's not too bad after a while. Compared to the academy, sitting in a tube didn't seem like a big deal." Sensing Kirsten's confusion, Nila laughed. "Tactical goes through military boot camp. Co-ed showers, co-ed bathrooms. Zero privacy."

Kirsten blushed at the thought.

"Trust me, hon. No one is thinking about sex for thirteen weeks. Even if they are, they'd be too tired to do a damn thing about it."

Kirsten offered an uneasy laugh and finished the pasta, but the unusual fear in Nila's face bugged her and wouldn't let go. Something here felt wrong. Maybe if she offered something personal, it would help the woman relax. After a long, awkward silence, she blurted the first— and most embarrassing—thing that came to mind.

"I've got a thing about people seeing me naked. My mother used to rip my dress off and spank me in front of her friends. They all found it hilarious. Whenever I'm exposed, I just expect people to point and laugh at me."

"I'm sorry..."

"Don't be. She was a psychotic bitch. My abilities started to manifest when I was six, but my mother believed I was the spawn of the Devil."

"That's horrible. Dorian and I used to respond to domestic situations all the time with psionic children rejected by their parents. What the hell is wrong with people?"

"I can't answer that, but I'm sure there is such a thing as true evil. What keeps me going is thinking about the people I help, especially kids." She teased her fork around the empty plate. "Not to pry, but do you really think there's a grim reaper waiting for you at the squad room, checking his watch?"

Nila shifted in the chair and put her leg down, fidgeted, flashed a false smile, and then broke out in a cold sweat.

"Mommy..." Shani ran over and clamped onto her mother's arm, glaring at Kirsten.

"It's okay sweetie. She isn't going to make me go back. She's a friend of a friend."

The girl continued glaring while standing protectively in front of Nila. The best disarming smile Kirsten could muster did little to dent the overt hostility in the tiny dark eyes pointed at her.

"Sorry. Forget I even brought it up. I was only trying to help Dorian feel better and get over some of his guilt. I don't want to hurt you or your daughter. If you ever need *any* help at all from me, here." She swiped at her NetMini, sharing her PID. From across the room, Nila's device chimed. "Just call, okay?"

The instant Kirsten went to stand, Shani bolted, running away as if about to be hit.

Nila jumped, startled by the reaction, and leaned half out of her chair, peering into the hallway after her. "That's... odd."

Kirsten frowned, offering an apologetic look.

"Don't take it personally. She's like that with anyone from the department, thinks they're going to drag me out of here to my death." Nila walked her to the door. "Thank you for the food, and please tell Dorian it's not his fault, and I'm fine."

5

TAINTED

W isps of steam lofted the beautiful fragrance of around Kirsten's face, flooding the car. She adored it. Though, she also disliked that it had overpowered the scent of Evan's just-washed hair. Dorian shot her a longing glance as she sipped it, then gazed out the side with boredom at pedestrians. Whenever someone noticed the black patrol craft and aborted jaywalking, he laughed.

"If you want a taste, you can jump in for a moment." She sipped again.

He waved her off. "That's okay. It would feel too awkward having boobs. I wouldn't even notice the coffee."

Kirsten choked on coffee.

The comm crackled to life as she rummaged for napkins in the Nippy-Nom bag. Captain Eze's holographic head appeared.

"Agent Wren, I see you aren't having much success with your endeavor to learn how to breathe coffee."

Kirsten tried to laugh, which made her choke more. Dorian laughed enough for both of them.

"There's a 21-11 in progress at the Hoyt Towers in Sector 204."

She gasped a few breaths and blinked the tears out of her eyes. "Think it's a telekinetic or an actual?"

"I'm hoping you will answer that," said Captain Eze.

"Understood, sir. I'm on my way."

His bright smile gleamed for two more seconds before his head vanished.

"The man has exquisite timing." Dorian settled into the seat.

She gave a rearward tug on the right control stick that caused the patrol craft to rise straight up. Twisting the stick clockwise rotated the car's nose upward.

"Interesting," said Dorian.

"What?"

"You have the lateral control on the twist and the roll on the stick. Most people do it the other way around."

Kirsten shrugged. "I never played video games. Was too busy digging through trash bins for food."

Dorian gazed at the roof. "What's got you in a mood?"

She activated the emergency lights, then pushed the left stick forward, jolting the car forward, accelerating up to 298 MPH. "I spoke to Nila last night."

He snapped his head left, glaring at her. "What? Why? I asked you to leave her alone. She's delicate."

Left stick left, right stick right, the car swung sideways out to the left while sliding around a right turn, skirting the corner of a high-rise. "I had a bad date."

"Do you ever have good ones?"

Kirsten squeezed until her knuckles creaked on the left stick. 350 MPH.

"You drive like you're in a video game," he grumbled, clinging to the seat. "Okay, sorry. Please slow down."

"What do you care? You're already dead."

An ad-bot whizzed by so close the car passed through the hologram.

"Whoa! Dammit woman, slow the hell down. I may be dead, but you are not."

"Nila's not delicate. She's guilty. She thinks she's next, thinks she cheated death somehow, and he's waiting for her...."

Dorian grunted as she wrenched the car into a hard left. "That shouldn't have pissed you off like this. Or upset you. Who did what to a kid?"

Kirsten stopped trying to crush the controls. "Shani. Nila's daughter. She stared at me as if I was some kind of killer there to take her mother away."

She hung a sudden right into an alley uncharted for hovercar traffic, and slowed to 200 MPH. Horizontal blocks of steel and glass connected numerous buildings along a ten-block-long area, creating a three-dimensional maze off limits to civilian hovercar traffic. Dorian emitted a constant nasal wail of alarm the whole few minutes it took her to fly an almost corkscrew pattern, dodging around the interconnected tubes and boxy protrusions jutting from buildings. Two ad-bots crashed into bracing struts to avoid the car, setting off showers of orange sparks behind them. She rolled sideways to squeeze past a narrow spot, rolled flat, and shot out into clear skies at the end of the 'tunnel of death.'

The route plot arc, a yellow ribbon on the NavMap, twisted and unkinked, recalculating. Dorian started to relax, but grabbed his stomach when she shoved forward on the right stick, causing the car to drop like a stone.

"Oh, come on. You don't have a stomach to get sick with."

That wry grin she loved/hated so much curled his lower lip. "You seem more confident since you've been taking hand-to-hand training."

"I won't crash. You should have thought of something else for a focus than a patrol car. Bit less risky."

"Choice wasn't exactly involved." Dorian waved dismissively. "Rene's mercs didn't seem too inclined to laser me to death at home on my couch. I think there's some bits of me in your chair still."

Kirsten lined up on the aperture of an enclosed roof parking deck, aiming for a landing in the emergency lane. She squeezed the patrol craft between the gap with inches to spare on either side, then tugged up on the left stick to slow the drop, buying just enough time for unfolding wheels to accept the car's weight. A gasp of Cryomil fog billowed out from beneath as the hover units powered off, drowning out the sigh sliding past her teeth.

"Sorry. I'm being shitty." She turned to face him. "Something's bothering me about Nila, and I'm—"

"Really pissed off, yeah I got that part." He shook his head before dissipating into a cloud of mist that reformed standing outside. "Question is, at what?"

Kirsten took a breath, let it out, and shoved the door upward. She waited until the soft hiss of its ascension ended with a *thunk*, then climbed out and stared at him. "I'm pissed Rene got away with killing you and turning Nila into a civilian afraid of her own shadow. Never mind the effect it had on Shani. And there's something really bothering me about the way they're acting. I can't put my finger on it."

He looked off to the side. "I'll find him sooner or later."

"By the time you're strong enough to be a threat to a living person, he'll be dead."

Dorian scowled.

"Excuse me, young lady. You can't leave your car there." A middle-aged Asian woman in an expensive suit approached from the door of a small office.

"Please stand back, ma'am. I'm responding to an emergency call at this address."

"You don't look like the police. They don't have black cars, and they don't wear black uniforms. Are you filming a holo-vid or something? You don't look like any actress I know."

An orb bot the size of a fist whirred out from behind her, clicking and beeping as it recorded still images of Kirsten, the car, and the area.

"Go back to your office. I don't have time to explain. Call it in if you want, this is a Division 0 investigation."

"Wait… the psionics?" The woman blinked.

Here we go. "Yes. Please let me—"

"Oh, my! You're a real psionic? What's it like? Were you born that way or did you decide to become psionic later?" The woman poked and pawed at Kirsten, seemingly enamored at touching her. "Can you read my mind? Do you know what I had for dinner last night? Can you tell what my son's name is?"

In Kirsten's imagination, she put the woman in an arm bar, and slammed her face first into the patrol craft's hood. In reality, she smiled. The overbearing curiosity bothered her almost as much as fear.

"Mrs. Koga, I really must insist you get out of my way before someone is hurt. I am sure Jimmy is fine, and the tempura was amazing. Now please."

With the grin of someone who had met a holovid star, the parking manager raced back to her office.

Kirsten didn't have time to sigh, and hurried to the elevators.

"Admit it, you enjoyed that a little bit." Dorian fell in step at her side.

She hopped in, faced the door, and pushed the button for the ninety-second floor, eight levels down from the parking deck. "Okay, maybe a little."

After a short metal-walled tunnel from the parking level, the clear capsule descended along a rail into a large atrium chamber. The high-end residence tower held only eight apartments per floor arranged around a central courtyard that simulated an outdoor suburban neighborhood. In essence, the middle of the building consisted of an enormous room where each wall bore the front face of two huge apartments behind the façade of freestanding houses, complete with flowers, bushes and lawns. Shimmering holo-projectors created the illusion of open sky on the ceiling.

The elevator column rode down the middle, offering a view of seven almost-identical 'micro neighborhoods' before stopping on the ninety-second level. Kirsten stepped out and followed a decorative footpath around to the west side, the address where the call had originated from.

In front of the left house, a man in a silk suit stood near an elegant woman in an ivory-colored gown. Between them, a girl of about twelve sat on the edge of the garden in a smaller version of her mother's dress. Mother and daughter had their hair up, held in place by an interlocking arrangement of delicate silver strips. All three were thin, dark-skinned, with high cheekbones. Both parents made Kirsten feel tiny, and if the kid stood, she probably wouldn't be much shorter than her. The daughter stared sullenly at the ground; her father appeared on the verge of screaming. The mother's body language and presence suggested she had prevented an all-out war.

"Careful," said Dorian. "I know how you get around rich people. You're already in a bad mood; keep it professional."

"Good morning, Mr. Greene. We got a call about possible paranormal activity? I'm Agent Wren, Division 0."

The man nodded at her, reluctantly accepting a handshake that ended as fast as he could pull away. "I am worried my daughter might be psionic. I need to know so we can get her fixed if necessary."

Mrs. Greene glared at him. The girl sniffled.

"Excuse me? Fixed?" Kirsten asked, barely holding her voice at an even tone.

"Well, you know." He waved his hand in a rolling gesture. "Cured. I'll not have psionics in my family."

"It's not a"—she paused, thinking *goddamned*—"disease, or a choice. You're either psionic or not. It doesn't happen out of the blue one day."

"Well, 'psionics' are not the sort of thing this family needs associated with it. I have a reputation to maintain," said Mr. Greene, nose held a little higher.

"Kirsten…" Dorian put a hand on her shoulder.

She closed her eyes and let the air out of her lungs. "Tell me what's happening."

"Well, things have been breaking. Plates, holo-bars, her younger brother's toys flying around." The mother continued describing symptoms appropriate to a classic poltergeist.

"I found it online. Sometimes this happens around twelve or thirteen with girls." Mr. Greene's eyes bulged ever so slightly from his skull. "Most times it goes away, but it's getting worse."

The daughter shuddered and shrank in on herself. Her body language apologized for her existence.

"It's every bit as common for boys, Mr. Greene. Girls are more sympathetic in movies. Where is your son?"

"He is staying with my mother for the time being," said the woman. "He was not taking the disturbance well. Before you ask, no, it did not stop when he left."

Kirsten approached the daughter. "Hi, sweetie. Can I bother you for a minute?" She turned to Mr. Greene. "Shall I assume if she is psionic you'll no longer want her and I'll be taking her back to the dorm?"

The girl burst into tears, covering her face with both hands.

"You can assume if the son of a bitch tells you to do that, I'll be taking my daughter to a new apartment, without him." Mrs. Greene sat beside her daughter and put an arm around her. Relief exuded from the girl. She leaned into her mother, glaring up at her father with hurt eyes.

Kirsten liked Mrs. Greene.

"Alexis. Will you please look at me?"

Alexis Greene wiped her cheeks dry, swallowed, and lifted her head. Kirsten gazed deep into her soft brown eyes, past the all-too-familiar shame. The young girl's surface thought chatter swelled and faded as she dove deeper, probing for the telltale signs of psionic ability. Dorian waved his hand past the girl's face, eliciting no reaction whatsoever. After a few minutes of concentration, Kirsten straightened up and glanced back and forth between the parents.

"Well, there is a problem. But it's not Alexis."

"What is it?" Both parents asked at once.

You're a miserable excuse for a father. She forced herself to keep a neutral expression and tone. "Alexis is not psionic in the least. That means you have an actual spirit in your house."

Mr. Greene flashed a broad smile at his daughter. Alexis glared, having none of it.

Dorian wandered around the garden to stand behind the girl and her mother, smiling at Mr. Greene.

"A spirit? Like a ghost?" Mr. Greene's voice went up in time with his eyebrow. "You don't honestly expect me to bel—"

Mr. Greene turned into Mr. Grey.

Kirsten stared into the fountain, trying not to laugh. By the time Mrs. Greene and Alexis looked behind them, Dorian had ceased his manifestation. Mr. Greene took a seat next to his wife and stared into space.

"I could help you with this issue, but, seeing as you clearly don't want psionics in your house, I'll head back to the station."

Mr. Greene raised his hand. "Wait. I'm sorry."

"Don't apologize to me. Apologize to the daughter you were ready to throw away for being different." *Dammit.* She cringed, hoping Eze wouldn't scold her later for 'not presenting the smiling face of psionics to the world.'

Dorian winced, though Alexis grinned at her.

He looked up with a numb expression. "It's been crazy."

Oh, screw it. Already opened that can of worms. "Don't make excuses. Make amends to your daughter. You realize you basically told me that I'm a sub-class person, and she would be too if she were like me." Kirsten turned, took two steps, and stopped. "The one with the door hanging open?"

Mrs. Green nodded. Her husband studied the ground.

Kirsten approached the residence.

Dorian went in first, smiling back over his shoulder. "You handled him pretty well. Are you okay? That seemed a little too close to home."

A few items in the living room looked out of place: a small vase on the ground leaking water, holographic picture bars knocked askew, and a spilled bowl of misshapen round lumps. She stooped to pick one up.

"What the hell is this?"

"Nuts. Well, probably Epoxil carved into the shape of nuts. You know, the kind of irregular strange-looking objects people leave in bowls on tables to look nice, not for eating."

She chuckled, dropped it, and peered at carvings of wildlife on either side of the primary holovid player, a life-sized wooden jaguar on the left, a majestic elephant on the right.

"Yeah, I'm not dwelling on that bitch anymore." She moved into the dining room, whistling at an onyx table big enough for twelve. "I think I'm going to find Rene."

"You don't want to get mixed up with him." Dorian shook his head.

A six-inch jade lion flew from a shelf, missing her by an inch. She ducked it, glaring at a spectral smear vanishing into an enormous animated electronic painting of a nebula.

"Yeah." She ran after it, down a corridor among bedrooms. "I do. He hurt you."

Dorian went wide, passing through the wall. She skidded to a halt by the door to Alexis's room, judging by the holo-posters. Inside, Dorian rolled on the ground atop a suspension of white vapor. The apparition had a defined head as well as two hands, with little more than smears of fog between them that suggested a human shape at the most rudimentary level. The shape of the head hinted at male. It punched at Dorian's chest; his smirk called it a minor nuisance.

"He'll have lackeys again. You will hesitate at killing them, since they're dominated." He grabbed the poltergeist about the neck, trying to hold it up as a target. The spirit's head flopped around like a lead weight atop a noodle. "Lash it."

Two points of white light hinting at its eyes flared wide. A teen's entire collection of concert holodisks rippled from wall-mounted shelves at her. Kirsten held up a hand to guard her face, but yelped and dove to the side when several hit her hard enough to break skin. They kept on pelting her as she darted to the left. By the time it stopped and she lowered her defensive arms, both the poltergeist and Dorian had left the room.

"Ow! Son of a bitch." She touched two fingers to a cat scratch on her cheek and called out, "I can suggest them to go away."

"What do you plan to do with him once you catch him?" shouted Dorian from the next room, amid the meaty *smacks* of repeated punching. "Command is quite wary of suggestives."

Kirsten dashed into the hall and left at the next doorway into a small boy's bedroom. Dorian grappled with the poltergeist on the floor. Threads of spirit energy wrapped around him, making a clean strike impossible. "They're not fond of Mind Blast either. Yay for me I can do both. We take Rene in alive. He can't suggest anything with an inhibitor on."

The poltergeist oozed away from Dorian's grip and dashed back through the wall to Alexis' room. Growling, he leapt after it. Kirsten sprinted back to the first room, calling the lash as she ran. She skidded to a stop in the doorway, hand raised.

As if in response to the power radiating from the glimmering white energy cord, the poltergeist emitted a keening wail and hurled Dorian straight up. He flew into the ceiling, causing a lamp made of three rose-shaped LED bulbs to flicker. Kirsten started a swing, but a sudden assault of school-issue datapads fouled her aim. The spirit wisped around Dorian's attempt to grab it again darted back to the boy's room. Dorian, too, leapt into the wall.

"Ugh!" Kirsten scowled. "Sometimes I hate being solid."

"I don't want to take him alive," yelled Dorian from the other room.

Kirsten rushed back to the boy's room. The poltergeist shrugged away from Dorian's grip and dove at Kirsten. Reacting with instinct to someone running at her, she performed a perfect ju-jitsu grab on cold air. The stunrod on her belt turned itself on and tapped her in the knee.

The rug tasted like foot.

When the flashing blue left her vision, she spat carpet fibers out of her teeth and growled. Pain cascaded in ripples from her right leg, which refused to move. The stunning effect of the neural shock set her muscles twitching. She snarled, grabbed the bed, and dragged herself up on numb legs. The crash of breaking glass motivated her into a limping run. She wobbled down the hall, back across the dining room, and into the kitchen, managing to fall over only once on the way when her right leg gave out. By the time she arrived in the kitchen, the after-nausea of a stunrod shock had reached full swing.

Dorian tried to get a hold of the spirit, grabbing and gathering it as if trying to collect a rope made from flying bed sheets. The head and both hands floated away while he pulled at its wispy midsection, stretching to the other side of the room, all the while hurling glassware and bottles at him.

"Dorian, you don't want to kill Rene. Not unless he's an immediate threat to your life."

"I think I'm a little past that point." He ignored the pelting of physical objects, which couldn't touch him, and yanked on the ectoplasm, dragging the disembodied head into a punch that sent it back across the kitchen.

Kirsten swung the lash, but missed the zooming swath of spirit by inches. The phantom another wail and streaked into the cabinets. "Wow, this son of a bitch is fast. Look, if you kill his ghost... You're already shitting ectoplasmic bricks whenever a Harbinger shows up."

He stopped running after it, breathing hard more out of habit than need. "I..."

Clinking and rattling migrated around inside the cabinets, whatever the poltergeist did remained concealed behind small imitation wood doors. Kirsten turned in place, following the sound, arm poised for another lash. "You deserve revenge, but I don't want them taking you. Last time was too damn close. I thought it was going to..." She choked up.

A door burst open, releasing a swarm of knives into the air. Kirsten let herself fall straight down, ass to tile. It hurt, but less than a dozen knives. Still, the jolt to the spine left her stunned, mouth agape. Dorian lunged armpit deep into the cabinet, and grabbed the spirit by the neck. He flung it out into the room, ignoring a barrage of spice jars. The poltergeist finally seemed to realize throwing physical objects at him did nothing, and stopped.

Kirsten rubbed the back of her neck, wondering how landing on her butt could cause her head to ache. She missed an opportunity for a lash due to lacking any desire to move. The food reassembler above and behind her went bonkers, spraying hot sauce, jelly, and peanut butter down on her. She raised an arm to shield her eyes.

"Yeah... I thought that too," said Dorian, adding a growl as he fought to keep a grip on the spirit. "This thing is bat-shit nuts. There's no rational thought left in it. Whack it."

"As soon as I can move." She groaned, scratching at the floor in an effort to restore feeling back into her legs. "If you kill Rene, I'm not sure I can beg them off you. Please let me handle him."

"What the devil's all that damn noise?" Mr. Greene's bellow filled the hallway.

The poltergeist wrenched out of Dorian's hands, spirit fog spreading around his fingers.

"Shit," rasped Dorian. "This is like trying to wrestle spaghetti."

Mr. Greene stopped short in the archway to the kitchen, staring at Kirsten—the only entity he could see aside from the mess. "Good grief, woman. What are you doing?"

The spirit elongated, stretching away from Dorian's grip, flying right at Mr. Greene. Shrieking, it raised its arms as if to claw him to ribbons. The man didn't react whatsoever to its approach, continuing to stare at her like he'd caught his three-year-old trashing the kitchen.

Oh, I am so done with this damn thing... and this idiot.

Kirsten slung kiwi jam off her hand, then re-summoned the Astral

Lash. Mr. Greene babbled at the appearance of the scintillating strand of light. She grunted, and swiped downward at the passing poltergeist. The whip struck the spirit in its approximate back.

Splat.

The poltergeist exploded in a massive shower of transparent, cold slime.

A weak sense of oblivion flickered across the Aether. Still, Kirsten shuddered. Mr. Greene looked as though someone dumped a bucket of egg whites over his head. Tendrils of goo stranded off his nose and chin. He blinked, stunned mute as if slapped. Somewhere behind him, mother and daughter gasped.

"What in the world?" Mrs. Greene poked him with a tentative finger, jerking her hand back from the cold slime. When she spotted the formation of knives impaled in the wall, she had to cover her mouth to stifle a scream.

"Poltergeist. It won't be bothering you again." Kirsten struggled to her feet, rubbing her tailbone. "Sorry about the suit."

Mr. Greene turned with the motion of a mannequin on a rotary platform, mouth still open, hand still held up. He blinked again at his wife, who moved past him into the kitchen, shaking her head at the carnage.

"Why did that thing come here? What did it want?"

Kirsten washed her hands in the sink, shrugging. "I can't even begin to guess. These sorts of spirits aren't true souls, more of a latent snapshot or a fragment of someone's personality that gathered enough power to start roaming around. Some think they are very weak demons."

"Do you?" Mrs. Greene began the process of collecting knives from the floor.

Dorian rubbed his chin, as eager for her answer as the family.

"Well." Kirsten dabbed at the cut on her cheek with a wet towel. "I know there's a place I call the Abyss, where evil spirits go when they are purged from this world. I suppose it's possible for energy to burp back out whenever something crosses into it. That might be what people call a demon, but it's really only a returned ghost. One who got out of jail, so to speak. I don't think there are real *demons* per se. Not in the biblical sense anyway. I'm sure those are stories made up by people who didn't understand the supernatural."

"And wanted to burn whatever they didn't understand." Dorian said in a somber tone.

"Yeah," she muttered, rubbing the back of her right hand.

"So..." Mrs. Greene swiped a finger at the counter, making a disgusting face at the slime. "What is this?"

"Ectoplasm or something. The spirit that had bothered you was a fragmentary piece of energy, not a true soul. This slime is what sometimes happens when spirit entities experience a violent interaction with something that disrupts their essence. We still don't really know what it is. No technological devices we've ever put it in have been able to determine its composition."

"Well, you damn sure disrupted the hell out of that thing," muttered Mr. Greene. "I've never seen anything like this in my life. So, what do we do with this gunk?"

Kirsten clenched and released her right hand. "I suggest mops and towels. Down the drain. Cleaning bots exposed to it have been known to exhibit strange behavior." She scraped her hand down her front and slung slime into the sink. "But, you can rest easy now. It's gone."

"It's *very* gone," said Dorian.

THE SILVER CIRCLE

Chrome spheres clacked back and forth, inches from Kirsten's nose. The farthest on the right swung into the hanging line, kicking the farthest left into the air. The endless repetitive motion created tiny fireflies of reflected light that danced across her workspace. Her right arm served as a pillow between her chin and the desk, her every breath fogging the gloss black surface. She tracked the Newton's cradle with her eyes: left, right, left, right, the tapping sound rhythmic—mesmerizing.

It stopped.

She blinked. All five spheres sat idle. *Did I fall asleep?* She reached out with her left hand—the electronic armguard made for an uncomfortable chinrest—and prodded the toy back to life. This time, two orbs moved on either side.

Click, click, silence.

Her eyebrows drew together. "Figures, I get a broken one."

The two spheres on the edges rose outward as if under their own power.

Nicole, right behind her, burst into laughter. Kirsten almost fell out of her chair.

"Dammit." She grabbed her chest. "Don't sneak up on people. And why is your face so red?"

"Better *I* find you sleeping than Eze." Nicole adjusted the fit of her uniform top, flashing an impish smile. "Oh, no reason."

"I'm not sleeping, I'm bored." Kirsten let her chin fall onto her arm again. "Nice. Same guy as last week?" She braced for the impact of the foam stress skull, laughing after it bounced away.

"I'm not *easy*." Nicole gave her a raspberry. "He's officially a boyfriend."

"Oh, nice. Finally found someone who made it to the second date? Who is it?" Kirsten sat up, reclining in her desk chair, turning her head left to follow the redhead to her desk. "Did you skip telling them you're psionic?"

"He knows. It's Jaden from Admin." She checked her face in a small hand mirror.

"Nikki, he's eighteen. That's still a kid."

"Oh, and I'm geriatric at twenty-one?" Another raspberry. "He's smart. He's good-looking. He's psionic too, and he's in *love* with me." Nicole blinked. "What do you mean you can't have the one you want?"

Dorian sighed.

"Nicole Logan, will you please stop—"

"Wren." Captain Eze's voice reverberated over their conversation. They both looked at his door.

Nicole grinned. "Well, he yelled from his desk, so it's not bad news."

"At least you won't be bored now," added Dorian.

Kirsten pushed herself standing, stretching the past two hours' worth of sitting idle out of her legs. A wobbling gait carried her into the office of Captain Jonathan Eze and the automatic door closed behind her without a sound.

"Good afternoon. I hope I am not keeping you up." He grinned, plucked a can of Qwikwarm Coffee out of his lower desk drawer and set it on the edge nearest her.

She took it, picking at fingernail switches in the base to set cream and sweetness levels before twisting the bottom of the can. The sharp crack of a broken ampule announced the start of a chemical reaction. Warmth spread into her hand a few seconds before the fragrance of cheap java filtered into the room. "If this is about the Greene case, it was a poltergeist. They throw—"

"It isn't." Eze raised one eyebrow. "What are you frowning at?"

"Do they think spelling quick with a w makes it trendier or something? Why do companies do stupid crap like that?"

Eze pulled his fingers over his chin and chuckled. His contagious smile always lifted her mood. "I think your question goes beyond the depth of the mysteries we deal with. But"—he slapped his desk—"I have something that needs your attention far more than protecting the coffee-drinking public from poor spelling."

The sudden noise and shift in mood from jovial to serious made her jump. Upright, she took on a military posture and nodded. He poked at his terminal, the lights dimmed, and a holographic screen spread over most of the wall to her right displaying an overhead map of West City. Amber gridlines denoting sectors appeared. At the far zoom, they appeared more as a faint gold tint than individual squares. Eze pushed a button on his holo-panel, shifting the big map's focus down to a region twenty sectors square, a hundred mile grid. The size of the map and the rapid zooming of a top-down view gave Kirsten a faint sense of vertigo. It came too close to when she'd leapt off the parking deck. The grid expanded to individual squares, each bearing a number.

"Watch Sector 637. This is from late last night, a few seconds past 0100 hours."

With a beep, the screen glimmered and went from static image to moving video. She locked on to the spot he mentioned, searching for anything out of the ordinary in the twelve-inch square. Blackness appeared in the south, left area of the sector. An inky dot grew to about a mile across, then smeared to the northeast, painting the city in a trail of gloom. The affected area expanded as it spread, fatter in front like a comet with a long tail. Eighteen miles later, it stopped, leaving a giant swath of nothingness over four sectors. After a few seconds, the blackness began to fade from the tail end, disappearing gradually along its length until only a round spot three miles across remained. Six seconds later, it shrank down to a tiny point and vanished entirely.

"The image makes me think of someone running a black paintbrush tool over the satellite feed. Are you sure this isn't a hacker messing with the Citycam system? They really should protect that better. Every baby hacker cuts their teeth on it."

He pushed a datapad across his desk. "There were over two hundred ninety thousand reports of power outages along the trail. A localized blackout is responsible for the path you see here. Everything from street lamps to city cams to NetMinis, it all went dark."

"Okay, that rules out a hacker. If a paranormal entity caused this, what the hell is it doing? Ghosts usually suck up power to restore themselves or build up for a big event."

Eze's chair creaked into a lean. "It gets better."

The image zoomed in further, sinking to street level. Kirsten gripped the back of the chair beside her for balance as the point of view plummeted to Earth, pulled up, and flew into one of the ubiquitous mounted cameras. Based on the condition of the buildings it surveyed, she assumed it was in, or at least at the edge of, a grey zone. A dark band circled one of the gleaming towers, as if someone sliced one entire floor out of a skyscraper-shaped cake.

"This is Sector 848, where the blackness stopped. Pay attention to the tower with no glass on one floor."

She leaned closer to the giant holo-panel. "I think I see a small fire inside. Maybe squatters cooking? That's not too unusual for—"

The flame roared up, bright as a magnesium flare, flickering and sputtering. The video flashed to a field of white static a few seconds before freezing.

"This is the moment when the blackout trail arrives. We lose about nine seconds of video." Eze un-paused it.

When the image crackled back to clarity, diagnostic text scrolled over it as the citycam went through a boot sequence. A column of 'PASS' slid up the right edge. Thick black smoke had filled the windowless floor, confined as if some sort of force field kept it from spilling out the edges. She blinked in confusion for a few seconds until all at once, the smoke drew inward as if sucked into an unseen vacuum. The phantom campfire was gone.

"That's—"

"Keep watching." He backed up a few frames and restarted it.

Again, she watched the smoke recede. This time, she didn't look away to talk. Thin lines of static banded down the image a second before a torus of distorted light expanded outward, flakes like shimmering ice at its outermost edge. The circular wave of energy grew until it passed through the walls of adjacent towers. The blur of its approach desaturated the colors in the video. When the approaching transparent wave reached the camera the video cut to black.

"I saw a similar effect when the Wharf Stalker died." She sank into the chair. "I mean, when I..."

"I know what you mean. What disturbs me isn't that it resembles your description of the obliteration of a powerful entity. What disturbs me is that *I* can see it"—he gestured at the display screen—"and the cameras recorded it."

Kirsten looked up with a gasp. She hadn't even thought of that. For the first time, she wondered if she would be strong enough to deal with something as powerful as this image suggested. "M... maybe it was just a blast wave from an explosion"—her voice fell to a mumble—"an explosion that didn't damage glass windows right next to it."

"I don't like that look in your eyes, Kirsten. I don't think I've ever seen you afraid of ghosts before."

A nervous laugh escaped her. "I don't think I've seen anything this freaky before."

"You shouldn't go alone. Sector 848 is a bad area."

I'm not alone.

"Take Logan."

She leaned forward. "I'm not sure bringing Logan is a good idea, Captain. She's not used to seeing paranormals; it might leave a mark." *This isn't the police to her, it's high school.*

"She can handle it. She reminds me a little of you. Innocent on the outside, tough inside."

Kirsten couldn't tell whether to feel complimented or insulted. Either way, changing his mind would take all day and accomplish nothing but waste time. She didn't want to be responsible for her only friend suffering mental damage. "Are you sure?"

"Eminently."

She exhaled the entire way back to her desk.

"Hey, Nikki?"

"Yo?" She swiveled around, grinning.

"Suit up. Eze wants you to go with me on this one."

"Cool." She jumped up.

Kirsten caught her on the bicep as she attempted to dart past to the garage. "Nikki, there might be some *strange* things here. If you wanna fake it, I'll tell Eze you went."

"Bullshit." Nicole grabbed and held her hand. "If he wants me to go with you, he's worried. I'm not gonna leave you without backup."

Four blue eyes locked. Kirsten gave in first.

"Okay." She tugged Nicole back once more. "Thanks... and, I'm sorry."

"TALK ABOUT CLOSE, THIS BUILDING'S RIGHT ON THE EDGE OF THE GREY." Nicole fiddled with the NavMap, magnifying it as far as it would go.

Kirsten frowned at the screen. "What difference does a few inches make?"

She regretted the question as soon as Nicole started laughing.

Dorian draped himself between the seats. "You really ought to watch what you say around her."

The ceaseless glimmer of West City dimmed as they flew into Sector 848. Officially, the grey zone ended a full grid square northeast from here, but the relentless creep of tired desolation had already set in. A slow exodus of civilized people left businesses closed or with armored windows. Gangs fought wars in the streets while the cops came in later and cleaned up the bodies.

Less work for them.

Dark spots appeared amid the patchwork of light. A vacant apartment here, a shot out lamp there, though the buildings' structures remained intact. Around a distant century tower, the electronic windscreen lit up with four green triangles hinting at a square. She drove straight toward #1998 City Road 130. One entire floor out of a hundred, the thirteenth, had been gutted, all the windows and steel molding on the outside blasted off by a powerful explosion some time ago. The plasticrete slab floors had withstood the blast, focusing all the energy outward. Kirsten nudged the patrol craft into a slight dive and slowed to a jogging pace near the building, flying in an orbit at the level of the damage.

Inside, a few walls remained intact, steel beams with clods of Epoxil planks, one or two still clinging to scorched drywall. Fortunately for the upper floors, the building's structural integrity didn't depend on the outer wall. Internal supports remained intact. The glass, pure fascia, represented only cosmetic damage. A three-story tall band of windows on facing buildings appeared newer than floors above or below, likely destroyed in the blast and replaced.

"This building is zoned as abandoned." Nicole's face turned blue in the terminal's light. "Looks like the title's under the name of a leasing company out of East City, uhh... Kukla Investments. No one has occupied it in about seven months."

"Whoever demoed this building knew what they were doing." Dorian whistled. "Complete eradication of one floor with minimal damage up and down."

"Think it was a professional job?" Kirsten brought the car to a hovering standstill, gazing into the building past flaps of translucent plastic drifting in the breeze. She activated the forward spotlights and rotated the car side to side, examining debris.

"Umm..." Nicole flipped screens. "Div 1 has a report of an unexplained detonation about seven months ago, four bodies recovered."

"I was talking to"—Kirsten sighed—"never mind. Shit, do you feel that?"

"Feel what?" Nicole looked over.

"Yeah." Dorian edged into the shadows of the backseat. "Harbingers?"

Kirsten stared into the building a few seconds more, then at the dashboard, then at her lap. "I... No, it doesn't feel right."

Nicole peeled her gaze away from the terminal and also looked into the building. "Just creep forward and land inside, the hole's big enough."

"I'm not risking the floor collapsing."

Kirsten pulled the car into a vertical ascent and set down on the roof a few minutes later. The air held a faint trace of foul between chemical and fecal. Stale industry picked at her throat as she crunched over trash and kicked synthbeer canisters out of her way. She stopped in front of the roof access and frowned at the dark interface panel. The building had no power. Without it, her police override code would do no good. She banged on the door three times.

"Anyone in there?"

Waiting.

"Hello?" *Bang, bang, bang.* "This is the police. I'm about to open this door with a laser. If there is anyone on the other side of it, yell now. You have ten seconds."

Dorian shook his head, walking past her through the door. After a moment, his head came back out. "It's clear."

"Sorry." She took the E-90 out of its holster. "I sometimes forget you're a ghost."

"Ghost?" Nicole whirled about. "Where?"

Kirsten bit her lip, raising the weapon. "It's a long story."

She aimed at the door, thought better of it, and backed up ten feet before firing at the lock plate. The first shot burned a hole in cinder blocks an inch to the right.

"Calm down," whispered Dorian. "Your hand is shaking."

Her second try melted the knob into a spray of hot metal. The third did enough damage in the right place to let the door swing free. Nicole grunted, and the flap of metal flew open hard enough to slam a huge cloud of dust off the wall.

Kirsten's jumped back, making a face worthy of the Wall of Derp. "Gah!"

"Sorry, that was me." Nicole offered a sheepish cringe, and stood up straight. "Hey, why are you so on edge?"

Kirsten walked around Dorian rather than through him, making him chuckle. "The video I showed you on the ride over here. That, and something doesn't feel right."

She crept past bare cinder block walls rife with the dry scent of aerosolized dirt. A vertical shaft ran the length of the building, leading down into the dark. Sudden light caused Kirsten to whirl. Nicole caught her hand, keeping the E-90 aimed at the wall. Panic melted to accusation in Kirsten's eyes as she glared at the strips of light on the sides of Nicole's helmet.

"Please warn me. Light coming out of nowhere can mean so many things…"

"Sorry," whispered Nicole. "You really need to calm the hell down."

Kirsten sighed a wordless apology and put the E-90 back on her belt.

"So…" Nicole peered over the railing from the seventy-fourth story roof. The lights painted long glowing streaks in air smoky with dust. "Thirteenth floor, huh? About that long of a story?"

———

"SERIOUSLY? *THAT'S* WHY YOUR PATROL CRAFT HAS A REPUTATION?" NICOLE grinned. "Cool!" She paused, biting her knuckle. "I mean… It's not cool he's dead, but…"

"Tell her not to worry about it, no offense taken."

"He says it's okay."

"So you, like see him all the time? Does he like watch you in the shower?"

"No." Dorian and Kirsten answered simultaneously.

"Is he the one you have a crush on?"

Kirsten stumbled over the last step on the fifteenth floor landing. "No."

"Liar." Nicole grinned.

Dorian found the wall to be rather interesting all of a sudden.

"It's…" Kirsten sighed. "Maybe if he were alive, but… Even as a ghost, he's still my partner."

Nicole shook her head. "They say it's a bad idea to get romantic with your partner if you're on field work. Leads to mistakes. I mean, it happens but they usually reassign people."

"Mistakes? Like what, getting him killed?" Kirsten cringed. "Sorry, that sounded bitchier than I meant it."

"Is it cool having a ghost for a partner? He can do all sorts of ghosty stuff the perps never expect?"

Dorian rolled his eyes.

"I think he'd rather be alive still, and no, he's not *that* old. He can't do too much to living people at all."

Nicole squealed.

"Except the old icy hand down the back bit," mumbled Kirsten.

The redhead seemed intrigued and freaked all at once.

"Whoa." Kirsten went rigid as her boot touched the thirteenth floor landing. "Damn."

A grey door, warped from the force of an explosion, fluttered in the wind, tapping against the frame it no longer fit with a repetitive *clonk, clonk, clonk*. Nicole slid past her and pulled it to the side, looking back with an uneasy lift to her eyebrows.

"K... I feel something weird in there. "

Kirsten's knuckles went white on the handle of the laser. "That's not a good sign."

"How bad is it?" Nicole pulled out her E-86. Green light pulsed back and forth along the sides.

"I don't know. Any psionic can sense the presence of an entity powerful enough to affect the living, even if they can't see them."

Nicole's alarm lessened. "I didn't feel funny in the car."

Maybe bringing her along was a good idea. She's keeping me calm. "Dorian's not old enough, or mean enough, to raise those hackles."

"Thanks." Dorian went first, looking around at the destruction. He stopped to examine a few scorch marks. "Whatever did this was conventional. Explosives had to be placed at several detonation points. Main charges near the center; shaped, probably. Bluish discoloration makes me think NE4. I think the blast was set up deliberately to shove everything out the windows."

"K?" Nicole swiveled toward her.

Kirsten cringed away from the bright helmet lights pointed at her face. "Yeah?"

"Did you just hear something? I thought I heard someone whispering over there."

Dorian shouted Nicole's name. She looked toward him.

"You're hearing Dorian. I don't understand how. This area is…"

"Wrong." Nicole finished her sentence. "I want to go home and hug my dad, hide under a blanket."

"Latent fear." Kirsten squatted, brushing her fingers over the dusty plasticrete. "Something happened here that burned fear into the fabric of the building. The dread that's affecting you isn't natural. You're picking it up from the environment."

"Does a giant friggin' bomb count?" Nicole pushed past a sheet of tattered hanging plastic.

"I don't think the people who died in this had time to even mess their pants," said Kirsten.

They fanned out, drifting among cracked concrete support posts, hanging wires, and exposed pipes. Boots scuffed, the wind howled, and soon, Kirsten stopped noticing the sour awfulness of the all-too-close black zone to the north. Ten minutes into the search, Nicole raised her voice, so close to the timbre of a frightened child, Kirsten worried.

"Kiki… I don't like this."

Kirsten ran toward her, stumbling over the debris of a few chairs and a desk. Past a still-standing section of wall, she rounded a corner and skidded to a halt with her mouth hanging open.

An area eighteen feet across glimmered with metallic silver paint. Someone had traced a circle on the ground, laced with intricate symbols resembling runes and pictographs. Half-molten candles—three white, three black, and one gold—stood at seven points around the exterior, lining up with the geometric arrangement of shapes within.

Lines divided the interior of the circle into sections, each filled with drawings that possessed a crude sophistication. The pictograms didn't appear childlike or primitive, rather simple. Kirsten squatted, hesitant to touch it. Fingertips hovering inches above the markings, she noted some of the lines etched deep into the plasticrete floor slab. This spot radiated an overwhelming amount of paranormal energy, forcing Nicole to back away, arms folded and shaking.

"Someone engraved this here; it was meant to last awhile." Kirsten whistled.

"Umm, isn't that plasticrete? That stuff's harder than armor." Nicole tapped her chest plate. "How did anyone do that?"

"It's composite armor-grade plastic mixed with concrete. The stuff isn't *that* tough. Our sidearms will go through it… eventually. Anyone with a portable welder could've done this, but the grooves are too precise. I"—she scratched her head—"can't explain this."

Dorian yelled off to the right, a fair distance away. "Found an M3 wire burned on the ground. Junction box out in the hall has a Tricor Fiber uplink, or what's left of one. Whoever lived here was a big time net head."

"What's that?" gasped Nicole, pointing.

Kirsten looked, seeing nothing. "What?"

"A shadow just moved over there. Big. Assault trooper big."

"Please don't be fucking with me here, Nikki." Kirsten stepped around the circle as an odd feeling in the back of her mind told her not to cross it.

"I swear I'm not." The redhead's tiny voice sounded as if it came from an eight-year-old.

"Who's there?" Kirsten shouted, her voice echoing off the bare floor and ceiling.

Nicole sniffled.

"You can wait in the car if you want."

The lights on Nicole's helmet swept back and forth with a rapid headshake. "No, I'm not leavin' you here alone."

A dry rasping chuckle rolled over the entire floor, thinning Kirsten's blood. It had no focus, no direction, reverberating from everywhere. She spun in place, heart racing as she searched for the source of the voice. Kirsten bit back a yelp when she spotted a shadow creeping along the far side of the room between columns and patches of still-standing wall. The figure appeared huge, maybe seven feet tall, and wide. Malice replaced the fear in the air.

Hate brimmed from the entity, focused on her.

Nicole screamed. Kirsten whirled. Her friend stared aghast at Dorian. He had moved closer, six feet away from the edge of the silver circle. His hair shifted in the wind. Faint transparency to his body told her he'd become visible.

Pain.

Agony paralyzed her. Kirsten howled. Her E-90 slipped from her fingers and clattered to the ground beside her as she collapsed to all fours. It felt as though someone poured Cryomil all over her and lit it on fire. No, someone shot her with a laser. No, burning iron spikes had rammed themselves into her kidneys and twisted. She scrabbled at the ground, crawling forward. Her knee bumped the weapon, she remembered it, and put a hand on it. The pain in her back increased to the point it didn't hurt anymore.

Gasping, Kirsten called on her psionic power, wrapping it around the paranormal energy invading her body. She growled past a clenched jaw and forced the invading entity out, diminishing the pain from mind-numbing to horrible, then raised the E-90 into her field of vision. Blue dots glowed in the dark, the holographic gunsight wavering in her trembling grasp.

Nicole slid to a halt nearby and helped her up. They both aimed their weapons around, but the shadow had vanished. Kirsten stowed the E-90 and opened her eyes to the astral world. Her left arm had chicken-winged up against her chest from the pain along that side of her body. If not for Nicole holding her up, she would have fallen.

Her Astral Lash unfurled from her hand, a shimmering thread of blue-white energy that coiled around her legs. The rest of the pain fled. Kirsten took a step, rolling her arm around to get blood flowing again while squinting at the darkness. Shadows slid long as if the moon fast-forwarded across the sky.

"Where are you?" asked Kirsten, her tone angry. "Show yourself."

The mood lightened. Wind no longer made the slightest sound.

Whatever the entity was, it had left, and taken fear with it.

"Holy shit, that noodly thing is so pretty." Nicole, back to her old self, shook her by the shoulder. "Are you okay? What was that scream?"

Kirsten relaxed her mind; the lash evaporated. "I don't know." She swooned off her feet.

Nicole held on, easing her to sit on a toppled filing cabinet. She grunted. A small spot of pain returned, as though someone held a single candle too close to her back.

Dorian jogged over, shaking his head. "I saw something move. It came out from behind the post, shot over to you, and went back so fast it looked like a blur."

"Wraith? Maybe it's pissed off I got its little brother." She grimaced. "Dammit, my back is burning."

Nicole pulled Kirsten's uniform top out of her pants, and gasped. Her bare skin glowed near blinding in the glare from helmet-mounted lights. Kirsten's armband chimed announcing an email from Nicole.

"Look at that... And damn, girl, get some sun."

Kirsten glanced up at her friend, and then opened the message. It contained a photo of her from behind, pale skin marred red by three vertical scratches about six inches long over the left kidney. The skin had welted, angry and red, looking every bit as hot as it felt. It didn't bleed much, the depth little different from what one might expect from a petulant housecat. The sight of wounds nearly identical to what had been on Adrienne's body infuriated her.

The damn thing that got away... But, wait... it couldn't be. This one felt much stronger.

"Just a scratch." Nicole patted her on the shoulder. "The way you screamed I thought you'd been stabbed."

Kirsten shuddered as she forced herself to sit up straight. "It hurts a shitload more than it looks. You like peeking into my head, check this bad boy out."

Dorian chuckled. "I wouldn't recommend you do that."

"Yeah." Nicole shook her head. "I won't, and what the hell? Did I just hear Dorian again?"

"Hey, Dorian... Help me out here?" grunted Kirsten.

He stooped and put a hand into her back through the wound.

"Ahh." She closed her eyes. "Nice and cold."

"Sergeant Icepack, reporting for duty." He saluted with his other hand, but his expression fell serious. "I feel something. There's a taint in the wound."

"Yeah. It's just like—"

Nicole, attempting to be helpful, applied a stimpak.

Kirsten belted out every known swear word and made a few new ones up on the spot. The scratches faded away and came back, in a repeating cycle. When it stopped, the marks remained as before. Agony left her curled up and bawling like a child.

"Maybe you need a priest?" Dorian cocked a grin.

A minute or so later, she unclenched her jaw enough to speak. "Priest my ass. That's all mind over matter stuff. Only works if you believe it, and you know my opinion. Same thing that happened to Adrienne. Energy in the scratches."

"I'm not sure *you* know your opinion anymore." He put his hand back into the wound.

"This is kinda freaky." Nicole giggled. "I'm not astrally sensitive. I shouldn't be hearing him. I'm gonna go take pictures and stuff of the weird silver crap."

Out. Kirsten closed her eyes. *Get out of me. Whatever you are, get out of me.*

Kirsten focused her psionic energy inward, searching for a trace of any presence. The attack had left dark energy behind. The miasma had a slimy, unclean quality that made her squirm, almost as horrifying as the puddle she'd fallen into in the Beneath.

Out! Her mind-voice screamed at the top of its non-lungs.

She pictured her energy wrapping around a thing that squirmed and fought back. Pain plucked at her back as though scabs peeled out of the claw marks. She clenched her psionic fist and crushed, pulled. A flash of pain came on as if someone tore a strip of duct tape away from her skin, followed by a sense of a tiny oblivion. Kirsten's eyes snapped open. She lurched forward and grabbed a charred column, panting.

Cool air over her back reminded her of three scratches.

After a few breaths, she straightened up and slipped a stimpak out of her belt case before flicking the yellow safety cap off the end.

Dorian's hand moved to her shoulder. "You sure you want to do that to yourself again?"

"Yeah. I cleared the energy from the scratches. Stimpak won't hurt this time." She eyed the shiny metal tip. "This place is filthy. I don't want to get an infection."

7

VAPORIZED

City Road 1804 and Morris Avenue belonged to Kukla Investments, LTD, after purchase via government auction seven months ago. The original owner, Westmoreland Properties, lost it during a legal battle. The insurance company refused to pay out, citing a technicality in the policy that claimed Westmoreland had failed to adequately prevent a tenant from using dangerous devices. Despite the relatively controlled nature of the demolition, dozens of other tenants on the floors above and below sued for injuries. The rest of the tenants filed a class action, seeking compensation for the expense of a sudden need to move to a new home. Ultimately, the government took ownership of the property and sold it at auction. Kukla purchased it for about a hundredth of its value.

Kirsten tapped her fingers on the side of her head; two coffees and a strawberry-filled crepe had almost cured the memory of the horrible pain. The financials made her want to say fraud, but she couldn't quite put together exactly what struck her as sketchy. Westmoreland collected no money on the deal, not to mention the barrage of lawsuits. Kukla bought the building from the government at a price so cheap it verged on criminal, but had done nothing with it. Perhaps what bothered her was how no other individuals or companies had even bid at the auction. After licking a bit of strawberry from the rim of her cup, she drained the last of the tepid brew.

"Any luck?" Nicole slid her chair over.

Seeing Nicole act like a normal person and not a sugared-up tween worried Kirsten. "You okay? You seem a bit off."

"I guess I'm still a bit scared. It felt like something followed us out of there."

"I didn't see anything," said Dorian.

Nicole didn't bat an eyelash at his voice. That felt normal enough to let Kirsten smile.

"Dorian didn't see anything," she whispered. "Please don't go yakking about him. Even here, talking about ghosts makes people look at you weird."

"I believe you... I mean, before an hour ago I..." She scratched her head and forced a grin. "Oh, I got some info on the hamburger."

"Lunch?"

Dorian rolled his eyes. "I believe she means the victims of the demolition work."

"Oh. Good, I'm sick and tired of chasing an accounting trail. It looks so suspicious but makes no sense."

"What does?" asked Nicole.

"Place goes boom. Owner's insurance company pulls a piece of shit move, refuses to pay out. The property management company refuses to pay out of pocket for the repairs. Tenants leave, Westmoreland stops paying taxes on an abandoned building, so the government seizes it and sells it at auction. Only one outfit bids on it, not a single other person or business tries. Kukla pays peanuts for the property, but then does nothing with it." She waved at the screen. "They're letting it sit there."

"That's weird," Nicole said with a nod of finality, as if her statement answered everything.

That's why you're tactical, sweetie.

Kirsten reclined, breathing warm coffee-air around her icy fingers. "Maybe they wanted to do something with the property, but the proximity to the grey zone scared off potential tenants?"

"I bet people got freaked out by the hit squad."

Whoa. She said something useful. "What hit squad?"

Nicole kicked off Kirsten's desk, shoving her wheeled chair back to her workstation. A second later, Kirsten's chair propelled itself to join her. She yelped and flailed her arms at the unexpected motion. Once the shock wore off, she glowered.

Kirsten caught herself with two hands on Nicole's desk. "Little warning, please."

"Check this out." Nicole pointed. "Forensics went over the scene for more than two hundred work-hours. They managed to piece together a grand total of four-point-two victims."

"Point two?"

"That must have been a big bomb." Dorian grinned.

"DNA said dog." Nicole sighed. "Poor thing." Her sadness evaporated with the next coherent thought to enter her mind. "Four people, three of which they traced back to the employ of the Lyris Corporation. Seems like enforcers or assassins or something." Nicole sniffed. "Is that strawberry?"

"The crepes. You don't remember?"

"Oh, right. I was too freaked to eat." She turned away from the terminal and took out her NetMini to order food.

"What about the enforcers?"

"Oh. Yeah. Division 2 figured out there had been three of them, plus the poor shithead they were sent to kill. Their leader went by the name Seneschal. Guess that's a nickname or something. Who names their kid that?"

The image of a man in his later thirties with mixed Asian-white features filled her screen. Black hair slicked tight to his head, sunglasses covered his eyes, and he wore a high-necked black trenchcoat.

"Call sign, maybe?" Kirsten studied him. "Was he military? Kinda looks it."

Nicole picked at the file. "Desmond Chen, according to their HR department. Not much info on his background. I couldn't find a face match in any military records. Lyris records have him as that team's squad leader, with the official title of 'issue resolution manager.'"

"Sometimes they don't even try to hide it," said Dorian.

"Next guy called himself Icarus real name Michael Coley." Nicole tapped the terminal.

The screen shifted, a muscular black man, early thirties, appeared. A thick mass of dreadlocks cascaded over the shoulders of a shiny black coat. His eyes hid behind wraparound silver glasses above a confident grin.

"This guy was ex-military, had some infantry training. His record has a lot of transfers in and out of 'auxiliary logistics,' whatever that is." Nicole shrugged.

Dorian looked up. "Covert ops would be my guess. He's probably the one who set up the demolition charges."

"Dorian says he might be covert ops."

"Good thing he's already dead. Sounds like a dangerous guy." Nicole flashed a cheesy grin. "Okay, so we got a question mark and a military assassin. You're gonna love the last one."

"Dare I ask?" Kirsten stretched.

The face of a twenty-something Asian woman appeared, staring at the camera as if she plotted six different ways to kill it in the span of two seconds. Something about the look made Kirsten uneasy, as if her eyes had no soul behind them.

"She looks deader than I feel," said Dorian.

"Mariko Moriyama. I found a reference connecting her to the Nippon Shōgyō-Kumiai, but she's also listed as an employee of Lyris Corporation. Says she was a *ninja*." Nicole waved her arms in a mock of martial arts so feeble even Kirsten felt skilled by comparison.

"You know they still use them." Kirsten mourned her empty coffee cup. "Real crap storm, if you ask me. Corporations over there actually kill each other out in the open, it's all ritualized and legal somehow. I don't understand it."

"It's all about prestige and profit," added Dorian. "Companies have become literal kingdoms with CEOs behaving like shogun."

"Okay. Remind me never to go there." Nicole jumped when her NetMini chimed. "Crap, food's here. Be right back."

Kirsten scooted back to her terminal, once again slogging over the financials as Nicole ran off. After another twenty minutes failed to give her an epiphany, she placed a vid call to the main PID for Kukla Investments.

The bust of a bland-looking man with eastern European features shimmered into being, a hologram floating above her desk. "Can I help you?"

"Good afternoon, I'm Agent Wren of the National Police Force, Division 0. I have some questions about a property your company owns, specifically, the building at CR 1804 and Morris Ave. It is a high-rise residence tower, involved in an incident a few months ago."

His expression remained unreadable. "Kukla Investments owns many properties in both cities. We primarily hold titles while leaving the management of each facility to local entities on a contractual basis. As a financial services company, we do not deal with the day-to-days at an individual property level."

"I see." She swiped her hand at holograms, pulling up her notes. "Can you tell me what local entity handles this address, please? It's a bit odd to me that only Kukla submitted a bid on it, and nothing has been done with it yet. The damage from the explosion hasn't even been fixed."

"Please hold one moment."

The floating head turned into a shifting geometric screensaver. Kirsten drummed her fingers on the desk, staring over the top of blue cubes and catching Morelli giving her the evil eye. She stretched, arms high, and savored the momentary shudder of her muscles releasing tension. Half glancing back at Morelli, she picked at her eye with a middle finger. He squinted and sank back behind his desk, averting his gaze. When the screen saver shifted back into the man from Kukla, she raised her eyebrows a little—enough to say she expected a smokescreen answer.

"Agent Wren, thank you for waiting. According to my research, the property is currently on retainer to a holovid production agency planning to use it in the recording of a big-budget feature. The blown-out floor is ideal for their needs. Renovations are scheduled to begin once filming is complete. Unfortunately, I don't have specific dates. That's all private with the media agency."

Crap. That sounds almost plausible. "I see. I don't suppose you have any idea why no one else bid on the place?"

"Miss Wren, you seem like a nice enough young woman. Are you naïve to the point of believing government auctions are above manipulation?"

"You admit you fixed the sale? A bribe?"

"I admit no such thing. I merely suggest certain parties who may convey the appearance of being beyond reproach might in fact be far from such a state. It may also be that the mechanism of action by which the building's fall into government ownership came about—an assassination if I must be so indelicate—frightened other investors away. Of course, there is always the proximity to an undesirable patch of real estate. A—what is the term? *Seraya zona*, I believe you call it?"

The words *Detected Russian: grey zone* scrolled across the lower edge of the terminal.

Crap squared. Well, this was a wild goose chase. "Yes. All right, that does make sense. Thank you for your time. Sorry to bother you."

"Always a pleasure to help the authorities." The man offered a plastic smile and dropped off the line.

Kirsten leaned back in her chair, rubbing the frustration out of her eyes. The suit made sense on the surface, but the answers came too fast, without hesitation, scripted. Something didn't add up.

Nicole glided by, returning to her seat. A small cup of coffee floated away from her bundle of plastic bags and landed in front of Kirsten.

"Saw you looking at your empty like you wanted to tongue kiss it." Nicole winked.

Slurp. Strawberry latte, exactly what she had been thinking about.

She sighed at the back of Nicole's head as the woman started on what appeared to be a grilled salmon salad. Her friend had boundary issues with skimming surface thoughts. Kirsten sighed; anger never quite formed, pity and sympathy shoving it aside. *Are you that desperate to endear yourself to everyone?* Kirsten cringed, regretting the thought right away, but relaxed. Even master telepaths couldn't eavesdrop without looking at someone. Both of Nicole's parents remained alive—and loved her—each other not so much. The divorce hadn't been easy on Nicole.

"Thanks, it's just what I wanted." Kirsten rolled her chair across the aisle, sliding to a stop beside her. "Did you find anything about their target?"

"Mmm?" Nicole turned with a fork in her mouth, blinking. She removed it, chewed twice, and swallowed. "Uhh"—she blushed—"you're welcome." Nicole cringed.

Kirsten patted her on the arm. "It's okay."

"Yeah." The redhead let her fork fall into the salad. "I did. Sorry for peeking."

"Don't worry about it. I really ought to just accept you are the way you are by now. Oh, the maître' d at Grimaldi's carded me."

Nicole giggled, a mood change on a dime. Kirsten embellished the story of her rotten date, making Armando/Brian/Douchebag sound worse than he'd been. A few minutes, and most of the salad later, Nicole prodded her terminal and the face of a twenty-something Indian man appeared.

Short hair, straight and neat, framed a face mixed with confidence and paranoia. The image shifted to profile, making his protruding nose seem bigger. Text scrolled in on the adjacent panel showing only a few traffic citations and minor cyberspace infractions.

Nicole mumbled around a mouthful of lettuce. "Vikram Medhi, twenty-four. He graduated from Victoria University with a bachelor's in virtual security construct design and counter-intrusion. According to this, he worked for Unicostal as a network protection agent."

"He had to be moonlighting," said Dorian. "Hit squads don't usually make a habit of going after defensemen."

Kirsten slouched. "Could be."

"He did work for Uni"—Nicole glanced at the empty desk—"oh, you were talking to…"

She reached over Nicole's arm, pawing at a few screens of holographic text. "The crime scene techs had a theory that Vikram had been in cyberspace for some hours prior to the detonation, and a dead-man switch triggered when they assassinated him."

Nicole raised both eyebrows. "So you're saying our Lyris friends killed themselves when they killed Vikram?"

"That would piss *me* off," said Dorian.

Kirsten tapped her chin. "Do you think a ghost could literally go into cyberspace? I'm wondering if the power outage might have been our friends from Lyris traveling back to the site of the bomb within the network."

"How the hell should I"—Nicole flashed an overdone expression of stupid—"Duh. Right, never mind."

Dorian paced about, his eyebrows shifting up and down. After the fifth circle around the desks, he came to a halt and pivoted on his heel to face her. "Doubtful. Essentially, ghosts are coalescences of electromagnetic energy. In theory, such energy *could* travel along wires, but I don't think a spirit would be capable of experiencing the illusion of cyberspace. We couldn't interpret the data the same way a senshelmet or M3 jack translated it all into images, sounds, and sensations. It would just be power on a line. I can't see any point to trying to figure out how to travel by wire when we can float through walls. I'm at a loss to explain the blackout."

Kirsten shoved herself away from Nicole's desk and rolled. She thudded into her desk, causing the holographic financial records to wobble for several seconds. After a few minutes of thinking, she looked up at Dorian and blinked.

"Maybe not, but you just gave me an idea about something else that has been bothering me."

8

GUILT

Endless streams of ad-bots created a swaying tunnel of glimmering holograms and zooming metal boxes. Kirsten threaded the patrol craft down the shifting tube, feeling a bit as if she played a video game. After a few minutes of nerve-wracking near-misses, she dashed for an opening in the top and climbed up away from the traffic. At a safe altitude, she slowed and leveled off, squinting at the golden sunlight on the mirrored surfaces of approaching buildings.

A ponderous trash-collection droid spat out from a port midway up a building on her left. She yelped and steered hard right to avoid crashing into it. Eight tiny (by comparison) robotic arms at the front end pushed at the garbage struggling to explode out its front end. It looked like a gluttonous, legless pig having eaten itself to the point it could no longer close its mouth.

She flew for a little while more until nearing her destination, heading toward a building with a large, rounded deck jutting out from the seventieth story of an office tower. It held a giant peanut-shaped pool surrounded by lounge chairs and perhaps fifty people sunbathing. Above the platform, the wall curved concave all the way to the top thirty stories higher. The thought that it looked like a giant cup holder, the cavity in the building a perfect match for an impossibly large mug, made her want coffee.

The sunbathers shielded their eyes from the fading sun, gazing up at her patrol craft passing overhead. A few shouted in alarm at someone so far out of the designated traffic lane. On the opposite side of the building, a similar deck served as a parking area for a few dozen hovercars. She landed in the first open space she saw, and went for the elevator.

"This is a bad idea," Dorian grumbled, jogging to keep up with her brisk walk.

Kirsten pointed at the door and shook her head. "No it's not. I'm sorry if you don't want to deal with it, but I can't let it go. He did something to her. Something's not right with the way she acted."

"I was thinking on the ride over, what if the thing that scratched you was responsible for the blackout?"

She stormed up to the sliding doors at the end of the parking deck. *Beep.* Police ID accepted. "I... Crap. If you're right, that means the entity isn't tied to that building." She stormed into a corridor where a bank of ten elevators lined the walls. The hallway continued to a matching glass wall leading to the pool area. Pleasant music fell like mist from the ceiling, as if watering the plastic plants. "If it's not stuck to the building..."

He gazed at the ceiling lights. "It'll be like chasing Albert all over again."

Silver elevator doors closed in front of her, leaving her staring at her full body reflection. She smirked, but swatted bits of lint away from her uniform. Dorian fidgeted in the manner of a boy about to ask his crush for a first date. Kirsten hit the button for the thirty-ninth floor, and the cab sank.

"I didn't notice the pool deck last time we were here. I guess this place is higher end."

He refused to make eye contact. "Below the fiftieth, it's not much more expensive than everything else in the area. Pool access is extra. You could afford to live here, you know. You're not as poor as you live."

She stared at him with sad eyes. "I don't want to waste it on stuff I don't need. I've eaten trash, Dorian. I've done things for food..."

"Hey." A cold finger tried to lift her chin. "That's not who you are anymore. You make good money with the force, and you don't have to live like a street urchin. Besides, you're taking Evan home now. You need more room. The boy needs a bed of his own, not a sleeping sack."

Thinking about Evan brought a smile out from under the cloak of shame she had pulled over her shoulders. "Maybe. If things work out, I'll consider it."

"Work out?"

Ping. The door opened.

"Yeah, my psych report. They're a little suspicious of my sudden recovery from the nightmares. I didn't tell them about the too-real vision I had while working out the kinks of how to project. They'll think I'm even nuttier."

He laughed, an emotion that died a hasty death when he saw Nila's door. Dorian folded his hands behind himself and fidgeted. Kirsten waved at the silver box, ringing the doorbell. A moment later, the door squeaked to the side, beige panel consumed by beige wall. Nila stood there in the same sweat pants but a different top. Off-pink sweater this time. Still barefoot. Pink toenails.

"Hi, Nila, can I come in for a minute?"

The woman paled at the sight of the Division 0 blacks; the silver belt, the E-90, boots; the whole of it seemed to trigger an anxiety attack. Nila staggered back, clutching at her face as if she had witnessed a person's guts spill out on the floor. With a scream, she ran into the apartment. The shriek drew Shani from the back hallway. She stopped at the end of the hall, her twig-thin body wrapped in a one-piece swimsuit. A towel fell out of her hands and off her shoulders when she looked at Kirsten in full uniform.

"No." The girl shouted. "Leave my mommy alone!"

As Nila disappeared into the kitchen, the little girl charged. Kirsten weathered a barrage of feeble punches in the chest and held on, immobilizing the writhing child in a forceful hug. Dorian cringed away and wandered to where he could see Nila. After a few minutes of struggling, Shani ran out of steam and sagged. Her rage useless, she resorted to sobbing and begging.

"Please don't kill my mommy." She sniffled, wiping her face.

"Shani, I only came here to help her. I'm not going to make her do anything she doesn't want to do. I think someone might have hurt her." *Such suspicion in eyes so young.* "You'll make a good detective someday, kiddo."

"Police are bad. They make people die."

Kirsten carried her to the sofa and set her down. "I promise you I am not going to hurt your mommy. I didn't come here to make her go back to work. I'm only here to make sure she's okay."

Shani's face switched from glare to plead and back again. The concern in Kirsten's voice broke through, and the child pouted at her lap. "Okay."

Nila arrived at the kitchen door, walking toward the sound of her daughter's voice. "Shani, is everything—"

As soon as she saw Kirsten in uniform, the panic returned and she sprinted out of sight. The girl started crying. Dorian radiated anger. Seeing Nila act like a terrified bimbo from a low-budget slasher vid grated on him.

"It's not your fault, Dorian." Kirsten patted the girl on the head and hurried into the kitchen.

Nila curled in a ball under the table, scooting back as soon as the source of her fear walked in.

"Nila, *calm down.*" Faint light from Kirsten's eyes reflected on the wall. The woman froze.

Kirsten stooped and crawled under the table with her, grasping the woman's head in both hands and staring into her eyes. "Listen to me, Nila Assad. I think Rene did something to you. All I want to do is fix it."

Shani wrapped herself around the doorjamb between the kitchen and living room, half her body visible, a distrustful glare at Kirsten.

"What are you doing?" Dorian stepped into her peripheral vision.

Kirsten fished around in Nila's brain for what she suspected—and found.

"Someone implanted a hypnotic trigger in your ex-partner. It had to be Rene." Kirsten's voice came out trancelike, slipped in between periods of focus. "He conditioned her to be terrified of working. I see Rene. After you died, she used all ten of her stimpaks on herself. He forced her to drive him away, helping him escape. I'm almost there… I can erase this compulsion."

Nila went catatonic, arms dangled to the tile floor.

Dorian surged with rage, growling. He stormed about in a circle and tried to punch the wall. When a hole smashed in the drywall with no apparent cause, Shani ran, her scream getting quieter the farther she went into the back of the apartment. Dorian shuddered, glaring at nothing in particular.

"Easy." Kirsten's concentration broke. "I know it wasn't her idea. He made her do it. Hey, Dorian."

He glared down.

"It is not your fault. She didn't *lose* her nerve, Rene stole it. The way she's been after the shooting was entirely *his* fault."

Anger fizzled off in the form of pacing. "Don't tell her I was trying to work up the courage to ask her out. She doesn't need anything else to upset her."

After diving back into Nila's mind, Kirsten ferreted out the telltale energy patterns of a long-term suggestion. Inflicting such a permanent imprint exceeded her understanding of Suggestion. She'd only ever used it for short-term commands. Those who excelled at Suggestion the way she excelled at Astral Sense could leave psychic land mines that caused enduring changes in behavior, sometimes even sleeper commands that could remain unnoticed for days, months, or even years before they triggered and forced the victim to do something.

In Nila's case, it appeared he had used her to flee the approaching army of police, and created a false dread about returning to work, making her think doing so would cause immediate death. *Surprised he didn't kill her.* Kirsten frowned. *Probably didn't want the heat of murdering* two *cops.*

Sweat ran down the sides of her neck, the exertion of repairing the hatchet job in Nila's mind more strenuous than five swipes of a lash. "I think I killed that implant. She should probably go talk to Lt. Cmdr. Ashford when she collects herself."

Dorian shivered at the name. "I don't think that's a good idea. He'll find out she helped him escape and wipe her back to infancy."

"Now you're the one being paranoid. She didn't consciously do that; it was Suggestion. I'm only a grade two telepath, maybe a three in Suggestion. I don't really like using it." *It just comes in so damn handy sometimes.* "For Nila's sake, she should make sure it's been cleaned out. I don't want to run the risk of there being some deep implant I'm not good enough to find coming out and doing something years from now."

"Ugh." Nila held her head. "Kirsten? How did you get inside? Where's Shani? What the hell happened to my wall?"

Kirsten helped her up, out from under the table, and walked her to the couch. "Do you remember me visiting you two days ago in a green dress?"

"Sort of…" She stared at the wall. "No. Not really."

She looked down at their clasped hands, brown fingers laced with hers. *Wow, I look so pale compared to her.* "I'm sorry to dredge up bad memories, but do you remember the day it happened?"

Nila's hand slid up her arm, rubbing where she had been shot. "Yes. Like yesterday. He figured the patrol craft's windscreen would block eye contact since it's not a real window. Classic Dorian, he was always so confident." A wistful smile parted her lips. "I miss him."

Dorian continued pacing, grumbling.

"I'm not telling you to go back to active duty, but he blames himself for your PTSD."

She blinked. "I have PTSD?"

He whirled. "Kirsten, don't torture her. Please just leave it alone."

"You've been acting like you do, showing a sharp fear of anything to do with the department. It verges on irrational. I just found a suggestive implant in your head from Rene. He'd forced you to be morbidly terrified of anything to do with Division 0. You were normal until you saw me in uniform, then freaked out like a little girl seeing the closet monster."

"I think you're overstating things. I feel fine. I suppose I could call Doctor Kim, see what he thinks."

A shadow moved in the hallway, but when Kirsten looked up, she saw nothing.

"Wait, did you say he blames himself?" Nila blinked. "He's not dead?"

Dorian lifted his chin, a slight side-to-side shake in his head. "Kirsten, please..."

"I told you the last time I was here he's a ghost. He's right behind me now."

He hung his head.

Nila barked a nervous laugh, but when Kirsten remained serious, she lifted an eyebrow. "Are you kidding me?"

"No. Don't you remember a few days ago when I came by with the food? Peek at my head if you want."

The telltale wave came, a cool band of energy like a gentle breeze that existed only to her brain. Kirsten let the feeling in, keeping her gaze on Dorian's chiding finger. Nila tried to look at the spot of room where he was, estimating by what she saw through Kirsten's memory.

"D... Dorian." She gasped.

He sat on the sofa next to her, and Nila reached into the space he occupied.

"I feel cold."

Kirsten had never seen him display much emotion before other than anger. Dorian looked about ready to cry. She found it difficult to contain jealousy as he stroked a vaporous hand over Nila's thick black hair.

"Tell her she is beautiful, and if she does decide to go back to active duty, she should never perform summaries."

Kirsten relayed the message.

Nila wiped her nose. "He only killed three. They all deserved it, what they did to innocent people."

Dorian found the floor intriguing.

"It's not that," said Kirsten.

"It's not what?" Nila looked up. "Div 1 officers perform summaries on Lace dealers, cop killers, some of them even on anyone who hurts a kid."

Kirsten squeezed Nila's hand. "I'm not talking about the law. I mean, yeah, we can *legally* kill people in some circumstances, but it's *wrong* to do that."

"You're telling me you've never killed anyone?"

"I have." Kirsten gazed down, her voice almost a whisper. "Only when I had to, when they were trying to kill me. Heat of the moment, immediate danger. Never premeditated, never with malice or vengeance. Never as some kind of judgement."

"Is that why Dorian's still here?" Tears slipped down Nila's cheeks.

Dorian tensed.

"He has unfinished business. Besides, he wasn't ready to retire." Kirsten tried to smile.

Nila nodded.

Dorian relaxed.

A child's whispering echoed in the hallway. Kirsten looked over, then back to Nila. "I'm afraid it could still be a mark on your soul to kill a defenseless person, no matter how evil they are."

"Some religious people insist on eye-for-an-eye," said Dorian.

"And others say 'turn the other cheek.' It's all guesswork, Dorian. None of us *know*. I don't wanna risk it." She faced Nila. "He wants to get Rene for what he did to you."

"Is that why he's haunting? Guilt?"

"Yeah, but not about what he did. He is worried about your recovery."

"Kirsten..." Dorian held up a hand.

Nila squeezed her arm again. "It's fine. The lasers made tiny holes. Bullets would have blown my whole arm off and I'd have a metal one now."

Kirsten shuddered.

"Bullets wouldn't have gone through the damn armor plated car. People can't carry ballistic weapons large enough to put holes in a PC." Dorian scowled. "It's bad enough they let everyone and their mother carry guns. How the hell did he get laser rifles?"

"He was holed up in a grey zone. There's about two hundred people in this city to every cop, and politicians are what they always have been—for sale," said Kirsten.

Dorian and Nila nodded. After a moment, he found the strength to whisper loud enough for Nila to hear him. Kirsten left them some privacy, heading down the hall to the daughter's room. She nudged the door open, finding the girl flopped on the bed on her stomach, still in her bathing suit, propped up on her elbows as if reading a datapad.

At the sound of Kirsten's approach, the girl flipped over, clutching a stuffed white unicorn. Her expression radiated guilt. She tried to block a small mound of stuffed animals with her body.

"What's wrong?"

She pouted. "I'm too old to play with dolls and make them talk."

Kirsten leaned on the wall. *Aww.* "It's okay, Shani. You're still little enough to have an imagination. I'm sorry for scaring you. My friend was angry someone hurt your mommy."

"You have an invisible friend?" The girl blinked, as if calling Kirsten nuts.

"Yeah, something like that. Were you talking to your invisible friend?"

The girl looked at the unicorn. "No. I was being stupid, talking to a piece of cloth."

Kirsten edged closer and took a seat on the end of the comforgel pad. "Your mom is feeling better now. Someone did something bad to her, but it's gone now."

"Can we still go to the pool?"

"That's up to her, but I think so."

Shani smiled. "Watch this."

She set the unicorn down on its legs and stared at it. A ripple spread over the plush white fabric an instant before the stuffed creature pranced around. The telekinetic animation was precise enough to make all the legs move independently, creating a near-perfect illusion of life.

Kirsten broke up, giggling. The kid's intense concentration lapsed as soon as Kirsten added a human-shaped rag doll to the mix. Her telekinetic effort was crude by comparison, the doll bobbed along as if held by a hand.

Playing with dolls for a few minutes seemed to take the girl's mind off the fright of a self-smashing wall. Nila walked in and put a hand on Kirsten's shoulder.

"Thank you."

Noticing a lack of Dorian, Kirsten paled. "Where's Dorian? He didn't just vanish, did he?"

"I think he said roof, or car, or something. It was hard to hear him."

Kirsten stood and the doll fell limp. "Yeah, he hasn't spent a lot of time trying to learn how to project into the real world. I should get going. I'm in the middle of a case and only stopped by to help. After the last time I was here, I couldn't get it out of my head that something didn't feel right. Glad I listened to that itch."

"I think I'm starting to remember things. It's coming back to me in bits and pieces. I'm gonna find that bastard."

Shani curled into a ball, frightened at the tone in her mother's voice.

"Don't do anything you'll regret, Nila. It's not worth it."

Tactical Officer Nila Assad shifted her eyes to Kirsten and gathered her daughter into a hug. "I have to think. I know I accepted the possibility that ghosts were real, but seeing him, seeing *proof* that gho"—she squeezed the girl tight—"seeing proof there's more than just this. It makes a lot of things different."

Kirsten's offer of a handshake became a long, silent clasping. "Beings far beyond the abilities of mortal police keep the laws of the dead. I don't really understand it either yet."

"Mom?"

They both looked at Shani, who showed no obvious reaction to the strangeness that had occurred around her.

"Can we go swimming now?"

9

THROWAWAY

It took a moment for Kirsten's eyes to adjust to the abrupt darkness that followed her terminal shutdown. Two hours' worth of staring at images left them pulsing. On the far end of the squad room, Morelli and Simons chatted about a dust up they had gotten into with a telekinetic shoplifter. Through the blinds, she watched Captain Eze gathering his things into a briefcase in preparation to go home for the night. Morelli wandered off, saying something about an anniversary dinner with his wife. Simons laughed, eager to get home to her husband. Both of them gave her only cursory smiles while hurrying by.

Mind Blast. They think I'll roast them if they piss me off. As if I couldn't control myself. She pouted at her terminal, trying to brush off the feeling of isolation even among her own squad. For a while, she sat there in a glum mood, watching Dorian, but he didn't look up from his screen.

"You shouldn't torture yourself, Kirsten. I'm flattered, though."

She glanced left at Nicole, in the office late due to being absorbed in a video game. She slurped purple tea up a straw, her frantic poking finger trying to guide a screaming cartoon squirrel around a burning city. Kirsten laughed; that *so* fit her personality. Nicole paused the game long enough to nibble at her dinner, and smiled with her eyes at Kirsten while sucking small gummy globs up the straw.

Maybe I'm going about this wrong. I wonder if I should try dating a woman instead. I could ask Nicole.

The redhead gagged and coughed tea, which ran out of her nose in purple trails as the holo-terminal flashed red with the death of her virtual rodent. She whacked herself in the chest twice, trying to breathe, and gawked at Kirsten.

"Just teasing." Kirsten winked. "That's not what I was going to ask you about, though. I found a lead on our friend Vikram. I think forensics might have been played."

Nikki does have a cute butt.

Choking, sputtering, and more coughing. Her friend's face matched her hair.

"Oh, come on, I'm messing with you."

After blowing her nose, she wiped her eyes. "What do you mean about forensics?"

"What if Vikram set the whole thing up? Maybe the bomb wasn't a dead-man switch. I didn't see him haunting the place. Most murder victims linger around the scene of their death. What if he got away and set a trap for the hitters?"

Dorian sounded bored. "If he killed the people who murdered him, there's no unfinished business to keep him here."

"Ooo. That's an idea," chirped Nicole. "So how do we find out? Did you get that net-pin I sent you? New dating site opened up."

"I found a record of someone that did—"

"It's just guys though, no girls."

"—some private work for Vikram." Kirsten massaged the bridge of her nose.

Dorian winked. "You're wasting your time trying to tease that one. One thought at a time, hon."

"What did he do?" Nicole swiveled in the chair, facing her.

"The guy seems to be a member of a hoverbike gang that lurks near the piers around Sector 313. I found some money going from Vikram's PID to this guy, umm, Ronnie's account. Only thing I can think based on the amount of credits is either he's buying a lot of drugs or hiring muscle."

"So what's that have to do with our Vik?" Nicole giggled.

"What about that is funny?" Kirsten scratched her head.

"Vikram… victim? I said Vik with a k. Oh well. I guess if he's not dead, he's not a vic."

Dorian groaned.

"I'm not sure if he survived. That's why I wanted to talk to this Ronnie. It's kind of a bad part of town. You up for a ride?"

Nicole jumped up, wearing an exaggerated, closed-mouth smile. "Sure. Don't wanna go alone?"

"Yeah." Kirsten grabbed her gear. "You know I'm afraid of living people."

SECTOR 313 SAT ON THE COAST, A WHARF DISTRICT ONCE BUSY WITH international shipping before shuttles replaced ocean-going vessels for heavy transport. Trade left the domain of the sea to pleasure cruises, scientific research vessels, and warships. No one bothered fishing anymore as even if they caught something not belonging to a protected species, it would be tainted to the point of inedibility.

The warehouses and docks, abandoned for about ninety years, experienced a brief rush of activity during a charged political campaign about a decade ago. Sheila R. Burke ran for the Senate on a platform of providing affordable housing by repurposing unused commercial properties. Her smiling mocha-hued face still littered the area on tattered plasfilm posters. Several detached from the walls as the car glided past, whipping around in a frenetic spiral before following lazy eddies to the ground.

"What are we looking for?" Nicole asked, forehead pressed to the passenger side window.

"Bunch of guys standing around hoverbikes. I think they call themselves the Skorpions. With a k."

"That's stupid," said Nicole. "Why do they always have to use mean things? Why doesn't some gang call themselves the chinchillas or something?"

Dorian cracked up. "I'd think twice about messing with a gang with the balls to call themselves that."

"Yeah, maybe. I dunno," Kirsten said, half paying attention.

She set the car down by a row of hoverbikes parked in front of a long, one-story structure. Not quite a building, it resembled an afterthought erected out of scrap metal in the parking lot of a shipping warehouse. Closer inspection revealed a construction of welded cargo containers. A handful of people outside propped up the front wall. Their attire ranged from light, civilian-grade, bullet-resistant armor to tattered scraps of gang couture. The most extreme individual, one of the women, pranced about bare-chested with sheer pants that left most of the outsides of her legs exposed. A lime green NanoLED tattoo of a mutant scorpion glowed over her sternum. Its twin tails coiled outward, circling beneath one breast each. Her neon green lipstick curled into a frown as she saw the police lights on the car.

"How can she walk around like that?" Kirsten averted her eyes, blushing.

"I know, right?" Nicole muttered, putting her helmet on. "That's gotta be damn cold. I don't know how those cyber-neko people can stand it."

"She's not a neko."

"Oh, you probably should've grabbed a set of tac armor for this," said Nicole.

Kirsten blinked at Nicole, flummoxed that her friend didn't seem to think it inherently wrong for anyone to run around naked in public. With a sigh, she decided against saying anything more. Dorian slid out of the car, walking between them. Conversation among the gang simmered out to the silence of a faint whistling breeze, too weak to hide the electronic firing circuit chirp from a few ballistic weapons turning on. At the sound, Kirsten put one hand on her E-90 and the other in the air.

"I'm not here to bust anyone's balls. I just want information. Where can I find Ronnie?"

"Hah." A sienna-skinned man, blue vest over his bare chest, stepped down off the porch wearing a massive grin. "You guys shouldn't have. Cop strippers, nice."

"Happy birthday, Sicario." A pudgy Asian in an armored vest raised a beer in salute.

The big guy sauntered over, stopping a few paces away.

"That's close enough. We're not strippers, jackass."

Scorpion-tits sashayed over, still frowning. "The police don't send young chick-meat out to a grey zone." Kirsten's face reddened, but she did not break her cop-face. "Cops also wear blue. So who are you?"

The one called Sicario put an arm around the woman, cupping her right breast and flicking at a gold barbell in the nipple. Kirsten suppressed the urge to cringe as her brain took a guess at what such a piercing would feel like.

"Back up, hands where we can see them." Nicole had her gun out, waving it at them.

More than half of them noticed the laser, and seemed confused. One man tilted his head at her, blades extending out from the tips of his fingers before locking in place with a *click*. Seconds later, the high-pitched presence of vibro inducers rattled Kirsten's teeth.

Kirsten whipped her E-90 out of the holster, aimed right at him. "You take one step, it'll be your last." Her voice shook a little much for her dignity, but maybe that would work to her advantage. If the gangers thought her scared, they'd believe she'd shoot.

"I only want to talk to Ronnie about some side work he did." Kirsten reinforced her grip with her left hand, keeping the weapon aimed at vibro-claw man.

"Yo, Rampart. Some funny cops are lookin' for you." Sicario yelled over his shoulder.

Glass shattered from inside the building.

"He's gonna run," said Dorian.

"Fuckin' kill 'em!" A deep voice boomed from inside.

Sicario went for a pistol on his belt, which leapt out of the holster and skittered to the ground at Nicole's feet. A tiny camera flash from the side of her helmet confirmed another addition to the Wall of Derp. The scorpion tattoo turned blue.

"Mood boobs?" Nicole asked. "That's kinda neat."

Six others reached for guns. Kirsten scorched a hole through the thigh of the man with the claws; his panic-stricken grab at the wound did more damage to his leg than the laser. He fell out of sight on the porch, screaming.

A huge man with a build like combat cyborg made of meat burst out a window on the far side of the bar and hit the ground running, no intention of participating in any fight. Others drew weapons while Sicario gawked at his empty holster. Wild with panic, he charged Nicole. The bare-chested woman ran past Dorian toward Kirsten, emitting a banshee wail.

Dorian drew in a non-breath. A pulse of energy wafted from him and the bar windows glimmered with the spectral light of his reflection, his skull glowing visible beneath his face. Men screamed, dropped guns, and ran. Another woman, short with black hair, raised both eyebrows.

"That's awesome... Holy shit. Is that real or a hologram?" She gawked, stepping closer. "Are you really there?"

Kirsten focused on the charging woman reaching for a belt knife. Nicole's laser spat a streak of green light across the periphery of her awareness. The tattoo turned bright red, glinting off the shiny blade swinging breasts coming at her. Kirsten should have fired, but laser on knife felt too close to murder.

She stepped back with her right leg, turning ninety degrees and letting the thrusting blade slide past her chest without contact. The woman's momentum carried her forward. Kirsten hooked a leg, put a hand on the woman's back, and shoved her face-first into the hood of the patrol craft. The gang woman crashed down on the hood with a meaty *smack*. Unlike a civilian car, the military plating offered zero give, even the windshield and windows, also thick armor plates with a few tiny holes containing cameras.

"Ugh, bitch," muttered the woman. She shoved away from the car and spun with a sideways slash.

Kirsten leaned back, the blade missing her face by an inch. When the knife came back, she sidestepped, grabbed the wrist, and twisted the ganger around in a pain-compliance hold. The screaming woman flew face-first into the door, losing her grip on the knife. An unexpected left elbow to the head knocked Kristen stumbling to the side, breaking her grip.

Scorpion glowing bright orange, the woman shoved away from the car again and flew in with a wild right hook.

Ducked.

Second punch.

Leaned.

On the third punch, Kirsten caught the woman's wrist and spun the arm up behind her back in a chicken wing before throwing her down over the hood.

Whap.

Bare chest squeaked on icy armored plating. Kirsten leaned all her weight on top of the taller woman, grinding her into the car. While the ganger might've had a six-inch height advantage and more muscle, Kirsten had leverage at the moment. At a loud *whack*, she glanced over at Sicario staggering away from a roundhouse kick. Nicole bounced her stance back and forth like a boxer, grinning. A laser wound in his shoulder oozed blood front and back, his left arm clearly out of the fight. Kirsten fumbled for binders.

The woman growled past clenched teeth. She almost stood straight up with Kirsten on her back. A twist of the arm hurt enough that the woman sagged limp, and slid a few inches down the hood. "Ow, fucking bitch, you're gonna rip my nips off."

"Not my fault you're not wearing a damn shirt. Should have thought of that *before* you pulled a knife on a police officer." Kirsten grabbed a handful of hair and bonked the woman's head into the armor plating twice. "I could have shot you. I'm trying to be nice here. Stop resisting arrest."

Kirsten's uncharacteristic aggression shocked Nicole's attention off Sicario. He yanked a bootstrap gun off his leg and shot her in the chest, the loud *snap* of the slug bouncing away from her tactical vest whip-cracked off nearby buildings. With one hand pinning the woman's wrist between her shoulders, the other crushing the back of her head into the car, Kirsten could only gawk as Nicole flew into a rage.

The gun rocketed out of Sicario's hand before he could fire it again, tearing the trigger finger off at the first knuckle.

Nicole held her arm toward him, growling. "You motherfucker."

Sicario's legs swept out from under him, leaving him hanging in midair, face down. Nicole thrust her arm down, and the man smashed into the ground hard. Still growling, Nicole sidestepped and telekinetically launched him headfirst into the front passenger wheel-guard. The impact to the armored shroud knocked him cold.

"Son of a god-damned bitch, you're so fucking lucky Kirsten's here, or I would have shot your ass." Nicole took a running two-step and drove her boot into the side of his unconscious head.

Seeing Sicario flying around sapped the fight out of the shirtless woman. Kirsten cuffed her and hauled her around to the back seat. After propping her chest-first against the car, she patted down the cloth-covered areas in search of other weapons.

"Are you going to admit to hiding anything in any body cavities, or do I have to go digging?" asked Kirsten, listening to surface thoughts.

"I'm sure you'd love that." The woman growled.

"Sorry to disappoint. Got a feeling you're clean." Kirsten shoved her in and slammed the door.

Nicole picked at a scratch in her breastplate.

"You okay? That was… umm."

Nicole panted, lifting her visor. "You've never seen me in the field before, have you? I hate asshats that shoot at cops. No respect." She pointed her weapon at Sicario's back. "Bastard." Her eyes lightened back to their usual sky blue as they shifted to Kirsten. "Relax, I'm fantasizing. Hey, where'd all the others go?"

"Dorian flashed a spooky face at them. They ran, except for that one chick making goo-eyes at thin air."

"Oh." Nicole cringed and put binders on Sicario.

She tried to lift him to his feet but couldn't move him. After a second try, and a mousy grunt, she gave up and searched him on the ground, tossing a few drug injectors, two knives, another leg-gun, and a few mags of ammo in a pile. "Damn, this guy was ready for a war." The helmet cam recorded the search, and evidence.

While Kirsten called for backup, Nicole opened the other rear door and focused an intense stare on Sicario. He floated again, toes dragging across the dirty metal ground. The woman screamed as the unconscious man levitated into the car. She released her telekinetic grip and sagged as if a great burden had been lifted from her.

Kirsten punted the door closed. "Backup's on the way. I'm going after Ronnie."

"Rampart." The topless woman yelled. "His name is Rampart. What the hell are you people?"

Kirsten cringed at the question. "Division 0. We usually deal with psionic crime."

"Psionics?" Her terror almost made the hovercar shake.

Consider yourself lucky. Ordinary cops would have shot you the second you pulled a knife.

The telepathic voice slapped her still. Kirsten shook her head at the dirt-smeared breasts and the matching pattern of clean on the hood.

"Nikki, can you watch these two? I'm going after Ram-whatever."

"Gotcha."

"Over here," Dorian yelled, about two blocks away.

She jogged after him past the warehouse and away from the shore. He led her down one alley, around another corner, and into a trash-strewn strip between two buildings where she waded knee-deep in old plastic cartons, empty cans, and unidentifiable scraps.

"He's in the trash box at the end, the blue one with the white rose painted on it." Dorian pointed.

"Thanks." She paused. "Hey, you're more than two hundred yards away from the car."

Dorian gasped, looked in that direction, and bit his knuckle. After a moment, he stopped faking fear and laughed. "I guess it's not such a big deal."

Kirsten's chuckle stalled at the sound of a soft feminine sob. "Ugh, what now?"

"You're just lucky, I guess."

Still thigh-deep in trash, she trudged a few dozen meters toward the noise, arriving at another passage too narrow for the term alley; even a one-seat Jian Feng microcar would be hard-pressed to fit down it. A mangled mass of woman paced back and forth, clutching entrails dangling over an emerald miniskirt. One blue high-heeled shoe danced around her left ankle, held on by a torn strap, her other foot bare. No trace of a shirt remained, or much of anything else inside her chest. Her hands worked in an endless battle to put her insides, inside.

They kept slipping out.

Kirsten sagged, staring at the ground. "Oh, no."

"Oof." Dorian cringed.

"I'll come back; she's not going to get any deader. Please stay with her?"

"Sure." He nodded, put on his cop face, and strode toward the spirit.

The trek through the sea of trash back to the dumpster proved arduous; she worked up a sweat.

"Rampart? I know you're in the blue refuse storage unit. I'm not here for you. I only want to talk about Vikram Medhi."

She jumped at a sudden loud *boom*. The initial thought was gunshot, but as her heart resumed beating, she figured he had startled and banged his knee into the side of the dumpster.

"All I want to do is talk."

A belabored groan echoed from inside the trash box. A dull green industrial canister, the type often used to hold volatile gas, rose into view. Trash slipped off the top as the giant cylinder wobbled higher, supported on the massive arms of a man close to eight feet tall. Veins bulged out of his biceps, forearms, and forehead. He might have been Caucasian, but had turned bright red. Breaths came in struggled gasps as he strained to hold it in while supporting such weight.

Kirsten drew her E-90 and aimed. *"Do not throw that at me."* Her eyes glowed for a second.

He blinked, making a disappointed face like a little boy told to go to his room. She half expected his response to be, "But I wanna."

Rampart kept staring at her, grimacing and twitching at the exertion of supporting so much weight.

"Set it down before you hurt yourself."

He shifted left and right, teetering as the exertion of bearing the load overtook him. Gravity gained the upper hand and he let it go forward. The volatile materials cylinder crashed to the ground with a deafening *clang* and enough force to make Kirsten stumble. She recovered her balance and looked up as Rampart vaulted off the rim of the refuse box, flying at her in a tackle.

Fortunately, the amount of trash on the ground made the landing somewhat pleasant, except for the corner of a box that caught her in the back of the right thigh. His hands slid over her chest on their way to her throat.

"*Freeze.*"

In an instant, Rampart went rigid, shuddered, and broke out in a cold sweat. "What the hell?"

"Will you please calm down? *Get off me.*"

Muscles, independent of his brain, obeyed.

She dusted herself off, rubbing the painful spot on the back of her leg. Rampart quivered, his body the victim of a raging contest of willpower. Confusion at why he couldn't move made him cry.

"Well that's just a sad, sad sight." Dorian chuckled, walking over with the gory girl behind him. "Felt that thing hit the ground, came running."

"I got him." Kirsten crossed her arms.

Nicole sprinted into view down the alley, sliding to a halt at an intersection and spinning in a circle. It took her two rotations to notice Kirsten two blocks away, and she dropped into a tactical walk with her weapon trained on Rampart.

"Don't kill me." He continued to shudder as he strained to move.

Kirsten relieved him of a pistol, four knives, and a three-foot length of chain, all of which she tossed into the dumpster. "I'm not here to kill you, Ronnie. I want to ask you about Vikram Medhi."

"Uhh, who?"

"You might want to step back, K. When your mind wank wears off, he's gonna twist you in half." Nicole came to a halt about ten yards away. "His arms are bigger than your thighs."

Rampart appraised his biceps. "She's got tiny legs." He shrugged.

"Yeah, she kind of does," said Nicole.

"You two can both go to hell." Kirsten didn't know if she should laugh or scream in frustration. She held up her left arm, accessing the embedded terminal in her armored guard, and projected the holographic head of Vikram Medhi, which spun in a slow, counterclockwise rotation.

"Oh. *That* dude. He called himself Diva or something… Dava, maybe. Heard he got himself dead."

"That's what I'm trying to figure out." Kirsten lowered her arm, the holo-pane vanishing. "Have you seen him since the explosion, any idea where he hangs out?"

His gaze darted between her and Nicole, lingering on the redhead who seemed eager for any excuse to fire.

"You real cops? Not Lyris? What's with the black?"

"Notice how you can't move?" Kirsten put her gun away. "Division 0. Normally, we handle psionic stuff. All I care about is Vikram right now, unless you're wanted for a major crime."

"He hasn't seen Vikram for months," Nicole added. "Negative on the serious crime, too."

Kirsten whirled on her. "Dammit, Nicole, you can't just go into their heads. It'll get thrown out of an Inquest, and they'll walk."

"What?" She relaxed enough to shrug. "It's for *his* benefit. He's not lying."

"So you don't know if Vikram survived the explosion?" asked Kirsten. "What did you do for him?"

Rampart managed to get his arms down. "He had the place wired up big time, carried a trigger button on him all the time. Me? All I did was loaf around eating his food. He hired me to watch his limp ass while he jacked in, and be there in case some shit showed up to start problems. The dude was slick, though. No one ever backtracked him. I got paid to sit on my ass."

"Lyris backtracked him." Kirsten turned at approaching lights, and waved at a trio of Division 1 patrol officers.

"Yeah, I wasn't there for that one, or I'd be kibble too. I ain't seen him since. Word on the street is he set himself off."

"He's not lying." Nicole lowered her gun. "Don't do anything stupid, Howie."

"Ronnie," said Kirsten.

"Rampart." He grumbled.

"Rampart?" Nicole scrunched up her face. "Isn't that like a part of a umm, castle or something?"

Kirsten gestured at the man. "Look at the size of him."

"Oh. I get it," said Nicole.

Ronnie gazed up at the smog, sighing.

All three of them turned at the scuff of a heavy boot approaching.

"Evening, Agent Wren, Officer Logan." A tall, muscular woman, as pale as Kirsten, saluted her. "What's this guy's story?"

"Officer Dietrich." Kirsten returned the salute. "I was hoping for information he didn't have. He bolted from the scene. Only thing I can tag him with is inciting violence against a peace officer."

Nicole replayed the recording of Ronnie's voice shouting "kill 'em."

"Understood. Your partner filled us in about the two idiots in the back seat. They're on the way to the tank already."

"K?" Dorian cleared his throat, pointing at the ghost next to him. "Name's Cara. Goes by Rush out here."

"One minute."

The burly female cop escorted Rampart down the alley, leaving the two male officers as backup.

"Okay, what happened?" Kirsten startled the ghostly woman by waving at her.

"I guess it was a few days ago. I was working a few blocks over, you know…" She stared at her one remaining shoe, pushing her aqua-colored hair over one ear.

"That's not important; you had to do what you had to do to survive."

"So this guy comes out of nowhere like, and shoots Rafael in the head."

"Their *guardian*," added Dorian.

"The girls scatter, the big fucker picks me. I run like hell, but heels, ya know."

Kirsten shifted her weight. "Yeah, I know."

"I trip in this mess, he drags me around here, I figure at first he's just gonna take a freebie… but he didn't seem interested in sex at all. Then I seen his arms. One's a big ass hook and the other just a block… A hammer like, with little stubby fingers, he was augged out to Mars and back. Carved me up like a goddamned turkey, singing like a loon the whole time. Opera or some bullshit old man stuff." Some of her insides fell with a glop.

"I'm guessing you understand you're dead."

Rush reeled in her inner bits. "Yeah. I'm not that smart, but I kinda figured that out."

"Any idea what's keeping you here? Do you have any family, friends, anyone you want me to contact?"

"None that give a shit. Mom overdosed a couple years ago, died. No idea who my father even is. He could even be dead, I don't know."

Kirsten offered a consoling nod. "Is your body still over there?"

"Yeah. This way." Rush drifted back into the narrow passage.

"Guys…" Kirsten waved at the Division 1 patrolmen. "Over here."

They trudged into knee-deep trash, following her to the less packed alley. Kirsten tried not to look at the bloody dangles trailing behind the dead prostitute. Eventually, Rush stopped, pointing at a pile of debris. The smell in the air left no doubt as to what lay underneath it. Nicole shoved cartons, tubes, tires, and other items out of the way telekinetically. Flies buzzed into a swarm at the commotion; the sight of a rotting body made the stench even worse.

Nicole turned away, woozy. "I hate maggots."

"Wow. That one's been there a few days." Officer Juarez put his hands on his hips.

Kirsten looked between them. "You guys got this?"

Officer Duncan offered a noncommittal shrug. "Yeah we'll scrape her up."

"I have a description of the killer. Assuming you're gonna like take notes or something? Maybe give half a shit?"

Rush pouted at the floor. "No one gives a damn about us, least of all cops. One walked right past me the other day and didn't even slow down."

Duncan took a few haphazard image captures of the scene with a portable from his belt. "No one reported her missing. Not surprised. These street rats aren't usually missed."

Kirsten fumed. The sound of Rush breaking into sobs poked a hole in the dam holding her back.

"Patrol Officer Duncan, are you going to stand in front of me and tell me someone's life is worth less because they don't have anyone to scream at your watch commander to find them? I can't believe you're standing here, looking at a murder victim like an annoyance only because life left them no choice but to walk the streets."

The tone of her voice sucked the nonchalance out of both officers and they snapped to attention.

"Someone killed this girl and left her here in a damned alley, alone." She continued to grow louder, taking on the cadence of a drill instructor. "You're looking at what's left of a nineteen-year-old who had no choices. Not one lousy person in this entire shithole of a city gave enough of a crap about her before it was too late. The least you E2s can do is treat her with a little god damned respect."

Kirsten dug her fingernails into her palms, too angry to cry, and too aghast to care if they saw her red-faced and out of breath.

"Right away, ma'am." Officer Duncan, who bore the brunt of the assault, saluted her.

"And don't stomp on top of her. There could be evidence anywhere." Kirsten tapped at her armband display until a dispatch doll's head shimmered into being. "I need a crime scene team to my current location. Homicide investigation."

"Thank you…" Rush reached to touch Kirsten, pausing as something made her glance down the alley. "Mom?"

Kirsten spun away from the patrol cops, not wanting them to see her eyes watering. "Go to her, Cara. There's nothing but pain for you here."

The dead girl offered one final smile back at someone who finally cared, and limped away. Her appearance gradually changed, all the gory bits sliding back into place, wounds closing. Her loping drag of a walk became a normal stride, and she vanished in a cloud of flickering silver. Kirsten swallowed the lump in her throat and whirled with the scowl of a displeased commissioned officer at the two enlisted men.

She wouldn't let them make more of a mockery of that woman's life than fate already had.

HOME

Flickering color painted the walls, changing the mood in time with the image of an emerald-scaled dragon flying above the tips of a pine forest. The man on its back, clad in white robes, hurled lightning from his outstretched hands at an army of glow-eyed, bat-winged creatures darkening the sky behind him. One landed in the saddle behind the rider, screeching, and sank a mouthful of yellow fangs into his shoulder. The dragon, reacting to his companion's grunt, torqued its body into a wicked roll that launched the unwanted passenger against the trunk of a passing tree.

Kirsten hadn't paid much attention to the video, or the increasing darkness in the hour since they got home. Evan sat on her lap, tolerating the hug she'd clamped on him when the movie started. She clung, feeling his breathing and the vibration of his voice in his bones as he cheered the great wizard Monwyn's victory over the forces of darkness. His hair brushed her cheek as he shouted with both arms in the air. The giant white T-shirt she threw on felt like a warm blanket compared to the uniform. She stared at her toes, at the size difference of their feet, and squeezed him tighter.

"This isn't a sad part. You shouldn't be crying. Princess Alsbeth hasn't been kidnapped and threatened with doom if she doesn't betray Prince Thiandren to open the gate of Kol'Namarr and let the Realm of Darkness invade the world yet," said Evan, speaking his lungs empty. He took a deep breath and twisted to smile at her. "*That's* the sad part."

Kirsten laughed, releasing one arm from the hug to wipe her cheeks. "Yeah, I forgot."

A shift in the music drew his attention. The high-tempo battle theme of the air chase gave way to the eerie ambiance of a landing in the Forest of Penumbras, the lair of the great demonic general of the Unwoken Army. Despite having seen *Monwyn the Wise* two dozen times, as well as its prequel, the forest scene still scared him.

From the safety of a thin blanket, Evan watched the black goblin fail to assassinate the great wizard. Kirsten grinned as he trembled with worry until Gring'nur the Shadow Slayer died to a well-placed light spell. Evan threw both hands up again and cried out in joy. She attacked the spot where his pajama top pulled out of his waistband, tickling him into a fit of laughter.

"Pause." he yelled, past peals of giggling.

The holovid player obeyed. A moment later, he lay still, sideways across her lap. He panted and gave her a look of mock annoyance for interrupting the movie before shifting to sit back on his heels, facing her, trying to catch his breath.

"You had a sad day at work?"

She fussed at his hair. "Yeah."

"Thought so. You get squeezy when you have a sad day." Evan settled back into her lap to continue the movie, but spun around with a worried face before he let all of his weight down.

"Do I have to go back to the dorm?"

She melted. "No, they didn't say anything like that. I'm sad because I met a dead woman no one cared about."

"Oh. I bet you helped her." His mood lifted.

"I hope so." Kirsten put an arm over his chest once he got comfortable.

"You did. You're like Monwyn… but more, uhh, girly."

Kirsten laughed.

He stared at the frozen image of the white-robed wizard's face, harsh in the shadows of a daybolt flying from his hand, for the span of a few breaths. "Are you too nuts to keep me?"

She hugged a groan out of him. "I don't think so, hon. I'm okay now, it was just bad dreams. You helped me get rid of them."

"You had a bad mom, too. Do they think you'd be a bad mom 'cause yours was mean?" He pulled his knees to his chin. "I want to stay here."

Kirsten patted him on the belly. "Yeah, that's what they're afraid of. They're just trying to protect you. I'm sure it will work out. A few more weeks and the caseworker will see we're okay."

His hair tickled her neck as he craned his head back to look at her. A huge smile crept over his upside-down face before he sat up and thrust his finger into the air.

"Resume play!"

The daybolt flew into a crowd of shadow goblins, dispersing half a dozen at once. Monwyn chanted, the bassy, magic-amplified voice shaking the apartment as he prepared a grand spell.

Doorbell.

"Pause." His fist smushed into his cheek as he leaned forward, grumbling.

She extricated herself from the seat and jogged to the door, hand on her gut to tamp down the butterflies. *The caseworker wasn't supposed to be here for two more days. Is this one of those surprise checks?*

A swipe of her hand at the silver panel created a low-res image of the hallway, a man in a grey coverall waited, holding a large slab of semi-transparent plastic with what looked like a mirror in it.

"Little late for a work job? It's almost nine." She let off the talk button.

The man leaned closer. "Yeah, I know, I'm doing it off the books. Kyle's a cheap bastard."

Guess the uniform worked. Kirsten opened the door, backing away as he came in, maneuvering the mirror with care. Once inside, he rotated it upright. His surface thoughts confirmed he'd only come here to install the bathroom mirror.

And he thinks I'm cute. Debating if he should ask me out. Doesn't seem like he wants a one-nighter. Oh, shit, the movie behind me, he can see my shape right through this shirt.

Red faced, she took two steps left.

"Hey," he said, offering a handshake. "I'm Julio."

The embarrassment faded, she returned his smile and handshake. "Kirsten."

"Bathroom's over here?" Julio pointed with the mirror as he walked past the bed to the inner door. "Yep, thought so. All these one-bedroom places have the same layout."

She leaned on the doorframe, watching him remove the pitiful shard from the wall and hang the new mirror. Julio's glance kept drifting away from his work to her bare legs, and he made idle chat about music and other things, winding up sounding more awkward than sexy. Kirsten found it strange to cause a guy to trip over himself, and stifled a giggle when he fumbled the mirror and almost fell over trying to stop it from shattering. He recovered, turned to smile at her, and lost a little color.

Crap, what did I do? I didn't even tell him I'm psionic yet.

"I made popcorn; I won't start the movie 'til you're done," said Evan from behind.

The sound of munching wandered away into the distance. Julio seemed to remember that hanging a mirror only takes about thirty seconds when the hooks are already installed. He excused himself and went for the door as if the room had fleas. She smirked, then used the mirror to make sure she still looked her age.

The outer door squeaked closed. Beep, locked.

For a moment, she felt indignant at the idea Julio thought Evan was her son and not her kid brother. She would have been thirteen when he was born. When her brain settled on the idea, really wrapped around his assumption Evan was hers, she smiled.

"Hell with you, Julio. Your loss." She flicked off the bathroom light.

"That popcorn still hot?"

"Yep," chirped Evan.

She hurried over and jumped on the couch beside him.

LEGAL GUARDIAN

Consciousness snuck up and pounced on her. Kirsten sighed, stretched, and rolled her head to the right. The holo-bar on the nightstand projected the clock the instant it sensed her looking at it—5:50 a.m. Fatigue had gone, but an indefinable feeling of unease settled in. She swished her feet back and forth beneath the sheets while picking at the material of her shirt. The maintenance tech had *finally* fixed the bed. Yet, she couldn't fully enjoy the feeling of a proper, functioning Comforgel pad that didn't force her to sleep in skivvies to avoid a sweat bath. Too much worry.

She rolled to the side and noticed Evan's empty sleeping bag. She shot upright, about to panic, but exhaled at the sound of a running autoshower. The light leaking out from under the bathroom door flickered, as though someone stepped past it.

Alarmed again, she slipped out of bed and grabbed her service weapon. Evan quoted the great Monwyn, his voice echoing in the tube as he chanted the Invocation of Arcane Dominion. She would have smiled if not for her fear of an intruder in the apartment. She crept to the door, brushing it aside with her left hand, aiming the laser with the other. Bright light within caused an involuntary squint.

The foggy cylinder blurred Evan's scrawny little body as he gesticulated and made lightning sound effects. He raised his arms over his head as the silver spray ring reached the floor, paused, and rose back up.

Two feet shy of the autoshower, Theodore, in mid-sneak, appeared about to stick a head full of scraggly black hair into the plastic. A rain of phantom droplets fell from his soaked and ragged trench coat, held out like the wings of a buzzard. His boots squished with each step, but the moisture existed only for him.

"Theodore," Kirsten muttered, careful to remain quieter than the whirring machinery. "So help me, if you do anything to him…"

He froze, whipping around with a surprised look that relaxed into an innocent grin. When she didn't smile, he straightened up. The dark stains on his olive drab pants glistened crimson in the light, still oozing from ancient bullet wounds. He trudged through her and walked out into the living room. Kirsten shook her head and followed, tapping the button to close the door behind her.

"Theodore, what the hell were you going to do to him?"

He bowed. "Sorry, heard the thing running and the room wasn't blocked off. I couldn't resist the thought you'd forgotten again. I was hoping to catch another peek of your luscious titties. Course, kids are fun to scare the bejesus out of."

"Please leave him alone. If you ever do anything nice for me, make it that." She stomped across the room and fell on the bed, tossing the E-90 on the nightstand. "Dammit, Theodore, I thought someone was in the apartment."

With an exaggerated hurt pout, he glided over, making a show of floating. "I'm not a person anymore?"

"You know what I mean, a criminal."

"Thank you for the compliment." He bowed, deeper this time. "That's a nice new mirror. It would almost be worth it to stick my head up the bowl again."

Kirsten blushed. Her elbow ached, remembering when she smashed the old one. "Why do you torment me like that?"

"It's not you. You're just the only one what sees me all the time."

Her face scrunched with disgust.

"Hey, I'm dead. I'm—"

Kirsten frowned. "Not dead. You've said that every time you've come here."

"Trademarked." He snapped nonexistent suspenders. "Anyway… I figured you'd like to know some of the boys saw some shit. Word among The Kind is something slipped out of the infernal darkness."

Consciousness arriving an hour early required a hand on the face, and an eye rub. "Give me that once more in English, please?"

He chuckled, pacing back and forth, trailing an effect of wet carpet that faded within seconds of his passage. "Group of my friends, we have a sort of community. Call ourselves *The Kind*. Spirits without any qualms, without any attachments, we're in it for the fun." He spun to face the sudden light from the door. "No hurry to go… through."

Evan emerged from the bathroom. He walked by, tugging at his briefs, and waved at Kirsten without looking. "Morning." He paused by his sleeping bag. "Hi, Theodore."

Plop. The boy fell to his knees on the padding, and let gravity pull him forward.

The ghost grumbled. "Dammit, boy, have the decency to at least act scared."

Face-first in his pillow, he shrugged. "You probably can't do anything to me. An' if you are powerful enough to hurt me, she'll splat you."

Theodore gestured at him, a wounded look sent at Kirsten. "Do you believe this? I've caused corporate assassins to cry; this little bugger ignores me like I'm a bit of carpet lint."

"Soggy carpet lint," Evan muttered, already half-asleep.

Kirsten giggled. "So what about this darkness?"

Orbiting the bed, Theodore made a series of faces at the almost-sleeping boy.

"Please, Theodore. It might be important."

He came to a halt, dripped a few times, flapped his arms, and sighed. "Okay, fine. You know where the Harbingers drag the bad ones off to? Well, sometimes the door don't close all the way and a couple of 'em get out." He leaned close enough for her to perceive flaking lines in his white face paint.

"Damn."

"Aye. Damn." A nod flung water at her before he stood up straight. "You're a right bit of a wordsmith, girl. *Damn's* a fine good way to put it. Never did understand that, how they grow *stronger* after they get taken. Them abyssals, they not ghosts anymore, they be somethin' else."

"Demons?" She frowned at the blood perpetually oozing from the gunshots that killed him.

"Some people call 'em that. That other place, it turns 'em into a whole other thing than just a ghost. Course, they ain't supposed to be *able* to get out. If'n you get run over and killed by a car, does it matter if it was a sedan or a coupe?"

Kirsten blinked. "A what or a what?"

Theodore waved at her. "Bah, damn kids."

"Aren't escapees the sort of thing Harbingers are supposed to deal with?"

"Those things?" Theodore laughed. "Nah. They go after ghosts, but the escaped ones, the abyssals, they're too strong. They have too much will to remain. There's rules, ya know."

"So these 'abyssals,' they simply run around forever?"

"Well, I'm sure your little party trick will work." He mimicked a whip-cracking gesture. "But the *other* ones, they get involved once them abyssals grow too powerful. Somethin' 'bout wreckin' the balance. Course, no tellin' how many people'd be dead by then."

"I'm not going to sit back and let them run amok. Please tell me already and skip the guilt trip." Kirsten curled up on the bed, under the sheet. "Can you make it quick? I still have another fifty minutes to sleep."

"What I hear, and this was from an old soul, is that if them abyssals get too big, they throw things out of whack and something *else* comes down to kill them. Kind of like a Harbinger, but it plays for the other team." He chuckled.

Kirsten's eyebrows knitted into a flat line of disbelief. "An angel? Seriously?"

He produced a spluttering noise with his tongue, shrugging. "Well, s'pose that's as good a name as any. Day and night, light and dark. Existence by contrast. No one would know what light was if they 'ad no dark to hold it up against. But, keep your eyes open, girl. Word from The Kind is a bunch o' spirits slipped free of the *bad place*. Might even be someone you sent there."

"Dammit, Theodore, now I can't sleep."

"Heh. Gotcha." He winked. "If they didn't come already, they ain't looking for you. Feel bad for whoever it is they want, though. Things what crawl up from the Abyss are not happy bunnies."

"Guess I'll just have to cast daybolt at 'em."

Theodore lifted an eyebrow. "What?"

Evan emitted a sleepy mumble and grinned.

"You know…" Kirsten made a whip-swinging gesture.

"Ehh." Theodore set his hands on his hips. "Hope it's that simple."

Kirsten stared at the ceiling. *Great. I'm never going to sleep again.*

THE SCHOLAR

Cheery electronic music nagged Kirsten out of a momentary nap. Her eyes cracked open, hurting from pale grey light saturating the city in front of her. A shifting mass of warped faces, hands, and dark clothing flowed by, though no raindrops ran down the virtual windshield. The downpour couldn't penetrate the armored slab.

She glanced to the right, cringing at the brilliant orange glare of a holographic sign on the building she'd parked next to. A vertical stack of Chinese characters shimmered above small English text reading 'Baozheng Trading Company – imported exotic goods.' Across the street, a large compound shadowed a courtyard. Round and white, the buildings resembled a scaled-up arrangement of hatboxes, dotted with windows and architectural ridges.

A hovering bot the size of a shoebox came within an inch of the patrol craft's door, the source of the jingle.

"Your food's here." Dorian smiled. "Good morning for the second time."

The 'window' motored down with a labored whine. A small mechanical arm jutting from the side of the delivery bot waved in greeting before its front end opened. She took a clear plastic box filled with steam from inside, tossing it back and forth between her hands to manage the heat.

"Thanks," muttered Kirsten.

Another happy *chirp* emanated from the bot, which flew off. She poked the button to close the window, and, with a smooth mechanical droning, the inch-thick panel slid back up, the illusion of it being transparent eerily perfect.

She popped the carton open and cradled a breakfast burrito.

"Well that smells a lot better than the crap you get from the Nippy-Nom. Egg? Smells a little odd."

"Jalapeños. Ordered it on a lark once with Nikki. It's grown on me." She took a bite. "You wanna taste it? You can hop in if you want."

"That's okay."

"Right, boobs."

He looked past her across the street. "So what are we doing at the National Archives?"

She held up a finger while trying hurry chewing. "Computer finally spat out a hit on the silver circle. It tagged some of the pictographs as ancient Sumerian. There's a philanthropist here who supposedly has experience in that sort of thing. I'm hoping to pick his brain."

Chomp.

"Either that's rather tasty, or you forgot to eat dinner last night."

"Boaf," she muttered, her mouth full. Once she swallowed, she sighed. "Actually, I couldn't eat. Rush got to me."

"You're not going to start moping about being alone and unloved again, are you?"

"No. Just upset at those two idiots for being such callous dicks about it."

Dorian scratched at his eyebrow. "Jaded. Sometimes the ones who see too much too fast detach from it all. It's how they cope. I guess it makes it easier to think of them as road kill than as people." He turned to face her. "Oh, turns out that they have been looking for that guy for quite a while now, almost two years. Same aug killed a cop last April, over a year now and mauled his partner."

"I met a Div 9 woman a couple weeks ago who asked me if her dead partner was haunting her. Rush's description of the killer sounded pretty familiar." Kirsten set the burrito down and thumbed a text message out on her NetMini.

"Found something?"

"Nah." She sent the message and grabbed the remainder of her food. "Just passing along the info to someone I think might want to know."

After stuffing the last three bites of her breakfast in her mouth, she stepped out into the rain, crossed the street, and jogged up a long, steep stairway to the outer courtyard of the West City National Archives. Part museum, part records hall, the vast structure occupied about two square miles.

Shimmering aqua-colored blobs of light danced in the air over the primary atrium. Rain died a sizzling death upon a dome-shaped energy field. Free from of the downpour, she slowed to a casual walk along the entry courtyard past several statues of historical figures from the late 2200s: Takeshi Nomura, the inventor of the first practical ion drive, followed by the team that developed faster than light systems, a diorama of cyberspace pioneers, and a mess of truly ancient people she didn't recognize. They all had something to do with pre-war history.

"So who is this philanthropist?" Dorian ceased bothering to avoid people, simply walking through anyone who got in his way.

A few shivered; most didn't notice.

"Konstantin Dobrynin. Old money. His family's been prominent in Europe for many generations. He emigrated from the ACC a couple months ago, apparently the guy had enough cash to buy his way out. Or they didn't want him around."

"Or he's a spy." Dorian shook his head. "Did he apply for residency, or is he visiting?"

"The file didn't say either way."

"Hey!" blurted a young man in a security uniform as she ducked around the weapon scanner by the main entrance. "You can't—"

"Is something wrong?"

He looked at her uniform, seeming confused but hesitating. Fear spread over him as he spotted the zero on her rank badge and understanding of the black uniform crept in. He shook his head, mute.

She turned away with a scowl. "I didn't think so."

"Uhh," he warbled, offering a clumsy salute. "Sorry, ma'am, the black caught me off guard, is all. Don't see you guys much."

I'm bitchy today. Kirsten slowed, tilted her head at him. That his fear came from potentially offending a police officer and had nothing to do with psionics allowed her to relax. "It's okay. I've been dealing with a lot of... *interesting* people lately."

Dorian cracked his wry grin. "It's nice when they're just terrified of the rank, not the brain, eh?"

She crossed a grand concourse filled with holographic reproductions of ancient artwork hanging among dusty curtains of artificial sunlight. "Why does mankind always have to isolate some group for scorn? Countries, religion, skin tone, gender, sexual preference, psionics... why do we seem to *need* people to hate?"

"It's 2418; except for psionics and countries, you're talking about ancient history. Most people don't even remember that." He paused to admire flecks of glimmering dust drifting about in a holographic reproduction of a painting projected from an emitter labeled 'Rembrandt.' "Two hundred years ago, people made a big deal about being proud to belong to a vilified group. Now it just kind of is, and no one notices. I'm not sure anyone even remembers."

"There're still some pockets of it." She turned a corner, now past rows of statues. "Some of the East City gangs have adopted pseudo-religious ideals and attack anyone who doesn't agree with them. Others go after people for not being white, some go after people *for* being white. How damn stupid can you be?"

Dorian laughed. "Yeah, especially since you can change your skin with a trip to Reinventions. It's like wanting to stab someone for wearing the wrong color shirt."

Kirsten waved him off. "Not everyone has a million credits to waste on a DNA rebuild."

She wandered on past marble, bronze, and stone reproductions of people and things. Being here annoyed her at how much she didn't recognize, making her feel stupid for having missed so much school. The high vault ceiling divided the room into sections, each with a moving hologram depicting some point in the past. Biplanes in one, soldiers from an ancient war in another, political faces, the first starship launch, the ribbon cutting of the first Moon colony, and others. The entire back end of the room was devoted to the Corporate War, and played up the military's role in restoring stability to what had once been the United States.

"You can't judge humanity based on a few dozen morons. People can be stupid. Look at that group of neko junkies trying to have 'cat person' declared an actual ethnic group."

"Yeah. They don't need to pick on other things because they have psionics to hate now." She shoved a heavy faux-wood door out of her way.

Opulence bathed the office beyond it. Wooden everything surrounded her, genuine wood and not Epoxil from the scent. Paneled walls held shelves of books interspersed with oddities including silver skulls, bronze spheres, and a stuffed raven or two. Her boots made no sound over the sand colored carpeting on the way to an immense U-shaped desk. The grey marble slab top deviated from the theme of wood, covered by an orderly array of the usual desk techno-gadgetry as well as bits of ancient history. At the right corner, a bronze fish perched upon a head-sized green marble sphere.

A transparent older woman in a blue dress appeared seated at the desk. "Do you have an appointment?"

Kirsten took a step back, hand on her weapon. The woman didn't feel like a spirit, nor did she possess surface thoughts.

"Grabbed the gun this time, not your chest." Dorian laughed. "You're almost a cop."

Wow, that's an expensive damn holo-emitter. She looks solid. "Yes. I called about thirty minutes ago. Kirsten Wren, Division 0."

"One moment, officer."

The elderly simulacrum sat idle, a pleasant smile on her face as if watching unseen birds. After a minute, the gestures looped.

"I think I'm on hold," Kirsten whispered.

One of the shelves wobbled, then opened outward, revealing a hidden door to another, even larger, office. A thirtyish man stood in the passage between the rooms, his teeth bright against skin accustomed to the outdoors. She had the odd feeling he might've been older than he looked. People with money often went to Reinventions to shave off time. Either that or a young man with an old soul. A suit of shiny blue silk offered enough of a hint at an athletic physique to suggest he didn't spend all his time in the annals of a library.

A coral-hued cuff peeked out from the sleeve of his jacket as he gestured for her to enter. She cocked an eyebrow at the fluffy white ascot beneath his neck, amused by the anachronistic touch it lent to his overall appearance. Two silver rings glimmered with sapphires on the hand holding the door, three carved gold serpents coiled about the fingers of the one waving her in.

"Good morning, Miss Wren. The VidPhone hardly does you justice." Konstantin Dobrynin gazed into her eyes. "Such a perfect, deep shade of blue often renders poorly in hologram."

He brought his hand back, as if to shake, but drew hers up to place a gentle kiss upon her knuckles. The warmth of his breath swam over her skin, his eyes half-closed. Her arm fell to her side like a hunk of firewood.

I'm still back in the car. I'm still napping. This isn't real. This is what happens when you skip breakfast.

The Division 0 blacks felt a little too form-fitting under his gaze. She tried not to blush as she followed him down the narrow, short passage. *At least on this side, it's an obvious door.* When it swung closed, she couldn't quite tell if she felt trapped or welcome. Her nerves brought the essence of jalapeño to the back of her throat. She coughed, patting herself on the chest. *Okay, maybe I didn't dream about eating.*

"Can I offer you something to drink?"

"I'm on duty, and it's not even nine in the morning."

"Water, then; you look like you could use it. Are you fond of coffee?"

"All right."

He gestured at a chair, and went to a bar on the far end of the room. She glanced around over wooden shelves in a deep reddish hue, laden with scores of actual paper books. Most appeared old, loaded with dust. Atmospheric retention fields over the shelves charged the air with electricity. Kirsten stepped across a huge Oriental rug set at a diagonal in the center of the room. Fringe on both ends had enough of a metallic sheen to make her wonder if it had been made from real gold. Leering gargoyles mounted to the bookshelf behind the main chair seemed to stare at her, a feeling beyond that of simple carved eyes. She sat at the edge of one of the off-white guest seats facing the desk, not comfortable enough to relax into it.

"Do you take cream?" He glanced over his shoulder, tiny ceramic pitcher in his hand.

His eyes seemed to have the same burnished color as the rosewood shelves, somewhere between brown and red.

"A little."

Dorian wandered the edge of the chamber. The clink of spoons rattled about before Konstantin pivoted with a tray in hand. He paused to sniff the contents of the cups. The timing made her wonder if he'd waited for Dorian to walk past him. Konstantin sniffed again and smiled over the delicate cups at her, then moved to her side and set the tray on a small floating platform table between the two guest chairs. An overwhelmingly strong coffee aroma filled her senses. After she chose a cup, he lifted the remaining one, holding it up as a toast.

Kirsten tasted it, barely managing not to cough at the potency. "Espresso?"

"Turkish." He took a sip. "They still grow real beans there in the *ground.* So, what can I do for such a beautiful lady on this dismal rainy day?"

"Real coffee? He's showing off. That's only about two hundred credits you're drinking in that small cup." Dorian poked her in the back.

He's not walking around the desk to sit. He's staying close to me.

"Miss Wren?"

She shook off her daydream. "Yes, umm." *Subtle, K.* "I'm investigating a paranormal event and found some things I can't explain. The database spat out something about ancient Sumerian. I've never heard of it, but when I tried to look it up, I kept finding your name attached to articles."

"Ahh, so you were one of the six people that bothered to read my work? I have somewhat esoteric hobbies. I am fascinated by beautiful as well as ancient things." He set his cup on the desk, tilting his head slightly to the side. "I have a certain fondness for anything which appears delicate on the surface but is, in fact, quite dangerous."

Her gaze ran over his chest, eyebrow climbing as a pectoral ridge swelled prominent beneath his shirt. She fumbled with a datapad, before holding it out to him. Konstantin took it in a manner that brushed his fingers over her hand in a lingering departure.

"The image scans we took are in there." She couldn't look at him anymore.

"His desk is large enough, the walls are thick, and no one would hear anything." Dorian wandered along behind her, hands clasped behind his back. "What are you waiting for?"

Crimson. *This isn't right. I want a relationship. I'm not a cat in heat.*

Konstantin tapped the screen and lowered himself into the other guest chair. Images of the silver circle appeared in midair, enlarging as he pinched and stretched at the intangible light. He studied one for quite some time, then flipped to the next. Kirsten sipped her coffee, still refusing to look at him.

"I have not seen anything resembling this since my arrival in the UCF. This appears to be an attempt at constructing an intraplanar bridge."

"A what? Like a portal?" She blinked at him. "Seriously?"

"Well," he said, lips parting into a confident grin. "Some people believe in this sort of thing. Cults, mostly, societies that died out quite a long time before the Corporate War."

Transfixed, she sat there staring at him. Her heart thudded at the back of her consciousness. The light in here made him seem younger, as if he only had her by a few years.

"Have you been here long, Konstantin?" She absentmindedly tried to sip from an empty cup, putting it back in the saucer and feeling foolish. "I didn't see any emigration documents."

"Fascinating." He held his hand to his chin. "I am here on a journey of information sharing, for the Archives. There is no political agenda. I operate in societal circles that don't have time for pettiness of that nature."

"So he *is* a foreigner." Dorian resumed his wandering.

"Let's suppose this stuff you're talking about is real. I've seen ghosts. I guess I'd be a bit of a hypocrite to discount anything at this point." When she made eye contact, she caught him glancing out of the corner of his eye. "What would something like this circle do, assuming it was real?"

Can he see Dorian?

His glance flicked back to her, then to the images. "From this, it appears as if someone attempted to contact an entity on the other side, from an alternate world. These ancient sects thought it possible to channel the energies that flow between and divide different planes of existence by using a combination of force of will and patterns traced in precious materials."

"Like silver?"

"Indeed."

"Why would a precious material concern the planes? It's only precious because humans decided to make jewelry out of it."

"Rarity." An aloof expression of interest crossed his face. "The pattern and the intent is what matters, the preciousness is an element of exclusion. When the implements cost more than peasants earn in a lifetime, fewer people attempt it and many discount it as a hoax. It is simply a means to achieve a degree of safety with secrecy and doubt."

"Peasants?" Kirsten giggled. "Did we slip back into the dark ages?"

"This sort of ritualism has been around for a very long time. Occasionally, someone with a gift tries it and gets something to work. Perhaps someone such as you, who can see other worlds?"

She shook her head. "No, I don't want to call anything out of anywhere. I have to send them back. Could that circle have enabled spirits to slip out of the Abyss?"

"If you believe in such things, perhaps." He stood. "I would love to discuss this with you at length; you are an enigma of splendor."

"Oh, you're too kind." She eased out of the chair, taking a step for the door. *Enigma of splendor... that's a compliment, right?*

"Wait, so you have a decent looking guy with an incredible amount of money who also happens to not care you're psionic, and you're ready to run like hell?" Dorian shook his head. "I give up on understanding women."

"Let me copy these files. I shall study them in detail and get back to you." Konstantin glided around behind the huge desk and eased himself into an enormous black leather chair.

"I'll need your PID." He leaned into the creaking leather. "So I can call you if I find anything."

"Of course." *Give him the department number.*

Beep. Her personal NetMini chimed.

Oh, shit, what did I just do?

13

A JOB UNFINISHED

The Archives faded into the distance on the rear-view monitors. Kirsten squeezed and released the control sticks to work out the tension in her body. After weaving through the ad-bot layer, she swerved hard to the right and climbed into the hovercar lane. The rain continued, appearing here and there as brief pixilation in the windscreen, digitally removed from the display. Silence pervaded, save for the steady thrum of the various electronics in the patrol craft's console. The pulsating rhythm of the ion drives ran down her back like massaging hands.

Kirsten settled into her seat, death grip relaxing. "That was strange."

"I'm honestly surprised you didn't—"

"Don't even say it. What do you think I am? Sure, he's tall, dark, and richer than hell. You think I'm going to fling my pants off and leap onto his desk?"

"Umm." He chuckled. "I was going to say peek into his surface thoughts."

A minute of silence.

"The red goes quite nicely with the blonde."

Kirsten wanted to scream in anger, cry from shame, and hide from embarrassment all at once. After a moment, she muttered. "It was just too good."

"You know, I think the man saw me." Dorian glanced at the console.

The heat ticked up two degrees. "Did you notice how he stopped with the tray when I walked in front of him?"

"I had a feeling. If I wasn't gawking at him like a cat in heat I might have eavesdropped on his head." She growled. "Nothing felt like he was doing anything to me, but I couldn't stop thinking about how amazing he looks. I'm such a screw up."

"I'm sure it's nothing. He might simply be an undocumented astral. Really, as a foreigner, he's out of our purview unless he does something criminal. Usually, ACC psionics come running to us waving their arms and begging for help."

"He wanted to put me off balance." She hung a left turn and climbed up a lane.

A teen rolled sideways and shot past on her right side. He started to flash an angry glower at the 'slow' car, but wound up with an 'oh, crap that's a cop!' stare. He slowed to the pace of a grandmother. Kirsten ignored him. *He'll be too terrified to drive like an idiot for at least twenty minutes.*

"Maybe Konstantin found you attractive? You are very pretty; you have those tragic Cosette eyes."

"What the hell does that mean?" Kirsten looked away from traffic in short spurts to pin him with a quizzical stare.

"It's from an ancient theater production you've never heard of. Whenever you're not doing anything specific, you seem to stare into space asking the world why it's so mean to you."

"I do not." She frowned. "I'm doing okay now."

"So where are you going?"

"Nowhere specific. I'm thinking."

"Agent Wren, please acknowledge," said a female voice from the console.

Kirsten looked at the console. "Guess we have a destination now." Poke. "Agent Wren here, go ahead."

"21-47 reported at PubTran monorail Terminal, Sector 1471."

A handful of small holo-panels opened: security camera footage of glass exploding for no reason, gunfire cracking out of thin air, and a man in a long black coat fading in and out as he walked down the concourse.

Kirsten whispered. "Seneschal."

"Copy that, I'm en route. I suspect astral entities involved. Please advise Division 1 not to enter the area. I don't know what we're dealing with yet. Also, give me a red dot on the station, I don't want any trams arriving until it's clear."

"Acknowledged."

Dorian glanced at the roof, the bar lights came on.

She yanked back on the right stick while twisting the left one counterclockwise and shoving it forward. The car shot vertical out of the hover lane and whirled around to face Sector 1471. Kirsten's body mushed into the seat from acceleration.

CHAOS PLAYED OUT BELOW. A ROW OF PARKED CARS ALONG THE STREET leading up to the station bore the marks of a roving gunfight. The fighting appeared recent due to the shattered remains of windows covering the road and sidewalk with twinkling crystalline glitter. People streamed down two large powered stairways that led from the small micro-park between the street and the station up to the elevated platform. The top of the long oval tube, the clear barricade over the monorail itself, peeked over the edge of the raised floor. Lights flickered inside.

A group of Division 1 patrol officers worked the base of the stairways, attempting to keep order among the fleeing crowd. Everyone ducked at once at gunfire within the evacuated station. Kirsten elbowed her way into the opposing mass of bodies, plowing through the crowd and up the stairs. At the top, she stepped into the squint-inducing fluorescence of an empty plastisteel-floored mall. Metal support beams flanked bench seats, a plastic carton slid across in spurts of wind, and a few of the shopkeepers on the street-side end remained to defend their possessions.

Kirsten swallowed. The sight of an empty PubTran monorail terminal was scary in a post-apocalyptic sort of way that tensed the muscles in the back of her neck. A dark feeling simmered in the air, announcing the presence of something paranormal. Dorian drifted right as they advanced, searching for any trace of activity.

Boots crunched on broken fragments of electronics. The damage in the terminal mostly appeared to be the result of bullets. The column the former display screen had been mounted to showed no sign of harm, not even scratched paint, as though the projectiles ceased existing as soon as they hit the giant monitor. She had seen a similar effect before. Some ghosts could learn how to cause direct harm to other beings, and that technique often manifested in a form of attack familiar to the ghost—like a gun. Of course, it didn't create real bullets, merely bursts of energy.

An Indian man darted out of an empty store, dark grey sweater and black pants glittering from adhering flakes of broken glass. He ran past an armed shopkeeper without triggering any sort of reaction. Someone in the store behind him fired a weapon; the sound, heavy and booming, suggested something huge like an ABR20.

Kirsten ran for cover behind the nearest metal column. She pressed her shoulder against it and peered around. "Vikram?"

The runner blinked at her in surprise, hesitating only for a fraction of a second before diving over a bench. At another deep *boom,* a shower of sparks scored dark gouges in the white paint on the column behind him. Seneschal stalked out of the store the man had run out of, holding a rifle-shaped weapon with an almost two-inch thick barrel.

"Oof. SPR-42." Dorian whistled. "Forty-two millimeter shotgun. Those come with a coupon for a free mop. Even Div 5 thinks they're overkill."

Kirsten ducked out of sight behind the column. "Five doesn't use them because a mess of little bullets won't scratch a cyborg. They prefer one big one."

"That's what she said," muttered Dorian.

She sighed. "Seriously?"

Boom.

Kirsten flinched.

A scattershot pattern of sparks ended another holo-screen showing arrival and departure times, leaving the post unscathed. Icarus rushed out of a store a quarter mile down the concourse, dreadlocks trailing him like a cape as he ran toward the sound of combat.

Vikram scrambled into a forward crawl, screaming as another blast from the huge shotgun tore the slats out of a bench above his head.

"Over here," Kirsten shouted, waving.

Dorian ran to the next column, taking cover. "Try shooting one."

"Seneschal," she yelled. "Stand down, we can't—"

Not hesitating in the slightest, he pivoted to aim at her and fired.

Boom.

She dove to the floor amid a rain of fragments. Dorian leaned out, firing his E-90, though rather than a blue beam it made a white streak. The energy spread over Seneschal's left shoulder, hitting him with the force of a punch. An annoyance.

Dorian ducked behind cover when Seneschal pivoted to aim in his direction. "They're strong."

"Guess it's true what Theo said. They're not who they were before."

"Oh, they are." Vikram appeared at her left, crawling. "They're still trying to kill me."

She waved a hand *through* his shoulder. "They already did."

"I mean, they're trying to kill me again." He curled up behind another column six feet away. "It seems they are somewhat upset with me for blowing them up. The dark things took them, but they came back."

Kirsten popped up, firing. The laser seared an ember-edged channel several inches long into Seneschal's chest. Flakes of ash blackened and drifted off in the wind, but the hole sealed. In the distance behind him, a small shop caught fire.

"Please, you can't let them get me." Vikram tried to grab her arm. "They murdered me once already."

"Stay down." She leaned around the column to take another shot.

Seneschal slid behind a vendomat. Kirsten kept her aim on the machine, nodding to Dorian, who ran to take cover at a closer post. Icarus emerged past the cloud of fire-suppression fog billowing out of the burning store, firing at a standard assault rifle at Dorian. Bullets clicked into the floor around him, but made no secondary ricochet.

"You do not seem confident." Vikram risked a brief peek.

Kirsten didn't take her eyes away from the floating azure dot of her gun sight. Vendomat and gun traded blurriness as her focus shifted back and forth. "I'm not entirely sure what I'm dealing with here. Ghost bullets aren't supposed to break physical things." She shifted her aim to the right, and fired at Icarus.

A diving roll put him behind the wall of a gadget store, leaving a glowing patch of plastisteel where Kirsten's laser scored the floor. Dorian sprang to his feet and charged, his gun seeming to teleport from his hand to the holster. He launched himself into a flying tackle, and disappeared into vendomat. A heavy *thud* echoed from behind it. Dorian slid into the open on top of Seneschal.

"Stay here, stay down." Kirsten leapt up and ran, switching the E-90 to her left hand.

Icarus popped out at the squeak of her boots. He aimed at her, but hesitated. With a hesitant grimace, he fired a few shots at the ground to her left, forcing her to slide into cover behind a metal-walled planter. Seneschal punched upward, knuckles mashing into Dorian's cheek with a strike that launched him vertical, a dozen feet in the air. The force of the hit stretched Dorian's head like a warping hologram. Seneschal dispersed into a cloud of mist and reappeared on his feet.

Kirsten popped up and fired. A thread of azure light lanced Seneschal's thigh as he reached for his rifle. The laser burned an ash channel through his leg, making him roar in pain. He glared at her, opening his hand toward the ground. The massive shotgun pivoted and flew into its master's arms, pointed at her.

Dorian, his head once again back to normal, fell on top of him, stunrod across the man's throat. The shotgun went off in mid-takedown, the blast shaving two lights off the ceiling. Dorian snarled, crushing the manifestation of his baton into Seneschal's neck and using it to flip the man over. They tumbled to the floor again, Dorian perched on the abyssal's back. Icarus swiveled aim to Dorian, but ducked when Kirsten fired at him, the laser melting a spritz of plastisteel out of the wall by his face.

Sensing opportunity, she ran across a large oval planter surrounded by benches and vendomats, taking three steps on dirt before leaping a bench on the other side. She called the astral lash in midair, boots touching down the same instant the tip hit Seneschal in the back of the head.

Dorian leaned away from her attack, barely containing the primal urge to flee from the disruptive energy. Seneschal's scream melted into a roar. His eyes lit with the dark crimson fire of the Abyss.

Vikram screamed. Kirsten whirled, finding Mariko having come out of nowhere, sword rammed into his back. The Japanese woman grinned with sinister glee, her eyes completely black, teeth pointed. A veil of darkness clung to her, as if her body didn't quite want to be solid. Her grin widened, and she twisted her sword, triggering an agonized howl from Vikram.

She enjoyed causing pain.

The dead hacker gaped at the shiny blade sticking out of his gut, whimpering. Kirsten whirled and took a second to aim. The sword jerked free, raised for another stroke. She fired. The azure beam caught Mariko in the face, melting her nose into a hollow and starting a fire in her mouth. She stumbled a step to the rear, shaking her head as if reacting to a sucker punch instead of a Class 4 laser opening a hole entirely through her skull. Mariko's face filled in, inky black smoke peeling from her nostrils.

With a wail, Vikram dove into the ground out of sight. Mariko hissed at Kirsten, a snarl so feral and deep it did not sound human. Her teeth formed a zigzag line of razor-sharp triangles, nothing even close to human. The once-woman circled to the side, spindly limbs elongated and narrow, her lithe body shrouded in black fumes. Kirsten raised the lash, coiling it behind her in preparation for a strike. Dorian and Seneschal grunted, still fighting behind her.

Mariko shrank away from the light with a hiss and darted off to the south. Like a human-headed spider, she leapt from monorail to monorail, elongated arms and legs carrying her out over a dozen parallel tracks. Kirsten shrieked from a sensation similar to a bucket of ice water hitting her in the back. Dorian's ghostly essence washed over her. He landed in a slide on the floor. Before she broke free of the paralytic cold, he vanished into the floor. Kirsten spun to the rear. Seneschal's hand grabbed her around the throat and lifted her off her feet.

Eyes bulging, she gurgled. The touch of his hand burned like fire. Her kicks passed harmlessly through a body solid only where he wanted it to be. Icarus nodded at Seneschal, lifted his rifle, and sank down into the platform, chasing either Dorian or Vikram. Seneschal pulled her in close, bright red eyes burning with hatred. The same aura of dread Harbingers carried radiated from him—the taint of the Abyss. She shuddered from her proximity to evil.

Still holding her up one-handed with his left, he pulled a large handgun out from under his coat and raised it to her forehead. "You are a pain in the ass. Welcome to the world of acceptable collateral damage."

Kirsten mentally swung the lash, charging it with fear. The energy tendril coiled up and around, striking him in the side and swatting him into the air. Seneschal careened in an arc, a living dart, before landing on his head and sliding a few feet while his body remained vertical. Momentum eventually carried him over to land flat on his chest. She rubbed her neck, thankful not to feel the tenderness of a real burn. His touch had burned only in her mind.

Kirsten charged at him, taking two steps and bringing the energy whip down again. Seneschal flipped himself over onto his back and caught the lash in one hand. He held the stream of brilliance in a smoking grip; his eyes brightened and he roared with agony. The flesh of his fingers boiled and bubbled. Bones glowed beneath the skin. Kirsten forced more power into it, left hand grabbing her wrist for support as she pushed down. The anger in his eyes flickered to fear for an instant; his grip on the spectral weapon faltered. The tip stabbed at his face like a furious cobra trying to bite him, missing by inches.

She screamed despite clenched teeth, trying to power her way past a contest of wills. Right as she started to sense the upper hand, he dissipated in a cloud of ink black vapor. The sudden lack of resistance sent her stumbling to her knees. Kirsten released the lash and landed on all fours, trying to catch her breath. The cloud that had been Seneschal sank flat to the floor, expanded into a wide field, and seeped into gaps between tiles.

Gunshots erupted outside. The barrage snapped her out of her fatigue and she ran to the stairs. A row of Division 1 officers fired with wild abandon at something beneath the platform, nine weapons creating a rapid strobe in blue muzzle flash. She ran most of the way down the steps before leaping over the railing and landing in a three-point crouch. Seneschal stalked along in the dark underside of the PubTran station, phasing through fences and wire conduits. Orange sparks flickered whenever a bullet struck him, insignificant holes closing as fast as they appeared. He didn't even bother to look at the officers.

"Ugh," Dorian moaned from the ground somewhere ahead of her.

"Stop firing, you're doing nothing!" she shouted at her forearm guard; the comm made her voice much louder in their helmets.

The barrage trickled to a few isolated shots, then stopped. When quiet returned, she ran to Dorian, who lay in a trench atop several cable runs. He didn't appear wounded, rather tired.

"Shit. Are you okay?" She climbed over pipes and boxy components, easing herself down by his side. Willing herself tangible to the astral world, she cradled his hand. "What happened?"

He squeezed her fingers, calming her. "Fine, but tired. They beat the snot out of me. Gonna take a while to recover, but I'm okay. I can maybe handle one of them, but two at once, no way. They're too strong." He chuckled. "It's really not fair."

"But they've only been dead for a few months."

"That's what I mean about it not being fair." He brushed broken glass of his chest. "They're not ghosts, K. They're... something else."

"Yeah, I guess so. I have to find Vikram before they do. They're going to obliterate him."

"Poor guy." He struggled to sit up. "Too bad there's not enough left of him to use the trick Ritchie showed you."

Lights flooded into the chain link darkness. Kirsten held a hand over her eyes as Division 1 officers approached behind their guns. "Everything all right down here, ma'am?"

A male officer lifted his visor. "Umm, are you okay?"

"Zeroes talk to themselves sometimes," said his partner.

"What happened here? Did you find anything?" A sergeant stowed her weapon and approached, hesitating at the sight of Kirsten's posture appearing to hug nothing.

"I'll be in the car," Dorian wheezed. His body faded out of sight, voice lingering. "I need a nap." Pale luminescent fog crept among the weeds and glided past the chain-link fence, and the legs of the patrol cops.

Kirsten stood, wiping dirt from her hands. She scowled at the distant cavern of power cables, water pipes, sewer lines, and fencing. "Yeah, I found something. I'm just not sure what it is."

14

THE SONS OF CHARON

Kirsten gazed into the sky, catching herself picking out the ad-bots displaying kid furniture, clothing, and certain electronic games. Thousands of the little bots coursed overhead, the blood of the city moving in veins defined by pre-programmed flight paths. She nudged vindaloo around her plate with a fork. Thinking of Evan took away the usual loneliness she experienced whenever she wound up staring at advert bots. They didn't quite make her feel like an outsider peering in on a life she wasn't good enough for anymore.

The patrol craft waited barely ten feet away, outside a three-foot-tall barrier of plastisteel separating the Kajuraho Restaurant's open-air seating area from the sidewalk. The eighteen-inch-thick barricade would theoretically be able to stop a ground vehicle moving at ninety miles per hour. Not that anyone could drive at that speed on the ground here to begin with. This part of the city had too much traffic and too many red signals.

Dorian hadn't reappeared all yesterday, and so far this morning, he remained absent. For whatever reason, he had fixated on the patrol craft as his focus, so there he 'slept.' His cremated remains occupied an urn somewhere, but he had chosen the car instead. Kirsten felt his presence during the ride, wondering how long it took a ghost to 'sleep' their way back to full strength.

The chicken went down slow. Despite her newfound tolerance to jalapeño eggs, the Indian food remained a little too spicy for her to devour fast. A man two tables away gazed into nowhere, his head and hand moving as if in a silent conversation. Thin silver wire stranded from behind his ear into a NetMini tucked alongside his plate. She imagined her dad's voice saying *implanted comm whatevers*, and let out a soft laugh.

A citycam ball mounted to the corner of the building ceased its endless panning, fixating on her. She set a piece of chicken between her teeth and pulled her fork out, staring at the orb of smoky glass. Seconds passed. She bit down, chewing. The camera continued pointing right at her.

Bet one of the techs is checking me out.

The camera disregarded, she continued her lunch and tried to sort out her current mess. *Okay, I've got a ghost who used to be a network security guy. Lyris Corporation sends a hit squad to take him out, everyone dies in a blast. Somehow, these assassins escape the Abyss and continue their original mission. Vikram's lingering around for some reason. But what about him pissed off Seneschal's crew so much they fought their way out of the Abyss to kill him a second time? What am I missing?*

"Mmm." She exuded contentment as a sip of her mango lassi put out the spice fire in her mouth. As she went to set it down, she froze, staring at a ring of condensation on the table from the cold cup. *The circle.*

Kirsten set the drink down hard enough to spill some. *Of course. Find who made the circle, and I'll know what the hell is going on.*

Loud rumbling pulled her attention into the street. A shot-up and battered van creaked to a halt alongside the patrol craft, stopping right in the traffic lane. The image of a skull-faced grim reaper had been autobrushed on the side. Two copper coins perched upon a tongue that protruded from the teeth.

Electricity sizzled around the front left wheel motor, as if one more bump would spell its demise. The driver door opened in time with the whirr of a mechanized sliding door on the far side. The man who emerged from the driver's seat had overdone it on black eyeliner, but otherwise appeared to ignore most matters of personal hygiene. Belt-long hair, blackened by a substance never intended to be cosmetic dye, clung to him. His torn pseudo-leather vest covered a stained white shirt, as well as a pair of submachine guns. He stared at Kirsten like a rutting bull about to charge.

She tensed, fork slipping from her fingers at the sudden blaring horn from a small car trapped behind the van, pinned in the lane by unforgiving traffic. Gulping down her unease, she stood, preparing to order the van to move.

Automatic gunfire shredded the calm. Men on the street side of the van riddled the offending horn-bearing car with bullets. Diners around her dove to the floor, sending tables, chairs, and food flying. The driver went for his weapons, an unblinking grin leveled off at Kirsten as though he didn't want to spook her into running before he could shoot her.

The woman in the car dove down into the passenger seat, her screams inaudible over the roaring chatter of small automatic weapons. Kirsten caught a glimpse of a dozen small braids in the back seat, each tipped with pink clip-on ribbons. As windshield peeled away and coolant fogged out of holes in the hood, Kirsten lunged toward the crash barrier at the edge of the seating area, E-90 in hand. Desperate to stop the men shooting at the civilian car with a child in it, Kirsten shot into the side of the van as fast as she could click the trigger, hoping to hit the men behind it.

The driver brought his weapons to bear. Men's screams rang out and the barrage of fire aimed for the car came to a halt.

For an instant in the pause of gunfire, the screams of a woman and her daughter became clear. The driver fired a burst from both weapons at her.

Dorian came flying out from the side of the van, leaping into the air toward amid a hail of bullets. A look of intense worry spread over his face, a snapshot preserved in adrenaline slow motion. He roared. She sensed his energy shift; when he hit her, he almost had the mass of a solid man. A hit like a plastic bag full of cold pudding crashed into her and knocked her flat. A rip of pain tore at her left arm, between elbow and shoulder. Kirsten hit the ground on her back. Dorian slid over her like a mass of gelatin and went sliding under several tables.

At a handful of chairs spontaneously falling over, people screamed.

She scooted up against the little wall, her left arm numb and disobedient. It wanted to hang there doing nothing. Cold seeped into her uniform as her back pressed into frigid plastisteel, thick enough to stop bullets. The driver fired again at random, laughing as his bullets tore up several people searching for cover under tables.

Men screamed; an older woman cried out. Without thinking, Kirsten popped up and took a poorly-aimed shot at the driver. The streak of light missed him by an arm's length left, igniting the front-end of the van. He swerved his automatic fire toward her as if watering the lawn. A thin line of pain scratched over her ribs on the left as she ducked. Kirsten used the tip of the E-90 to poke the emergency call button on her left forearm guard. The arm still wouldn't move.

"Stay down!" Dorian screamed, as he ran to her side. "You're shot through the arm, bone's probably broken."

Anger held her fear in a headlock. "He's shooting people!" *Shock is wonderful.*

The scuffing of the other men shuffling around the van preceded a few random bullets into the seating area. One of the large windows in the restaurant shattered..

Dorian scowled. "I don't know if I have enough strength to scare them; knocking you down about tapped me."

She smiled, grimacing at the pain that only now radiated from her arm. Hot blood slid down her triceps; she blinked. After stuffing pistol between her thighs, she pulled the stunrod off her belt and laid it across her lap.

"Nonlethal?" Dorian blinked. "Are you kidding?"

Kirsten's sapphire eyes darkened. "There's a kid in the car. I can't just sit here. This is all I have."

She pressed her right hand over her wounded bicep, screaming from the pain, but coating her hand with blood. Focused on her desire to fuse the astral echo of the stunrod with is physical form, she smeared the blood over the baton. Wisps of luminous white vapor coalesced around her hand in response to her power. The blood smear glowed for a second before it soaked into the stunrod as if absorbed by a towel.

"Here, take it. Gimme a distraction." She shifted to her knees, facing the wall. "I don't use this trick too often 'cause it needs blood and I'm a wimp. But... I seem to be throwing blood all over the place right now, so... On that note." She rushed two stimpaks, which, although they didn't give her feeling back in the arm, stopped her bleeding.

Dorian noticed the change in the weapon right away. For a time, it would be tangible to both ghosts and mortals. He picked it up, awestruck at a physical object solid in his hands.

"Come on, man. Before I faint."

A little voice in the car screamed, "Mommy!"

The desperation in the cry made Kirsten pop up again, facing four men with six submachine guns and a cheap assault rifle. Dorian ran at them. A trickle of gunfire went almost in Kirsten's direction as one man spooked and fired at the floating stunrod coming at them. The one with

THE SONS OF CHARON | 125

the old rifle found it hilarious and laughed, right up until the thing hit him in the nose and sent him to the ground in convulsions.

Two felt it a good idea to shoot at the weaving eighteen-inch rod with the glowing blue tip, and started throwing bullets all over the place. Kirsten sighted on the driver, and put one pulse straight through his chest and into the van. Steam and smoke wisped out of his mouth a second before he fell forward like a plank. Dorian set upon one of the others, not even using the stun electronics. He swung the stunrod like a club, smashing it into the side of the man's knee, collarbone, head, and chest twice. The thug collapsed, down for the count from the beating—plus more than a few bullets from his idiot friend still trying to shoot the baton.

Other cars swerved and crashed where errant fire went into traffic. Kirsten pivoted and fired at another of her attackers. Blood sprayed from two finger-sized holes, one on either side of his chest. He wheezed, dropped his guns, and doubled over, cradling the wound.

Kirsten forced herself to stand, one-arming her E-90, which she kept pointed at the man coughing up blood. Dorian applied the stunner again to the rifle-bearing ganger for good measure, then smiled at the novelty of holding an object all over again.

After kicking weapons out of reach, she backpedaled to the car while keeping the man in view. A series of quick rightward glances made her heart skip a beat. Both the woman and a girl of about ten in the back seat had taken hits. Blood spattered the interior of their little silver car. The girl lay on the floor, sweating and breathing in shallow gasps. The mother had passed out.

"Dorian, stun that last son of a bitch."

She holstered her weapon to free her only working hand, but found the door locked. Disregarding the door, she clambered up the hood and slid in via the destroyed windshield. The broken bones in her left arm ground over each other as she tried to get a stimpak out of her left side belt case with her right arm.

"Officer, is my momma gonna die?"

Kirsten looked up at the voice, pinned in place by innocent brown eyes peering past a hanging curtain of tight braids. Finger trails of blood smeared over the chocolate-hued skin of the child's cheek, staining the collar of a white shirt with big-headed caricatures of a boy band. Kirsten stared at the girl, her right hand shaking with rage. She scowled at the men laid out on the road.

"Now you know why I did some things I've come to regret." Dorian's voice filtered in from behind. "If that girl was dead, would you finish off the survivors? Would you punish them?"

She snapped out of her daze. *Shit. I've lost a lot of blood.* "No, sweetie, I think she's gonna be okay. Where are you hit?"

The child sank into the seat, whining. Kirsten stifled the urge to scream in pain as she forced her hand into the awkward case, fingers scrabbling at a stimpak.

"My side and arm." The girl pulled her shirt up, revealing a graze over the hip and a few nicks from flying glass. She also bled from a grazing shot near the shoulder.

Lot of blood, little danger.

Kirsten's relief almost let the light-headed urge to faint from pain win. She handed the girl a stimpak. "Do you know how to use these?"

"No," said the girl.

"Press the small end into your leg and hold it down until it stops hissing." Kirsten struggled to pull out another stimpak, bit the safety cap off, and stabbed it into the mother's thigh.

A soft hiss came from the back seat. "Ooh! It's cold!"

"Agent Wren, please respond, what is your status?" The small silver bud in her left ear vibrated.

Oh, shit, how long have they been trying to comm me?

"Shots fired. Numerous civilians wounded. I'm hit, but okay."

Palpable relief carried in the voice. "Roger that, Agent. Hold on, backup is one sector out."

"I can hear them already."

The woman moaned. The girl tried to climb forward, but Kirsten held her back.

"Medics are coming; your mom's gonna be just fine."

Kirsten held the girl's hand until the area swarmed with Division 1 officers as well as medtechs. Once the medics had the woman extracted from the car and took the girl, Kirsten staggered toward the confused ghost of the van's driver. Another medic came up behind her and gently grasped her unhurt arm.

"Come on, we've got the civilians taken care of. Damn lucky thing you were here."

"No, it isn't." Kirsten groaned at the pain of pulling away from him. "They were after me."

"You've lost a lot of blood, and it looks like your arm is broken. We need to get you to the facility."

She all but dragged the medtech to the side of the van. "In a minute." She pointed with her good arm at the ghost. "You. Shithead."

The medic blinked. The new spirit lunged into a choking grab, but flew right through her.

"You're a ghost, you jackass." She turned to face him. "You do this for ha-has? Why me?"

Smoke poured from his nostrils, an aftereffect of death-by-laser. Kirsten glared at him, surrounded by the shimmer of emergency lights dancing along plastisteel and glass. Traffic had ceased, the entire area cordoned off as a crime scene. More flashing red and blue lights came in overhead as additional patrol craft set up a hoverlane exclusion zone. The advert bots rerouted their path, except for a few that tried to sell stuff to the police.

"Nothing to say?" asked Kirsten, glaring at the ghost.

"Come on, Agent Wren. If you are hallucinating, we need to get moving."

She let the medtech hold her, bracing some of her weight against him. "I'm not hallucinating."

The dead ganger looked around, put his hand into the wall of the van, and stared. His murderous glower melted away to genuine fear as the reality of what happened to him sank in at last. Two patrolmen walked past, dispersing him into a cloud of mist. When he re-formed, he took an angry step at Kirsten, pointing.

"What the fuck did you do to me?"

She would have folded her arms, but for one thing, she couldn't really act tough while in that much pain. For another, folding her arms required both of them being able to move. Also, since only the dark-skinned medtech in white kept her on her feet, she didn't even try to be menacing. "What did *I* do to *you?* What did you try to do to me?"

"We'z 'sposed to kill you."

She smiled a saccharin grin. "Well, there you have it."

"I'm dead?" He looked at the street and back at her. "You bitch!"

A ripple of anger ran down her back. *What balls! This asshole tries to kill me and is angry at me?* She narrowed her eyes, wanting *them* to pay him a visit.

"Did you decide to shoot at me because I was a cop for some kind of initiation rite? Or are you really just *that* damn stupid?"

The sense of mood changed, darkened. Dorian wandered back to the patrol craft, whistling. As the shadows grew more intense, he dissipated into his car. The dead ganger coughed a cloud of smoke and looked around, addled by the approach of dread he couldn't see.

"Someone gave us a pile of swag and an image cap of your face. More swag if we got you."

"Did you get a name?"

"Yeah, but I don't remember it. Dude had a girl's name, though."

"Rene?" She started to fall over as strength left her legs.

The medic hauled her up. "Okay, that's it. You may outrank me, but I am still a medtech. You're about to faint. Whatever you're doing is over." He turned to his right. "Jen, need a slab, stat."

"Yeah. Renee. It's a girl's—"

Three Harbingers welled up out of the ground beside him and his answer twisted into a primal scream.

Kirsten surrendered to the medtech pulling her backward, and gave up fighting to stay conscious.

DEBRIEFING

Placid warmth surrounded Kirsten. A street full of flashing lights, loud voices, moaning citizens, and pain had become quiet calm. She remembered Kendall, the medic, holding her hand inside the MedVan. She enjoyed the weightlessness of the breathable gel, savored the lack of pain, but didn't much care for being suspended nude in a floor-to-ceiling tank of slime with two men outside.

Tickling built up into a sensation similar to a dozen mice nibbling on her arm. She looked. Her toes instinctively curled at the sight of a gory hole in her left upper arm. Bits of her flesh floated like chum around the wound. Fragments of skin and bone drifted under control of invisible tugboat nanobots.

A voice filled the gel. "Agent Wren, please try to hold still. It will take longer if you keep moving around."

Yeah, yeah. You said that last time, too.

When the initial shock of seeing a hole clean through her arm faded, she watched with the awe of a curious child. Slivers of bone swam out of the wound as if on their own, melting away to nothing as the microscopic machines scavenged them for material. Snaps came from within, a high-pitched cracking as if someone popped their knuckles underwater. She cringed at the sound, expecting pain, but none came. Her entire arm felt *wrong*, as if everything below the gunshot wasn't part of her anymore. Over the course of the next twenty minutes, the diameter of the channel gradually shrank until it closed. She looked away as nips of discomfort from her ribs, legs, and cheek gave away where other repairs occurred. A cluster of automotive glass glimmered above and to her right. Nanobots, unable to dissolve glass, carried it to a disposal port in the center of the floor. She watched it fall, slow-motion snow, past her toes. A wisp of blood trailing out of her calf stole her attention away from the tiny fleet.

Damn, I didn't even feel the one in the leg.

The outer door hissed open, startling the two doctors. Two men in long, sand-brown coats, black everything below them, dark sunglasses, and with the same perfect hair walked in. Both had the telltale lines of neuralware on their left cheek, a thin strip of somewhat darker skin that trailed down from an indentation where the implant clung to the outside of the skull.

The man on the right looked every bit the image of the traditional government agent. Nondescript, corpse-white, short hair, maybe late thirties. Little about him would linger in the memory for more than a few minutes after he left. His partner had darker skin and black hair, and also seemed more muscular under the coat. His features had a Latin touch that tweaked her embarrassment to a brief tawdry thrill.

Division 9.

Gel flew out her nostrils. Her attempt to squeal in embarrassment produced no sound. She scrambled to cover herself as the doctors protested the intrusion. For an instant, Kirsten felt a surge of gratitude at them for trying to defend her modesty. It fell flat when they acquiesced at the presentation of ID badges. Both doctors backed away from the badges, hands up. The pair of agents approached the tank, emotionless faces appraising her like something on display at a medical museum. Neither man showed the slightest bit of arousal at the sight of her. She wondered if they might be dolls or synths, though didn't dare risk a surface thought peek. Rumor had it Division 9 had mysterious cybernetic implants that caused telepaths great pain.

She braced for them to start laughing at her, the way Mother's friends always did whenever they watched her suffer a paddling. Fear gripped her and kept her arms at her sides instead of trying to guard her intimates.

The one on the right looked her up and down with a detachment that made her feel less than human. "How much longer?"

The gel blurred his voice, mixing it with the subtle thrum of the pumps filtering the fluid. The doctor's response came from too far away to pierce the Lexan shell around her. Both Division 9 agents offered a single curt nod and glanced at her again. They stood with the stillness of statues, cardboard cutouts of the stereotypical government spook. If either of them had any emotions, any excitement at all at seeing her naked, they kept it buried deep. Paddling with one hand, she managed to turn her back on them.

She found it quite challenging to sniffle with a gel-flooded nose.

Why are they here? Did I do something wrong? Couldn't they wait until I'm dressed?

"We would like to talk to you about the incident at the Kajuraho restaurant, as soon as possible."

The voice flooded the B-gel, silky and cold. It sounded like the voice of a man who could kill without remorse, who could torture a trapped woman with an unblinking stare. She shivered.

Kirsten hung in silence for another twenty some minutes, although it felt more like two hours. Head bowed against the rear wall of the tank, she wanted Captain Eze to barge in and read them the riot act for violating her privacy. She tried to focus on the thought they were military men, used to showers of a hundred soldiers at a time, men and women. She tried not to feel stared at.

"Agent Wren, please put your feet down. We're going to drain the gel now," said one of the doctors, via speakers in the tank.

She straightened out, both hands over her crotch, back still to the room. The mechanical noise permeating the gel intensified, sound waves rode the fluid right to her eardrums. Her toes touched down on the tepid plastisteel base. Soon, her weight settled onto her feet as the surface of the gel descended past her head, over her shoulders. Freezing cold air flooded the top of the tank, chasing away the nice, warm gel.

She sank with it, wanting to delay the embrace of arctic winds as much as possible. Soon, she sprawled on the ground, arms curled around her legs. With her back to the room, she fought the urge to blush. Kirsten braced for another wave of crippling shame, memories of Mother's punishment, but it didn't hit her that hard. Straightening, she turned to peer over her shoulder.

The agents looked down at her. The doctor stood a few feet behind them holding a white robe made of towel material. Although mortified, her present situation didn't carry the same feeling of helplessness that it had so often done in the past. Kirsten curled in place, cheek to knees, holding her breath, lungs still full of pink goo. Her eyes tracked a wisp of blood in the peach-colored fluid as it circled the vent ports before vanishing into the grille. Her mother's cruelty had gone down the drain of newfound resolve. This humiliation was normal, not crippling.

She merely had four men staring at her.

Kirsten tried to speak, but gel burbled out of her mouth. Panic at having lungs full of liquid gripped her, and she forgot all about being naked. Coughing, sputtering, flailing, she scrambled around on the slick surface. Tractionless gel sent her sliding onto the icy floor; attempts to scream only worsened her choking.

Having had enough of watching her struggle, the doctors grew enough backbone to push past the Division 9 agents. "Give us a moment, please."

She clamped onto one of the white coats, adoring the warm cloth against her skin. For a few minutes, he would do as a father substitute. Hands patted her on the back, pushing her down into a posture conducive to expelling the substance. Her body took over, convulsing as she coughed up mouthful after mouthful of warm breathable gel. When it stopped, they let her kneel there a moment, forehead pressed against the wonderful, cold floor, a white towel-robe draped over her. They helped her up and over to the waiting Comforgel pad and handed her some towels to wipe the remainder of the gel away from her face.

Blessed warmth.

The two government men shadowed the doctors, buzzards waiting for a carcass. They kept quiet while the medics checked her over with handheld scanners to ensure the nanobot repairs had completed without any problems. Kirsten accepted an offer of hot tea with lemon, shivering while clinging to the steaming plastic cup. Satisfied at her recovery, the two doctors left with the usual notice about hitting the call button if she needed them again.

She sipped the tea, looking over the rim at the two emotionless men. Their sunglasses made it impossible to tell where their eyes pointed. Both had the appearance of plastic figurines from some kind of government conspiracy board game. Hot liquid slid down her sore throat, triggering a minor cough.

"Agent Wren, I'm Operative Perry. This is Operative Castillo."

D9 Operatives... They're lieutenants, shit.

She released the mug into her left hand and saluted them.

"We have reviewed surveillance imagery of the event at the Kajuraho restaurant."

Air entered her lungs without a sound. *What did I do wrong?* A tiny trickle of gel ran down the inside of her throat, triggering another cough.

"This event is a matter of concern for us," said Perry.

Why? She trembled, trying not to look terrified. "How can I help?"

Operative Castillo plucked a tissue from a wall box and offered it. "The event appeared to be a targeted attempt to assassinate you. Division 9 responds to cases of attacks on police personnel."

"We take a dim view of such things." Operative Perry could have been the narrator for an hour-long Nat Geo special on the formation of dust.

Holy shit, they're not investigating me.

Her relief exhaled into a slouch. She sucked down more tea. It hurt inside, but it hurt good.

"We'd like to hear any thoughts you have on who might have wanted to kill you. The aggressors in this fire event appear to have belonged to the Sons of Charon," said Perry. He may as well have been describing the mating habits of an African sand spider. No, sand mite; spiders were at least a little interesting.

"I've never heard of them." She cradled the beautiful heat to her chest.

"They operate out of Sector 304, one of the older disavowed areas. They follow a sort of quasi-mythological mindset based on death."

She wished Perry would move a little when he talked, maybe pace, maybe blink. The statue routine came off as super eerie. "Right. Charon the Boatman, he was sending me a message. Wait, disavowed areas? You mean black zones?"

Operative Castillo cracked the faintest of grins. "We prefer the term disavowed. They were quite far away from home. If they had been out cruising for a random victim, they would not have gone as far out of their comfort zone, especially into the city proper."

"They were coming for me. The man I killed told me who sent them."

The operatives exchanged a glance. Castillo's android mask cracked enough to let sympathy leak out for an instant.

She frowned at him. "I'm not nuts. I'm an astral sensate; surely you guys have files on us. I see ghosts. I have since I was a little kid."

Another glance traded.

Perry's eyebrows ticked up a millimeter. "Let us assume ghosts exist—"

"You know psionics are real. Why is it so hard to accept we don't understand the world nearly as much as we like to think we do?"

He cleared his throat. "Let us assume ghosts exist. Operating on such an assumption, what would he have said?"

"A few years ago, a Division 0 tactical unit tried to apprehend a psionic suggestive. The man had about a half-dozen mercenaries under his control, armed with energy weapons. The tactical team had no idea what they were going into. One man died; his partner was wounded and further exploited by the individual."

Neither man moved. She assumed they both took notes via cyberware. She remained silent until Perry offered a slight nod.

"Rene Bollard is the suggestive responsible. He escaped, overpowered the surviving officer, and forced her to drive him somewhere. I'm not enough of a telepath to dig the memory out of her, but I was able to undo a hypnotic suggestion he'd left behind to cover his trail."

"Who was this officer?"

Kirsten smiled at Operative Castillo; he seemed more human than his partner. "Tactical Officer Nila Assad. He'd conditioned her to be terrified of returning to work, setting up the belief that if she did so, she would die the same day."

They offered grim nods.

"Dorian Marsh, her partner who was killed, he's umm…" Kirsten drank half the mug as it rapidly lost heat. "He's lingering behind, a little peeved with Rene for killing him."

Perry responded with no facial inflection at all. "We are aware of Sergeant Marsh's murder, Agent Wren. It is an open case. We are currently tracking the credit trail of the M-99 Barrager assault laser rifles back to a black marketer on Mars. Trust me, Agent Wren, anyone remotely connected to this will be held accountable."

Notice how the female mite takes great care with her eggs, burying them in the sand to keep them out of reach of predators. "Open case? He's *dead!* He's still here, still hurting, because no one gives enough of a shit to hunt the bastard down."

Neither man much reacted to her outburst.

"I'm sorry, I…" She stared down into squares of ceiling light reflected upon the tea. "He's kind of my partner now, as a ghost."

"I… see." Perry's words had the dry crisp of ancient wax paper.

"I'd show you, but I hear you guys have stuff in your head that'll hurt a psionic trying to go in."

"We can neither confirm nor deny—"

"Right, whatever," she grumbled. "Do you have any idea where Rene is hiding? Is he still even in the city?"

"It is our belief he is still inside the city." Perry glanced at the door, as red hair tinted the tiny window. "We have not located him at this time."

"Do you have any evidence beyond the word of a"—Operative Castillo raised one eyebrow—"ghost, that Rene Bollard ordered the hit on you?"

"Not yet, but I haven't pissed anyone else off recently. Maybe Intera still has a bit of a grudge."

"We checked the Intera angle already, Agent. We found no evidence to indicate their continued aggression or involvement with you. However, we did turn up a vid trace originating from Officer Assad's home to an unassigned NetMini two days ago."

"A PID-less mini?"

"It has a PID." Castillo glanced the door, someone outside furtively tapping. "Your friends are anxious." He almost smiled. "It's a throw-away phone, a bogus PID not owned by anyone, hacked into the system. We could not triangulate the position of the receiving device because it bounced the communication to an audio-only stream and funneled it via the GlobeNet to a backbone host in Mexico City. There was no live recipient. The call was left as a message, and we were unable to move fast enough to penetrate an ACC system and trace it before it was retrieved and deleted."

Kirsten set the empty cup down and smiled despite her blush at Operative Castillo. She shrugged out of the robe as she stood, then walked to the autoshower. As soon as she turned her back on them, her confidence evaporated and she bit her lip in shock. *What the hell am I doing?* Pant. *Too late now, just go with it. He's cute, even with the sunglasses, and he's not scared of me at all.*

Perry glanced at Castillo. A tiny smile lifted the corner of his mouth as the autoshower started up. They took a few steps closer to the tube. She hoped because it would make it easier to continue talking.

"So, Nila placed a call to a dump phone? That does not make any sense. Maybe I missed something in her head. I put in a request for Lt. Cmdr. Ashford to do a deep dive and make sure I cleaned everything up."

With fog on the tube, she felt comfortable enough to look at them. These two Division 9 agents appeared unsettled at the mention of Cmdr. Ashford's name. Even the high and mighty Nine feared someone noted for mental abilities that strong. The spray ring descended, hitting her from all sides with hot soapy water. She straightened away from the side, running her hands over herself in rapid swipes to get rid of the sticky residue of dried B-gel. For once, she felt thankful someone out there unnerved people more than her. Compared to Ashford, she was a fluffy white bunny rabbit everyone wanted to hug. Then again, if her Mind

Blast equated to a Class 1 pistol, Ashford probably ranked somewhere around artillery.

At the end of the dry cycle, she pushed the tube open without hesitation and walked straight at Operative Castillo. After brushing past him, she retrieved her clothes from the table and hurried into uniform. Exasperation at their imposition held her humiliation down while her infatuation with Operative Castillo punched it in the head. By the time she clicked her belt in place and secured the E-90, she felt calm.

"Dorian wants to kill him. I don't think he needs that stain on his soul. I'm going to try and find this guy. Ghosts can go places even Division 9 can't. I *will* bring him in."

"We cannot guarantee official support on a one-officer manhunt, Agent Wren. Consider sharing any information you obtain."

"As if you'll believe me?" She scoffed. "By the time I convince one of you I've found him, he'll have moved. I appreciate you trying to help, but you guys aren't equipped to deal with someone rated as high as he is in psionic suggestion. Your operatives will be masturbating in the street while he walks away laughing."

Operative Castillo opened the door for her. "I am sure we can be of more assistance than you think."

Kirsten halted in the doorway, inches away from him, one eyebrow raised with half a smile. *Maybe you can show me what you mean?* She bit back the thought. "Thanks. I'll, let you know if I find anything."

She walked over to Nicole, the only one there. "What, no party this time?"

"They only throw parties for the first time in the tube—or if you almost die."

"Lucky for me I qualified for both last time." Kirsten shivered.

"Aww, you just got a little nick on the arm." She glanced at the two operatives, muttering. "Walking dead man and… oh, hello hotness. Hey, he's cute."

The Division 9 operatives went down the hall, in lock step, not glancing back. Kirsten stared after him until they vanished behind the corner of a white wall. "Yeah, but they aren't going to be much help."

"With the shooting or with your sex life?" Nicole rubbed her chin.

Kirsten blushed. "Both."

16

PAYBACK

Hot water cascaded in waves over Kirsten's body. Arm braced on the autoshower tube, she leaned her head against it and sighed as the heat melted the tension out of her muscles. Her left hand slid up and down the small of her back over where that *thing* had scratched her. Smooth, unhurt skin met her touch. Somehow, the memory of the scratch lingered. She had to keep rubbing the spot to prove to herself it had gone away.

She turned into the spray, squeegeeing the soap out of her hair with her fingers. A dark shadow of bruise circled her left bicep, and it hurt to touch. The doctor said the discomfort should fade before the bruise.

"Call for you," said Evan, right outside the tube.

Kirsten whirled, grateful for the fog, gawking at the pajama-colored blur drawing closer.

"Evan! I'm in the tube, tell them I'll call back."

The boy didn't slow down. Her NetMini hit the outside with a sharp *click*, and Captain Eze's holographic head appeared inside the shower after a brief fit of rainbow static. His eyebrows lifted for a fraction of a second, and he turned away, loosing a hearty laugh at the result of a child's sense of urgency.

Kirsten wanted to crawl into a hole and never come out.

"Call me when you are done, Wren. I need you to check out a site. There is some urgency, but the event is over."

"Yes, sir." Her voice shook more than her hands.

He hung up.

The Evan blur moved away to the door, closing it.

Shit, he broke the blockade. She pounded the dry cycle button, hoping Theodore didn't notice the opportunity. Fortunately, no one else—living, child, or spirit, invaded the bathroom before the shower finished.

After donning a new pair of undies from the white box on the wall, she gathered a towel about herself and walked to the main room. Evan sat on the edge of her Comforgel pad, kicking his feet in lazy swishes, his face lit blue by the datapad absorbing his attention.

She sat next to him. "Evan?"

He looked up, grinning. Upset as she was, she couldn't stay mad at that face.

"If someone calls for me, next time can you please just yell through the door?"

"Why?"

Kirsten attempted to explain the indelicacies of just walking in on someone in the shower. "Your"—she exhaled, pausing—"mother might have walked around the house with no clothes on all the time, but I'm not like that."

"She's not my mom." He swung his pout back to the datapad, legs still.

"I'm sorry." She pulled him into a hug that brought his mood back to normal. "You embarrassed the Captain. It's not proper for him to see me in the shower."

He threaded his arms around her. "He said it was important police stuff."

"I understand. But next time, let him know I'm in the shower. Speaking of showers, your turn." She stood, shooing him at the bathroom.

"'Kay." He hugged her once again, then darted into the bathroom.

As soon as the whirr of the autoshower kicked in, she finished getting dressed. By the time Evan emerged from the bathroom, she'd made breakfast and pointed at the tiny table where a plate of 'sem eggs and toast waited for him.

It felt so strange having more in her cabinets than a dusty, ten-month-old packet of NinNin Instant Noodles.

DORIAN STOOD AT THE EDGE OF THE ROOF, ARMS FOLDED, AS IF HE HAD BEEN watching the sunrise and kept staring in the same direction after it had come up. The wind howled, though his hair didn't move. At the sound of the door opening, he turned. Kirsten staggered as soon as the wind hit her, not even bothering to try gathering her hair into a clip as she forced her way through the gale to the car.

When the door whumped shut, she gasped, enjoying the stillness. "Feeling better?"

He materialized out of the passenger seat. "Quite. The thing with the stunrod was rather enjoyable, aside from the problem of you having to bleed to make it work."

Kirsten fixed her hair up, then brought the car online. "Well, I seem to be getting a lot of practice lately."

"You should have shot the man aiming a weapon at you." He shook his head. "I understand what you wanted to do, but a dead cop can't save anyone. Prioritize threats, react tactically."

"There was a little girl in the car behind them, I didn't even think about the guy shooting at me." Kirsten grunted from the force with which she dragged the patrol craft vertically into the air.

"Careful, K. Thinking you'd rather die than live with the guilt of wondering if you could have reacted faster, done something different"—he looked her in the eye—"might turn into a self-fulfilling prophecy."

She picked at the comm panel for a moment in silence.

Dorian held a hand over her arm. "Evan's different. Every mother should be willing to die for their child."

She opened her mouth to say something, but stopped. She wanted to say she couldn't value one child's life more than another's, but her voice failed her when she thought about Evan's face.

"Wren?" Captain Eze's head shimmered in over the console. "Am I interrupting?"

"No, sir." She shook off her emotion and straightened up. "Sorry, I meant to call in… was just caught in a conversation."

Eze glanced at the empty passenger seat, then back to her. "Spirit?"

She nodded.

"An inexplicable attack occurred at the Lyris Corporation building last night, causing several fatalities." Two panels opened, one on either side of his head, with security video. "The attackers strolled right through gunfire as though it wasn't there."

"Combat synthetics?" She blinked at the screens when Seneschal and

Icarus strode into view on the left screen. "They're on camera... How is that possible?"

"There's been photographic evidence of spirits for centuries," said Dorian.

She leaned close to the screen. "Yes, but they *look real*, not like ghosts."

"You know them?" Eze's right eyebrow crept upward.

"It's related to the blackout trail, I think. Those men are dead, but they're not ghosts. I think they're something worse, abyssals."

Captain Eze glanced about as if searching the archives of his memory for meaning. His face took on a grim stare after a few seconds. "You had better get over there soon."

"On my way, sir."

Kirsten punched in a NavMap pin for the Lyris building and spent the ride watching the security vids on loop while the patrol craft auto-drove. The two abyssals had, it seemed, taken on solid form and marched straight into the lobby. When security attempted to stop them, Seneschal shot them. She cringed at the confirmation of her fear from the PubTran platform; their bullets *could* hurt living people. Other camera views spliced in as they moved deeper into the facility. Seneschal took the lead, shooting anyone who dared show themselves in the hallway. Icarus watched the rear, firing on a few security guards attempting to chase.

Incoming bullets passed through them, dots of light winking as the slugs hit without effect. A second after the shot, their clothing mended as if nothing happened. Five minutes into the video, the Lyris guards got the hint and disengaged, fleeing in terror. Lights flickered and died as the abyssals went past. Employees cowered under desks and in closets. Finally, they arrived at an office that appeared to be their objective. Seneschal kicked in the door, vanishing out of sight of any cam. Kirsten stopped play, backed up a dozen frames, and traced a square with her finger on the terminal. A tug at the corners of the glowing box magnified the image of a nameplate.

Grayson Kendrick
  Director, Issue Resolution and Problem Management.

Kirsten leaned back, wiped her face with both hands, and resumed active control of the patrol craft. "I guess he had a labor dispute with his boss."

Dorian chuckled. "Hmm. They didn't get as good a retirement package as I did."

She bowed her head. "Sorry."

"Stop feeling sad over me."

"Can't help it." She chuckled at herself. "Guess I put the 'sensitive' in astral sensitive."

He snickered. "Yeah, no kidding."

A minor course adjustment brought the nose of the car around to point at the Lyris corporate campus. The main building stood 106 stories tall, flanked on either side by a ninety-story sub tower. Curved arches connected them, giving the trio the appearance of a central building hugging its siblings close. All three gleamed in the early morning sun, slabs of mirror against the sky. She circled, looking for the telltale flashing yellow that identified an entrance for hovercar parking. On the back of the left tower, a heavy armored door occupied a space three car-widths across at the center of four rotating warning lights. Kirsten pulled up, front bumper two feet from the door, and looked around for some way to open it.

An orb bot the size of a basketball floated up to the driver window.

"Open the door, please. Agent Wren, Division 0. I'm here in regards to the shooting last night."

Lens covered the majority of the orb's face, trails of distant reflected ad-bots crawled over the curvature. Amethyst light glowed from deep within its core, oscillating brightness in time with a placid voice. "No employee identification detected. Entry to the Lyris Corporation employee parking area is restricted to Lyris Corporation employees. Please clear the area."

Why do they have to program these things to sound so damn arrogant? "That's because I'm not an employee. I'm with the police."

"Please stand by."

Kirsten scowled at the fluttering purple light. Absent any emotion, the voice taunted her with a blasé attitude, indifferent to five people dying here less than eight hours ago.

"I am sorry, miss. The police have already investigated the scene. I cannot"—the orb shuddered, the inner light shifted to orange—"I'm so sorry, Agent Wren," said a different voice. Natural, human sounding. "Stupid automatic programs, one moment please."

The yellow lights around the door spun faster and a few red ones came on. Seconds later, the massive portal split into four segments, each sliding into one of the corners. Kirsten nosed the car past the gap before they had opened all the way. The orb followed as the same human voice shouted over the hydraulic whine of the multi-ton door.

"Please follow me. Use the emergency parking area."

It zipped ahead, over the hood, and zoomed down a lane between rows of parked cars. Other bots lazed about in the air, occasionally cleaning a windshield or collecting a discarded cup.

"Free car wash while you work. Nice place." Dorian looked out the window on his side as a shoebox-sized robot sprayed foam over the front of a parked car.

Kirsten navigated the columns, chasing the little sphere until it came to a halt over a section of plastisteel floor covered in crisscrossing reflective yellow paint. The way it wobbled made her imagine it waving 'over here' with an arm it didn't have. She extended the ground wheels and brought the patrol craft in for a landing.

The orb floated over to her as she got out. "So sorry again for the bother. They skimped on the sentry programs."

"I keep getting the feeling corporations think they're above the law. Haven't been feeling a lot of respect lately." Kirsten wanted to slam the gull-wing door, but the pneumatics absorbed her anger.

"Please understand, it was a program error. I'm David Ling, head of security. I took over this bot as soon as I became aware of what was going on. Please follow it. I'll meet you in person at the desk."

The orb's inner light returned to violet. She wondered if that meant it would be annoying again. It didn't speak, merely rotating away before floating off at the pace of a brisk walk. Kirsten followed it over a small curb to a glass-walled elevator large enough to hold forty people. Motors at each of the eight corners hauled it along four metal tracks in an exposed central shaft. The giant window offered a pleasant view of offices arranged around the open middle, plants everywhere. Artificial birds swooped and darted past hazy rays of sunlight pumped in via fiberoptic lines from the outside to feed the plants.

Dorian whistled. "Is this an office or a mall?"

The elevator stopped, having descended only four floors. The orb hung a left as it exited the cab and went for a wide opening with an inclined motorized floor. As soon as she entered, Kirsten realized she'd entered the archway connecting two of the high-rises. People glanced at her, as many checking out the gun on her hip as did her figure. One or two recognized the significance of the black and speed-walked away. She continued to walk rather than let the moving sidewalk do all the work, and reached the crest of the archway in a few seconds. The orb lingered at the end, waiting for her. As she neared, it drifted off to the right.

Another elevator took her to the ground level of the main tower, past dozens of floors of plants, rerouted daylight, and somber employees. When it stopped, the familiar yellow glow of holographic crime scene barriers strips came into view at the end of a hallway to the right. She paused, staring through the glass wall of the elevator at Division 2 techs checking out a bloody trail along the grey carpet.

"Officer?"

She looked ahead; the orb hadn't waited for her and had to double back to let her catch up. *Strange how even corporate* robots *seem impatient.* It led her away from the investigation scene, north instead of east, and stopped by a large black reception desk in the security section. The man waiting for her appeared to be Chinese, possibly early thirties. His plain black suit looked unassuming, not at all as pretentious as she had expected from the VP of internal security.

"David Ling?" she asked, extending a hand.

"Ah, Agent Wren, so nice to meet you face to face." The voice matched the orange light.

"I trust you understand why I'm here, as opposed to the other officers?"

He paused, measuring his response with a sideways glance at the receptionists. Hand extended off to the right, he took a step. "Please, this way."

She followed him to a glass-walled office at the corner of the next hallway. Opaque blue glass separated it on both sides from adjacent offices while the ones facing the outside and the hallway were clear. Holograms of Chinese art, watercolor on paper, shimmered an inch off the transparent walls. The small, egg-sized projectors that created them stuck to the walls directly behind each piece of false floating paper. A few swords, a naginata, and a pair of bo staves hung on pegs. Dorian looked around, shaking his head.

"Hard to do naughty things with the secretary in an office with glass walls."

Kirsten shot him a look.

David Ling turned to face her, wearing a serious expression. "I do understand the nature of your presence here, Agent Wren. I spent an hour this morning talking to Greyson Kendrick. *After* he had been murdered."

He doesn't feel psionic. "Do you normally see ghosts?"

David shook his head. "Not usually. I had arrived early as I do every day, so I can hit the gym before I start work. After, I returned to my office and settled into my morning meditation. Just as I grounded myself, I heard him talking."

"Fascinating."

"The mind is a powerful tool if you know how to wield it." Mr. Ling offered a slight bow. "I have been told you are able to see spirits with much less effort involved. Mr. Kendrick was quite insistent something terrible was afoot and wanted me to do something. Unfortunately, the shock of hearing him broke me out of my state and I"—he chuckled in a whispery rasp—"must admit to being a little too rattled to try again."

Kirsten glanced around, but spotted only Dorian in terms of ghosts. "He's not here now. I recognized the two men who attacked from another case I'm working on. Can you tell me what, if any, relationship Desmond Chen or Michael Corley had with Mr. Kendrick?"

"Grayson was their immediate supervisor. Well, Mr. Chen reported to Mr. Kendrick. Corley and the Moriyama girl were direct reports of Mr. Chen."

"Mr. Ling, I apologize if I'm being too blunt here, but we both know Seneschal was the lead on a *problem resolution* team. I usually take that particular euphemism to mean assassins. Lyris sent them to kill someone, correct?"

"I cannot comment on that." Mr. Ling walked around his desk and fell into the seat, elbow propped on the edge, fingers over his mouth.

She squinted when he sent a worried look out the window. "No, I'm not going spelunking into your head. Unless you're killing innocent people, I don't have jurisdiction on corporate espionage."

"Liar," said Dorian with a smile.

Mr. Ling folded his hands in his lap. "Door, close."

A soft rush of air puffed behind her.

"Greyson was Seneschal's handler, responsible for giving him tasks. They were not always assassinations, Agent Wren. Most of the time he rescued abducted employees overseas, or retrieved stolen property, or facilitated the extraction of defecting talent."

"But he *was* sent to assassinate Vikram Medhi?"

Immediate recognition flickered on David Ling's face at the name.

She raised both eyebrows at his look of shock. "You seem surprised. We've already established I can see ghosts. I met Mr. Medhi at the PubTran station a few nights ago when what was left of Seneschal and his team tried to kill him... again."

Ling thrummed his fingers on the desk. Kirsten had seen that face before, the desperate want to disbelieve despite having seen or heard enough to have doubts.

"Anything at all you can tell me might help. I think Seneschal might have come back to take revenge on Greyson for sending him on a task that resulted in his death."

"Is that typical? He's only been dead a short while. I've never even heard of such a thing. Hauntings are usually, umm..." Ling waved his hand as if searching for what to say.

"You're right. Most hauntings are far more subtle. Seneschal has become something beyond a simple haunt, and I'm trying to understand what and how. Please, what do you know?"

"Lyris Corporation did employ Mr. Medhi on a contract basis for several electronic infiltration operations. While he was working for us, he decided to help himself to confidential data belonging to Lyris in violation of our trust. Mr. Medhi then attempted to use said information to extort twice the agreed upon fee in exchange for not selling it to our competitors."

Dorian shook his head. "Translation: Medhi got some dirt on Lyris and wanted to go to the Newsnet with it."

"So, rather than pay the blackmail to buy his silence, they sent Seneschal's team to silence him for good."

Ling touched his fingertips together. "That would be illegal, would it not? The team was sent to get the data back. However, if they needed to defend themselves..."

Kirsten frowned. "It's a little late to sugarcoat it. Doesn't much matter what their orders were now. The man who ordered the hit, Greyson I assume, as well as the people who killed Vikram are already dead. There's nothing to prosecute. A surviving relative might sue the corporation, but you're lucky. He doesn't have any."

David offered a mute nod.

"I doubt they'll be back." She set her hands on her hips and grumbled at the uselessness of her visit here. "They got what they came for."

An older Caucasian man in a black suit, as pretentious as she had expected David's to be, walked in through the glass interior wall, a bloody mess from neck to crotch. At least two dozen finger-sized holes, and several larger ones, exposed his guts and in a few cases, the room behind him.

Kirsten pivoted toward him. "Grayson Kendrick?"

He nodded.

David stiffened. "Is he here?"

Dorian looked him over. "SPR-42, less than ten feet away. Probably two shots." He paced around behind the man. "Fuzz in the exit wounds, probably got it while sitting in a nice, expensive chair."

Grayson grumbled, rotating to stare at Dorian. "Hmm. I didn't realize they had ghost cops. I want to report a murder."

Dorian smiled at Kirsten. "He wants to report a murder."

"Which murder would that be, Grayson? The one you ordered on Vikram, the murder of your hit squad, or the revenge killing that claimed you?"

Grayson glared at her. "There's no need to be so hostile."

"Did it even bother you when your squad got wiped out?"

He fidgeted.

"I thought not. You were more concerned with the stolen data than their lives. That's probably why they came back to kill you." She scowled at him. "They're still a threat I need to take care of. What can you tell me about this whole mess?"

Grayson glanced at Mr. Ling, who remained happily outside the conversation. Kirsten turned away so as not to giggle at Dorian's eye peering at her through one of the bullet trenches.

"Vikram stole some of our data. I sent the team in to recover it and teach him a lesson. I am not being deceitful when I say I did not order his death. I don't know what happened that night, missy."

"Watch your tone. You call me Agent Wren, or possibly Kirsten, if you can stop being a puffed-up ass for five minutes."

Dorian snickered into his hand.

Mr. Ling also chuckled. "Kendrick always was a bit over the top; SVP attitude, Director's chair."

Grayson frowned at him. "Will you tell him to kiss my ass?"

"He wants you to kiss his ass," quipped Dorian.

"Oh, that's cute. He can't hear you, either." Grayson grumbled.

"What do I need to know about the team?" Kirsten stepped in front of him, blocking his view of Mr. Ling.

"Seneschal was their squad leader. A consummate professional, he did a lot of work for various European firms before we acquired him due to his exemplary record."

"I suspect that means he could kill without hesitation, obeyed orders without question, and never got caught." Dorian leaned on the desk.

Grayson scowled.

Kirsten smirked. "It's a bit late for corporate obliqueness, Grayson. You're dead."

"Fine. We recruited Desmond Chen for his ability to get done what needed to get done. He was loyal to his contract. As soon as he signed a new one, previous employers were no different than any other potential adversary. He had no family, no attachments, no hesitation."

Dorian laughed. "Sounds like a nice guy."

"He wasn't fond of sloppiness, and rather frowned on Mariko for enjoying her work so much."

"She enjoyed killing?" Kirsten thought back to the shadowed face, the glowing red eyes, and that look of pure glee as she caused pain.

"Yes, especially men. I only glanced at Michael's report in brief, but I remember something about her having been indentured to a Japanese Keiretsu from a young age. She was not treated well, I believe. Desmond had traveled to Japan on an extraction run and she attempted to interfere. Michael, rather Icarus, let his conscience burden him into feeling bad for her. They wound up stealing her as well as extracting the defecting technician. It took several weeks, but we eventually broke her conditioned loyalty to Nippon Shōgyō Kumiai."

Kirsten scrunched her face. "The NSK isn't a corporation. Why would they care about an extraction?"

"They are a facilitator allowing the fragmented, warring prefectures within Japan to continue to trade with the outside world and keep their internal battles hidden. As such, they maintain a security force available to any corporate entity for assistance, especially with outsiders. Mariko was one of their ninja."

"Ninja?" Kirsten sighed. "I've never seen one; I'll have to hope that the stories about them are pretty much exaggerated."

"Most people think of ghosts the same way, do they not?"

Greyson had a point.

"This is the opening of a bad joke," added Dorian. "A mercenary, a ninja, and a Special Forces dude walk into a bar..."

"Stop." She held a hand up. "What about Icarus?"

"He used to be UCF military. His records were sealed, even from us.

When he came looking for work, he claimed experience in clandestine operations, mostly wetwork. He was one of those *best of the best* types, highly motivated, highly physical. Health food... quinoa, wheat germ, blenders full of green ooze, his office always stank like moldy shoes."

"It seems as if you have your work cut out," Dorian muttered.

Kirsten shifted, gazing past the glass wall at four office-worker ghosts watching the inspection of their murder scene. "Yeah, you got that right."

17

LINGERING

Kirsten slouched back in the chair, too tired to even put her feet up on the desk. Evan slurped noodles from a take-out container, making silly faces. Giggling, she stuffed another forkful of mei fun into her mouth, glancing at Captain Eze's empty office. *He asked me to meet him, the least he could do is show the hell up.*

"How come you're here so late? You got homework?" Evan tilted his head.

She smiled. "Don't rush to grow up, hon. This job is nothing *but* homework."

Kirsten's smile faltered to a flat line as she stabbed her food. *He's an astral, too. They're gonna put him out on the street with me someday.* Kirsten forced herself to keep smiling at him when worry crept into his eyes. *No, they wouldn't do that. Too awkward to have a mother/son team. They don't even let siblings pair together.* Evan's eyes crossed as he tried to watch a noodle slide through his puckered lips. Kirsten laughed, deciding not to worry about ten years from now.

As if they'd wait for him to be an old man of nineteen.

Light pierced the darkness of the room from the far end of the hallway that led to motor pool. Captain Eze's silhouette appeared in a nimbus of glowing orange. The door closed, cutting off the glare from outside and allowing color and detail to fill in on his face and uniform. He went by at a brisk stride, apparently not over the embarrassment of the shower call earlier in the day. Kirsten scooted forward, two quick forkfuls shoved into her mouth as she got up.

She tried to speak with a full mouth, but food dribbled out. She paused to finish chewing. "Okay, almost time to go home. Get started on your homework. This shouldn't be long."

Evan nodded, digging into his backpack for a school-issued datapad. Kirsten stretched, then sagged forward. After a deep breath, she summoned up the strength to trudge across the squad room to Eze's office.

"Sorry, sir. Evan just meant well, he didn't—"

"It's all right, Wren." He turned to face her, looking a touch haggard. "I just got out of a meeting with Division 9. They wanted to ask about the death of Sergeant Marsh and the investigation into the man responsible. Do you have any idea why they seemed to think I might have some information we were not sharing with them?"

Dorian walked in, both eyebrows up, his interest piqued.

"Bastards walked in on me at the hospital." She blushed.

"When I became aware of that, I conveyed our mutual displeasure." Captain Eze sat behind his desk. "I would have been back here half an hour ago if not for the argument it caused."

"Let me guess, they accused you of coddling women without military experience."

"Something like that. They don't understand the unique position some of you are in, growing up here..." Eze rubbed his face, as if trying to wipe away the distrust of others.

She matched his smile, fatigue and all. "I escorted the victims at Lyris across. Only one left. She has some stuff she needs to tell her brother before she's willing to cross over."

Eze nodded. "What interest do you have in Sergeant Marsh? I noticed you were picking through his things a few weeks ago, and you paid a visit to his partner a few days ago. Did you really send in a form referring her to see Commander Ashford?"

"Yes. Rene Bollard, sir. He is the suggestive responsible for Dorian's death. He put a suggestive condition in Nila's head." She explained how he programmed Nila to fear the police, as well as used her to facilitate his escape. "I was hoping Commander Ashford could dig a bit deeper and find out where she took him and make sure I didn't miss cleaning anything up."

"You think you missed something?" Eze lifted an eyebrow.

"She called Rene to warn him after I left, after I deprogrammed her. He had to have buried it way down in the subconscious. Maybe she only started vid call to his NetMini without saying a word. The Sons of Charon came after me because of that call, I'm sure of it. Rene knows I want him, and I'm not planning to disappoint the son of a bitch."

Captain Eze's glance hardened. "It is admirable you take offense to the murder of one of our own, even though you never knew him, but I am concerned. You don't have the combat experience or tactical training—"

"Captain, sorry to interrupt, but no one else is going after him. I've got a rating in Suggestion; I can fight him."

His glower softened to a patronizing smile. "Kirsten, your rating in Suggestion is far short of what we believe Rene capable of. You're not even on the watch list." He chuckled. "Rene held six men in thrall for months, a small private army."

"Rene is going to attack Nila again. He's sending assassins after me. He'll do anything to get away from us, and I owe it to Dorian to…"

"Avenge him?" Eze sighed. "Revenge is a bumpy road, Kirsten."

The chill presence of Dorian's hand circled around hers. "Don't get yourself killed because of me."

Kirsten looked at Dorian, too angry to cry. "I'm not so smitten I'm ready to die just to be with you."

They both laughed despite the mood.

"Are you…" Eze's head leaned to the side, at empty air.

"Dorian is still here, sir, right in the room with us. He's restless because Rene got away and he's worried about Officer Assad."

"You'll not be rid of me so easy," said Dorian with a wink. "I'm not going to leave you alone, even if you do get Rene."

She grinned. "I'm not trying to get rid of you. I just want to do what is right."

"Okay, Kirsten. Perhaps you have been working too…"

The lights flickered. Eze's voice trailed off as he glanced at faltering LED bulbs in the ceiling. They dimmed even further before fading out to darkness. Officer Morelli trudged in the door, nose buried in a datapad of reports. A coalescence of white fog hung in space, and Dorian stepped out of it, an incredible look of intensity upon his face, as if manifesting required extreme effort.

To Kirsten, the real-looking Dorian faded to transparency.

Morelli's datapad hit the ground with a *clack*; he shrieked like a cheerleader and ran in such a panic he tumbled over a desk outside.

Evan's wild cackling pushed Kirsten over the edge, and she joined him in laughter. Eze's other eyebrow rose to meet the one that had gone upward at the fog. He looked Dorian up and down, then stood, rendering a funerary salute.

"You're getting stronger..." Kirsten gawked at him.

Dorian returned the salute. "I'm still with the team, sir." His voice seemed to float in from the edges of the room, from no specific direction.

Speaking caused the manifestation to evaporate, the effort a breath held to the point of bursting. Solid again in her eyes, Dorian slumped into a chair, seeming winded.

The lights fluttered back to life. In the distance, aluminum desks banged as Morelli scrambled back to his feet and ran off down the hallway, wailing.

"Tom never did like me." Dorian glanced after him.

Kirsten giggled. "Well you *were* his T.O. Your comment about him being a hothead kept him in training for an extra three months."

"He was. Still is." Dorian folded his arms. "Trying to chase a suspect down a crowded hover lane at 285."

"Is *that* why you put the patrol craft through a window?"

Dorian cringed. "No, he did that trying to fight me for control. All I wanted to do was slow down to 250."

"Well you've probably just sent him to psych for at least a week."

Eyebrows fluttering, Dorian leaned back and put a hand on his chin. The thought didn't seem to plague his conscience at all.

Captain Eze lowered himself into his chair, pondering, showing no outward affect from seeing Dorian. He nodded once at something in his head. "So that's what you meant when you said he died before you met him."

"Yeah."

"Heh. I should've figured that out given your particular talents. Kirsten, please. Be careful poking around the Rene issue. Suggestives can be extraordinarily dangerous once they get to his level."

"Understood, sir." She stood to leave. "Did you get a whiff of anything from Nine? Think they'll find him?"

"If they have anything, they aren't sharing. You think you need another protection detail?"

"Tell him I got it. Just take the car home." Dorian smiled.

"I think I'll be okay. Rene doesn't have the resources of a corporation behind him, and I have a partner who doesn't sleep."

18

SHOWDOWN

The patrol craft came in low over traffic, four or five feet above cars that had skewed into collisions with posts, vendomats, and parked vehicles. Kirsten drifted along a touch faster than a jogger's pace, studying broken glass, skid marks, and blood.

On the primary windscreen, the computer inserted neon lines of green and yellow resolving the flight path of bullets it extrapolated to be responsible for several holes in the surrounding environment. The results of her scan corroborated the witness accounts of the unbelievable. Two cars, driverless, had raced down the street. Citizens heard gunshots and witnessed showers of debris, but saw no guns—or people using them.

The citycam recording, open in a side panel display, showed the chase from an elevated view. A small green car weaved past traffic, empty, and sometimes using the sidewalks to get around logjams and red lights.

Behind it, an ordinary mid-sized passenger sedan fought the river of cars, frantic to catch up to the little green car. Like the people, the citywide surveillance network had picked up the sound of automatic weapons fire. Commuters crashed in their panic to escape as the backs of their cars disintegrated amid a hail of unseen bullets. She wondered if any of them even noticed at the time what shot at them.

According to the map, the chase had persisted a little over seven miles. She accelerated and climbed. Six miles later, the smoldering ruin of the sedan melted into the street. The Division 1 patrol craft that had lasered it in half had parked nearby. Kirsten slowed to a floating halt before dropping straight down to land next to the officers.

"Morning. Got anything on the car?"

They both saluted. A short woman with skin the color of creamed coffee lifted a gold-tinted visor. Early morning sunlight streaked parts of her blue armor with white glare as she moved up to the window. "It was reported stolen by its owner, but they had no description of the thief. We arrived on scene during the roving gunfight. The car ignored three warnings, so we hit it with the Starburst."

Kirsten eyed the bulge on the roof of their car, above the passenger seat. "Nice shot, Sergeant, right in half."

"I was driving; Simms took the shot."

The other officer nodded.

"We found no one in it, but the car smelled of propellant. Someone was definitely firing weapons inside it. I have no idea how the hell we missed them, or how the frick they got away from this without being injured."

"Uhh, Sarge?" Simms looked up from a datapad. "I'm going back over the scanner recordings during the pursuit."

Kirsten and the female officer looked at him with expectant faces.

"The car was empty the whole time." He scratched his helmet. "Think a hacker got into the Navcom?"

"I could answer that for you, but I don't want you to take up heavy drinking." Kirsten smiled.

"Hit me." Sergeant Summers radiated confidence.

"Ghosts."

To Kirsten's surprise, the patrol sergeant didn't seem rattled or even look at her as if she were crazy. "Ghosts?" She shook her head. "You don't think it was a hacker?"

"Unless he could hack the stink of ballistic propellant into the car."

Officer Simms went quietly back to his car.

Sgt. Summers pondered, then nodded. "That's a good point. Well, go do what you Zeroes do then." Sergeant Summers smiled and looked off into space while the buzz of radio chatter filled her helmet.

A rush of camaraderie washed over Kirsten. She returned the smile, thrilled at feeling like part of a team for once and not some freak on the outside.

"Agent. We're getting reports of gunfire at Prospect Mall, down the street where the other car crashed, they're asking for you."

"Crap, they're still here. Sergeant, have them evac the mall."

"Already—"

Kirsten leapt back into the patrol craft and accelerated, staying on the ground. The mall was only a few blocks away and Division 1 had it blocked off from traffic. It would take longer to transition between hover and ground mode than simply drive such a short distance. After weaving around the debris left in the wake of the chase, she hung a squealing left turn onto the approach ramp for Prospect Mall. Black streaks on the charcoal-hued traction coating led over the incline, stopped abruptly at the top, and resumed about twenty feet later. Ahead, the tiny green car lay in a crumpled, smoking ruin, smashed into the shopping plaza wall at the end of the squiggly trails.

Two dozen patrol officers milled around a row of blue-and-white patrol craft. The entire area shimmered in the glow of flashing lights. A sizeable crowd, perhaps a hundred and a half people, pressed into the police line with a mixture of annoyance and curiosity. Kirsten squawked the siren, opening a gap in the spectators, and pulled up to the barricade.

As soon as her door opened, gunfire erupted inside.

"Corporal." Kirsten approached the closest man in blue. "Let whoever is in command of this squad know to keep their men out of the mall. There are paranormal entities involved. I don't care if you believe me or not, no one goes in."

Not waiting for the reply, she grasped the handle of her stunrod to keep it from bouncing against her leg and took the long stairway to the mall's front entrance two steps at a time. Four capsule elevators flanked the door, continuing to glide up and down along their tracks despite being empty. Automatic glass doors slid out of her way when she ran for the entrance, but they closed through Dorian—not that he cared. The deserted interior lent eeriness to the building dread she felt at dealing with these beings.

Even Dorian had a look of concern. These things had enough power to obliterate him.

She halted at a three-way intersection packed with stores and kiosks, a cloud of two dozen or more idle ad-bots hung in midair. "If you're still feeling weak..."

The bots all whirled to face her. Kirsten imagined yellow exclamation points of glee above them a second before they all descended upon the only living person in the mall. An explosion of advertising holo-panels surrounded her.

"No way in hell I'm leaving you alone in here." He pointed northeast. "That way."

"Gah!" she cried, swatting at the evasive floating nuisances. "Stupid bots."

Kirsten, trailing a cloud of commercialism, jogged to the end of the concourse toward voices emanating from around the corner. A silver-tiled column outside a holovid shop provided some cover. She leaned out enough to peek with her E-90 around the corner. Icarus and Seneschal stood with their backs facing her, about twenty paces from the corner. They flanked a fountain made of fiberoptic line and glass dolphins frolicking in a rainbow of light and water. Two more passages packed with shops led off in a fork on the opposite side of the glowing installation.

Icarus squinted into the distance. "I got nothing. We lost him."

Seneschal growled low in his throat. He swung a compact assault rifle sideways, aiming past rows of shops. "I can still smell him. We wait here for Mariko to flush him out."

Kirsten lifted her weapon, aiming at Seneschal's back. Once the glowing sights lined up, blue dot inside blue ring, she called out. "Seneschal, Icarus, hold it right there."

"Smooth. What do you intend to do, haul them downtown?" Dorian shook his head, and ran into the wall.

They turned. She fired. Ad-bots scattered in an eruption of shimmering plastisteel and glowing holograms.

The streak of azure energy struck Seneschal in the back. His body collapsed inward at the point of contact, as if molded from wet sand. The brief pulse bored a roving trench down his body as he whirled, leaving a narrow opening with the glow of embers along the edge. Black smoke exuded from both sides. For an instant, he reacted with alarm which gave way to anger. Unlike bullets, the energy weapon could hurt him.

She lined up another shot, but aborted, rolling behind cover with her back pressed into the wall as Icarus sprayed automatic fire at her. Kirsten suppressed the urge to scream while flakes of silvery tile shattered and popped around her, a rain of ceramic bits falling on her head. Bullet holes offered a weak view of the two abyssals. Like any modern slug, his attack had drilled a neat hole in the two-foot square column and gone out the other side.

Oh, shit.

Kirsten edged to her left in case he fired again.

"Stay out of our way. This does not concern you," growled Seneschal. "You are clueless. If I see you again, I *will* kill you."

She clutched her E-90 with both hands, close to her shoulder, and yelled, "It's not so simple. You don't belong here, and I will not allow you to hurt any more innocent people on a demented mission of vengeance."

"Innocent?" Icarus joined in, half chuckling. "There's no such thing as innocent."

"Look, I'm sorry you died." She crouched, peering through the lowest bullet hole at them. "That doesn't change the fact I have to send you back where you belong."

"Oh, listen to this one, Ic." Seneschal's laugh raked down her spine, cold as a torrent of icicles. "She wants to play." He whirled with a flare of his coat and strode toward her, unconcerned that she might shoot him.

Kirsten backed off and stuck the E-90 into its holster. When Seneschal rounded the holed column, his eyes shot as wide as his skull would allow. Half of Kirsten's body glowed in the stark blue-white glare of the lash; her eyes flared the same hue. As soon as he stepped into view, she snapped the tendril at him. Her face twisted with resolve, she growled, tapping her grief from helping the dead office workers for extra power.

The Astral Lash snagged in his chest, plumes of ebon vapor boiling out from the point of contact. Seneschal howled, knocked to a knee in pain of it. She leaned back, yanking at the ethereal cord and tore it loose. A great blast of heat and blackness poured out from a fluttery, gaping hole in Seneschal's chest.

His expression was unmistakable—abject fear.

"Tag. You're it." She winked.

Icarus yelled in surprise, followed by the scuffing of boots and the dull thud of body blows. Dorian grunted, then a heavy slam. She imagined him judo flipping Icarus to the ground, or maybe Dorian had gone down. Punching noises continued amid growls of pain and anger from both sides. She couldn't worry about that right now. Before Seneschal could recover from the shock of the first hit, she swiped the whip across his chest a second time.

Her strike hit him with the force of a truck, knocking him six feet airborne. He hit the ground on his chest, sliding, leaving a trail of black ichor over the polished white floor. Kirsten ran after him, winding the lash behind her in preparation for an overhead swing. She stepped into the swing, but Seneschal dissipated into a cloud of dark fog, and her strike found no resistance.

The sheet of vapor sucked itself into a vertical column behind her. Seneschal coalesced back into his solid form in mid swing, cracking her across the back of the head with the stock of his rifle. The hit felt less than solid, as if made of inflexible rubber rather than metal. Dazed, she stumbled forward and fell to her knees. Behind her somewhere, Dorian gurgled.

"Man, pity they don't teach cops how to fight worth a da—"

Icarus's taunt cut off with an *oof*. Kirsten rolled to her side, startled out of her daze by the rattle of a weapon. Seneschal aimed at her back. Her eyes focused past him for a split second; Dorian's fist in Icarus's gut lifted him inches off the ground. The demonic mercenary fell over backward and Dorian pounced on him.

Kirsten rolled to the side. Seneschal's weapon erupted in a thundering barrage. Floor tiles stripped away to bare concrete in chunks, a path of destruction racing toward her. Sprawled on the ground, she had nowhere to hide. Kirsten shoved her fear aside and reached out with her mind, grasping at his essence. Her arms shook from the effort of fighting him. Seneschal stopped firing, roaring as he strained to aim at her. Psionic energy welled out of her with such intensity a shroud of luminous vapor burst out of her hand. The white fiery glow crawled up her arm to the elbow. She pushed him back, working her way to her feet as their battle of wills surged back and forth.

"You..." Seneschal took a step back, grunting, struggling. Grey eyes dilated. A sudden fear of her seemed to take hold in him, though it sparred with anger.

Icarus rolled out from the hold, sweeping Dorian's legs and dropping him hard on his back. Dorian sprang up, his three quick punches deflected with ease. Kirsten screamed, face reddening with determination as the strange fire crept over her shoulders. Her hands flared as she thrust them forward at Seneschal. The phantom light vanished in an intense flash. He sailed airborne, flying backward into the tile-covered column, which broke, crunching under the force of his impact. Groaning, Seneschal slid to the ground in a fall of silver ceramic chips. She ran in, unfurling the lash, taking advantage of his disorientation to score a clean hit into his chest.

Seneschal's roar broke all the windows within fifty yards.

Dorian leapt at Icarus again. The former covert operative leaned to the side and caught him in the shoulder with a knife as he went by. Wisps of energy drifted from a slice that sealed within seconds. Icarus whirled and pounced on him from behind, stabbing Dorian twice more for three tries. Dorian staggered, groaning.

Kirsten fixed her eyes on Seneschal, who appeared drained to the point of near-delirium. He looked less than real, but his eyes had taken on a soft crimson glow. Thick shadowy darkness leaked from his body, pooling around his legs where he knelt at the base of the smashed column.

She called them.

Her left hand pointed at Seneschal, focusing her power to hold him down. She cringed as his desperation mounted, every ounce of her strength tested. Seneschal struggled as if chained to the ground, growling at the force trapping him. His every attempt to move poked her in the brain.

Dorian shouted, landing a lucky punch to Icarus's chin that sent him staggering. The ambiance shifted. The dim crimson light in Seneschal's eyes flared bright. Shadows thickened and dozens of whispering voices filled the air. Forms welled up from puddles of darkness seeping in along the gaps in the floor tiles.

Harbingers approached from every side.

Emboldened by their presence, Dorian found a second wind and leapt at Icarus, baton aimed for the back of the head. The commando whirled, trapping his arm. He threw Dorian forward and dropped to kneel behind him with a knife at his throat. Dorian groaned, trapped in the expert grip of a military-trained assassin.

"Send them away, or he dies," rasped Seneschal.

Kristen glanced at her partner. A pang of worry weakened her focus long enough to let Seneschal stand. Feeling him move, she regained her concentration and pushed him into the wall. "I can't... I can only call them," she said, forcing the words out.

Dorian elbowed Icarus in the gut without effect. "Finish it, I'm already dead."

Seneschal stared into her eyes. "First, we will kill your partner."

Icarus dragged Dorian backward, shying away from the mass of approaching silver eyes. They seemed less interested in him, likely because his strength had not diminished as much as Seneschal's. Icarus sent a baleful glare at Kirsten, at the traces of white vapor simmering along her shoulders, the faint hint of luminosity in her blue eyes, and swallowed. Kirsten tilted her head, wondering why out of nowhere, he seemed terrified of her.

"Then we kill your little friend." Seneschal's lips curled into an evil smile, black fog leaking through his teeth. "Evan, is it?"

Fear, desperation, and anger burst out from within her. Her concentration faltered; Evan's face filled her mind.

Icarus relaxed his grip, retreating from her. Dorian squirmed loose, grabbed the wrist holding the knife at his throat, and jammed it up to the hilt into Icarus's chest armor. Dreadlocks shifted as he looked down at the knife, regarding the wound as a triviality. A quick, but powerful, punch to Dorian's throat knocked him flat.

Seneschal hissed at Icarus, a demonic rumble manifest in his voice. He leapt past Kirsten's distracted effort, catching her across the cheek with a punch that put her headfirst into the ground. Growling, he stalked after her, but a curtain of Harbingers rushed forward. Vaporous shadows engulfed her. Sixteen flickering silver specks stared out of the darkness. Seneschal halted, his expression a mixture of rage and fear. Icarus took off along the concourse, diving into the ground some distance away. After a momentary staredown, the mass of Harbingers advanced. Seneschal backpedaled, gaze darting around at the creatures closing in. Their whispering intensified, and they reached for him. Seneschal staggered off, forcing himself to run.

Kirsten sat up, cradling her face, shivering as the mass of shadows swarmed after him into a cyclone of darkness that slid down the bright mall corridor. Whispers quieted. The ring of black grew distant until it vanished into the same point of floor where Seneschal had gone. The Harbingers' presence receded. With them and the abyssals gone, the constant dread hanging over the area faded away. Kirsten looked up at Dorian, who staggered over to her.

"Almost got him." She wiped a bloody nose.

"You okay?" He appraised the developing bruise on her cheek.

She pressed a stimpak into her shoulder. "Yeah, I've had worse. Think they'll get him?"

"Here's hoping, but..." Dorian cast a worried look at the spot of floor. "That would be too easy. Nothing's ever that easy."

19

BEACON

K irsten wound up in tears by the time she hung up the vid call. Not a loud, sobby sort of crying, but silent tears streamed down her face. Evan was having a great day at school and had no idea that a creature out of the Abyss had threatened him. She warned Eze about it, but wanted to talk to Evan anyway. She couldn't get the joy in his eyes out of her mind, and it made the tears come harder.

"Dammit, Dorian. If he…"

The cool presence of his hand settled into her shoulder. "Abyssals are vicious, but they are single-minded. They will use anything they can to get to you. If Seneschal seriously means to harm Evan, he won't do anything until after they destroy Vikram. He can't help it."

She looked up, gathering her composure as an army of police and techs invaded the mall.

"Thanks for the all-clear, Agent." An older man in a blue Division 2 jumpsuit saluted her. "Frank Martinez, Tech Four. I'm in command of the CSI team." He scratched his head, glancing around at the damage. "Word is I'm not gonna care for your explanation of what happened here."

"Heh." She chuckled, surveying the damage. "What's not to like? Just a pair of demons determined to destroy the ghost of the man who killed them. You're going to find hundreds of what appear to be bullet strikes, but you won't locate a single projectile." She stood, surprised to find Martinez at eye level. "Was anyone hurt?"

He nodded. "Yes, about two dozen people if you factor in the incident in the street outside. Fortunately, no one died. So... demons?" He blessed himself. "Seriously?"

After the short-short version of events, Tech Four Martinez wandered back to his crew, shaking his head.

"Stopping paranormal entities and making alcoholics. I think your work here is done." Dorian tried to pat her on the shoulder, his hand whiffed through.

"Maybe in another hundred years, people will stop looking at me like *that*." She crossed her arms, watching the crime scene techs scurry about in search of forensic evidence for several minutes. "We can't let them kill Vikram again. If they get him before I stop them, who knows what they'll do. Right now, they have a common motivation. Without him, they might go their separate ways and do all sorts of horrible crap. It could take decades to track them all down." Kirsten shivered at the thought.

"So how do we find an undead deck jockey?" Dorian grinned. "Not as if he's going to be logged into the GlobeNet. We can't just ping him."

Kirsten blinked. "Yes we can. I just need some quiet."

A hundred yards away, at the primary intersection of the mall's two main passageways, she escaped the bustle of the investigation. Twenty abandoned merchant pushcarts surrounded an enormous round area packed with soil, flowers, and trees. Holographic birds danced among the oasis of nature stuck smack dab in the center of the mall. A great skylight let the sun flood down all six floors, gleaming from the silvered sides of motorized stairs around the perimeter of a vertical channel. Devoid of people, the courtyard possessed a degree of serenity quite out of place for West City.

"If you have an idea, better get on with it." Dorian glanced over his shoulder. "They're going to be letting people back in soon."

She sat on a bench, closed her eyes, and concentrated on the name Vikram Medhi. Much the same way Darksight allowed her to see without light by opening her eyes to the astral realm, she pushed mental energy out instead. A silent calling directed at him, spread out into ether. Dorian heard it right away, nodding with immediate understanding of what she did. Kirsten gave him a waypoint, a lantern in the dark to seek. She couldn't *summon* him, but he might choose to answer her call.

"Hello."

Kirsten relaxed her mind, opening her eyes to find a nervous Indian man in front of her.

"What the devil did you do to them?" he asked, shifting about.

"Thank you for trusting me." She stood. "I'm sorry. I almost got Seneschal but..."

Dorian grumbled. "You should have finished him off. Don't worry about me."

Vikram looked between them. "I saw him running with those... things chasing him."

"Yeah. They got away. You should be safe for a little while, at least while he is weakened."

"Probably a few days," added Dorian. "I'm not entirely sure how it works for them compared to normal ghosts, but abyssals don't have remains or attachments to go to in order to recover their energy. It will quite likely take him some time to recover his strength."

"I'd like you to stay with me, if you can." Kirsten's innocent smile seemed to ease Vikram's fidgeting. "They're bound after you for some reason. You are safest with me."

He gnawed at his fingers, eyeing the atrium, jumping at any moving shadow. "They killed me once already. I had a feeling someone was coming, so I rigged a dead man switch. When my pulse stopped, the entire floor turned into a fireball."

"Took them with you." Dorian rubbed his chin. "I wonder if that counts as killing?"

Kirsten shrugged. "We don't have time for philosophy class."

"No, we don't," said Vikram. "They're quite upset at me. That Seneschal had a reputation for being a perfectionist. I think he's angrier he failed to anticipate the bombs than he is about being dead."

"Do you know anything about what happened there after you died? Who made the silver circle?"

Vikram shrugged. "I am not certain, it appeared one night. I didn't see anyone draw it."

Dorian squinted at him.

"Okay." She sighed. "Will you stay close to me for a few days?"

Vikram cringed at a change in light. "You can protect me?"

"I'll do everything I can to keep you safe. Of course, the best thing you can do to protect yourself is to move on."

"Move on?" He tilted his head.

"Transcend to the next world... go through the silver light." She waved her hand in a circle as if to emphasize the point. "Do you hear the voices of any of your family calling you?"

"No."

"Do you know why you are lingering behind? It can't be related to your murder. Everyone responsible for it is already dead."

Dorian moved his hand off his mouth long enough to speak. "Maybe he wants the whole company to go down, like Albert."

"Oh, for"—she mumbled, almost dropping the G word—"shit's sake. What do you feel is keeping you here?"

Vikram thought it over, stuffing his hands in his pockets. He looked away, then down at the floor. "I had some evidence, on my Nishihama, data proving Lyris Corporation complicit in the deaths of several thousand people in the Middle East, Africa, and western China. I wanted to expose them to the world."

"Why didn't you send it to the Newsnet? Why sit on it?" Dorian's gaze hardened. "You were trying to make some money off it in the process, weren't you?"

"I wanted to verify it." Vikram looked up, eyes tracking a holographic bluebird across the atrium. "If it proved to be spurious, it would have ruined my career."

Dorian continued giving him a distrusting look.

"Were you ever able to verify it? Maybe we should look for the data?" Kirsten tapped away at her armband console, searching the site reports for the blast.

"The deck is toast." Vikram sighed. "My copy of the data is gone."

"Well then." Kirsten let her arm fall to her side; the holo-panel turned itself off. "I guess we can worry about it once he's no longer being hunted."

Dorian folded his arms. "So this is your plan? Dangle him as a lure and just wait?"

"Basically. We know they are going to come after him again." She stared sympathy at Vikram for a moment before firing a pointed look at Dorian. "The best we can do is be there for him when they show up. Unless you have a better idea."

Dorian pursed his lips. "Unfortunately, I can't think of anything."

20

KUNOICHI

K irsten sat in the patrol craft, NetMini held to her chest. She thumbed the edge while staring out the windscreen across the unnatural square patch of grass, trees, paths, and benches comprising Sanctuary Park. Branches swayed in an unsettled breeze, visible here and there in the glow of a handful of standing lamps.

One entire sector, five miles square, had been sectioned off into a nature preserve of sorts. Few people had the time to bother with it during the day. Mostly students or the elderly came here, but at this hour, it was empty.

Disappointment in Evan's face when she asked him to stay at the dorm tonight haunted her. She didn't want to leave him alone at the apartment, and had 'work stuff' to do. While he'd given her a sad look, he didn't cry or protest at all. His level of maturity at bad news made her feel even more guilty. All she wanted to do was fly to the school and squeeze him.

"What are we waiting for?" Vikram leaned in from the back seat.

She put the device in her pocket. *Calm down, K. You're acting like a child, it's only one night.* "Since we're stuck waiting for Seneschal to make a move, I'm trying to help Dorian with another problem."

Dorian blinked. "Me? Is that why we're sitting here in the dark?"

"There." Kirsten pointed.

Out in the grass, two men walked from the shadows. One in the clothing of a tattered vagrant, the other a well-to-do executive. They crossed to stand in a patch of light cast by a streetlamp, both striding through a park bench. More figures appeared as the minutes ticked by, men and women from various parts of life: rich, poor, cybered-up, and intact. By the stroke of midnight, about two dozen spirits had collected in a group. Kirsten stared at Theodore as she exited the car.

She found it hard not to feel a twinge of anxiety while crossing the grass. Some of these ghosts were quite old, one or two rumored to have been rather famous before the war. A muscular older man in a nice suit looked her up and down, then greeted her with a curt nod. The mass of them turned, a mixture of shocked, curious, and indignant stares fell on her.

The Kind.

"Kirsten." Theodore held his arms wide as if to embrace her. "Who are your friends?"

"Forgive me if I don't hug you. You'll just grab my ass." She winked. "You know Dorian. This is Vikram."

"Dark energy upon that one," said an old man in a cowboy hat, pointing.

"The abyssals you told me about are chasing him, but that's not why I'm here."

The assembled spirits murmured amongst themselves, the muscular old man in the suit took a step closer, gesturing at Vikram. "Bringing him here could draw them to us."

Theodore laughed. "Calm down, Governor. They won't bother an enclave this large, not here in Sanctuary."

"I won't stay long." Kirsten offered a respectful bow at the ancient spirit. "I wanted to ask you to help me find someone. The man that killed Dorian."

Dorian gazed at the stars. "For heaven's sake, Kirsten. You're going to get yourself killed."

"Great, then I can hop in the sack with her." Theodore winked. "Assuming she's not an old maid when she bites it."

Kirsten pinched the bridge of her nose. "Theodore, you are a penis with legs. Dorian, I'm just trying to help you."

Theodore bowed, accepting her compliment. "Rene, is it?"

"Yes."

"Don't," said Dorian.

Vikram fidgeted. "This is not getting us any closer to destroying Seneschal."

She infused her body with astral energy, and put a hand on his shoulder. "Relax, Vikram. We could run all over the city and never find him. When he shows himself, I'll be ready."

Kirsten relaxed the power before Theodore could grope her chest. "Too slow."

"Aww." He faked a bashful shrug. "Can't fault a man for trying. I'll help you, but you know my price."

Immediate crimson face.

"You don't have to do this. Don't do this." Dorian shook his head.

Burning embarrassment saturated her. She looked at Dorian and then back to Theodore. "No contact."

He held his hands up. "No contact, I promise."

She focused on her feelings for Dorian, and closed her eyes. "Fine."

At that instant, she sensed a shift in the energy. Danger.

Kirsten spun, arm whipping out as the lash unfurled. Mariko sprang out of nowhere, rolling into a tight ball under the passing tendril. The Kind moved as a mass, taking a step away all at once. The dark form creeping over the grass whipped her head up. All-black eyes showered Kirsten with hate, tempered with shock. The once-beautiful face of a young Japanese woman, not much older than her, twisted with an inhuman grin of pointed teeth, as if her mouth had been cut two inches wider on each side. She exhaled a raspy hiss that lofted the scent of sulfur on the wind.

"Impossible... Gaijin girl." Mariko tilted her head to the other side, hands held out like claws as she scuttled sideways. "How! Tell me how you saw me! You have no training."

Vikram almost fainted.

Kirsten frowned. "Ninja or not, you're still dead. I can feel you."

A monstrous growl came from the tiny woman, beyond the vocal range of a mortal. She blurred into a streak of black. Kirsten brought the lash up to defend herself, but miscalculated Mariko's aim. She landed on Vikram, sinking her teeth into the crook of his neck and knocking him to the ground.

Dorian whirled and grabbed Mariko, peeling the wispy shadow away from the screaming hacker. The wounded spirit curled on his side, both hands over where she bit him as if ashamed of it.

Mariko melted into a cloud of black vapor, appearing at Dorian's right and punching him in the side. Poof. She reappeared on his left, kicking him the back of the head. Poof. Appeared behind him, sword drawn; all in three seconds.

The lash sizzled through the air between them, sparing Dorian an impaling strike. Mariko's semi-ethereal form slid backward into a crouch, avoiding the whip. Her straight-bladed ninjato caught the moonlight, gleaming. Kirsten moved to stand over Vikram as Dorian shrugged off the assault.

"Good thing I don't have internal organs anymore." He winced. "I think those were supposed to be hits on pressure points."

"You are both fools," snapped Mariko. "Get out of my way or die."

The ninja floated skyward, coming apart into four duplicate copies of shadow. Kirsten swiped the lash at the one with the strongest sense of energy. Three false images landed on Vikram, making him howl from fright, but doing little else. The real Mariko twisted in midair, avoiding the searing weapon. Growling, the demoness hit the ground in a three-point stance, sword held straight to the side in a one-handed grip.

"You have no idea the pain I will cause you, *Gaishō*." Mariko's mouth seemed to grow even wider, sharpened teeth glinting. "I shall devour your precious little boy next. You shall hear his screams in your nightmares."

Mariko leapt to the side cackling, her body flowed like liquid darkness with limbs. Sinister laughter turned into a perfect reproduction of Evan's voice screaming. "Mommy! Help! It burns!"

Two shots from Dorian's laser caught the apparition unaware. The projection of Dorian's desire to harm it took on the form of his old familiar sidearm. Mariko's head lolled to the side, glaring at him sideways, unimpressed. Neither shot appeared to have an effect.

Kirsten's howling cry startled Mariko's gaze back to her. She hammered the lash down with such fury it doubled in width. Aimed more by desire than physical motion, the energy whip scorched a jagged path through the demoness, splitting her from forehead to crotch. The gap between two halves of ninja widened for an instant before thousands of crisscrossing tendrils of black vapor shot across, weaving together. They interlaced, thickened, and pulled her whole.

Mariko slinked away, the malice in her eyes replaced with mortal dread.

Kirsten stalked after her, speaking in a cold, chilling tone. "You fucking touch him, and there won't be anything left for the Harbingers to throw in the trash."

Dorian leapt at Mariko in an attempt to tackle her, but she effortlessly guided him into a broken-neck landing on the ground behind her. At least, his neck would have broken if he still had a spine. Kirsten lunged, swinging the lash into an insubstantial mass of smoke. The inky cloud raced over the grass, coiled around the side of a building, and vanished into the night.

Vikram rubbed the bite mark, hiding it from sight until he had reintegrated. Dorian picked himself off the ground and adjusted his apparition back to rights. Kirsten couldn't look at him until his neck no longer appeared broken.

"Calm down. They're only using him to get to you, to goad you into getting reckless. You'll do Evan no good if you get killed out here."

"Seems like it backfired." A bare-chested scrawny man with a massive beard, long hair, blue jeans, and sandals smiled. "Her feelin's fer that kid made her stronger." He winked before he rejoined the spirits.

"What's that smell?" Kirsten sniffed.

"Marijuana." Dorian laughed.

She released the lash, which shrank back into her hand as if it retracted into her arm. The world seemed darker for its absence. She covered her face with both hands, eyes open, nodding and breathing in search of calm. "You're right… Mimicking his voice was just…"

"One of their favorite tricks." Dorian attempted to stretch away soreness. "Wow. Fast and flexible. I bet she was fun at parties."

"Girls what can move like that make big money in some places." Theodore chuckled. "Kirsten looks pretty flex—" He stopped, raising his hands as both Dorian and Kirsten glared at him.

"Thank you." Vikram approached, offering a deep bow. "I see that you *can* stop them. I pray you will *destroy* them before they harm more innocents."

"Kirsten," said Theodore, wandering closer. "Word among The Kind is your friend Rene is holed up in Sector 187, an abandoned hotel building at the middle of city road 2044."

"Oh, hell." Dorian shook his head. "No. You are not going there. Absolutely not."

"One more thing." Theodore held up a finger. "As Dorian can likely corroborate, Rene has a habit of padding his surroundings with thralls. He has about a dozen people with him now. Of course, they're only local gang types. No mercs with high-end military gear."

Dorian grew paler. "Kirsten, no."

"Black zone or not, I won't let him get away with what he did to you… or Nila."

"Let it go, Kirsten. The law has trapped him in the black zone. For a high-society fluff like him, that's even worse than death."

She nodded at Theodore. "Thanks."

He made finger-guns at her and winked. "Oh, you'll be thanking me later."

She blushed.

"But you can wait 'til you confirm my info's good." He stuffed his hands in his coat pockets. "I trust you. You ain't got it in ya ta lie."

21

VENGEANCE DENIED

The patrol craft rose over the edge of the apartment building roof, kicking up a cloud of dust where the ionic downblast scoured a patch of metal. Thin sparks spidered across the ground, lapping at the car's underside. Kirsten twisted the right-hand control stick enough to rotate the vehicle parallel with a flat spot between two ventilation units, then flicked the switch for the wheels. When the mechanical droning noise stopped, she set the vehicle down in the nest of tiny blue lightning bolts.

Captain Eze's holographic head appeared at the center of the console, eyes half open as though he had recently been asleep. "Wren, I got your message. What's the situation?"

"I have a lead on where Rene Bollard may be hiding." She shut down the drive system. "I want to go check it out."

He ran a hand over his face and shook off the last vestiges of sleep. "All right, let's hear it."

"He's using an abandoned hotel as a hideout, has maybe a dozen gangers under his influence."

"It's in Sector 187," Dorian yelled, though Eze couldn't hear him. He glared at Kirsten. "Tell him where."

"That doesn't sound too difficult. We can assemble a tactical response team and go in after him. There's no need for you to get involved. You don't have tactical training. I trust you have obtained an address?"

She opened the door and got out. Eze's virtual image leapt from the console to float above her armband, half the size. Kirsten squinted into the wind, her hair fluttering.

"Wren... What aren't you telling me?" Eze's voice sounded smaller, tinny.

"He's hiding in 187, sir."

Jonathan Eze's pupils shrank; he pursed his lips around a sharp exhale. "That is a complication."

"It was the first area to be blacked out on the NavMap, K." Dorian put a hand into her shoulder. "For some reason, it attracted the worst of the gang warfare, then as soon as the police backed off to let them fight it out, it got worse. Illegal augs flocked in, it..." He looked her right in the eyes. "I cannot even imagine what kinds of spirits lurk there."

She glanced at Dorian and made herself solid to him. He took her hand and squeezed it.

"The stuff hiding out in there is..." Ad-bots whizzing by distracted him for a second. "It's... too dangerous. The military won't even go in there. The grey perimeter around it has a standing Division 5 detachment to keep what's in there, in there."

"Wren, you know the sector is off limits. I..." Eze's lips curled into a frustrated snarl. "As much as I want to see this son of a bitch fry for killing a cop, I can't authorize any operation going into a disavowed sector—especially *that* one."

Disavowed... He sounds like one of them *now.*

"But, sir." She held her left arm up, bringing him closer to her face. "If we keep letting those areas rot, they're only going to get worse. It sends a message that they are havens from the law."

The cadence of fingers drumming on a metal desk came over the comm. "Decisions have been made. Retaking those areas failed a cost/benefit analysis—"

"But—"

Captain Eze's look stalled her interruption. "If the military *were* to retake the disavowed regions, it would force the criminal element into the Beneath. Down there, they could cause real damage to the city infrastructure. Command wants them up top where they are contained and relatively harmless to the city as a whole."

"Captain, with all due respect, I don't think it's right to let a cop killer go free simply because the military is too chicken to go where he's hiding. If I have to do it on my own time—"

"No." Dorian shook her. "Those *disavowed sectors* are worse than prisons. Let him rot there."

Eze leaned closer to the VidPhone, enlarging the illusory version of his head. "Wren, it is only out of concern for you that I forbid it. Do not, under any circumstances, approach or enter Sector 187 in pursuit of Rene Bollard." He leaned back, worry evident on his face. "You are too young to"—his face flashed orange from an unseen blinking light—"Oh, bother. Hold on, Wren. I have an official channel coming in."

The head faded. She let her arm fall limp. Dorian slid his hand across her back to the far shoulder. Her mood swirled with anger, sadness, and frustration. She leaned into him, the scent of his cologne grew stronger.

Vikram emerged from the car, fidgeting. He paced around, occasional stares shot their way. Several times he seemed about to speak, but held it back.

"I would rather you didn't risk your life to avenge me." Dorian put his arms around her from behind, chin over her shoulder. "It would pain me more to see you die than have him go unpunished."

She clasped a hand over his, pulling his arm tight to her body. Light from the distant city caught in the smog, diffusing into a violet haze among the silhouettes of distant towers and streaks of glowing ad-bots.

Dorian glanced down as her thumb traced the back of his hand. "You can do much better than me. Stop torturing yourself."

She leaned her head back against his shoulder. One small twist and she could kiss him. Kirsten stared into the deep green of his eyes, basking in the feeling of a man's embrace. Her eyelids drew heavy; the urge to go for that kiss grew.

His finger met her lips. Her eyes popped open, and she looked away. He had the smile of an amused older brother. He relaxed his grim around her and she moved to the railing, leaning on it while watching the parade of ad-bots go by.

"Kirsten..." He took a step after her. "I'm old enough to be your father... not to mention dead."

The absurdity of it made her laugh. "Yeah, I'm sorry."

"You deserve a full life, a family. I know you want one or two of your own someday." He winked. "There is a man out there for you, somewhere. What about Templeton? You got his PID, but haven't called him."

She shrugged. "I dunno. I got the same kind of 'big brother' vibe from him that you give off. He's in his thirties, *later* thirties."

"Kirsten, you're twenty-two. You need to live a little, to lighten up."

Leaning against the railing, she turned to smile at him. "Are you suggesting I do a Nicole and swap boys twice a month?"

"Not sure. She seems pretty keen on this new guy…Jaden?"

"Excuse me?" Vikram held up a hand. "Is this pertinent to the issue of three *demons* trying to kill me?" He flashed a weak smile that faltered back to a flat line. "Again."

Dorian fixed him with a hard glare that sent him wandering back toward the car. "Ungrateful little bastard, isn't he?" He stared plaintively at her. "Please don't do anything silly. Listen to the Captain, stay away from Sector 187."

She pulled threads of wind-tossed blonde away from her face. "Rene tried to kill me, too. Maybe if he succeeds, they'll actually go after him."

"I tracked the bastard for eight months. I know him. If you rattled him enough to chance an attack like that, sooner or later, the arrogant son of a bitch will make a mistake, and then we can take advantage of it."

"You think so?"

"I'm sure of it." Dorian walked to the car, staring down. "Please promise me you won't make a mistake before he does."

She shivered.

22

CLOSE CALL

Kirsten draped herself over the counter of a small coffee shop two days later, her eyebrows scrunched together. She stared at the machine processing her order, spewing brown liquid and beige foam together with a squirt of chocolate syrup at the end. She wanted it so much the cup tilted a hair toward her. The synthetic stuff would have taken half the time and been a quarter of the cost. Still, forty credits for her once (now twice) a month splurge seemed a small price to pay for the little escape.

"Easy." Dorian patted her back. "Don't yank it off the machine or you'll spill it."

"My TK is too weak to lift a cup of coffee."

Dorian grinned. "You shouldn't have ordered one big enough to swim in."

She let her head fall on her arms, the tip of her nose touched false jade. "Vikram is going to drive me nuts. He was up all damn night bitching and moaning about me doing nothing. He doesn't have to sleep anymore, so he doesn't think I do, either." She stopped, staring bleary-eyed at the wall. "Bathe in… bathtub full of coffee… mmm." Head down.

Dorian peered out the window at Vikram, still in the back seat of the car, glaring into the coffee shop as if late for work and the taxi driver took a random break.

Kirsten straightened out, rubbing her back. "It's not like we can do much else but wait for Seneschal to try again. If they have some way to sniff him out, the best chance we have to find them is to use him as bait."

"Sore?"

"Evan crawled into bed with me last night; something spooked him. For a little kid, he takes up a lot of space." She stretched and crumpled over the counter again.

"I had a dog like that once," said Dorian, chuckling.

The hollow plastic skiff of a cup sliding toward her over acrylic made her head snap up. She flashed an adoring smile at the clerk and gathered the cup to her chin. The wonderful fragrance of coffee and chocolate overwhelmed her senses as she supped of the nectar of the gods.

"Any man would kill to be that cup," quipped Dorian. "Except maybe Armando."

She snarfed foam, giggling. The clerk gave her an odd look, the sort of odd look one reserves for odd people who burst out laughing for no apparent reason in quiet places. He kept giving her the same incredulous squint as she grinned, waved, and went outside to the car.

Ten minutes later, the coffee was three quarters gone, and they sat seventy stories up by the side of an office building. Kirsten glanced at the mirrored glass, wondering if anyone inside questioned the presence of a patrol craft hanging there.

Riotous sounds came around the corner, projected from a billboard-sized advert droid bearing a Newsnet feed. On its screen, a small cadre of people waved metal poles projecting holographic signs with fear-mongering slogans regarding psionics. A frazzled middle-aged man with wild white hair and a tan coat rasped an interview with reporter Kimberly Brightman.

"So, Reverend Harris, why is your congregation here today?"

"The Lord says suffer not the presence of Satan in your midst. Society has become blind, my dear. The minions of The Devil walk amongst us and yet they are welcomed! They are welcomed by those too afraid of *offending* people to speak out. The Dark One has poisoned the minds of our people such that those who speak the True Word are shunned as bearers of hate."

Kirsten's glare could have cracked glass. *Damn bot is lucky this car doesn't have a Starburst pod.*

"Most scientists believe psionic abilities are the result of natural evolution. Reverend, what do you have to say to those who believe you are on the fringe? That you and your" —Kimberly gestured at the sign-wavers—"dozen or so followers are perhaps paranoid?"

"Scientists are under the spell of Lucifer. It is part of the plan, you see. If they succeed, and convince us to accept psionics as normal, society is dooming itself to Hell!"

The immense droid lumbered past, so big it had running lights like a shuttlecraft. Kirsten scowled, a low growl rumbled in her throat.

"Don't pay them any attention," said Dorian. "Even the reporter thinks he's a kook. He's so far out in left field he makes fun of himself every time he opens his mouth."

She closed her eyes, releasing all the air in her lungs in a controlled meditative breath. "Yeah."

"Command, this is Officer Nila Assad, I'm under" —a shriek crackled over the comm—"ediate backup at my home" —gunshots in the background—"I'm hit..." Agonized screaming lasted two seconds before the comm cut out.

Kirsten spun the patrol craft and rammed the left stick forward. "Son of a bitch."

Dorian's face darkened. He activated the emergency system, bar lights and transponder that created a siren in any nearby hovercar. "Rene."

"Command, this is IO-44 en route to Officer Assad's location. I'm close."

"Copy that 44. Attention all Division 0 personnel, officer down at..."

Kirsten tuned out the rest of the announcement, focused on driving. The patrol craft edge past 300 MPH. She didn't need the Navcon, knowing the address already. The distinctive 'cup-holder' shaped design of the building helped it stand out as well. Ad-bots whistled past as she spun the car up on its side to slip around another slow-mover. Dorian's lack of protest at her rough driving was an obvious clue how he felt about the situation. Vikram remained in the back seat, smirking at them while kneading his hands. His head moved as if on a swivel, expecting attack at any moment.

Two minutes later, and with the parking area full, Kirsten circled around the building and brought the car in over the pool deck. Sunbathers clambered away, some screaming, some yelling. A cushion of cloud filled the area beneath the black patrol craft. Mist fumed out of the water, following the hovercar across the pool, dissipating almost as fast as it appeared. The rush of air as she jammed to a hard stop shoved four lounge chairs, and their occupants, into the water. As soon as wheels hit metal, she leapt out the door and ran, armband held to her mouth.

"Implement police override. Lock down elevators and outer doors. Send an express."

The armband emitted a pleasant female voice. "Processing."

Red lights flashed in the hallway as a recorded male voice announced a police lockdown in progress, and asked all citizens to stay calm and remain in their apartments. One elevator waited for her in the hallway between the parking deck and the pool. She jumped in. It accepted her Police ID and whirred toward Nila's floor.

She looked at Dorian. "Where's Vik?"

"With the car."

"Shit, if they come for him now…. Will you please go get him?"

Dorian glared; worry for his former partner boiled out of his eyes.

"I can't fly through walls, and you can't do much to help her."

"Fine."

He zipped into the ceiling, as if he stopped and the elevator kept going. Seconds later, it chugged to a halt on the thirty-ninth floor. She sprinted down the corridor, wall-mounted lights streaking like glowing comets past her vision. The door to Nila's apartment had stuck partially open, the panel shot out. Kirsten took her E-90 in a two-handed grip as she edged up to the twitching slab of Epoxil. A brief peek past the edge revealed little more than a quiet room and the fragrance of ballistic propellant; sharp, acrid, and laced with carbon. Beneath that awful smell, the aroma of pancakes wafted by.

She clasped her left hand around the sliding door and pushed, attempting to force it open into the wall. The dead actuators offered a substantial amount of resistance. Kirsten managed to shove it an inch or two before it became evident her one-armed strength couldn't handle the task. She stuck a leg made in the gap, but even with her slight build, she couldn't fit.

The snivel of a terrified child came from inside.

Kirsten re-holstered her E-90 and put both hands on the door. Kirsten grunted and shoved, overpowering the hydraulics enough to slip past. Stumbling two paces in, Kirsten gasped a few breaths, readied her sidearm, and advanced. On the far side of the couch, Shani cowered in the corner of the living room. Still in her nightgown, she trembled. The child's hands clasped to her chest, toes digging into the carpet. She looked unhurt, but terrified.

Kirsten ran to her, lowering her gun. "Are you hurt?" she whispered.

The girl shook her head no. Terror faded to calm, and then to suspicion, then to accusation. Several seconds passed as they locked eyes, and the child pointed. Kirsten whirled about, gasping at the sight of the kitchen floor. With one hand over her service weapon, Nila lay face down in a puddle of blood oozing from her thigh. A few steps past her, a man in a long black coat slumped against the cabinets, dead. Small candle flames on his back wisped the scent of burned flesh into the air.

She got him.

"Nila!" Kirsten rushed over, examining her.

A nimbus of green wavered on the white tiles around Nila's E-86 as the ready light swept back and forth along the housing. The indicator read 59.

She only got one shot off.

Nila's sweat pants adhered to her leg, darkened by blood. The woman's breathing came in labored gasps, at the edge of consciousness. Kirsten tore at the fabric, exposing skin around a clean through-and-through wound in her thigh. Nila's shaking hand flew up and grabbed hers. She wheezed, fighting for air.

Kirsten fumbled with a stimpak. "Nila, shh. I'm here. Don't try to talk."

Nila tried to sit up, eyes searched for focus. "K…"

"You've lost a lot of blood, but you're going to be okay. Just relax." Kirsten pressed the autoinjector down, then hit her with a second one. Nila's bleeding lessened. pink foam exuded from entry and exit wound.

"No… K…" The woman struggled to raise a hand, as if trying to point toward the living room.

"What? Is there another one?" Kirsten shifted her right hand onto the grip of her weapon.

The chirp of a ballistic firearm's arming circuit came from behind. Kirsten froze for a second, a slow turn bringing her gaze upon Shani standing in the archway separating the kitchen from the rest of the house. She looked cute in her knee-length pink nightgown, bare feet, and disheveled black hair—the quivering gun in her tiny hands made for an adorable accent.

Kirsten's arm moved on instinct, reluctantly aiming at the girl. "Shani… What are you doing? Please put that down."

Small hands adjusted their grip; she almost smiled. "You wanna kill my mommy. The nice man says I have to shoot you. The nice man said I should kill anyone in the black suits."

No. She's gonna do it. She can't help herself. Kirsten's finger tensed. She stared at the seven-year-old pointing death at her. Guilt swam over her before she even did anything. One tear crawled down her cheek. She couldn't kill a little girl, even one pointing a gun at her.

Bang.

Kirsten lurched backward as a slug winged across the outside of her left shoulder. The recoil bounced the gun off Shani's forehead and knocked her back a step. Dorian sailed in from the ceiling and whirled about, taking in the scene. Left hand braced on frigid tile, Kirsten wanted to cry at the little pink target on the other end of her gunsights.

"Shani, drop the gun!" shouted Kirsten.

The girl raised it. Kirsten hesitated.

The soft *click* of an electric trigger sounded deafening over the silent kitchen.

Dorian dropped his hand; wisps of electrical energy threaded to him from the pistol. The exertion in his face from phasing through so many solid floors seemed to lessen as he absorbed it. Shani pulled the trigger again, frowning. Vikram covered his mouth with a hand, mirth in his eyes.

"Shani, what's gotten into you?" asked Kirsten.

"She shot me..." Nila rasped.

Shani threw the dead weapon to the ground with a childish snarl of contempt.

Kirsten gawked. *Rene, you motherf—*

The E-90 leapt out of her grip, as if someone Templeton's size had grabbed it and yanked. The weapon spun end over end, straight into Shani's grip. Kirsten blinked at the child. The little girl grinned with delight at the silver weapon, fascinated by the dots of azure light that moved in a constant sweep on each side.

"This one's shiny. I like this one more." She aimed.

"Shani, don't! It'll—"

Sparks crackled around the girl's arms when she tried to pull the trigger. The gun emitted a disharmonic squawking buzz. Shani's thigh-length hair stood straight out, forming a giant sphere coated in flickering lightning for an instant. She sailed into the air, away from the weapon, and landed on the couch a few yards behind her. The E-90 clattered to the floor.

Vikram laughed into his hand. Dorian grabbed a fistful of his collar, fist cocked.

"Sorry. I know it's a kid, but you have to admit that looked damn funny."

Dorian hit him. The dead cyberspace pirate staggered to the side, holding his nose, raising his hands in surrender against further assault—but still snickering.

Nila moaned and sat up, helping herself to two more stimpaks from Kirsten's belt. Dorian ran to her side, trying to be comforting and reassuring to a woman who couldn't hear or see him. Kirsten clutched the gash in her shoulder and staggered into the living room, blood leaking between her fingers. As she neared, an unconscious Shani came into view past the arm of the couch. The tiny body suffered sporadic twitches. Smoke pooled in her gaping mouth. A smear of blood ran down the cushions from where a tiny, burned trigger finger brushed it.

Kirsten put a hand on the girl's neck, beginning to breathe again when she felt a pulse.

"Rene, you son of a bitch. To hell with Eze's order... I'm gonna nail you."

A man in Division 0 tactical armor forced the broken door all the way into the wall. One handed, he slammed the door open hard enough to fry the console and send a shower of electrical sparks into the air. Three more entered behind him plus one woman. The lead officer approached Kirsten while the others set about clearing the apartment.

"Agent." He saluted, and then noticed Shani. "Oh, no, what happened?"

Kirsten relaxed. "She's alive... but could be dangerous. A suggestive got to her. It's not her fault. One dead in the kitchen, Officer Assad is hurt."

"So are you, Agent." A square of light appeared on his visor as his armor scanned her wounded shoulder.

"It's just a nick," she said, pausing to read his chest. "Parker, it can wait."

23

INNOCENCE RESTORED

Kirsten lifted Shani off the couch, easing her onto the carpet. Straddling the girl, she gathered the child's hands together and held on, pinning her wrists. Officer Parker offered flexi-cuffs, but she waved him off.

"If I can't overpower a seven-year-old without those, I should stay behind a desk."

Parker laughed. "Well, you are kinda little yourself. Any idea what to expect?"

"Telekinesis, at least." Kirsten found the girl's surface thoughts scrambled, likely an aftereffect of the zap. "Nila never brought her in for an assessment."

He shook his head. "That'll be a write up. Cortez, need you here."

One of the other armored men emerged from the back hallway. "Corporal?"

"Kid's a TK. You got containment."

Officer Cortez nodded.

"I have cause to believe a wanted psi suggestive programmed her to attack. I don't think it's her fault. She was terrified of anyone in the uniform." Kirsten looked down at the girl, gripping little arms tighter. "Okay, do it."

Parker pressed a stimpak into Shani's exposed shoulder. A faint hiss, and the kid's eyes snapped back to focus. She snarled, then thrashed.

Cortez shuddered, engaged in a battle of wills. Random pressure from telekinetic force pushed at Kirsten's body, trying to fling her away. Shani shrieked like a wild thing, squirming and kicking. When it became clear her TK could not brute-force its way past the more experienced officer, she bawled and screamed. The perfectly age-appropriate reaction to frustration reassured her.

"Stop." Kirsten's eyes flared with luminosity.

Shani went still, her caramel skin paling with fear. Cortez relaxed. Kirsten focused on the girl's eyes, mental fingers reaching into her head for the telltale signs of psionic programming. Sure enough, she found them.

Whispers, faces, ideas, and nightmares swirled in a milieu of color and sound. Sweat beaded on Shani's face as her upper lip curled, a snarl that never finished. The child went limp, gaze unfocused, mouth agape like a corpse. Only the feel of her breathing kept Kirsten from panicking. After forcing her way deeper into the girl's mind, she found a smear of intent. Protect Rene. Warn him if someone comes.

Nila didn't call him... you did. With me in the damn apartment. That's what you were hiding under the stuffed animals.

When the bad man failed to kill her mother, Rene's order made her try. She'd witnessed Nila holding a laser pistol and act like a cop, which set off her programming to kill anyone part of Division 0. Shani had taken the man's gun from the kitchen floor when Nila's back was turned, but she'd fought the compulsion to kill her own mother. Love battled with the psionic order, making her tremble. Rene had a lot of power. The child couldn't overpower the urge all the way, but she hit her in the thigh instead of the heart. Hearing her mother's scream of pain and seeing blood provided enough emotional power to break her free from the suggestion. She'd run to hide in the living room, afraid of getting in trouble for what she'd done.

The child already didn't like Kirsten, perceiving her as some horrible woman in black who wanted to take her mother away to a place that would kill her. Upon seeing her walk in moments ago, Shani had thought it Kirsten's fault Rene forced her to shoot her own mother. Pulling the trigger on the evil blonde was easy. She protected her family.

A tunnel of shifting blue light rushed past Kirsten's vision from behind. At the end, reality awaited. Kirsten sat back on her boot heels, gasping for air. Like the girl, she'd wound up soaked in sweat from the effort of undoing the suggestive influence.

Shani blinked off a disoriented haze. Two seconds later, she burst into tears. Kirsten lifted her into a hug, patting her on the back.

"It's okay, Shani. Your mommy's just fine."

The presence of medics came as a surprise, as did the lack of damage to the girl's finger or her own shoulder. Kirsten glanced at Cortez since Parker had wandered off. "How long was I in there?"

"About ten minutes."

"Where's Nila?"

"In the bedroom. Div 2 is going over the kitchen."

Kirsten gathered the sobbing girl and stood, carrying her down the hall to the main bedroom. Dorian paced by the edge of the bed, straining to speak to Nila while a medtech busied herself removing a portable nanogel sleeve from a now-intact thigh. Shani squirmed until Kirsten set her down, then ran into her mother's arms.

"Mommy! I'm sorry!"

Nila scooped her up, staring at Kirsten with a frightened, bewildered expression.

"Agent?" asked a woman.

She turned. The female tactical officer held out her E-90. Kirsten took it, exchanging a salute, and replaced it in the holster belt. *I wonder if I made a face like those people on Nicole's wall.*

Kirsten sent her telepathic voice into Nila's head. *We need to have Lt. Commander Ashford look at Shani.*

Nila shivered, squeezing her daughter close. "Why?" *What, he's a mind-blaster, why?*

Rene put a hypnotic suggestion in your daughter's head and turned her into a sleeper agent. I don't trust myself to have erased it all. Ashford is also one of the best telepaths we have. He's not a suggestive, but he will be able to tell if I missed something.

Nila looked at the door, the medtech, Kirsten, and then buried her face in Shani's hair. *He wipes memory. I don't want him to erase my daughter.*

Kirsten put a hand on Nila's arm. *He won't. It's not worth taking the chance he programmed her to do something else. Keep a close eye on her until you can see him. He's not as bad as people say. How would you act if the entire world was scared shitless of you?*

Nila cradled her daughter, attempting to soothe the sobs away. "Thank you for not..."

Her stomach did a backflip, she knew Nila couldn't bring herself to say *shooting my daughter.* Kirsten forced the thought out of her mind, she simply squeezed Nila's hand and smiled in the mutuality of words unspeakable.

BY THE TIME THEY REACHED THE ELEVATOR, KIRSTEN COULDN'T TAKE IT anymore and shot a stare at Dorian. "Why are you giving me that look?"

"I'm thanking whatever it is on the other side of the silver light Shani missed." His gaze softened. "You could've died, hesitating like that."

"I..." The opening doors startled her. "I couldn't live with the guilt of shooting a kid. Those two idiots from the Nippy-Nom were fourteen, and I'm not sure I could've fired on them if I had to. Shani's only seven. Never mind she's the daughter of someone I sort of know. I... there's no way I could've shot her even if it would've killed me to freeze."

"It's one of the hardest things any cop has to deal with. Some of those gangers are pretty damn young." Dorian exhaled his non-air. A wisp of fog formed in front of him as he searched for meaning in the rug.

"Did you..."

"I didn't kill him. It's pretty damn hard to leg an eleven-year-old with an E-90. Sliced it off at the thigh."

Kirsten gasped.

"He's fine now. You know as well as I do, under eighteen the government covers full regeneration."

"But... I've seen children with cybernetic limbs," muttered Kirsten.

"Either ACC immigrants, Mars colonists, or people born with missing limbs. Regeneration only follows the programming in the DNA. Anyway..." Dorian's jaw stiffened. "I killed the *leader* of his so-called gang, even after he surrendered."

"I can't believe you shot an eleven-year-old boy." Kirsten gasped.

"He'd already drilled Nila in the gut with a rifle, was aiming to finish her off. What choice did I have? By department policy, I should have killed him. You're more bothered that I shot a kid in the leg than you are that I performed a summary execution on the man responsible for arming him?"

She folded her arms across her gut, gurgling. "I dunno, you could have killed the boy, but took a risk trying to wound him."

"Youth isn't a guarantee of innocence," said Vikram, bringing up the rear. "In the ACC, many of the resistance fighters have dozens of kills before they're able to grow beards."

Kirsten put a hand on the door to the pool deck and turned to Dorian. "I…" She hung her head. "I almost died back there, and I was just gonna let her do it." A trickle of bile ran out of her mouth. The idea she came so close to death made her breakfast want to come up.

"Hey." His finger passed through her chin.

She raised her head as if he had moved it.

"You could have compelled her to drop it."

Shit. I'm such a dumbass. Too emotional. "Yeah."

"Me wanting everyone to be safe includes you." Dorian ran a hand over her hair.

Vikram gazed at the ceiling.

24

THE FOOLISH AND THE DEAD

C aptain Eze looked up from behind his desk as Kirsten stormed in. She waved her hand at the silver panel on the wall, closing the door. Vikram and Dorian oozed through it anyway. Eze sat up, and leaned back into his chair.

"Kirsten, I just saw your report on the incident at Officer Assad's home. I'd like you to take an hour or two today and have some time with Doctor Loring."

The shrink? Oh, dammit. "I'm fine, I just hesitated shooting a seven-year-old. I'm"—*he's not buying it*—"fine. I'll see her, but I am going after Rene."

"You know how I feel about that, Kirsten. You went right from the dormitory cadet program to Investigative Operations. Your astral sense ability is rare enough that they skipped you over most of the academy to put you out there."

"Hank was causing too much damage at the shipyard. They needed a ghost dealt with faster." Kirsten smirked. "So you think I'm helpless because I didn't do tactical first?"

He laughed. "No, I'm not saying you are helpless. You are far from helpless in situations that fit your talents."

Kirsten approached the desk and leaned on it with both hands. "So I'm fine to go chase wraiths, but the bastard that killed Dorian and almost made me shoot a goddamn little girl is too much?"

"You are talking about the oldest, most severe disavowed zone of the lot. Even if the military were to go in there, they'd take fifty men in assault armor with mechanized support."

"Shouldn't you be worrying about the three demons running about?" asked Vikram.

"I wouldn't..." Dorian held a hand up to Vikram. "Just let her vent."

"A platoon going in with heavy equipment will attract everything out there to come play. One person and a couple of ghosts won't be noticed. They don't have any defense against psionics; how do you think Rene is still alive? Sector 187 is teeming with augs. They don't have much brain left." She shoved off the desk and paced. "I could make them do whatever I need. What's Rene going to do next time? What if he learns about Evan?"

Dorian cringed. Vikram paced about, shaking his head and muttering.

Eze frowned. "What good will it do the boy to get attached to you only to have you go get yourself killed? I don't want to see that, either." He reached forward, putting a hand on hers atop the desk. "I don't care for official funerals. Wren, I've seen you go from a scared little girl to a strong woman." He sighed. "I'm not sure I could take that kind of bad news."

Nausea bubbled out of the pit of her stomach, churning anger and worry into syrup sliding up her throat. In her mind, Evan had a gun at her. She smiled at Eze's hand, dark against her pale skin. He'd wound up somewhere between a father figure and protective older brother.

She glanced out the large office window at the squad room. *Would he give Morelli the same treatment? I'm too cute.*

"If you're wondering if I would take the same stance with any of the men under my command, I would."

Her head turned back to him, eyebrow up.

He smiled. "No, you're staring at Morelli. I guessed."

Eze's terminal beeped. He shifted, reading something on the screen. The pleasantness of his smile faded way. The skin of his cheeks hung like those of a dead man. He pursed his lips, sighing out his nose.

"What? What is it?" Kirsten straightened up, biting at her lower lip.

"Kirsten. I strongly urge you not to pursue Rene Bollard into Sector 187." The glower he shot into the terminal screen moved to her, and softened. "However, if you are insistent upon it, I will not stand in your way."

Dorian yelled. "You won't? Dammit man, don't let her do this!"

"He is right," added Vikram. "This is taking away from the time you could be spending destroying the demons before they kill me."

"You're already dead, Vik." Kirsten whirled, hands shaking. She felt like a kid denied the ability to stay out late finally getting her wish, and then being terrified of going outside after dark.

Who was on the terminal? What did they tell him?

"Right after I ran away, when I was below the city, I sometimes felt as if I wasn't alone. I had a feeling that something was there watching out for me, leading me to food, leading me away from danger."

"I've heard nothing converts an atheist like being caught in a war," said Dorian with a wry grin.

Captain Eze lifted an eyebrow. "A ghost?"

She frowned at Dorian. "I don't know. I felt it again at the parking deck. Eleven stories up, two seconds away from a dozen hand grenades going off, I had this bizarre feeling that it was safe to jump. Somehow, I just knew I'd hit the advert bot and not die. It was almost as if something helped me."

"An angel?" Dorian grinned. "That Theodore fellow seemed pretty convinced the Harbingers have a counterpart."

"I don't know." She folded her arms.

Both Eze and Dorian took her answer as directed at them.

"Harbingers I've seen, often. If there is such a thing as their opposite, why don't I ever see them?"

"Maybe they're afraid of the dark," offered Vikram, sarcasm obvious.

Dorian shot him a glance. "I'm starting to see why Lyris wanted to kill him."

"Kirsten." Captain Eze got up, walking around the desk to put both hands on her shoulders. "I'm not sure what you're talking about, or what hope you think you have out there. I would advise you to leave chasing Rene to people who have combat training and experience."

"But…" She looked up at him.

"I won't stop you." His teeth creaked.

She hugged him. "I'll be fine, sir."

He eased her to arm's length, grinning. "Careful, Agent, that's how rumors start. I hope you know what you're doing."

Don't say 'so do I,' don't do it. "I do." She thought of the horror in Shani's memory at almost killing her mother. "I'm going to get the bastard."

A knock came from the door, turning two live heads as well as two dead ones.

"Enter," said Eze, returning to his chair.

Tall and wiry, a man in an I-Ops uniform glided in the door. Dense wavy hair, as black as his government-issue coat, clung tight to his scalp. His skin looked pallid and corpselike, his eyes surrounded by sunken shadows. A matte-black oak leaf pin adorned the right breast of his coat, above a silver nameplate.

Eze shot to his feet, rendering a sharp salute. Kirsten followed suit, as did Dorian. Vikram rolled his eyes.

"Commander Ashford," said Eze, snapping his arm back to his side.

The living phantom returned the gesture casually. Kirsten couldn't tell if his expression was caused by fatigue, boredom, or annoyance. Wherever this man went, conversations stalled and people scurried away. He endured a harsher form of the worry her small rating in mind blast earned her; in a way, she felt bad for him. Not only was he a mind-blaster of no small degree, he belonged to Division 0's internal affairs group. She made it a point to project camaraderie at him, even edging closer as if she *wanted* to be near him.

He noticed, almost even smiled. "I've just finished meeting with the Assad girl, and her mother." His lips curled a little more into a smile as he shifted his gaze to Kirsten. "You were pretty thorough. I didn't see any further latent commands."

"You should ask him to make you forget about Rene," said Dorian, folding his arms.

"Thank you, sir." Kirsten nodded once.

"I need a few minutes with the Captain if you don't mind, Agent."

"Yes, sir." She scurried out, making no effort to give him a wide berth like everyone else did. The pleasant feeling faded when she saw the office, and two connecting squad rooms, empty.

KIRSTEN SPRAWLED ON THE COLD TILES, ONE ARM DRAPED OVER THE TOILET. Trails of OmniSoy ran down her lip from her nose, pooling on her chin in droplets before they fell. Once an omelet, it had returned to the base from which it had been reassembled. Any second now, she felt another wave coming.

I almost died.

Stomach muscles contracting, she bent over the toilet. Just a dry heave.

The image of little Shani behind the glowing blue ring/dot gunsight hovered in the dark of her memory.

Another dry heave.

She imagined an azure streak from the E-90 tearing the diminutive threat in half.

Bile flew out of her mouth, several subsequent convulsions became bawling. Kirsten clung to the toilet like a well-meaning friend, sobbing against the plastic seat.

The familiar fragrance of her father's ambiance surrounded her. She sniffled her tears under control. Trembling, however, was another matter.

"You don't have to do it if you don't want to, sweetie."

She closed her eyes and smiled at the cool presence of his hand on her back. A quick mental impulse made her solid to him. "It's not that, Dad. I came close to being killed today, and I couldn't do a damn thing about it. A little kid pointed a gun at me."

Heave.

He crouched alongside her, frowning. "What has society come to? Couldn't you just shoot the gun out of the kid's hand?"

"That doesn't work, Dad. E-90's the biggest laser they can cram into a handgun. At that angle, it would've gone right through her gun, through her, through the house…"

Another dry heave shook her. Crying flooded her nose, sending dribbles down her chin.

Her father patted her on the back, rubbing up and down.

"I couldn't do it. I just froze up. I knew it wasn't her fault. That made it so much harder. That son of a bitch programmed her to do it. If I shot her, I'd have been killing an innocent."

More bile gurgled in her throat.

"I think you more than anyone should know not to dwell on what-ifs." He grabbed uselessly at the paper, unable to touch it. He sighed, shaking his head. "Wipe your face, hon."

She gathered a few feet of toilet paper and dabbed at her chin.

"After what your mother did to you… after what you endured below the city, you should be better apt to cope with this kind of—"

"Dorian was right. I could have just suggested her to drop it." She squeezed herself tight to her spectral father, burying her face in his chest. "Dad… I don't wanna die."

He held her for a moment in silence until she sobbed herself quiet. "You're still young, sweetie. You haven't become jaded like Dorian. You survived, no one got hurt, and you learned."

The kiss he planted atop her head made her feel six years old all over again. She adored and hated it in equal parts. She wiped her face and stood, flushing the toilet with her boot. Her father was gone when she reached for the stall door, a wisp of his old-man scent teased at her nostrils. She adjusted her belt, checked her uniform for spots, and took a deep breath.

Okay, Rene. It's just you and me.

25

PAYING THE BOATMEN

F og rolled over the street a distance ahead of where Kirsten landed the patrol craft. She gazed at the shattered faces of abandoned buildings, a miles-long tunnel into the heart of a world forgotten by civilization. Some shiny, some black, most devoid of intact windows, the misery of blight wrapped all of them in its baleful embrace. Despite it being early afternoon, a pervasive gloom hung over the area a few blocks distant. She leaned against the center of the hood and steeled herself in an effort not to let the foreboding sense of apocalyptic dread cloud her resolve. Fidgeting, she tugged at the psi armor she still couldn't get used to wearing.

Black panels of DuraFib composite molded to her body, attached to a flexible bodysuit. She shifted, trying to breathe under the annoying tightness of the chest plate and stop the crotch guard from digging into her thighs.

Dorian and Vikram approached on either side around the car. Vikram glanced over his shoulder at the intact city, swiveling back to the decay with an amused grin. Kirsten held up a hand at the glare Dorian leveled at Vikram and tucked her hair up to put on the helmet. As soon as the rigid armor surrounded her skull, a strange presence caressed her brain.

Psi armor, a recent addition to the Division 0 arsenal, could use the mental energy of its wearer to power a deflection field that increased its protection. Some even maintained that it could, when charged, deflect paranormal attacks. She held her arms out in front, made fists, and twisted them to examine the lay of the plates. Sized for a woman two inches taller, the suit she'd put on was the only one available for loan on short notice.

I hope Nila won't mind I borrowed it.

"I'm not doing this for you. I'm doing it for Shani and Nila." She fixed her eyes on Dorian. "You know he'll kill them."

Hands on his hips, he cast a stare into the mist. "If you had just left her alone like I'd asked you to, they wouldn't be in danger." He softened. "But I did see a little bit of the old Nila peek out."

Kirsten pushed off the hood. "I know. You don't have to remind me, I'm beating myself up enough. They're in danger because of me; that's why I'm here now. But, the programming he put in Shani would've made her a threat at any time in the future. He made them both ticking bombs."

Unable to admit she had a point, Dorian simply stared into the distance.

Vikram jogged alongside. "Maybe it would be safer to wait until the three demonic assassins coming after me are dealt with first? It would be somewhat inconvenient if they were to ambush us in this place."

She kept walking. "They will come when they come. The things that live out here won't stick around if weird crap starts happening. They're as superstitious as priests."

A half-block later, Dorian caught up to her, moving with renewed purpose in his stride. His lip curled into a determined frown, fists clenching and relaxing.

"Dorian, we're not going in there to kill him. I don't want you to make yourself any more appealing to a Harbinger then you already think you are. Don't give them more of an excuse."

His eyebrows drew close. "What exactly do you think we're going to do to him? The only chance you have is to catch him from a blind angle without him seeing you. If you knock him senseless, he can't tell you to shoot yourself. The instant you make eye contact with him, you're going to die." He stopped. "That is, assuming of course, you can somehow get past the dozen punks he's enthralled."

"This really is not the best time to do this," said Vikram, paranoid gaze to the rear.

"I have something he'll never expect," added Kirsten with a wink. "I have a Dorian."

He sighed at the clouds while Vikram gesticulated out of frustration.

"No, really. You can creep around his whole place and tell me exactly where everything is when their backs are turned. They can't see or hear you so it's like having perfect intel. As if I had a RD-92 overhead that can see through walls."

Dorian blinked. "I... Yeah. It seems more than one of us let their emotion get in the way."

Vikram grumbled. "Will you two get a room?"

The stink of chemicals and waste tangled in the air, making Kirsten regret not bringing a rebreather. She adjusted the fit of the helmet, looking around, noticing how the faint amber tint of the visor clarified the details in the environment. Any object that moved had glowing amber lines around it within a split second, attempting to identify what it was, and classify the threat level.

Kirsten held her left forearm up, reaching for a terminal pane that didn't appear. She froze, staring at a faint strip of dull grey trim along the gloss black armor.

"It's in the helmet on those," said Dorian. "Glance up to the left for utilities, up to the right for combat assist, low left for comms, low right for terminal."

Her eyes went up and left. A menu scrolled out in front of her, appearing as a billboard six feet tall. She pointed at the NavMap line, but nothing happened. After a few seconds, she figured out it tracked her eyes rather than her hands.

Theodore had mentioned city road 2044, so she plotted a route to the spot. The hotel building in question sat on the last block before the official start of the blacked out area of the navigation system, as close as the grey got to the worst black zone in the entire city.

Seems Rene isn't as confident as I thought. Even he won't go into the heart of 187.

She took a left turn at the next corner, gliding among old dead cars and skittering bits of paper and drywall. Curtains fluttered in window frames decades devoid of glass. A whisper, a chatter, and a clunk of wood hitting the ground made her spin with her E-90 raised. Red letters spelled out *overpenetration* across her field of view when she stared over the bright blue dot. The armor knew what kind of weapon she had. Nothing moved.

"You're going to get yourself killed in here, and then I'm royally boned." Vikram walked in front of her.

She almost shot him.

"Dammit, man." Her arms flew down as she puffed her chest out. "Watch where the hell you're going. This thing will hurt you, too."

Dorian pulled him back. "Easy, pal. If you're in so much of a hurry to handle Seneschal and his friends alone, you're free to wander off at your leisure."

Vikram tugged his arm out of the grip, grumbling.

Infuriated, she stomped along the floating green line leading her closer to her programmed destination. Around a corner to the right, she took ten steps before a pile of debris against the wall exploded into the air. She whirled, aiming at the spot. A man roared with a wild-eyed cry. Except for his head, the entirety of his body sparkled chrome, metal limbs and torso sculpted in the image of bulging muscles. Exposed Myofiber bundles swelled and moved, making him appear to be a skinless man carved from silver. Thin lines separated plastisteel panels on the smooth parts, and faint grey light glowed from between a few that damage had knocked askew.

"Uhh, that guy's naked," said Kirsten.

"He's a forklift," said Vikram. "Who puts clothes on machines?"

Dorian chuckled. "The man's got a point."

The man's bald head—the only skin anywhere on his body—reddened as he emerged from his bed of piled junk. His eyeballs all but popped out from their sockets as he stared at her.

"Pussy time!"

Kirsten set her stance, raising the gun. "You don't even look like you've got the equipment for that anymore. Get lost."

Saliva slipped past steel teeth. He cackled. "Nice little pop gun you got, *chica*. Won't scratch this." He tapped his metal chest twice. Four narrow metal strips on each forearm split open and folded inward. From within each gap, twelve-inch blades extended down into loops along the backs of his fingers, and locked in place. Taser-like sparks crawled down their length, snapping off the end with a flash. As if slicing paper, the augmented arm cut the steel wall of a dumpster with ease as he walked closer. Kirsten did a good enough job hiding her terror, clinging to the confidence that her psionic abilities would make oatmeal mush out of a brain loaded with cyberware.

He bellowed in anger at her lack of reaction.

She took a step back.

This thing has a mind... almost.

"Why don't you *put those claws away?*"

He shuddered, his body twitched.

"Just shoot him," said Vikram. "The man's obviously out of his mind. You'll be doing him a mercy."

"Aaaaaagh!" The silver behemoth screamed, his body shuddering in protest. One by one, the blades came loose from the finger locks and vanished back into their protective doors. "I'm gonna twist your freak head off!"

The aug lunged forward one step before she shot him in the chest. The beam hesitated on the polished plastisteel for a fraction of a second before it burned all the way through him. Hand clamped over the glowing hole, he stumbled to one knee. A few seconds passed in silence. He gawked at her, realizing the little 'pop gun' wasn't the ballistic nuisance he expected. Roaring, he staggered back to stand. Kirsten fired again, her second shot reflected back off the chromed chest, smoking a trace in the traction coating between Dorian and Vikram.

They both leapt to the side, yelling.

"Narrow your angle," shouted Dorian. "If you hit him at less than an eighty-five degree angle of incidence, the beam is going to reflect."

Vikram gestured at the cyborg. "Shoot him in the damn face. That's not a mirror."

"*Stop,*" she ordered, light dancing in her eyes.

The enormous man shuddered to a stop, fury darkening his cheeks. So angry he cried, his fingers fluttered in pantomime strangulation as his body protested whatever compulsion kept him from placing his hands around her throat.

The glow in her eyes lingered brighter for a few seconds. "You're going to *surrender at the perimeter,* now."

He clenched his hands to his head, the entire shining body warped and convulsed in his effort to resist. Plodding, step by step as if he fought strong magnets holding his feet to the ground, he trudged back the way they entered from.

"They're just going to shoot him, you know." Dorian stood next to her. "As soon as they see that thing come around the corner, they're going to light him up with the thirty-millimeter."

"That might be interesting to watch," said Vikram, wandering off to follow.

"So what, you want *me* to kill him instead?" She gawked.

"You could mind blast him a little bit, leave him loopy." Dorian tapped his head. "Of course, who knows how much damage he'll do to other innocent people... maybe it's better for the world at large they put him down."

Kirsten walked backward for several paces until she felt certain he wouldn't break the psionic coercion and come running back at her. As soon as she faced forward, she moved up to a jog. "I had him under control with Suggestion. You know I can't execute someone. If he comes after me again, I'll shoot him."

"What about Rene?"

She smirked. "I can resist him. I have a rating in Suggestion."

"Don't kid yourself. That's his primary focus, like you and astral sense. Compared to him, you dabble. You 'resisting' his Suggestion would be like holding up a dinner plate and thinking it's going to protect you from a bullet."

"Now's not the time to undermine my confidence." She stopped to give him a mournful glare.

"I'm trying to be realistic. Too much confidence is as bad as none. I don't want you walking in there expecting to just fight off his influence, and wind up dead."

Kirsten offered an apologetic stare.

Whatever Dorian said next drowned under the distant rumble of a heavy automatic cannon and a thundering series of explosions.

"Guess he didn't hold his hands up." Dorian faced to the rear.

About a dozen gangers filtered out of the buildings up ahead, drawn by the noise. In the middle of the street, Kirsten's police armor stood out like a 'kick me' sign... a ten-foot-tall, bright pink neon *kill* me sign.

"Oh, shit."

Kirsten sprinted to the side and dove to the ground on her chest below a light drizzle of bullets. Her sleek, armored body skittered over the traction coating without friction and she went headfirst into the side of a rusting car. Gathering her legs under herself, she leaned into the old metal hulk. The visor heads-up display drew amber ghosts, approximate outlines of men moving to cover on the other side.

She popped up, holding her E-90 in both hands, and shot one right in the chest. A spritz of red vapor burped out around the bright azure line, front and back; he dropped in place. Kirsten ducked down as the others returned fire. One slug burst out from the quarter panel and bounced off her thigh.

"Ow! Shit!" She rubbed the spot.

"If you get winged again, hand me the stun rod," said Dorian, grinning.

Vikram appeared around the corner, still laughing from the sight of the cyborg's encounter with a Division 5 assault vehicle. At the sight of Kirsten hiding behind the car, he sauntered up to her. "Natives seem restless, kiddo."

"Who're you calling kiddo? You're only twenty-five." She glared at him.

Spotting an opening via the holographic apparitions, she jumped up and aimed over the roof and took two quick shots at two reloading gangers. One caught it in the face and died on his feet, the other suffered a three-inch trench cored into his right bicep. A slug hit her in the left breast with a loud *clack*. She fell like a sack of wheat, crumpling to the ground.

"Fuck!" shouted Kirsten.

Dorian raised both eyebrows. "I don't think I've ever heard you swear that much before."

She leaned against the car, gasping breaths between throbbing pain wrapping around her left side. "Feels like a cyborg punched me in the tit. Figures he hit the same side the wraith did." She grunted, forcing herself to sit up. "Think you could help out a little?"

Seriousness returned to Dorian's face. He nodded once and walked through the car. The endless peppering of bullets into the husk slowed. One by one, he drained their weapons' power cells. Kirsten's sigh of relief came short lived as a screaming idiot with a pair of blades leapt the car. He landed a few feet past her and whirled.

Vikram stepped toward him, surrounded by a wisp of ethereal vapor. The ganger's bloodlust melted away to panic, gaping at the apparition before him. Vikram flashed a dark smile and lunged. Blind with induced panic, the man in the Sons of Charon jacket sprinted into the debris-strewn street. Vikram followed, outpacing the man with ease. The ganger kept looking back over his shoulder, screaming at the dead hacker—and ran straight into a jutting mass of concrete and rebar.

Kirsten flinched away from the sight of six steel rods lifting the painted grim reaper away from the man's back. He jerked about, twitching and gurgling before going still.

The aura of energy around Vikram disappeared, and with it, so did his reflection in a nearby window. He clapped his hands as if wiping off dirt. "Got one."

"What the fuck is wrong with my guns?" A man shouted, on the edge of inebriation.

Kirsten stared at Vikram. *He didn't think anything of killing that man. No hesitation at all.* "Vik, I know you're dead and all maybe you think you can do anything without worrying about the police but… if you kill people left and right, *they* will come after you."

He waved her off. "Defense of an innocent girl. Besides, you're killing these cretins as well."

He enjoyed that too much.

"Screw this lousy piece of shit." A gun clattered to the ground. A blade scraped out of a sheath.

Kirsten popped up, firing at random into the approaching gangers. All but two broke and ran. *They're killers. They want to kill me. I'm not shooting the ones who run away.*

A scintillating stripe of azure light connected the tip of her pistol to another man's chest. A split second later, the beam burst out of his back. His cheek squealed to a halt on the plastisteel ground, dead before he could scream. She jumped away from loud crumpling metal as the second man leapt onto the car. Her boot came down on something that shot out from under her and rolled away with a metallic ringing. She flailed her arms to keep balance, continuing to stumble backward. The man pointed a rifle with a barrel as thick as a small pipe at her. With no time to dodge or shoot him first, Kirsten concentrated on pouring mental energy into the psi armor. The the dull grey trim on the arms and legs lit up violet, surrounding her with an amethyst field of energy that teetered at the edge of being visible.

Boom.

Tremendous recoil knocked the man on his ass.

The impact to her chest smashed her flat, sending her into a sliding rearward spin. Her brain felt the hit as much as her chest did, the mental exertion similar to that of using mind blast. Unable to breathe from the hard hit, she stared at dancing spots in the air.

Laughing, the Son of Charon flipped the breech-loaded weapon open and slipped in another round the size of a hen's egg. He rolled back to his feet, still chuckling. As he went to jump down off the car hood, Vikram swiped at his foot. The man tumbled over forward. Vikram palmed his skull and rammed his face into the ground, breaking his neck on impact.

Kirsten sat up, pounding a fist into her chest in an effort to get air back into her lungs. Concentration waned, the luminous violet stripes faded back to grey. Dorian ran over, brushing a hundred flechettes from her.

She blinked. "You moved something."

He managed a worried smile. "They don't weigh much."

Kirsten let gravity pull her flat on her back, taking a few breaths before struggling to stand and putting a hand over her helmet. "Yeah, I'm fine. Little woozy, not used to this armor. It's kind of tiring."

Dorian locked eyes with her. "Are you sure you want to do this?"

"Yes. He's only one block over." She squinted at Vikram and lowered her voice to a whisper. "Watch him."

26

TRUE COLORS

Kirsten crawled in the rear doors of an old white van, abandoned with two tires on the curb and the nose wrapped around a pole. The windshield had enough grime to offer a decent bit of cover from the people milling around in front of the hotel three buildings down the street.

The locals circled a nonfunctioning fountain in the center of a courtyard of black tiles with bronze lines inlaid in diamond patterns around it. Across the main archway, the shadow of letters spelling 'Echelon Guest Suites' remained, drawn in less advanced corrosion compared to the rest of the surface. It was anyone's guess how long ago the locals shot the letters off the wall.

"The bastard even squats first class," grumbled Dorian. "Wait here. I'll go check it out."

She opened her mouth.

"No arguments." He held a finger up. "This is your idea. You suggested I scout, I am going to scout. I want you to stay right here, hide in the van, and be alive when I come back."

She closed her mouth.

"Good, now that we have an understanding…" Dorian jumped out the side and hurried at a brisk walk past the courtyard defenders.

Vikram chuckled past fingers over his mouth. "Don't you outrank him?"

"Stuff it." She leaned back, straddling the console. "Rank doesn't mean he's not right. Maybe this was a stupid idea, entering this sector alone." *What's that old joke about sergeants and lieutenants... If I even live long enough to get promoted to lieutenant.*

"I thought the other cops by the perimeter were about to drag you out of here."

"Heh." She pulled her helmet off to wipe the sweat from her forehead. "If I wasn't a Zero, they probably would have. Guess for once it's good people are afraid to get too close."

"You are too soft." Vikram paced about the small area. "You let things get to you too easily. You suffer guilt about killing someone who wants to kill you. It would seem to me that is a detriment to your chosen line of work."

Kirsten crossed her arms over the helmet in her lap. "The line of work chose me, I didn't—"

Vikram vanished, yanked by a hand through the street-facing wall.

"Shit."

She crunched over debris to the back of the van while trying to get her helmet on with one hand, and shoved harder than necessary at the door. It swung out with much less resistance than she expected, dumping her to all fours on the street amid a trash-fall.

A wail drew her eyes to Vikram, hauled around by Icarus's two-fisted grip on his collar. Dreadlocks trailed in a graceful arc as he flipped the dead hacker over and drilled him into the ground. Kirsten sat up, still kneeling, and shoved her hands forward, projecting a wave of astral force. Icarus flew into the air as if hit by a speeding car, tumbling to the ground in a series of sideways rolls until he came to a halt on his chest.

Vikram turned into a cloud of mist, which reformed standing. He sprinted at Kirsten, screaming once again as Icarus produced a compact assault rifle out of thin air and fired. She flung herself to the left, against the van's rear bumper. The barrage of spirit bullets flung Vikram off his feet.

Vikram skidded to a halt beside her, seven holes in his torso wafting vapor. He gazed off into space, moaning. Kirsten ducked around the flapping door and squeezed off several pulses from the E-90, chasing Icarus behind a broken bit of wall.

Vikram gagged, as if coughing on blood. He crawled under the van while Kirsten's attention focused on Icarus. She sent mental energy into the armor once more, activating the protective field, and rushed out from cover surrounded by a reassuring violet glow. She jogged across the street, leapt a fallen vendomat, and headed for cover by a wall of grime-covered concrete panels next to a parking garage entrance. A deep rumble inside vibrated the ground at her boots. When the noise stopped, she leaned out and peered down the ramp, pointing her E-90 at a row of cars long ago crushed by a falling ceiling support. Other than some dripping water, nothing moved.

I don't have the best luck with parking garages.

Icarus reached out of the wall, grabbed her helmet, and jerked back, pinning her head to the wall. His other arm wrapped around her throat and squeezed. Kirsten abandoned her grip on the E-90 and called the Lash. The glowing panels on her armor flared bright as the mental energy field resisted his effort to phase through and grab her unprotected neck.

She flicked the lash behind her, into the wall. Icarus receded into the building. She stumbled away from the wall and whirled to face the garage, arm high and psionic whip poised. Her heart raced from the scare of the sudden grab, but within a few seconds, fear shifted to anger—but then confusion. *That felt like a knockout hold. What is he doing?* She stooped to recover the E-90, holstered it, and trotted down the ramp.

When she reached the underground floor, Icarus dove at her from behind a giant slab of plasticrete. She dodged with a sideways leap. He landed a few steps away, raising his arms at her as if holding a rifle—that appeared out of thin air. Before he could fire, Kirsten rushed at him swinging the energy whip in a hard sideways swipe. He leaned over backward, evading it by inches, eyes wide as the blinding glow lit his face in harsh shadow for an instant.

Overextended, she lurched a step past him. He spun into an elbow strike that caught her between the shoulders and knocked her forward in an ungainly stagger that left her hugging a crumbling support column. Two loud gunshots went off behind her. Spectral bullets slammed into her back, knocking the wind out of her and spraying saliva on the inside of her visor. Her brain pulsed from the armor draining mental energy to power the protective field.

"Oof," rasped Kirsten.

She clung to the pole, stunned legs giving out from under her. A hunk of plasticrete came off in her hand, dumping her to the floor on her chest. Kirsten rolled over on her back, bringing her arms up in a defensive posture.

Icarus shook his head, the thick mass of his ropey hair swaying as he walked up to her limp body. His rifle flickered and shrank into a massive handgun, which he pointed at her head. "I told you, girl. Stay out of this. It does not concern you."

Kirsten hurled herself to the right while sweeping the lash sideways at his shins. Her whip caught him off guard and pulled his feet out from under him. She scrambled to her feet and swatted the energy whip at him in a downward stroke. He dove aside, narrowly avoiding her attack, which sank into the floor for a brief moment. Proximity to her spirit weapon seemed to throw him into a panic. He scrabbled at the floor, trying to crawl off to the left.

"You don't belong here," she screamed, and swung again.

Shani's face flashed in her mind, loading the lash with enough force to blast Icarus into a projectile. The former commando rocketed across the ground, plowing a clean trench in the scattered trash for a short distance before his body became immaterial. He slid to a halt about twenty feet away. Kirsten started to stalk after him, but he sat up, firing at her, so she leapt behind a car.

The shot clanked into metal somewhere behind her. She huddled against a deflated tire that reeked of piss. Vikram appeared on the ramp, some thirty yards back. Icarus shifted aim, snapping off a quick shot in his direction. Kirsten sprang up, ran over the hood of the derelict she'd been hiding behind, and flung herself at him. Icarus whirled toward her. His gun fell from his grip, vanishing before it struck the ground. He caught her by both wrists, holding the lash away and swinging her around to the left. She growled, futilely trying to overpower him with brute strength. He stared at her, expression calm, silent.

She squirmed, trying to make the lash flick into him. Her arms went wherever he wanted them to as they danced around and around. Kirsten narrowed her eyes at him. *He's fighting me like I'm an annoying little sister...* Indignant, she tried to kick him in the groin, but his body offered no solidity as he swung her around toward another column. Hard plasticrete turned out to be a rather painful thing to drive a knee into.

He sprang forward, shoving her over onto her back and pinning her arms to the ground on either side of her head. Unable to move with him on top of her, a new form of terror clawed at her heart from the implication of what their position resembled. Icarus hovered over her, staring past the amber visor into her eyes.

Four seconds of silence passed between them, gazes locked.

Whimpering futile struggles became growling convulsions. Fear became anger.

I'm being stupid again.

Rather than attempt an impossible contest of physical strength, she shoved with her gift, the say way she had pushed the soul collector back in the Saguaro Asylum. His semi-solid body shuddered; if not for her psi armor, his grip might have crushed the bones in her wrists. She strained with so much effort a headache bloomed at the core of her brain. Gradually, the weight pressing down on her lessened. Icarus had a *lot* of power for such a recent death, but he wasn't exactly a ghost.

Bit by bit, she gathered her fear under control and replaced it with focus. Icarus leaned away, losing a contest where she had a mild advantage. He continued to hold her arms, pulling her into a sitting position as she forced him away. Almost nose to nose, her confidence met his confusion.

Vikram, wailing, sprinted in as best he could with a hand over a new bullet wound in his side. He leapt on Icarus's back, dragging him away from Kirsten and sending them both gliding through the back end of destroyed old cars. She sagged forward, panting. Her head spun, the room shifted, and for a few seconds, she momentarily forgot where she was.

Squeaks and thumps of boots mixed with the meaty *thuds* of a brawl snapped her back to rights. She looked up at Icarus, who had Vikram in a grapple from behind, head drawn back in preparation to slit his throat. A wicked combat knife appeared in his hand amid a flash of spectral light.

"Icarus!" Kirsten lunged, risking a lash despite the two spirits being so close.

He ignored her, jamming the knife into Vikram. Her energy whip burrowed into Icarus' chest, paralyzing him in agony. Vikram shoved away and fell to one side, clutching a wound at the base of his neck. He scampered off in a crawl. Icarus swooned to the side and tried to scramble away but she lit into him with a second lash.

The instant the whip hit him, a deafening quasi-spectral roar blew out all remaining car windows within a hundred yards. Her helmet display exploded with static and error messages, then shut down. Intense red light shone from his eye sockets and mouth, radiating outward in a ring that reminded her of when she obliterated the Wharf Stalker.

"Eep!"

Expecting the same horribleness, she leapt for cover behind a pylon, hoping to avoid winding up unconscious for two days again.

Seconds passed with no massive spiritual detonation.

"What the hell are you doing? Finish him!" shouted Vikram, sounding every bit as hurt as he looked.

She peeked out from behind the column at Icarus.

He swayed on his knees, one hand pressed into his stomach. Fissures like lava cracks all over his body glowed crimson. His dark brown skin gleamed with sweat. At the sight of her, he raised a hand. "Wait."

Vikram pointed. "It's a trick, kill him."

"I know who you are." The red light in his eyes faded, leaving them brown... and sad. "I had no right to strike you. It was not my place." Icarus bent forward, arms limp in his lap.

"He is stalling. Whip him." Vikram gestured as if using a whip. "Do it!"

Kirsten edged a step closer, keeping her Astral Lash coiled about her legs at the ready. "What do you mean you know who I am?"

"I was sent where I belong." His voice, silken and deep, reverberated over the abandoned garage. "Call the ones who gather the hateful. I will not offer resistance."

"No. Don't believe him. He's trying to fool you."

She held a hand up at Vikram as if stopping traffic, still staring at Icarus. "You *want* me to call Harbingers? You think I can?"

He lifted his head in a slow, nonthreatening way. Meditative acceptance in his eyes appeared genuine. "I know you can. You are the one. You were right. I do not belong here."

"What *one*?" She wanted to trust his face, wanted to believe the sorrow in his stare. "I will call them, but tell me what you mean first."

Vikram howled, flinging himself on Icarus with the fury of an injured wombat. The two men grappled; the drain of being lashed left him Icarus to Vikram's furious clawing onslaught. Strips of red light flared bright within jagged claw wounds.

Obliteration cometh.

She glared. "Vikram, *stop*." The suggestion had no effect on a spirit. She raised the lash. "Vikram, so help me, do not destroy him. He is repentant."

"He lies," wailed the hacker. "If you will not finish this, then I must."

Icarus clutched at Vikram's shirt, trying to peel him off, but lacked the strength. Instead, he braced an arm across the hacker's throat and shoved. The man gurgled, bending backward, clawed hands in the air.

She whipped the lash across Vikram's shoulders, launching a billowing blast of energy vapor from the point of contact. The strike knocked him away from Icarus and sent him tumbling over the floor.

Kirsten stomped after him. "What's wrong with you? If the Harbingers take him, he won't be a threat to you anymore. There's no need to destroy him."

Vikram loped to his feet, stumbling to the left in a sidelong circling gait, arm clamped to his battered and smoking chest. He fixed her with a dark glower. "For the same reason you are hunting that man, Rene. I want revenge." He blurred at her, a tangle of glowing yellow eyes and shredding claws.

Kirsten yelped in shock and dove to the ground. Vikram passed clear over her. She landed in a somersault and sprang back to her feet, but he'd vanished.

So had Icarus.

She looked around for a moment before slouching with a sigh at not sensing anything paranormal in the area.

"Dammit." Her voice echoed in the empty garage.

The lash shrank back into her hand and went out.

27

A SHEEP IN WOLF'S CLOTHING

K irsten sat on the rear bumper of the dead van. Bracing her sore knee, she watched slow-drifting forms in the smog above change shape. Stillness settled over the desolation. Even the wind decided to abandon this place. With every breath, her back ached from where Icarus' bullets had hit her. His words drifted around in her thoughts. She wanted—no *needed*—to know what he meant by her being *the one.*

Damn, Vikram. What was he going to tell me before you chased him off like an idiot? Could he have been sincere, or was I about to walk right into another trap? Why am I so gullible?

The scuff of a boot on the footpath made her lift her head out of her hands. She drew her legs into the van, hooking a finger at the peeling inner lining of the door to pull it closed.

"Fuck you, Noz," said a young-sounding woman. "Why'd you have to give me this shit? You know I don't wanna do this shit no more."

Huddled against the door, Kirsten stretched up on her knees to peer over the bottom of what had once been a window, no longer any glass in it. A woman with bright lime hair stumbled down the sidewalk to the right. She wore a way-too-big Sons of Charon jacket that fit her like a short dress. A compact sub-gun dangled from a strap over the image of the robe-clad skeleton. Her loose grey pants wobbled, suggesting heavy, small objects filled the thigh pockets.

Kirsten used her helmet to zoom in on the woman's leg. *Ammo, maybe drugs, maybe grenades.*

"Noz. Fuckin' Noz." The woman swayed back and forth like a little girl singing a children's song. "Why Noz give Leaf drugs, Frenchman's gonna be pissed at Noz. Leaf wants to quit. Leaf pissed at Noz."

The woman stopped walking and opened her hand, gazing down at a mass of black crumbles. Rainbows gleamed on the surface of tiny rocklike bits like coal glass fragments.

Nightcandy. Kirsten cringed. *Poor thing, that's nasty shit. Hard to kick.*

I won't tell the Frenchman if you won't. Kirsten sent her thoughts into the woman's head.

Leaf clamped her hand closed over the drug. Arms to the sides, she went wide-eyed and looked at the sky. "God?" She stared for a moment before cackling. "I always knew you were a girl, too!" The green-haired waif spun in a giggling circle, as if trying to will herself to fly.

Kirsten bonked her helmet on the door. *What the hell is she doing here? Never mind, I can guess what they use her for.*

The girl stopped spinning, took a step farther away, and peered straight up. "Clouds? Why did you stalk talking to Leaf?"

Kirsten slipped out from the van and tiptoed up behind her. Chances were good even the silver cyborg from before could have snuck up on this one. She pulled the stunrod from her belt, reached out, and tapped the girl upon the head like a faerie with a magic wand. Blue light at the tip of the rod flickered.

Leaf fluttered to the ground.

"Sorry," muttered Kirsten. She put the stunrod away and dragged the unconscious girl to the van.

Once inside out of sight, she took the girl's submachine gun and removed the huge leather jacket before cuffing her hands behind her. The Nightcandy, she hurled into the junk pile under the front seat. Kirsten removed her helmet, straddled the unconscious woman, and brushed neon green hair away from a grime-streaked face.

"You poor thing."

She forced the young woman's eyes open with her thumbs and dove into her mind. Sure enough, Rene had etched his thralldom onto her neural pathways. Unlike Nila and her daughter, the effect on Leaf hung closer to the surface. Direct and immediate, it resembled the type of suggestions Kirsten could use, the main difference being hers lasted for a few minutes while Rene's approached permanent. She didn't know that technique—nor did she much care to. Suggestion came in damn handy for things like 'drop your weapon,' but beyond using it to save lives, that power unnerved her.

What Rene did to Leaf was more obvious, simpler, and easier to remove than what he'd done to Nila and Shani. Kirsten spent a few minutes unwinding the suggestion. Once satisfied the girl wasn't a loyal drone soldier of a rogue psionic, she decided to try a deep telepathic dive. The pathway to inner thoughts felt as if she slid naked down a plastic tube full of warm jelly.

Kirsten shivered. She'd never tried to go further into someone's memory than surface thoughts before. According to Division 0 research, using Telepathy to read minds worked much more easily on an unconscious person. The combination of having time to kill waiting for Dorian, worry for this girl, unanswered questions, and a test subject proved impossible to resist.

Within a moment, images drifted out of the blackness. Drugs of various kinds, a desperate want to be free of them, but she kept sliding back into their skeletal embrace. This girl appeared to be somewhat better off than Rush. Somewhat. She let the Sons of Charon take her under their decrepit wing for personal use rather than sell herself or suffer the control of a pimp. From the snippets of memory Kirsten found, the gang treated her okay at least in terms of not beating her. She still had to submit to sex whenever they wanted it, as well as run around like a live-in waitress.

Why are you in this sector? Her voice echoed as whispers in the unconscious mind. Scenes rebounded as if the words had bounced away from a wall and come back as pictures.

Perfect white teeth smiled from the well-groomed face of a man in an expensive suit.

Black.

The same man appeared on top of her, slapping and screaming.

"Failure..." *Whack.* "...amount to anything..." *Whack.* "...good thing your mother's dead."

"Daddy, no." Leaf's voice begged in the dark.

The same man crushing down on top of her, then pain inside her. She couldn't breathe, choking on fumes of alcohol.

Black.

The image of him asleep, face aglow in the dim orange light of a comforgel pad. A female silhouette appeared in a stretched rectangle of light spreading across the floor.

Gunshots.

Relief mixed with horror.

Kirsten recoiled; warm tears streamed over her cheeks even though she didn't want to cry. She slumped on all fours, her hands grasping the rotten carpet on either side of Leaf's head. Kirsten sagged forward. Eyes closed, she drew labored breaths trying to force those images—those *feelings*—out of her mind. She had something in common with this girl. Both of them had a *first time* they didn't want. He'd hurt Leaf taking it by force. The man with the new ration can had been gentle, but he'd hurt her for other reasons. Overcome by shame, Kirsten closed her eyes and shuddered, trying to stop thinking about the taste of beef stew.

Lips met hers. Kirsten's eyes snapped open, her startled yelp muffled by a tongue. Leaf continued kissing her. Kirsten froze, paralyzed for an instant by the sheer startlement of it, as well as the repulsive flavor of whatever this girl last ate—possibly grilled rat.

"Gah!" Kirsten sat up, pushing the woman down by the shoulders while spitting to the side. "What the hell are you doing?"

"Sorry, Leaf thought we were making out," said the young woman in a childish voice.

The dazed look in the girl's green eyes from the stunrod hit faded. She tried to sit up but found her arms locked in handcuffs. She stared at Kirsten, finally noticing the police armor.

Kirsten barely got her hand over the girl's mouth in time to muffle the scream.

"Quiet." Kirsten fought to hold her down for a full minute before she slouched with defeat. "*Quiet*," she commanded.

Leaf went limp.

"Good." Her voice fell to a whisper. "Listen to me, Leaf. I'm not here to hurt you. I'm not here to arrest you. I want the Frenchman. I'm going to get off you now. Can you stay calm?"

Leaf nodded.

Kirsten shifted herself to the right and sat on the floor. Leaf struggled in an attempt to sit up until Kirsten grabbed her dingy excuse for a shirt and pulled her up. The girl scooted back and shrank into a ball against the side of the van.

Silence hung between them for a moment. Leaf shivered, staring fearfully at her past a curtain of emerald green hair.

Kirsten rubbed the bridge of her nose. "Rene got into your head and forced you to serve him. I cleaned it out. I also saw what your father did to you." Her arm fell away from her face, hanging limp over her knee. "... and what you did to him."

Leaf almost vomited.

"I'd have shot him, too." *Liar, you'd have run away. Maybe* they *will understand. Even creatures like Harbingers could forgive her that one; they damn well better. Do they care* why *someone kills? Is one murder enough to get their attention at all?* "Honestly, I don't know how much Division 1 knows. I won't say anything unless I get called in front of an Inquest." Kirsten summoned a weak smile. "Don't worry, brain spelunking psionics aren't admissible. You're safe. And I... kinda understand."

Leaf wheezed, her lips doing an impression of a fish as she tried to talk. Kirsten removed the compulsion to be quiet.

"You spoke to Leaf out of the sky. Leaf not scared of psionics," whispered the girl. "Frenchman's got psionics. He gon' be mad at Noz. Noz give Leaf Nightcandy." She fidgeted at the handcuffs. "Are you God?"

No, I'm just psionic.

She shivered as the voice entered her thoughts. "Oh." Leaf sank, dejected.

"What's your real name? I'm Kirsten."

"Jennifer Ruiz, but people call Leaf, Leaf 'cause of green hair." The dangerously thin girl shook her head, making her lime-hued locks dance around. "Leaf have green since leaf little."

"Are you eighteen yet? Do you have any family left you can trust?"

"Eighteen inna couple months. Grandma on my mom's side, but she won't want Leaf 'cause Leaf is bad girl. Leaf can't stay clean. Leaf steals and Leaf buys bad things."

This kid has brain damage. Damn Nightcandy. I wonder if they can repair it. Kirsten flashed a tiny portable light in her eyes, pulling them open one by one. "You said you're not quite eighteen yet. Yhat means you're still a minor, and the government will pay for the detox... and any, umm, repair work you might need."

"Yeah, and put Leaf's ass in jail for killin' the dad."

"There is a very good chance it will be considered justifiable considering your circumstances. Besides, that was two years ago... and if it was up to me, I'd call it self-defense. They will treat you as a minor. You don't like where you are, you want off the shit, and you don't want to die before twenty, do you?"

Leaf stared at the floor.

"Did you kill anyone when you were with the Sons?"

She shrugged. "Leaf no shoot. Hang out with Sons for drink and sex. Sons feed Leaf. Protect Leaf... but kinda don't like Leaf."

"Who's Noz?"

"One of the Sons. He's got people inside Realtown, can get candy and other stuff. Leaf told him don't want no more, but he just gave it." She looked away at the ground, mewling. "Noz knows Leaf can't stop. Leaf doesn't like Noz."

Dorian's taking too long.

"Okay, Jen. I'm going to go deal with Frenchie. If you're still here when I come back, I'll take you with me back to... umm, Realtown and do as much as I can to make them go easy on you. I know I'm a cop and you don't think I give a shit, but you don't deserve this life. I've seen too many girls like you wind up as ghosts. I don't want to see another one."

"Why care 'bout Leaf?"

Kirsten sighed. "You... kinda remind me of where I almost wound up. If I wasn't psionic." She started to choke up, but logic got in the way. Had she not been psionic, Mother wouldn't have tortured her.

"You have asshole dad like Leaf?"

"Nah. My mother beat the shit out of me almost every day for being psionic."

Leaf's eyes widened with eagerness. "You kill 'er?"

"Nah. I was only ten. I ran away."

"Aww." Leaf sighed. "Sad. Too little to hit."

Kirsten took the giant Sons of Charon jacket and shrugged it on over her armor, shuddering at all the fleas and creepy-crawlies she imagined permeating it. After slinging the sub-gun over her shoulder, she slipped out the doors.

"Hey." Leaf scooted forward, tugging at the binders. "Leaf don't want tied. If finded, Leaf is fucked, for realz."

With a hand on the door, Kirsten stared at the pathetic creature in the van, aghast at the damage the drugs did to her. She wanted to leave the girl cuffed to the fan so she'd be here later, but knew the girl was right—in a literal sense. Leaving a young woman defenseless in a black zone exceeded her ability to be cruel. She leaned in and entered the code, removing them. Leaf reached for one of the jacket pockets, but Kirsten caught her hands.

"Look. I know this seems like a shitty choice between getting killed out here or possible jail time. If it were me, I'd take the nice clean cell and free food and be happy the bastard got what he deserved."

Leaf pouted at her. "Leaf no want chems, but Leaf knows she has chems and can't stop."

"Please wait here for me. I promise I'll help you as much as I can."

"Okay," whispered Leaf.

I could compel her to wait, but I'd be no better than Rene.

Kirsten picked up her helmet and backed out of the van, easing the doors closed to block Leaf's imploring stare. She removed her hair clip and fluffed her mane out into a curtain of wild blonde with both hands. After tucking her helmet under her left arm, she rested her right hand on the hanging submachine gun and did her best mimic of Leaf's strung out stagger.

The men hanging out around the courtyard didn't pay too much attention to her as she walked into view. She ducked into a narrow alley to the left of the hotel before anyone noticed the gloss black armor on her legs.

"What'cha got there?"

Kirsten whirled at the man's voice coming from behind her. A Son of Charon lurked in an alcove against the left wall in the shadow of a rectangular protrusion that blocked him from sight when she'd walked past. Bald with fluffy eyebrows and an unruly goatee, he folded his immense arms across his chest, his jacket creaking in protest.

"Huh?"

He pointed at the helmet. "Fancy."

"Oh..." *Holy shit that was close. Maybe I sounded high to him.* "Found it by a dead cop."

"Careful, they got trackers in 'em."

She belted a nervous giggle. "Yeah, right. Cops'll come in here. Bullshit."

The giant laughed his face red and his eyes into thin wrinkles. She hadn't noticed his combat rifle until his joviality tapped it against the wall.

"Hey, grab me a cold one, kid."

"Uhh, sure."

His surface thoughts surprised her with his motivation. He hadn't asked the girl to fetch him a beer as a sign of a female being subservient— the gang code kept him from leaving his watch station. *Wow, these guys are organized more than I thought.* She lifted an idea of how to go about getting inside from his thoughts before hurrying onward past the stacks of junk in the crammed alley. Piles of ancient computer terminals melted into discolored stains in various shades of white and green.

Holy crap, these things don't even have M3 sockets. They've got to be over a century old. How can the government just let this place rot so long?

Thirty feet later and around a corner, she found a dull brown door that she remembered from the sentry's thoughts of where to go. As soon as she opened the door, a man—painfully absent from the sentry's thoughts—grabbed her by the collar of the jacket and hauled her inside. He swung her around, put her back against the wall, and forced his tongue into her mouth.

Kirsten gagged on the taste of street whiskey. "Mmm!" The foulness of a body who hadn't seen the inside of an autoshower in years watered her eyes. She struggled with little success to shove him away as he squeezed the jacket into her armor over her breasts.

"Hey, what the shit? You got some hard-ass titties." He grabbed her again, made a grunt of confusion, then knocked. "Fuck, daz armor."

"Yes it is." She grabbed the handle at her side. "And this is a stunrod, asshole."

"Wha?"

Bwong.

The blue glowing tip emitted an eerie electrical chime as she cracked him across the side of the head. Kirsten couldn't help herself but whack him with it as payback for the forced kiss. The brief contact with the element only staggered him. He fell backward scratching at the wall for a handhold. Kirsten pounced, thrusting the tip into his chest. Bright azure sparks lapped at his T-shirt. He convulsed, flailing and trying to grab the air. His eyes rolled into his skull. Gurgling, he slumped and went still.

She spat, twice, trying to get the taste out of her mouth. Since she'd made it inside and did *not* want anything else going into her mouth, she put her helmet back on. *No sense hiding now.* Despite the risk it posed to be obvious, she happily shrugged out of the flea-infested jacket. More to keep someone from picking it up and pointing it at her, she kept Leaf's weapon. The psi armor gave her more confidence dealing with mortals, even if it she found it uncomfortable, heavy, and pinchy in all the wrong places. If she requisitioned a suit that fit—instead of borrowing Nila's— perhaps she could get used to it. Nicole certainly seemed to like her armor. *Too* much even. The woman didn't wear much more than a stim suit under it, claiming it became too hot.

Thinking about overheating made Kirsten feel too warm.

The helmet came back online in time to identify two figures on the other side of the wall before Kirsten opened another door. She hesitated, observing the three-dimensional amber silhouettes. *Oh, this is wonderful. Now that is damn handy.* One man and one woman leaned on either side of the doorway she needed to use. A pair of combat rifles leaned on the wall next to each figure, and both of them held a cylindrical object, probably a Synthbeer. Their motions suggested they carried on a rather flirtatious conversation.

I'd rather not kill them, SOC or not... They're compelled.

Kirsten eased her E-90 out of its holster and lined up the cobalt-blue sights on the woman's rifle. *If the sensor can penetrate this wall, so can a laser.* She aimed at the midpoint and fired. The beam sliced the rifle in two and its amber outline shimmered away. No longer a recognizable shape, the helmet electronics lost it amid background clutter.

"What the fuck was that?" shouted the man.

The woman's holographic image spun and looked down. "Fuckin' thing just exploded."

Too brief, they didn't see the laser. Kirsten's smile grew wider as the man backed away from his weapon, expecting the same thing.

Kirsten obliged him.

Unfortunately, that time, they both saw the streak of blue and came running. The woman burst through the door first, knocking it straight off its hinges. She pulled a small sword from a thigh sheath and rushed at Kirsten, hate burning from her eyes. The man followed close behind, without a weapon aside from his size and fists. Kirsten decided to take him out first; a Mind Blast peeled away from her brain with a sense of spine-wiggling discomfort similar to stepping barefoot in cold cat puke.

Her thoughts collided with his, and for a brief instant, her mind stuttered. Snippets of his recent past flashed by, back-feeding down the link as his brain came to an abrupt halt, choking on the overwhelming mass of information she forced into it. His charge became a stumble, which became standing and drooling. The woman, shrieking, dove at her.

Kirsten raised the stunrod, catching the incoming weapon. The woman's speed and bodyweight pushed her back into the wall. The edge of a UCF C39 BDB (boarding-party defense blade) hovered an inch from her faceplate. Growling, the woman shoved harder, almost forehead-to-helmet with her. Yellow light from the armored visor glistened in the sweat over her attacker's dark skin. Kirsten grunted, barely able to hold her back.

Is everyone stronger than me? Kirsten scowled, twisting. *Not like I ate well growing up.* The snarling woman pressed her into the wall, cracking plaster and shoving Kirsten downward toward the floor. Desperate for a distraction, Kirsten navigated the helmet interface with eye motions, going for the searchlights. The unexpected glare blinded the large woman. Kirsten shoved her up and left and slipped away to the right. The woman lurched into the wall, the gladius half buried in the old plaster.

"Bitch," yelled the gang woman, before wrenching the weapon free.

"*Stop.*" Kirsten leaned on the wall. "*Kneel.*"

Her brain reverberated with a brief shock, a membrane pierced, as the potency of a short-term suggestion overwhelmed Rene's lingering thralldom. Kirsten didn't have the time, nor the energy left to deprogram them right now.

"Sorry, but I'm in a bit of a hurry."

Kirsten became the Sleep-With-a-Side-of-Migraine faerie, and daintily tapped the woman on the head with the stunrod, then did the same to the still dazed and drooling man. Both gang punks collapsed unconscious. Dorian came out of the wall while she took a moment to socket a stimpak in the armor's injector port. Though she hadn't been injured, the shot would give her a boost of much-needed energy.

"There you are." He tromped over, circling her. "You hurt? What's with the girl in the van?"

Kirsten explained, euphoric for a few seconds at the rush of synthetic adrenaline. "You find anything?"

"He's on the thirty-sixth floor, and the stairway has a couple of IR mines in it."

She tapped the visor. "No problem."

"K… this is Rene. I still don't think you should do this."

"We're already here. Do you really want to let him get away *again*? His programming would've killed Shani someday when she pulled a gun on a cop. He forced Nila to help him escape and turned her into a mouse. He *killed* you. He sent these thugs after me who killed innocent people at Kajuraho. He almost made me shoot a little girl. This isn't *all* about you anymore. I want this son of a bitch."

"Yes. He killed me, but I don't want him to kill you, too."

Kirsten stared into his eyes. "Then watch my back."

TAKE NO CHANCES

D orian led the way up the stairs, pointing out the presence of a half-dozen detonators. Fortunately, the helmet's optics allowed Kirsten to see the infrared beam triggers. Each micro-charge projected a gleaming line of light across the stairs. Tiny flakes of broken glass from destroyed ceiling lights littered the concrete stairway in a glittering field of razor sharp snow. Empty autoinjectors and dried-out narcotic derm patches gathered in clusters of dust strewn with paw prints.

"I feel bad for these cats."

"Those are rat tracks." Dorian chuckled.

She drew in a breath, tensing.

"Really? After hanging off the side of Intera tower, taking a nosedive out of an exploding parking deck, a large rat scares you?"

"They're icky." She pouted like a nine-year-old, and then laughed. "Kidding. I'm no stranger to rats, but these are like twice the size of the ones I'm used to."

"Shh. Men around the next corner."

Serious face. Kirsten drew her E-90 and edged toward the end of the stairs. At the next landing, she whirled around the corner and aimed at four men in Sons of Charon jackets, all standing amid a thick haze of yellow vapor from narcotic inhalers. The air reeked of Flowerbasket.

"Nobody move," said Kirsten. "Drop your weapons and keep your hands where I can see them."

A little over ten seconds after she appeared, the first one reacted to her, and blinked.

"'Zat a cop?"

The other three looked.

"Naw, man, you're seein shit," said a skeleton wrapped in skin and hair.

"I see it, too," added another.

"Wait, you're right." Skeleton reached for a gun.

"Don't do it." She aimed at him.

Dorian sauntered up to them, waving his hands over their weapons and drawing the power away. A dead energy cell couldn't activate an electronic firing circuit. Kirsten relaxed.

As casual as if on a range, the four men pulled weapons and pointed them at her.

"There's four of us and one of you. Tell ya what." The pudgy one shifted toward her. "Bend over and we'll let you outta here."

"I don't think so." She smirked. "Might want to look behind you."

All four turned, squinting at the empty hallway.

White vapor rippled up Dorian's legs, surrounding him as he forced his essence into the material world. For a moment, he took on the appearance of the pile of meat that had been slumped in the driver seat of his car that awful day.

Even expecting something drastic, Kirsten cringed away from the sight with a howl of revulsion. Once the shock wore off, the realization of *what* she saw hit her, and she choked back tears. The pudgy man fainted, the other three barreled past her, screaming as they hurried down the stairs. When Kirsten risked a peek, Dorian had gone back to normal. He offered an apologetic frown.

Her pathetic stare of pity caused him to turn away.

"I made it look worse than it was for shock value. Come on, don't be like that." He took a step. "Rene is just down this hallway."

She pushed aside her grief for him and hurried up the stairs and past the door. Dead lights jutted out from the wall every twenty feet on curved bronze rods carved to resemble plants. Stains of every imaginable shade of brown covered everything, accompanied by the cloying stink of rotting food. The fading maroon carpet muted her steps as she crept forward, gripping her E-90 in both hands.

"You almost look like a cop today."

Her eyes narrowed. "I'm doing normal cop stuff today," she whispered. "Going after a living man. Dorian, please try to make sure he stays that way."

His face flared with anger. "You sure care a lot about the bastard that killed me. Never did understand how people get so wound up about the *rights* of murderers and how much they suffer. They didn't give a rat's ass for the rights or feelings of the people they killed."

"You're wrong." Kirsten softened her gaze at him. "I care about you. I don't want you to lose your... I don't want to lose you to the Harbingers. People make a big deal about that because if we don't, we're no better than they are. What's that saying? Eye for an eye and everyone goes blind?"

Dorian turned on his heel, stomping to the only closed door in their section of hallway. "Need I remind you I am already lost? You're still alive. Stop agonizing over what can never happen."

"Fine then. I want Ashford to mind wipe him so he spends the rest of his life sucking his thumb trying to remember what conscious control over shitting was like. I want him to forget what being psionic is."

"I can live with that."

She blinked at him.

Frustration seethed out on a sigh. "You know what I mean."

Kirsten hurried over to the indicated room and took a covered position by the doorjamb. She nodded once. Dorian stuck his head into the room despite the closed door.

"I think he recently finished having sex. There's a noncombatant on the right side about twenty yards from the door on a bed. If the look on her face is any indication, he's programmed her to worship him. Other than the woman, he's alone. This door leads to a small entertainment room. The bedroom is beyond. Balcony on the left side, windows are op—make that gone."

Kirsten took three heavy breaths and stepped away from the wall, facing the door. She raised her leg to boot it open, but stalled at Dorian holding up a hand.

"Please don't hesitate. Don't try to butt heads with his power. Promise me, the instant you feel him trying to do anything to your brain, you will shoot him."

She stared at the warped reflection of her face along the silver housing of her sidearm. The little metal prong she always ignored gleamed. With an expression like a kid at Christmas finding one more present, she pulled a length of microfilament wire out of the weapon's handle and tugged it out to about four feet. A few seconds of fumbling around the side of the helmet found the socket. Soon, a tiny display window appeared in her vision containing a view as if from the laser's barrel, complete with cross-hair.

"That's perfect." He grinned. "No line of sight and—"

"No suggestion," she finished.

Kirsten kicked the door open—right through Dorian—and charged in.

"Rene Bollard! Police! On the ground. Don't move, don't speak!"

She shouldered into a pea green wall at the far end of the entertainment room, poking the E-90 around the arch into the bedroom. The floating window in her view blurred as she panned to the right, finding Rene at the side of the bed with a woman in a headlock—gun at her temple. The woman wore only a sycophantic grin, her legs threaded among white silk sheets. She stroked Rene's arm, adoring even the touch that used her as a human shield. Inside, the fragrance of jasmine and incense overwhelmed the everpresent foulness of the building, so strong she tasted it.

He shifted to stand behind her more, pulling her in front of himself by the hair. "I must commend your determination, though I lament your foolishness."

The woman moaned as if turned on by his rough handling. She rubbed her breast with one hand. "Yes, Rene. That feels *so* good when you do it like that."

Kirsten's mind raced. She couldn't see his the weapon behind the hostage. "I'm not here to kill you, Rene. I'm here to bring you in alive."

Dorian stomped toward him, shaking with rage.

"You are a natural blonde, I see. Do you think I'm an idiot?" Rene jerked the woman's head back, making her moan in ecstasy. "There's no 'bringing in alive' here. Nice little fascist police state you people have going here. Only problem is whenever someone stands up to it, they execute them."

"You killed a police officer!" shouted Kirsten.

"Don't you mean an agent of oppression?" Rene chuckled.

Rene's grainy image in the targeting window tilted his head. The well-practiced, disingenuous grin of a con man a decade past his prime wrinkled his cheeks. He edged behind the head of the bed, pulling the woman up to her knees, drawing forth another moan of ecstasy.

"Oh, Rene… you're being silly. Stop poking it in my back. You're quite a ways too far up." The woman grinned and slid a hand down between her legs, massaging herself.

Kirsten tried to put the virtual cross-hair on his face, aiming for a four-inch-wide space that wouldn't strike the hostage. She held her fire, not trusting her aim.

"Rene, you know as long as there is an innocent life in danger I won't hesitate to shoot. If you kill her, you only guarantee it."

"I don't believe you." He tightened his fist in her hair. The woman emitted a gasp of passion. "If I kill her and you shoot me, it's murder. I know how you are. You don't want the stain on your soul. It's amazing what a god can learn from his worshippers."

"Can't see the gun," said Dorian with a hint of growl in his voice. He circled to the left for a better angle.

"I'm going to kill this whore and make you watch. Then I'm going to pay a visit to that little whelp of yours, what's his name?" Rene tilted his head in contemplation. "No, I'm not going to hurt the darling little boy. I'll make him kill you."

Rage boiled in her gut; somehow, she found the strength to swallow it. "Now you're the one who's lying. You won't dare leave this sector. You're scared, Rene, scared out of your mind. You can't go near the city proper because every police officer knows you're a cop killer. You know what they do to cop killers don't you, Rene? There won't be enough left of you to fill a synthbeer can. Your only ticket out of this shithole is me."

The woman squirmed, craning herself up to kiss Rene on the neck as she continued pleasuring herself. Kirsten tried not to watch. Rene seemed equally as disinterested at that moment.

"So why now? Why you? After all these years, they finally found someone stupid enough to follow me here?"

"It's deliberate misinformation, Rene. We want people to think we avoid black zones. That way, we know right where to look. And stop lying to yourself. We both know you can't stand it here in such squalor. You're more miserable in this filth than you would be in a holding facility."

Kirsten still didn't trust using a virtual targeting system to put a laser blast into a two-inch section of forehead. *Come on, come on, stand up a little more.*

"I don't think so. You know the thing about police officers' brains? They're small. Not a lot of room in there. I've been in enough cop heads to know the truth. You're all petrified of the *real* world. Laws? Your fake society? It's all smoke and mirrors. Everything is politics. This is *old world*. Like the Badlands. *This* is how humanity is meant to be. The strong rule the weak. Power is the only true law. I've seen something greater than you can imagine. It's out *there*, waiting for those who understand how the world is supposed to work."

"Rene, whatever drugs you've taken, they're pretty damn strong."

He barked a condescending laugh. "Stupid girl. Why did you really come out here? Were you that dead cop's side bitch? I thought he was bedding the nice little thing he had in the car with him. She was quite accommodating actually, gave me a ride, cooked me dinner, we had great sex... pity she doesn't remember it."

Fury leaked from Dorian's eyes as a spectral glow.

Rene jumped as a portable food reassembler to his right sparked and shut down. Two freestanding construction lights went next.

"Why don't you ask him yourself, Rene?" shouted Kirsten. "He's right in front of you."

She swiveled around the corner. Dorian blocked her direct view, but didn't appear in the digital targeting box.

The hostage moaned, reaching for Rene's nether regions. Her other hand moved up to rub her breast. "It's cold in here, Rene, my love. Why don't you warm me?"

A blaze of white vapor billowed around Dorian's outline; he stepped closer, out of the astral realm. His apparition scared any trace of flesh tone out of Rene's cheeks. The Frenchman shoved the woman forward onto her chest and jumped back, firing twice at Dorian. Two emerald laser streaks sizzled in the air, holing the wall at Kirsten's left. She yelped and dove into the room, taking cover behind a marble-topped table that she knocked over forward.

Rene fired again, the first shot going high, the next disrupting Dorian's left shoulder for a second. Showing no reaction at all to the hit, Dorian leapt at Rene, emitting a primal growl of hatred. Kirsten huddled behind the table as wild laser blasts streaked overhead. Seconds later, the firing paused, and she popped up, trying to get a bead on Rene who circled the bed in an effort to evade a furious ghost.

A chance step on a piece of loose rug spared Rene from Kirsten's first shot by dumping him on the floor. When he spun to face her, she ducked, breaking eye contact. Her helmet tried to show his position as an amber outline, but it flickered in and out, bits of errant pixels. A slab of two-inch-thick stone too dense for the sensors to penetrate.

Dorian let out a war cry. Kirsten pictured him diving over the bed. She popped up and aimed at Rene the same instant Dorian flew into a tackle. He hit Rene hard enough to knock him staggering, but lacked the solidity to take him down. His ghostly body phased through Rene, leaving him coated in a thin layer of clear slime. Dorian landed on his chest, gasping for breath. The wispy vapor around him—and his transparency—stopped.

Rene looked around, unable to find him. "What game is this?"

Kirsten ducked as Rene spun in her direction, but kept the E-90 over the top of the table to watch him.

A thin line of spittle flew from Rene's lip. "You. You're in my head, making me see him."

She startled as he fired at the table, testing the laser's chances at penetrating marble. Three small glowing orange spots appeared one after the next in front of her. The sight didn't fill her with confidence.

"No, Rene. I'm not making you see things. That's really Dorian's ghost. He's a little angry with you."

A fourth orange glow swelled an inch to the left of the first. "You don't expect me to believe in ghosts, do you?"

"She might not, but I do," said Dorian, projecting his voice into the world. The deeper-than-normal timbre and eerie echo made even Kirsten shiver.

Rene startled, aiming toward the open balcony doors. "How are you doing that, bitch?"

Kirsten shifted her E-90 left, following him, using it more as a camera than a weapon. The next time Rene startled and jumped to look at something else, she popped up.

Dorian manifested again.

"Jusqu'à ce que nous reverrons, mon ami," said Dorian in the same haunting voice. He stalked at Rene. "Do you remember when you said those words to me?"

The Frenchman screamed, falling into a stumbling backpedal. "You...." He stared at the woman on the bed. "Shoot the bitch. Kill her." Rene's eyes flared with a brief amethyst light. The woman's amorous smile faded away to a zombie's emotionless face. Still backing away, Rene tossed the pistol into the naked woman's lap before running for the balcony, as if ready to fling himself to his death to get away from Dorian.

Kirsten fired two quick pulses, trying to leg him, but missed both times. A green beam streaked past her eyes. Her body limp save for one raised arm, the woman on the bed fired a second time into the wall over her head. Kirsten ducked behind the table before the woman could figure out how to aim.

Every three seconds, the soft *bzzz* of an E-86 laser pistol broke the silence. The glowing orange spot in the marble grew.

A sudden wet *splat*—like a watermelon dropped from great height—made her jump. *What the hell was that?* Three seconds later, a *boom* thundered in the distance. Kirsten gawked at the wall above her head spattered with small gory chunks and droplets of blood racing each other to the floor.

The unmistakable crumpling *thud* of a dead body falling shook the floor.

She recoiled, trapped between a horrifying wall and a glowing slab of marble. "What the hell happened, Dorian?"

A brief pause of silence settled over the room, broken only by two hums of a laser pistol firing.

"Rene's head just exploded," said Dorian. "It's completely gone."

"Greetings from your guardian angel, kiddo," said a woman over her comm link.

I know that voice...

29

RECKONING

Kirsten knelt behind a two-inch slab of marble, whimpering at the growing collection of burning orange spots ranging from new and bright to almost too dim to see. The naked woman, the right half of her body spattered red with what had once been inside Rene Bollard's head, didn't react at all to the gore. Once, every three seconds, she triggered a blast of emerald laser into the marble table with the precision of an assembly line doll. A thumb-sized fragment of brain slid from her temple over a cheek, fell to her chest, and slipped into her lap. The shots continued, not realizing or caring that she etched only shallow grooves in the dense material.

"We meet again, Rene," said Dorian, seconds before the sound of a fistfight started.

Rene, hollow and echoing, screamed. Fear became confusion. Grunting, cursing (French and English), and more grunting rattled around the back end of the room to the metronome of a laser pistol set to repeat.

"Dorian… Little help here, I don't want to shoot this woman."

Kirsten kept herself low, listening to the brawl happening out of her sight. Laser blast, punch, laser blast, groan, laser blast, cursing, a punch; another laser blast.

"Dorian," she shouted. "I need backup, now!"

Rene's face came through the marble, transparent. She rolled away with a gasp, flattening against the wall. She cringed, at having pressed herself into gore. The sight of ghosts had become a matter of routine. As a little girl when she had to think about turning it on, they looked like transparent apparitions. When her skill increased and she started seeing them all the time, ghosts appeared opaque, barely distinguishable from living people. Only her psionic talent to sense them as ghosts broke the illusion. Whenever they breached a solid object, they became transparent again. Seeing a ghost look like a *ghost* harkened back to bad childhood scares. She despised her mother again for a few seconds. *What kind of parent blames their child for creating the monster under the bed rather than comforts her?* Another laser blast into the marble reined in her wandering mind.

Rene's writhing form slid closer, groaning. Dorian flung him down and pinned him in a perfect perp-hold.

Bzzrt. Another glowing orange spot appeared.

Kirsten scooted lower, back against the wall, boots apart. "Dorian? Would you please?" She gestured with the E-90 at the table.

Dorian twisted around to peer at the source of the rhythmic electronic noise. More marble glowed orange than didn't. The woman had had been hitting the same spot often enough to make it rather bright. The metronome changed from thrums to soft clicks.

"What the hell is this?" yelled Rene. "How did you pull me into this dream?

"Got it." Dorian resumed throttling Rene. Years of pent up angst released in the form of Rene's face bouncing repeatedly off the rug.

Rene wailed, swatting feebly at Dorian. "This is not real."

Kirsten peered over the edge with the gun cam, confirming the laser pistol dead before she stood. "Any idea what happened to him?"

"Sniper, I think." Dorian paused the beating long enough to glance at the balcony.

"Stop this at once!" shouted Rene.

Kirsten squatted over him. "You can't suggest anymore, shithead. You're dead."

"Kill yourself. Go dive out the window."

Dorian grumbled, digging his stunrod into Rene's throat. "I miss being able to use a decent pain submission hold. Doesn't work without joints."

Rene scrabbled at the carpet. "I'm gonna wake up from this, bitch. When I do, that little bastard of yours is…" His voice trailed off as he noticed the fibers didn't react to his clawing motions.

Kirsten scowled at his threat to Evan.

She beckoned.

They heard.

Dorian, leaning all his weight on Rene to hold him down, lifted his head to look up at her. The emotionless 'I win' look on her face appeared to scare him. She toned it down at the worry in her partner's eyes, and set her E-90 back in its holster. The incessant clicking from the bed continued. Seconds later, the room dimmed and grew ominous.

"What the hell is this?" Rene shrieked.

The shadows thickened and roiled, bubbling out of the walls like smoke. Whispers rose out of the corners.

Dorian leaned back, peeling the screaming Frenchman off the floor. "Maybe soften him up a bit for them?"

"No. He's too new, and I'm too pissed off. He wouldn't survive one hit."

A solitary harbinger spiraled up out of the floor as a plume of black energy that gradually thickened and took on a quasi-humanoid shape, so tall its head reached the ceiling. Wisps of darkness scuttled about as it glided closer. Shimmering silver eyes, unblinking, regarded Rene.

Dorian shivered, but wrestled his killer up to stand.

"What the fuck is that thing?" shrieked Rene, his form blurring from abject terror.

"They go easier on you downstairs if you accept it." Kirsten bowed in deference to the Harbinger.

All too willing to distance himself, Dorian released his grip and took a step back. Rene ran for the door, skidding to a halt as a second, smaller Harbinger appeared. He doubled back and skirted around the huge one to the balcony, almost falling over in his attempt to stop as three more Harbingers came up out of the patio and glided in the window. Another four emerged from the right side wall, phasing past the oblivious gore-spattered woman.

Rene whirled, darting about in search of escape, but the Harbingers had formed an impenetrable wall around him. With nowhere to go, he let off a crazed scream and charged at the smallest one. The swarm engulfed him; shadowy claws tore his ethereal flesh. A mass of darkening shadow gathered close, dragging the wailing soul down into floor. Kirsten turned her back on the sight, shivering and closing her eyes. After a moment, the phantasmal whispering ceased and the mood returned to normal.

The woman on the bed kept aiming at Kirsten as she walked over, finger still clicking even when the barrel touched Kirsten's armor.

"Stop shooting me."

Without a word, the woman let her arm fall limp into her lap. Kirsten sat on the edge of the ancient queen-sized bed with a solid mattress—the kind of thing people slept on before Comforgel (and its competitors) took over the world. A few minutes of eye contact later, Kirsten broke the mental link and sagged forward.

"Clear, left. Elements two, five, breach," said the same female voice that called herself a guardian angel, muted and distant in the hallway.

Weary, Kirsten lifted her head to look at two men fast-walking in the derelict apartment's front door. Head to toe in black with individual opaque lenses over each eye, the men advanced while sweeping compact rifles over the room. Infrared beams from targeting optics glinted in the dust. One aimed at her; she raised her hands.

The man nodded at her after a second and lowered his weapon, then moved to check the bathroom. He returned, letting his rifle fall to hang on an automatic harness, which pulled it against his chest. "Confirm clear. Suspect neutralized. One friendly, one civilian."

"Elements one, four, pull it in," said the same woman.

A high-pitched whine, unspooling cable, came from the balcony. Two more men in similar suits landed without a noise and walked in, followed a second later by a tall white-haired woman entering via the front door. A blank slab of black metal covered most of her face, with two small camera lenses at the corners. The armored visor whirred and lifted on thin motorized struts, exposing her face.

"Carter?" Kirsten's memory found a match for the voice. "Senior Operative Carter?" Used to dealing with enlisted Tactical and Division 1, it took her a few seconds to remember the woman outranked her. She blinked, stood, and saluted. "Ma'am."

The woman returned the salute almost casually on her way past Kirsten to appraise the body. A rifle as thick as a woman's forearm perched snug and vertical against the right side of an ultra-thin armored backpack. Lines and grooves in the weapon's housing hinted it could extend from its current length of three feet to perhaps six.

She shot Rene...

One of the men appraised the spatter on the walls and the mostly headless body. "Think Hardin will take this as your sniper qualification?

1784 yards with an MSP-18? Those modulars are a bitch for anything past 1200."

"Yeah, gimme a dedicated longball gun any day. Can always carry a sub for close-in work." Another man kicked the body. "Can't tell if you hit the nostril or not, ain't enough left. Bet's off."

Carter laughed in a sort of haughty high-society way that rankled Kirsten's distaste for the wealthy. "You still owe me lunch. I have scope video, and it was 1792 *meters.*"

"Where the hell did you find a shooting platform with line of sight on this shithole from that far away?"

"Airlift cable, ten feet below Whisper 12..." Carter stepped over the body, in line with the window and pointed with a karate chop gesture. "That way."

The largest man shook his head at the ground. "Horseshit. You expect me to believe you made this shot hanging off a goddamn cable from a whisper?"

Carter tapped her visor. "I've got scope-cam video."

All four men looked at each other.

Kirsten leaned to Dorian and whispered at a mouse's volume. "Division 9 must be nice. I can't imagine officers taking backtalk like that from enlisted."

"They're *all* officers, K. Plus they're covert ops. Wetwork stuff. It's soul-crushing work, so they blow off steam in various ways."

"Not as nice as it looks." S.O. Carter swung around and stepped over Rene for the second time. Her expression could have been amusement or annoyance depending on how the light hit her lips. "I do owe you a bit of thanks for leading us to him."

Rene's former lover whimpered, trying to grab the sheet without moving fast enough to attract attention.

Carter yanked the sheets from the bed, giving them a flip to check for hidden weapons. Satisfied, she threw it over the trembling figure. "Get dressed."

"I'm sorry I didn't trust you guys were really trying to find him. It happened so long ago."

"It's tricky to pin down someone with his talent set. Usually, we leave this sort of thing to you guys, but I've never seen a Zero with the testicular fortitude to set foot in a place like this."

"Umm. I'll accept young and foolish." Kirsten stood off the bed. "Umm, Carter, can I ask a strange question?"

"Go for it," said the woman, toneless.

"Are you related to Director Carter?"

S.O Carter chuckled. "If I had a credit for every time someone asked me that... No. She's not my grandmother. And I'm about as psionic as a brick."

Kirsten managed a nervous laugh.

The former hostage streaked across the room to the sofa, from which she grabbed a T-shirt and jeans.

"It was you on Eze's terminal, wasn't it? You told him to let me do it."

"I can see why you made I-Ops so young." Carter winked.

Dorian turned away, stifling the urge to laugh.

"So that's it then? You shot him in the head." Kirsten sagged.

"It's the only way we have to deal with someone with his particular talent set. I don't care what kind of psionics someone has... from 2000 yards away, a sniper rifle wins every time. He killed a cop; he would have been executed anyway. I merely saved us some tax credits. And I know you're squeamish about it, so I spared you the hassle." S.O. Carter winked, turned, and traced a whirlybird gesture with her right index finger. "Okay people, wrap it up."

In the time Kirsten had been speaking to Carter, two of the men had black-bagged Rene's remains. They hauled him to the balcony and attached the sack to lines that pulled it up and out of sight.

"The front's clear. You should have a safe trip out if you move soon." Carter went for the door in the same mesmerizing graceful ballet she called a walk, every tiny motion calculated and perfect.

Dorian leaned to the side to keep her in sight a few seconds longer, making no subtle act of staring at her tight-fitting ballistic stealth armor. "For once, I almost regret being dead."

"You hound," Kirsten muttered, then waved at the former hostage. "Come on. We are leaving. I have a feeling you'll want to keep your eyes closed when we go out the door, probably going to be a courtyard full of bodies."

"We stacked them nice and neat," said one of the Division 9 operators, offering a butler's bow on his way out the door.

The woman gave up searching for her shoes and stared at Kirsten. "Will someone at least tell me where I am and why I was naked? And what day is it?"

"Ugh." Kirsten walked over and put a hand on the woman's shoulder. "You've been abducted by a psionic criminal. I need to bring you back to the station to get checked out and go over any testimony you can provide. If you need some time to gather yourself before talking to us, we'll provide you a place to stay."

"I don't remember much," said the woman. "But I'll try."

Dorian cringed, glancing at the bed. "That's probably a kindness."

KIRSTEN YANKED ON THE VAN'S DOORS, DRAGGING THEM OPEN WITH A RUSTY squeal. The pile of trash stacked against the front seats fluttered in the wind. She hung her head and sighed.

"Poor kid. I hope she knows what she's doing."

"Leaf's not a kid." The trash moved. Bright neon green hair emerged from between two slabs of waterlogged cardboard. "Leaf is seventeen, and hiding."

Kirsten sighed with relief, then leaned in to help the girl out of the broken van.

"Where's my jacket? I had some…"

"Sorry, I lost it."

"Wren, stop dawdling. You have two hostile augs coming in from the west." An unfamiliar man's voice crackled out of a speaker in her helmet from a phantom channel.

"I have two civilians to escort out and one's barefoot."

No answer.

She looked at the crying woman and Leaf. "We gotta move. Borg coming at us."

Kirsten shoved the two civilians ahead of her, keeping an eye to the rear as they scrambled down the street. Howls and whistles echoed from the buildings everywhere.

A deep voice from the right called out, "Here, titty, titty!"

She drew her E-90 and swung to aim at a seven foot tall man covered in a suit of armor made of various scavenged parts. He hefted a small over-the-shoulder anti-armor missile, somewhat pointing it at her.

"Stop runnin', bitches. Unlike you, I *don't* care if you're alive for the fun part."

Shit. Kirsten put her gun away and dove into the former hostage, lifting her over one shoulder to spare her naked feet from running over a minefield of dangerous sharpness. On wings of fear, Kirsten managed up to a loping sprint despite the extra hundred-or-so pounds. Leaf ran beside her in a disoriented sway, sometimes flinching from things that didn't exist. The missile-toting man let out a scream of anger and chased after them, banging his hand on the launch tube. She couldn't tell if he beat on a malfunctioning piece of junk or simply wanted to make nose.

One block over, she hung a left turn at random to break line of sight.

Heavy rumbling drew nearer, vibrating the road. Kirsten decided to gamble and turned left, heading toward it. Seconds later, a huge six-wheeled A3V came skidding around the corner a block away.

"It's friendly, go!" Kirsten shouted, setting the woman back on her feet and shoving at their backs. "Run to the A3V!"

A ring-mounted cannon with two short barrels swiveled in their direction. Behind it, a blue Division 5 helmet peeked up from a hatch. Two flares of brilliant blue flames shot from the stubby barrels with a deafening growl. Tracer ammo streaked overhead, setting off a rippling array of explosions among the ranks of twenty or more men running up behind them.

The former hostage screamed and hit the ground in a ball at the tremendously loud barrage. Leaf tucked low and sprinted hard, heading toward the A3V—and right past it. Kirsten grabbed the woman by the hand and dragged her along. A couple cyborgs came out to play, so Kirsten also ran right by the armored vehicle. Two blocks later, she found Leaf standing in the middle of the street frozen, petrified at the sight of the police line at the edge of the black zone.

Kirsten jogged up to her. "It's okay, Jennifer. They're not going to hurt you. They'll understand why you did it… if they even think to investigate."

"You not tell them what Leaf did?" asked Leaf.

Kirsten bit her lip, again hoping the Harbingers cared *why* people killed. "If I was in your position, I can't say I would've been tempted to do the same thing. I'm too squeamish though, so I probably would've just run away. But… I understand. No. If you want to tell them, that's one thing. I won't make trouble for you. Not over a piece of human garbage who could do *that* to his own daughter."

Leaf hugged her and burst into tears.

"C'mon, kid. That Nightcandy has done some real damage. I hope it's not too late for them to fix it." Kirsten threw an arm around Leaf, and walked both women toward the waiting cops.

"You confuse me, Kirsten." Dorian walked up beside her. "All your whining"—he winked—"about not wanting to kill, and you're making plenty of excuses for what this girl did. Can you understand why I did some of the things I did now?"

"Oh, he's gonna try and make it," shouted the A3V gunner, a second before opening up with another burst. Kirsten cringed at the rumble of the heavy cannon and distant explosions. "Yee haw. Got 'im."

After handing the former hostage off to Division 1 with a transport request—she wanted to have Ashford check her out. Even though, she half expected he would erase all memory of being kidnapped. Rumor had it, victims of psionic crime often had their memories cleared to reduce the number of people who viewed psionics as a threat. Whether or not it really happened, she didn't know for sure. The idealist in her didn't believe the stories, but she couldn't fully put it aside either.

She comforted Leaf for a little while brought her over to the medical team stationed a safe distance behind the permanent barricade. Eventually, she returned to her patrol craft and glared at the clouds.

"Eye for an eye and all that? I don't understand. They say peace and love, and forgive and turn the other cheek. It all turns to bullshit when they see something they don't like." *My, these boots are shiny.* "What happened to the whole 'he who is without sin cast the first stone' thing? Or She who is without psionics burn her own hands on the stove first."

Dorian leaned on the car at her side, gazing up at the same blob of smog. "I executed four people. One was similar to Rene. Piece of trash named Eric Holm. He made women do whatever he wanted, kept them for days or weeks as pets. When he finished with them, he made them forget. His youngest victim was thirteen."

Dorian sighed. "I can still see his face the moment he realized he was about to die. But no, I don't regret doing it."

"Four? Nila said three." She tilted her head.

"Farhad Rahman was an astral. He would project and inhabit the body of living people. He started with civilians, but worked his way up to where he would possess patrol officers and commit crimes. Two of them died." He pulled his gaze back down from the sky and flashed a wistful smile. "There were six of us there. Not one of us wanted to take that bastard back alive. I'm pretty sure mine was the kill shot."

Kirsten put a hand on his arm.

"Number three... Kevin Andrew Baxter. He wasn't even psionic, just a med school washout who figured he could make a living by jumping people in dark alleys to steal cyberware. Sometimes he would harvest organs. Son of a bitch had a particular fondness for teens. Younger parts sell for more money."

Kirsten choked up. "If he wasn't psionic, how did you get the case?"

"The case walked up to me in a pair of torn jeans and a stolen shirt. I think the boy was fourteen. Saw the uniform, didn't understand what kind of cop I was. Said some creepy man was following him. I checked it out. Kid thought he was being stalked by a perv, so I peeked into the bastard's head and saw what he really wanted to do to the boy." Dorian's glare hardened, perhaps the same expression he had on when he killed Kevin Baxter. "I explained it to Captain Lee, was totally honest with her. They wrote it off as the suspect pulling a weapon on me. Hey, the boy's alive still."

"I'm sorry you had to do that. Do I even want to know what the fourth one did?"

Dorian's eyes froze over with a thousand-yard stare. "Shani."

Kirsten clamped a hand over her mouth to stifle a gasp. Only one thought came to mind of what someone might have done to her to warrant execution. "Oh, no…"

A spectral tear glimmered at the corner of his right eye. "No. Not that. No one hurt Shani. I killed the son of a bitch who attacked Nila seven years ago."

30

DEAD MAN HACKING

Evan whined into the pillow at unwanted consciousness. A few seconds later, his right eye peeled open. Whining again, he rolled over, narrowing his eye at the clock. He closed it and let out a heavy sigh. Hands balled into fists, he stretched, arching his back with a tiny grunt of displeasure at no longer being asleep. When the post-stretch paralysis faded, he sat up and pulled the sheets off his legs. For some minutes, he stared at his toes past a curtain of sand-colored hair.

His brain at last registered the chill of the room and he loosed a disgruntled moan of protest before standing up. One hand pressed to the side of his face, he staggered into the kitchenette, grabbing a chair as he passed, and dragging it to the counter. He hiked his pajama bottoms up, then used the chair as an impromptu stepladder. Still ready to pass out, he swayed on his feet atop the chair for a few seconds, staring at his reflection swaying side to side in the gloss black door of the food reassembler.

Evan reached one finger forward until it touched his reflection. The device beeped with each tap at its control panel. He tottered forward, forehead against cold glass, and napped for ten seconds while the machine worked. A louder beep that indicated it had finished woke him up. He snapped his head away from the door and stared at the offending machine, forgetting why it made noise.

"Oh, yeah."

He pulled opened the 'sem and seized a mug of coffee in a two-handed grip. Holding it under his nose, he took in a great breath, savoring its scent with his eyes closed. After two slurps of the too-hot-to-chug liquid, he set the cup on the counter and climbed up next to it. Balancing on his knees, he reached into the cabinet for a bowl and lowered himself back to his unsteady perch. He placed the empty bowl in the reassembler and dialed up sweetened oatmeal with honey and blueberries. He stood on the chair sipping coffee while the machine printed out his breakfast. Once it beeped again, he carried the bowl to the table, sat, merrily munching hot, sweet oatmeal while sipping coffee.

The coffee woke him enough to realize how badly he had to pee. He fidgeted and squirmed, swishing his feet back and forth while sending an annoyed glare at the bathroom door and the continuous thrum of the autoshower. With a whimper, he squeezed his legs tighter and focused on eating. As soon as the machine noise stopped, he looked up with a wide grin and bounded out of the chair.

The bathroom door slid open. Kirsten stepped out wearing a white robe, her face bright red. The sight of her stopped him in his tracks; head cocked, he blinked up at her.

"Why are you red? Is the water too hot?" He tilted his head to the other side as she made a strange noise and the color in her cheeks darkened.

"Uhh." Her voice quivered. "Yeah. The water was too hot. It's okay now. I fixed it."

Not having the patience to delay the urgency keeping him bouncing, he ran past her into the bathroom.

———

KIRSTEN TOOK ADVANTAGE OF THE CLOSED DOOR TO FLING OFF THE bathrobe and wriggle into her just-cleaned uniform. By the time she'd finished getting dressed, Evan draped himself against the doorframe wearing a stupid grin of relief in addition to his pajama pants. He ran into a hug; she picked him off his feet and sat on the foot end of the Comforgel pad with him standing between her knees.

"Is that coffee I smell?"

"You said my face needed coffee." He shrugged. "So I made it."

"You're too little for coffee." She pulled him up, dropping him on the bed with a gelatinous *splat*, then tickling him into a giggling fit. "I meant you had a face that looked like a person in dire need of coffee."

As his gasping laughter subsided, he stuck his tongue out. "What's the difference?"

"The difference is you're nine. We can talk about coffee again when you're closer to twelve… or sixteen."

"Aww, but I like it."

Maybe he is *my kid.* She ruffled his hair. "Did you finish your breakfast?"

"Yeah."

"Okay, get cleaned up and dressed."

He gathered clothes and disappeared into the bathroom. Soon, the autoshower whirred to life. Kirsten stretched out on the bed, trying to resist the lure of sleep as she gazed at ceiling tiles. Arms stretched to the sides, she lay quiet, listening to Evan recite lines from his favorite holovid wizard.

"I can't believe I'm going to say this." She exhaled and swallowed an ounce of disgust at her mother. "If there *is* anything up there, please watch over him."

DORIAN PEERED INTO THE BACK SEAT FOR A FEW SECONDS BEFORE GIVING her a quizzical look with his thumb pointed over his shoulder. "What happened to Vikram?"

Kirsten let go of both sticks long enough to throw her hands up in the air. "He's a damned idiot." She guided the patrol craft out of the parking deck, shifted to hover mode, and climbed. "While you were scoping out the hotel, Icarus decided to pay us a visit."

He paled.

"Relax. I had it handled." On a gentle ascent, she poked at the NavMap console and programmed a route to the Local Regional Tech Center, then stared in silence at the car in front of them. "He knew."

"I wouldn't worry too much about it. According to legend, demons can sense a person's deepest fears. When they try to use your mother against you—"

"No, not about Mother. Icarus knew I seem to be able to call Harbingers." She absentmindedly flicked her thumbnail over the button on the stick. "He wanted me to call them. Wanted to *surrender*."

"Probably trying to fool you into lowering your guard."

"Vikram said the same thing… right before he went completely nuts." The navigation system chimed, warning of an upcoming turn. "I believed Icarus. He seemed genuine. Vikram wouldn't stop… I had to smack him."

Dorian laughed. "I've been wanting to smack that guy for a while. You, umm, got rid of him?"

After she rolled level out of the turn, she exhaled. "No, I didn't hit him that hard, only enough to get his attention. He ran off. Icarus, too."

"Great. So much for hacker on a hook. What does the RTC have to do with this?"

Kirsten dove out of the hover lane, flying down toward the blinding white sprawl of the Division 2 Regional Tech Center. From the air, the building resembled an asterisk, a central node with five wings stretching away. All manner of antennas, dishes, and equipment studded the roof, as well as an enormous transmitter dish at the center, big enough to link with Mars.

"I want their help finding Vikram again."

"How would the eggheads possibly help you find a ghost?"

Kirsten winked, aiming for an open parking space on the southwest arm. "Never underestimate the power of a geek on a mission."

AN ELEVATOR AND TWO PALE GREY HALLWAYS LATER, HER MOOD WOUND UP in step with the dark cloud following behind and above her. The last time she stopped at a tech center, word got around within seconds of her landing that a Zero had entered the building. People peeked around corners and out of cubes, as if curious about a wild tiger roaming their hallways. As in, they wanted to see it, but simultaneously feared attracting its notice.

Sheets of light, about the size of a datapad, extended from silver strips mounted to the wall at each corner. Holographic signs contained lime green letters and directional arrows guiding her through the maze of corridors toward the network operations team. A swipe of her ID beeped the door open, allowing her in to a dim room filled with the glow of three dozen terminal screens and about eleven people. Each desk had a spider-like mounting rail with numerous panes of light looming over the operator, a wall of information threatening to engulf them. Most appeared to be sleeping. The wires running from behind their ears into their systems said they'd already sent their minds into cyberspace.

Dorian whistled, surveying what appeared to be naptime. "This looks to be a cushy job. I wonder how many of them fake working to catch a few zees."

The joke lifted her mood. She gazed from one operator to the next, skipping five limp bodies as well as two men who looked away in a panic as soon as they saw her uniform. She considered approaching a tiny, fuchsia-haired woman, until the woman threw off a glare of territorial challenge.

"Guess she feels threatened. She's not the prettiest girl in the room anymore." Dorian winked.

Kirsten felt herself blush and tried not to laugh. The last two techs not lost to the pseudo-dream of cyberspace were a slender white man in his middle twenties and an Asian guy about the same age. The thin one frowned at her as soon as she looked at him. His immediate assumption she had to be an idiot because she wasn't a tech plastered itself all over his face. He bristled, as if expecting her to come over with some banal user question about how to change the workspace background image on her terminal.

The last man had been staring at her since she walked in, though not in a creepy sort of way. He froze in place, half twisted in his chair, unable to peel his eyes from the silhouette of black in the doorway. When she made her decision, trotted down the three steps into the sunken tech room, and headed right at him, he whirled to face his terminal. His fumbling attempts to appear to be in the middle of something struck her as cute.

"Are you busy?" She leaned over his shoulder to look at his chest. "Tech Chang?"

"Sam," he blurted. Amid his confusion, his right hand flipped like a drunken moth between offering a handshake and a salute. "It's actually Samuel, but people I work with call me Sammy. My parents call me Samuel, but only when they're upset. Usually it's just Sam. Technical Lieutenant Saunders calls me Chang."

Dorian snickered.

"Hi, Sam." She returned his clumsy salute, and pulled over a chair. "I need a little help with a case."

He grinned; a little color appeared in his cheeks as his roundish face glowed. "What do you need, Agent?"

"I'm trying to find a dead man. He used to be a deck cowboy, and I need to find his ghost before something horrible happens. I was hoping you could use this IPv12 address and maybe come up with a list of places he used to log in from so I have some kind of idea where to start looking."

The thin guy, having expected some idiotic stupid-user question, guffawed at the mention of ghost, and went back to his terminals. Dorian wandered over, concentrated, and typed 'boo' on his command line. He swatted the holographic keyboard to delete it. Dorian retyped it.

"Okay, you are quite unamusing whoever you are," the tech announced, before paging among several different screens with feverish determination. "I will find you."

Thirty seconds later, Kirsten finished giving Sam all the data about Vikram's deck and the angry tech two desks over stared ashen at his screen. Kirsten sat with her chin in her hand and elbow on her knee, huddled close to Sam, watching the same monitor.

'I'm standing right behind you' appeared on the command line.

The thin tech stormed over to Kirsten, halting with a heavy stomp and a finger pointed back at the screen. "Are you doing things to my head or my computer? You're one of those... those... Telekinetics aren't you? Typing on my workstation from here."

She didn't look up. "No. Telekinesis can't type on holographic keyboards. There's no solid matter to manipulate. It's my partner, Dorian, messing with you. He's a ghost."

"You don't honestly—"

The tip of Dorian's finger became transparent as he tapped the man on the shoulder. Stiff as a toy soldier, the tech pivoted in place and marched out of the room.

"Eze's going to chew me out for that, you know," said Kirsten, shaking her head.

"You can't tell me it wasn't funny." Dorian laughed at the abandoned workstation. "Oh, he forgot to lock his station. That's a violation of security protocols. And you didn't do anything. If Eze gives you grief, tell him it was me."

Dorian wandered over to the terminal and extended both hands toward it. All six screens went dark. After hearing Kirsten claim a ghost present, the sudden shutdown of an abandoned workstation caused the only two conscious people in the room (the fuchsia-haired woman and a middle-aged man with dark skin) to gasp. Sam didn't notice, too engrossed in his task.

Text flashed by on one of Sam's terminals, images appearing one after the next on the panel above it. Citycam stills of various points where logins occurred. Sam turned to say something, but froze at noticing she sat close enough to touch shoulders with him.

She glanced at him. "What? Did you find something?"

He mustered a dopey smile.

"Sam?"

He blinked. "Uhh, yeah. I, umm." Blushing, he sat up straight and sent an indicative wave at the screen of text. "Got a few hits on the IPv12, physical locations where your guy logged in. The log files tell me this deck signature is associated with the net-handle Dvandva93."

"Only five places. Well, that shouldn't be too bad to check."

Sam lapsed into staring at her eyes again. She straightened. His head tilted back ever so slightly, his gaze following her face. An amused curl settled into the corner of her mouth.

"Thank you, Sam. It's nice to get real help for a change. Whenever I come here, I feel like the psionic exhibit at the zoo."

"You're welcome." He grasped her right arm in both hands, precipitating an awkward fumble from two-handed grip around her wrist to a normal handshake, only it continued for well past the standard customary duration.

Beep.

Sam dropped her hand as if it burned him, sensing his rudeness. A third terminal screen lit up with a citycam view of a coastal warehouse, drifting patches of fog, and broken windows. Below it, a flashing line went between red text and block highlight.

"What's that?" She leaned in for a closer look.

He turned his head toward her, again freezing at noticing her cheek less than six inches away from his face. His breath made her eyelids flutter, and her gaze flicked from the screen to him.

"Sam?"

"Sorry." He blushed as red as a stimpak. "Someone must have taken the deck, or maybe spoofed the IPv12. It's showing as active right now." He pointed at the image of the decaying warehouse. "Someone in this building is using it as we speak."

"Sector 1405." She frowned. "Grey zone."

The chill presence of Dorian's hands landed on her shoulders as if trying to give her a reassuring rub. "After 187, this should be a walk in the park."

"Think Carter will help out this time?" asked Kirsten.

"Chasing ghosts? Doubtful."

"Who's Carter?" Sam tilted his head. "Are you talking to me?"

"Div 9, and no. There's a ghost with me, remember?"

"Anything else I can do for you?" Samuel Chang flashed a hopeful grin.

Kirsten stood, shaking his hand again. "I'm not sure, to be honest. I'll know more after I check out the warehouse. My best chance is to get over there before they log out."

"No problem." He deflated onto his desk. "Glad to help."

She smiled at him. "Thank you, Sam. I owe you one."

ON THE ELEVATOR BACK TO THE ROOF, SHE CAVED IN TO DORIAN'S unceasing glare. "What? Why have you been staring at me like that?"

Dorian folded his arms, breaking eye contact. "If you need me to point it out, then maybe I shouldn't bother."

"Oh, Sam?" She shrugged. "He's just, I dunno… It's a techie crush on a female who actually spoke to him."

"Not up to your standards?" Dorian lifted an eyebrow. "He's not exactly a cover model for a trashy romance."

Her turn to blush. "No… I want sincerity. He only seems enamored. Any girl that gives him more than two seconds of conversation probably gets the same reaction."

Dorian tapped the side of his head. "Did you peek?"

"No." Kirsten emerged from the elevator into a brisk, cold wind howling among the parked hovercars on the roof. A gust almost stole her hair clip.

"So you don't know what was on his mind."

Distant orange warning lights came on at the end of the southwest wing, flashing around an elevated landing pad intended for larger VTOL craft. A whining roar of engines increasing thrust grew louder from the distant smog.

"I can guess what was on his mind." She pulled the patrol craft door up. "I can't think about this now. Vikram might be possessing his old deck."

"Bet that's his focus," said Dorian.

"Makes sense." She fell into the seat and pulled the door closed. "Not like he had any physical remains."

"Oh, he *had* physical remains." Dorian chuckled. "He just spread them over a very large area."

She cringed.

BETRAYAL OF CONSCIENCE

A row of five small boxes at the center of an otherwise black holo-panel cycled color in a slow march from silver to dark blue and back again. Kirsten tapped her fingers on the control sticks, waiting. After thirty seconds the 'please wait' graphic faded away and Nicole's face appeared in a 2D panel.

"Hi, whoever you are," she chirped. "It's Friday and I'm burning vacation days. By the time you hear this message I'm going to be exploring the historic First Colony on Mars with Jaden and—"

Kirsten killed the comm. "Drat. She didn't say anything about going on vacation."

"Ahh to be young and spontaneous." Dorian glanced at her. "You're young, but not spontaneous. What about Morelli?"

She grumbled. "Sarcasm much? He'll make up an excuse. Even if he *does* fail to talk his way out of helping me, he'd be neurotic and useless. To him, I'm a lesser shade of Commander Ashford, and now that you scared his pants brown..."

"You could request a Division 1 escort?"

"To chase a ghost?" She stared down at her hand while flipping her NetMini over and over. "They'd never go for it."

"Are you sure everything's okay? It's odd watching you look for help to do anything." He winked.

Kirsten flicked her finger at the NetMini until Templeton's contact info appeared on the little screen.

"Oh, now I understand." He glanced at an ad-bot sailing by on the right, a little too close to the patrol craft. "Trying to turn it into a date?"

"No, that's not it at all. I'm… I don't want to get killed now that I have Evan to look after."

"Even if you do, you could still watch him. He *can* see ghosts."

"That's not even funny." Kirsten slipped the device back into her pocket and paid full attention to the hover lane. "You're right. He wouldn't even be interested. I'm more than ten years younger than him and he'd probably look at me like I'm a little girl playing dress-up as a cop."

"More like kid sister. I think." Dorian winked and made the NavMap scroll to the area in question. "He did seem to throw off somewhat of a protective air about you last time you met. Besides, Sector 1405 isn't too bad as those places go."

Kirsten fished the NetMini out again. "I suppose I should either live the daydream or kill it before it drives me nuts."

Beep.

Threads of light weaved together above the gloss-black device, stretching into a three-inch bust of a man with broad shoulders and a large mass of hair bundled in two-inch-thick ropes. Kirsten bit her lip at the shape of a carved-from-rock jaw and broad, thick lips. He still had on the same olive drab coat, but on a vid call, looked paler than she remembered. In the absence of a dark alley, his face shimmered bronze. Like the bulk of the population, his ancestry was far from obvious.

"Hi, Templeton?"

"Oh, yeah, I remember you. Officer Wren. How are you?"

Agent. She swallowed the correction. "Fine, thanks. I was umm, wondering if, umm." She closed her eyes for a second. *Can I sound less like an awkward schoolgirl please?* "I have to go into Sector 1405 and I need some backup and…"

"The department is letting you go alone?" Even over the tiny speaker in her palm, the deep timbre of his voice thrummed in her bones.

"I'm trying to find a ghost. Officer Logan is on Mars and it would take too long to talk anyone else into it."

"And she wants to see you." Dorian leaned over.

Kirsten's cheeks burned. She slapped her hand down and crushed the holographic bounty hunter into the NetMini before glowering at Dorian.

"Relax, only you heard that." He chuckled. "Of course, now you'll have to explain why you're the color of a fire suppression bot."

"Hello?" asked a muted Templeton.

"Uhh." She slid her hand to the side, allowing his visage to fade into view from right to left. "Sorry, thought there was a bug on the screen." *Oh, yeah. Real original.*

Templeton's baritone laugh pulsed up her arm as the miniscule speaker struggled to cope. "Sure, I can meet you in Sector 1353, just south of it. How about ten minutes?"

"Great." She made a sound somewhere between a squeal of delight and a giggle. *I'm so pathetic.*

The light from the vid call faded. Dorian reached over and pawed at her hand until she let him hold it. "You need to be ready for this not working out the way you are hoping it does. He's thirty-six, you're twenty-two. To him, you're a kid in need of a guard dog."

She waved dismissively and accelerated to a speed that made Dorian nervous. A few minutes later, she veered northward to approach Sector 1353 from the south, an area dominated by huge warehouses. Most of the buildings were of similar size, long, rectangular, and in various shades of white. Sector 1509 bordered it to the north, crumbling and blackened. The sight of it brought to mind a dark cancer eating the horizon, a spot where the fragmented skeletons of collapsing skyscrapers folded into the center of a festering ruin.

A police vehicle, even a solid black one, coming in for a landing chased away about two dozen people hanging around a chain link fence on the west side of the street. Most sauntered away at a casual pace—or at least faked it. Two sprinted, but Kirsten had little interest in giving drug dealers a hard time. She shut down the car's drive system and leaned back in the seat. Various sections of console dimmed, letting the dark blue glow of the navigation panel flood the cabin.

Ascending rows of numbers formed a line north along the coast on the NavMap: 1353 (where she was), 1405 (*grey*), 1457 (*grey/dangerous*), 1509 (*black*), 1561 (*grey*), 1613 (*grey*). Sector 1509 contained no subdata points, the entire sector as black as a hole in space.

Kirsten poked the one-inch square representing 1405. Her finger pierced the hologram with ripples that spread out in a pretty, mesmerizing animation. Information popped courtesy of a side panel, listing about eight small-time street gangs. Only one struck her as worrisome: the Angels, a mostly Latin group that occupied the area above what used to be known as Los Angeles.

"Might run into Angels here."

"Well, that would make things a lot easier." Dorian watched shadows creep between the warehouses to the right.

"You are such a comedian." She gestured at the terminal, laughing. "I'm talking about the gang. You still think there's such a thing as real ones?"

"Harbingers exist, don't they? Besides, the gang isn't that bad. They know enough not to get into a pissing contest with the police. They work most of their frustrations out on other gangs trying to cut into their territory. I don't see you wearing *Táng-Long* colors, so you should be safe."

"I'm wearing worse." She poked herself in the breast.

Dorian chuckled. "Not all gangs grab any woman they can get their hands on. Around here, it's all about territory, merchandise, and a sort of quasi-politicking bred from having the people who live here actually support them. Both the Angels and *Táng-Long* are more like loosely-structured corporations than street gangs, except they tend to trade in illegal commodities. Though, you might find the *Táng-Long* interesting—they'd be apt to believe in ghosts." He winked.

"Something's coming up behind us." Kirsten looked at the rear-view screen.

A battered, two-seat *Chīsai* compact took a corner two blocks down and turned toward them. Most of its beige paint had flaked off in patterns suspiciously reminiscent of repaired bullet holes. It rode low on the driver's side, a severe lean made worse for an instant as it changed lanes to get right behind them. Kirsten could almost hear the motors in its twelve-inch wheels screaming for mercy.

The instant it lined up with them, she poked the console to run a scan. Light levels balanced out, and Templeton's face became clear beyond the windshield. He sat in a scrunch, his shoulders almost at the level of his ears. She burst out laughing.

"Why do huge men always seem to have tiny cars?" Dorian cackled, then drifted out his door without opening it. "Good grief, the man doesn't get *into* that thing, he puts it on."

Kirsten pushed her gull wing door open and stepped out amid a blast of lingering Cryomil fog. A moment of self-consciousness came out of nowhere. She checked the fit of the utility belt around her waist, brushed dust from her arm, picked at her hair. When Dorian started snickering at her, she forced her arms still at her sides and tried hard not to blush. Templeton drove up behind the patrol craft and parked. The *Chīsai* groaned as he disembarked, a mechanical sigh of relief as it no longer bore the weight of an enormous, muscular man. His boots clunked on the metal sidewalk as he approached. She looked up at him and stopped breathing.

Having the guardian angel who had come out of nowhere a few weeks ago in front of her again caused a collision of embarrassment and desire. Waist-long chestnut-brown dreadlocks trailed in the air behind him, fluttering along with his long olive-drab coat. He'd grown a bit of a beard as well, though she couldn't tell if he intended to or had been lazy and forgot to shave for a couple days. Her brain slam-shifted down two gears to a processing speed below the ability for verbal communication.

Dorian looked over his shoulder, twisting side to side as if surveying the street. "I don't see a holovid crew. They're going to miss the romantic moment."

Templeton stopped at handshake distance, extending an armored glove. In her mind, she reached out, tiny hand grasping only one of his gargantuan fingers. It took her a few seconds to move for real. That his hand didn't dwarf hers as much as she expected surprised her.

"So you're chasing a ghost?" The full force of his deep laugh fell over her, without the protection of a tiny speaker. "If you weren't a Zero, I'd expect you mean someone hard to find, but I'm assuming you are being literal."

Kirsten closed her mouth and opened it. A trace of cologne mixed with the scent of the ocean. She stared.

"Are you all right, Officer?" He waved a hand back and forth in front of her eyes.

"Yeah…" She spun her back to him. "I was just thinking about how to go about this." *Crap. I really am a rotten liar.*

"How much information do you have?"

She gave him a quick rundown of the situation. "… and the IPv12 trace showed activity from a building a few blocks in."

"All right." He slung a large over-and-under rifle around from his back. Laser on top, 42mm shotgun on the bottom.

Dorian scowled at it.

"Lead the way, officer. This is your show." He gestured with his left arm.

So formal. Officer… "You can call me Kirsten if you like." She smiled back at him.

"Agent... Sorry, didn't notice the rank." Templeton offered an apologetic nod.

Kirsten trudged forward. Not a single spark of anything but friendliness glinted in his eyes. She couldn't bring herself to look at Dorian, expecting the I-told-you-so face he so adored giving her. Keeping her head down, she watched shiny metal walkway turn to dark traction coating as she crossed an approach lane that ran beneath a rolling mechanical gate in front of another warehouse yard. Another block passed in silence.

"Peaceful here," said Dorian. "No ad-bots."

Kirsten paused at the end of the next block, leaning against the wall to peek around as if observing a potential threat, but the street held nothing but bits of trash skittering about—no people. When Templeton arrived behind her, also against the wall, she leaned into him.

"The building is another block up, on the wharf property."

Templeton looked around the area with a slow pan of his head. His right eye glowed orange under his dark glasses, painting his cheek and forehead with light. "There is some kind of EMF in the air, sensor sweeps, I think. Your boy seems to have set up a defensive perimeter. I'll need a closer look."

He didn't react to her leaning against him.

When her mind ran away with the imagination of turning around and kissing him then and there in the street, she took a step forward. *Hopeless. Daydreaming is gonna get me as dead as my daydream. What the hell am I doing?* She grumbled in her mind and marched along with a determined glower. Abandoned buildings passed on the right, though this place had few dead cars. This outer edge of the grey zone seemed more like an area people simply got up and walked away from rather than one destroyed by some horrible event. Flickering light reflected on the storefronts of a passing side street where a cloud of holographic tacos danced in the air, almost making her change course.

Damn. I'm hungry. Later. "Well, it's not totally abandoned."

Kirsten hooked a left past a long building full of garage doors in varying degrees of open. At the third, someone sprang from the dark and grabbed her from behind. The handle of her E-90 clanked into a metal crotch guard a second before the thick fragrance of motor oil and unwashed body fell on her. Strips of gloss black cloth fluttered around the arms that spun her around and shoved her back against the wall. Sleeves shredded to the point they resembled unspooled magnetic tape covered spindly arms with thin strips of metal grafted to the flesh. Tiny green and blue lights flickered from within the electronics. The upper half of his narrow face gleamed in plastisteel, still-human cheeks bore a steel-wool excuse for facial hair.

"Sweet." The man's metal eyelids blinked horizontally.

The effect stunned the words right out of her.

"That's a cop," said a wheezy voice to her left.

The man squeezed his fingers into her shoulders. "Just means we can't let 'er leave."

Templeton walked up behind him, and slapped his large, armored hand down on the man's shoulder with a painful *whap*.

Kirsten collected herself from her surprise, but hesitated at using Suggestion. The menacing punk's sudden look of worry amused her. His metal eyes extended out of their sockets on thin segmented rods, then swiveled around either side of his head to look behind him.

"Ugh!" She cringed. "Dude!"

"And that's a problem," added wheezy, another punk who'd moved up to stand close to Kirsten on the right.

Templeton took a step to the rear, grunted, and swung the man off his feet. His fingers ripped away from Kirsten's shoulders without damaging the uniform. He screamed as Templeton hurled him like a discus across the street in a graceful arc, his extended eyeballs fluttering on either side of his head. The punk hit a window on the second story of a warehouse, smashing the glass and disappearing inside. When Templeton recovered from the spin, he leveled his rifle off at the other man.

Clumps of coarse black hair stuck like steel wool to a pallid, emaciated chest. Legs covered with multiple layers of torn camouflage, denim, and something that may once have been leather, quaked. A delicate crackle like distant breaking glass rattling in his rapid inrush of air made it obvious he abused Icewhisper. The man probably couldn't run twenty paces without becoming exhausted.

"Get out of here." Kirsten waved him off.

The wheezy ganger took off as fast as his ruined body could carry him. Kirsten smiled at Templeton, and peered into the broken window across the street, listening for traces of life. A faint moan indicated the man hadn't died, so she felt okay leaving him there.

"You did that on purpose, didn't you?" Dorian leaned on the wall.

"What?"

"Hmm?" asked Templeton. "Are you sure you're okay? Your heart rate is way up."

"Let that shithead grab you so your hero could save you," said Dorian.

"I'm fine. Was talking to my partner. He's a ghost."

"Ahh." Templeton gave her a gentle pat on the shoulder with the same hand responsible for tossing a normal-sized man through the second story window of a building on the opposite side of the street. She wondered how much of Templeton remained human. *Could just be Myofiber combat boosts... the arms don't look replaced.* She grasped his forearm.

He smiled, noticing her subtle squeeze test. "Haven't gotten shot up enough to need all-metal ones yet."

"I'll be okay. Just startled. I didn't expect anyone to be in these storage bins." *One more try.* "Thanks... guess that's twice you saved me. I should make it up to you sometime. Dinner?"

Templeton chuckled. "I don't mind at all, agent. Just doing my part."

Somewhere in her head, a scene from an old holovid played—*Disaster on Colony Four*. Specifically, the last twenty minutes during which the military dropship on its way down to save the survivors malfunctioned and burned up in the atmosphere. Her mind leapt to the part where the dying dropship turned into a flaming comet that streaked out of the sky, crashing to a brilliant, flaming death amid jagged onyx rocks.

"Just thought I'd offer." She managed a pleasant smile despite feeling rejected. Though, in a few seconds, she felt foolish for getting herself so worked up over a man she'd met once. *I'm too young for him. Forget it, K. Focus on the mission.*

Dorian rubbed her back, his cold hand making her shiver. "For what it's worth, he's fourteen years older than you. Don't take it personally."

"Yeah. No worries. It's handled," said Kirsten.

"What is?" Templeton glanced at her.

"Another case I'm working on that panned out exactly how I expected it would, but I've been frustrated about."

"Ahh." His tiny grin suggested he probably caught her true meaning, but didn't make an issue of it.

Kirsten hurried another half block to the target address, another giant warehouse. Four men in dark grey armor stood guard by a mechanized gate in the fourteen-foot-tall fencing around the property. The once-drab plastisteel barrier bore the scars of a protracted graffiti war among at least six gangs. Some of it still smelled wet. She paused at a safe distance and picked over their surface thoughts.

"Promacor Biotech Corporate Security." She muttered. "They're protecting a CET, whatever the hell that means."

"Cyberspace Event Team. Probably a small cadre of deck cowboys holed up in this off-the-grid warehouse to make it harder to trace back to Promacor," said Templeton. He stepped up beside her, also studying the guards. The light emanating from his eye shifted from orange to dim green.

"Hmm. Not many gangers out and about." Dorian walked on by, approaching the gate.

"Yeah, you're right. There's like no one out here," said Kirsten, eyeing the streets and alleys.

"It's only two in the afternoon." Templeton chuckled. "Most of the locals are asleep, and the ones who aren't are busy warning everyone to stay away from this spot because a corporation with deep pockets has moved in."

She frowned. "I don't see Vikram anywhere."

"Could be inside. Gimme a few minutes." Dorian jogged through the gate.

Damn, you left me alone with him. She tried to peek beneath Templeton's sunglasses, unable to tell if they were worn or implanted. "Sorry to waste your time. I really thought this would be a lot more dangerous for me because of the gangs."

"Well." He laughed. "I did pull *one* moron off you."

Kirsten giggled. "Yeah, you did. Not to mention a whole pack of them a few weeks ago."

"I wound up in a lucky place at a lucky time. Did you ever find the punk?"

"Yeah, I got him."

"Good."

"Umm, nice car."

"It's a lot easier to sneak up on bounties in something they won't look at twice."

"Yeah, so do you have a—?"

Dorian came out of the wall between them. "A girl inside is using Vikram's old deck. There's some energy on it. You might be right in thinking he's used it for his attachment."

Dorian, you have either awful or perfect timing. Maybe someday I'll figure out which it is. "Okay."

"What?" One eyebrow peered over the top of Templeton's black lenses.

"Do you have an idea how we can get inside?" She glanced at the gate. "Oh, screw it. I'll try the obvious way first."

She walked up to the barricade. The four men startled and gripped their rifles, but didn't point them at her.

"Private property, get lost." The third man from the left angled his rifle toward her leg.

"That weapon rises any higher it's going straight up your nose." Kirsten glowered at him. "Do you make a habit of pointing weapons at the police?"

He froze, a note of suspicion in his eyes. The other three leaned back.

"Division 0." She used her armband terminal to flash a holographic ID. "I need to talk to one of your network operators. If all that is going on here is inter-corporate backstabbing, I couldn't care less about it. I'm trying to find a ghost. An *actual* ghost, as in spirit."

The men exchanged glances with each other, pale grey helmets swiveling back and forth. One of them mumbled, no doubt to a communicator.

Kirsten squinted at him, tuned into his head. "Tell Kincaid to relax before he has a stroke."

Dorian sidled up next to her. "The woman you're looking for has two-tone hair, top half cherry red, the rest jet-black. Wearing a Netßunny shirt."

"All I want is to have a chat with the redhead in the netbunny shirt." She dropped her voice to a whisper. "What the hell is a netbunny?"

"Famous deck jockey, some kind of cyberspace folk hero or celebrity, I think," said Dorian.

A few minutes passed in a cold, awkward silence, broken only by the occasional sound of sheet metal flapping somewhere in the wind and an unseen can rolling. Kirsten gazed past the guards, watching the glimmer of the mid-afternoon sun play with the ocean. A hundred yards in from the gate, a small rectangular section of the warehouse wall turned from white to black as a door opened. The motion drew her attention away from the sea. A muscular man stormed out, walking at the foot end of his elongated shadow.

He wore the same armor as the rest of the guards, but lacked a helmet. Gleaming silver threads wavered in the air behind two large pistols, one per hip, evidence of a cybernetic targeting link. White hair, too short to notice the breeze, glowed as he moved through a patch of unobstructed sun.

"Wow, he's old school," said Dorian. "Physical wires connecting his head to his weapons. Guess he's paranoid about jamming or eavesdropping."

"What?" whispered Kirsten.

"Wireless signals can be hacked."

"Oh," she said, still staring at the approaching man while nodding.

The man came to a halt inches from the mesh gate, hands on his hips. "So they weren't bullshitting me. A single cop shows up at the gate asking to see one of our assets."

I never did care for anyone who referred to other people as 'assets.' "That's correct. You must be Kincaid. I'm investigating a paranormal event and have reason to believe one of your *contractors* may be in possession of an item that used to belong to the spirit I am pursuing. I don't care what you're doing here. I just want to find this ghost."

Kincaid made a face and drew in a deep breath as if about to scream at a teenaged daughter for sucking down too many pills. Red flooded his cheeks and faded, and then he took a step back. "Ugh. Goddamn psionics always make my goddamn testicles itch. Tell me, kid, you ever get a case of Martian Nut Fleas?"

She glanced down at her form-fitting uniform. "Nope. Never been to Mars, and I don't have—"

"You don't need actual balls, girl, to get them fleas. You look like the kind of nail-picking, pale-faced, prissy, bottled-water-drinking, sushi-eating, salad-munching, sixty-credit-latte-slurping, shaved-beaver kinda bureaucrat what never has anything give them an itch like I'm talking about." He pointed at her chest. "Well then, you don't have a damn single idea what I'm talking about. Itch so bad, makes you wanna just tear them off." He mimicked the gesture of plucking something away from his groin. "Psios are the same way. They're like those fleas. Makes 'em itch, and not in a good way."

Kirsten leaned close to the fence. "I don't think there *is* such a thing as a Martian Nut Flea. You're only trying to scare me off with some ex-military 'oh, boy I've seen some shit that'll turn you white' chest-puffing macho crap you think will send me crying home to my bitch mother. Whatever you saw on Mars, trust me, it's got nothing on what waits on the other side of the living world. I've run into things that will make *you* suck your thumb and wish you were dealing with something as tame as mutated scrotal parasites."

Snickering corporate security men turned away from their boss, trying to hide their amusement.

Kincaid's hard expression remained for another ten seconds before he cracked up laughing. "Not bad, kid. I almost believe you. I'll give you a quick tour, but your attack dog's gotta wait here."

"I don't trust it." Templeton shifted his weight onto one leg.

Nothing in Kincaid's head caused any worry about her safety. "It's all right." *I peeked at his thoughts, he's worried you're a hitter for the competition.*

Templeton had little reaction to Kirsten's voice in his head. "All right. This is your show. If you want to take the chance, go right ahead."

"It's fine. I can handle it. Thank you for coming out here, I wasn't honestly expecting them to be willing to talk. Corporates don't usually believe me when I say I don't give a crap what they're up to." She faced Kincaid again and nodded.

"I'll wait for you here." Templeton folded his arms as if daring the corporates to try to move him.

With a droning whirr, the motorized gate slid open enough to admit a single person. She stepped in and followed Kincaid across forty yards worth of discolored plastisteel tiles bearing stains where old cargo containers once stacked. About halfway to the warehouse, he stopped unexpectedly, raising a hand.

"What?" she asked, a touch annoyed.

The retired soldier stared approximately at Dorian. "I'm bein' told there's a thermal anomaly following us. You got a tail, maybe a cloaking suit."

"That's my partner. He's a ghost." She put an arm across Dorian's shoulders. "Let me guess, you're seeing a cold spot right about here?"

"So much for the element of surprise," said Dorian.

"Oh, like they're going to believe me anyway."

Kincaid stuck his hand through Dorian's chest and waved it around.

"So tempting…" The corner of Dorian's mouth curled up.

After a few more passes of his arm failed to find a solid spy, he gave up. "Ghost, huh?"

"I said I'm here trying to find a ghost. I brought another one to help."

Kincaid's right eye twitched, and he scratched his balls.

THE UPPER FLOOR OF THE PRIMARY OPERATIONS FACILITY RESEMBLED A temporary military command post. Kirsten followed her escort past a dozen more rifle-toting individuals in identical grey armor. Automated sentry guns swiveled; the awful chirping buzz they emitted as their aim swept over her made her feel a little better. The company hadn't disabled the police ID lockout. Knowing the sentry guns *couldn't* shoot her eased some of her worry. Then again, owning a sentry gun with that lockout removed carried the same charges as actively shooting at a cop.

Sheets of hanging plastic, tinted metallic green from thousands of embedded wires, draped over a scaffold of thin pipes and enclosed a work area once used for shipping clerks. Twenty-eight desks and two empty spaces had been arranged around support columns and old office equipment. Six people lounged about, all watching her walk in behind Kincaid.

Every network interface deck and terminal screen appeared dark, suggesting all the operators had logged out. Kirsten moved among the desks and nodded at a pair of Jamaicans in red military pants and black jackets before offering a pleasant smile at a short Hispanic man in normal street clothes. He had his boots up on the desk by a shiny black Nishihama deck, tapping a sheathed knife against his thigh.

At the desk past him, an older man with silvery stubble and an old-fashioned tobacco pipe blew smoke into the blank dimness of a holo-panel. Wrinkles gathered and bunched about his mouth as the stubble undulated into a smile. Deep-set eyes pierced her, glimmering bright in contrast to his old military coat.

Three desks pushed together gave him a horseshoe workspace, each containing a deck plugged into the back of his head. Large and indelicate like the man, the drab green hardware bore the scratches and wear of many years. Both sported the logo of Titan Corporation in heavy metallic lettering.

"Wow, a multi-boarder. Two alchemists and a Titan Ultra… gotta be a former military operator, might even be burned out C-Branch," said Dorian.

She shot him a 'was that even English?' stare, making him laugh.

At a desk on Kirsten's left, a woman in her early twenties draped herself over a matte-black deck, as if trying to listen to the machinery's heartbeat. Staring sideways at the wall, she whispered in rapid pulses. Half her hair was white, the other hot pink. A four-inch-tall strip of black cloth wrapped around her otherwise bare upper body, barely concealing her breasts. From the waist down, she vanished beneath the largest, most cumbersome looking mass of frilly, lacy blackness Kirsten had ever laid eyes on. One boot tip, painted with green cat eyes, poked out from under the hem. On the side of the deck, a sticker bore the silhouette of a charred man on fire with a fragment of wire dangling out of his head.

The woman twitched, muttering "comeoncomeoncomeoncomeon" in an endless repeat. When she spotted Kincaid, she flew upright in the chair. "Wanna wanna wanna wanna wanna login. The electrons are calling me."

Kincaid glowered. "I'd appreciate it if you made this quick. Lorelei dosed some high-grade boosters for the run. They're wasting."

The frenetic woman held her hands (with black lace fingerless gloves) up as proof, two silvery-blue octagons about an inch across gleamed, one pasted to each wrist.

"I think she took too much. That girl's tasting time right now." Kirsten frowned at him. "Please tell me you have a medic?"

"She'll be fine, and yes."

Kirsten stepped over the bulky skirt. "Really, I'm not here about what they're doing online. You can let her do her thing."

Lorelei clasped her hands together under her chin, gave Kirsten an adoring look, and then promptly fainted over the desk. She'd gone back inside without waiting for permission.

The last contractor, a surly-looking girl who appeared younger than twenty, sat with her arms folded across her chest. As Dorian described, she wore a charcoal-grey shirt so tight it looked painted on. Cloth-covered buttons ran from the side of her neck over the left shoulder and down to the start of plain black fatigue pants. Yellow circuit lines traced the image of a psychotically cute ax-wielding rabbit with pink hearts for eyes, a stream of cables out of its ears into a dozen net decks. Glittering pink-purple letters spelled the word 'Netßunny' in a curve above it.

Her deck was abnormally long, almost four feet from end to end—as big as a concert-style electronic keyboard. The right third had a different style, suggesting Vikram possibly grafted two units together. Melt blur and char marks covered it from end to end. At a spot where a small cosmetic flange had snapped off, dark blue metal threads gleamed.

"What's with the funny b?" Kirsten leaned back to whisper in Dorian's nonexistent ear.

"Something the hackers do. I don't understand it, either."

Kirsten leaned closer and picked a finger at the gleaming threads. "Vikram molded a case out of DuraFib armor. Explains why it survived."

"This the one you wanted?" asked Kincaid.

"Yep."

He faced the room. "Okay, everyone back in. Keep it all wired. No open terminal screens until we're secure."

"Get away from my deck, lady." The girl shifted sideways, her boots sliding off the desk and dropping to the floor.

"I only need to touch it. Promise I won't break it." Kirsten rested her right hand atop the deck and reached out with her mind in search of paranormal energy.

"Diva gave it to me."

The girl grabbed Kirsten's arm. Reacting on instinct, she spun the teen around and drilled her face into the desk with a smooth ju-jitsu flip.

"Oof!" yelled the girl.

"Guess you are learning something from Gabriel. Nice reversal." Dorian clapped.

Kirsten narrowed her eyes, holding the girl down.

"Ow! You're gonna break my fucking arm!" A subtle hint of imminent tears skimmed below the anger in her voice.

Kincaid lunged at Kirsten, but stopped himself before making contact. "Is that necessary?"

Kirsten leaned over the girl. "You just assaulted an officer of the National Police Force. Can you keep your hands to yourself, or do I need to restrain you?"

The girl clawed at the far edge of the desk with her free hand, whining while nodding. Kirsten let go. She braced for a punch or kick, but the pouty glare that came back at her caught her off guard. The hacker slid off the desk and flopped back in her seat, pulling her boots up and hiding most of her face behind her knees.

"Can you hurry this along?" asked Kincaid, giving her the side-eye. "Or are you going to rough up all our talent?"

"Only the ones who get in my way or grab me," said Kirsten, before looking back at the girl and softening her tone. "What's your name? How old are you. Don't lie to a psionic cop, it's a bad idea."

"N0ra, with a zero not an o. I'm ei—sixteen."

"Sixteen? Parents?"

"Dad went to Mars, never came home. Don't know if he's dead or just ditched, don't much care either."

"Mother?"

"She emptied dad's credit statement on some cosmetic surgery place. She's fifty, but looks your age now. Found a new man who hates kids. 'Course, it's awkward to have a sixteen-year-old daughter if you're trying to act twenty-one. She took off and ditched me. I got thrown out of the apartment last month when they repoed it."

"Guess mom expected her to pick up the rent," said Dorian.

Lorelei popped awake again, chattering on about something called a 'loop-replicating Bitsmasher' soft.

"It's no big deal. Sarge took me in." Her hair swirled about as she smiled at Kinkaid.

Kirsten raised an eyebrow. Kincaid's glare flattened.

"No! Eww." N0ra shivered. "He's a better dad than the sperm donor."

"Oh. Sorry." *That explains his almost ripping my head off before.* After verifying the girl showed up in the system, Kirsten lowered her left arm and gestured at the deck. "So how'd you really get this? You said someone named Diva gave it to you?"

"Divanda... something Indian sounding."

Kirsten checked her notes, the holo-panel floating over her arm throwing off bright green light. "Dvandva93 maybe?"

"Yeah. We hung out in the same group when I was on the street. He, uhh... got out of the biz, gave it to me when he quit. So his name is really Vikram?"

"*Was*, Nora with a zero." Kirsten prepared to console her. "He's dead."

N0ra picked under her fingernails, and then fidgeted at the deck. "That sucks, I guess."

Lorelei's endless chatter ceased with a giggle, and she collapsed over her desk like a smashed gothic faerie. Kirsten looked over to check on her, but relaxed when the woman's active surface thoughts filled with the rapid streaming images her flying down a hallway somewhere in cyberspace.

"What do you know about the guy?" asked Kirsten, turning back to the girl.

"Diva was an asshole." N0ra's face reddened. "No, he didn't touch me. He killed thousands of people."

"What?" Kirsten and Dorian both blurted at once.

"I found some shit on him. He did a hack on Antheus Biochem about a year ago. They ran testing and fabrication facilities somewhere in Africa and India. Another outfit paid him to sabotage stuff. He rerouted pumps that caused a whole mess of experimental shit to leak. I can't even pronounce the crap, the words were *this* long"—N0ra held her hands about four feet apart—"the clouds wiped out a lot of people before the company got rid of it."

"I remember seeing something about that on the Newsnet. The older reporter who just retired was talking about some industrial accident," said Kirsten, frowning. "Damn, I can't remember her name."

"Funny, isn't it? That woman used to be everywhere. Couldn't walk ten feet outside in the city without seeing her face plastered on a dozen different screens any way you looked; now you can't remember what her name was." Dorian pondered. "I guess it is possible to be *too* famous. Donna something, wasn't it?"

"Yeah, Antheus almost went down in flames. Billions in fines." N0ra kept smoothing her hands down her thighs, her expression lost somewhere between furious and wanting to cry. "I found out he did it for like three hundred grand. All those people dead just for money. I sent everything I found to this other company, Lyris. They own Antheus. I sent them the proof it wasn't an accident."

"Shit," said Dorian, eyes wide.

Kirsten froze. *Well that explains why Lyris really sent Seneschal to have a chat with Vikram.*

Dorian set off to wandering the room. "If Vikram finds out, he's going to come after her. Not only is he going to be pissed at her for setting up his death, he apparently trusted her enough to bequeath the deck to her."

"He's only been dead a few months." Kirsten glanced around the room, annoyed at not picking up any paranormal traces. "I'll have time to confront him before he's strong enough to harm her."

"Harm who? Me?" N0ra sat up. "What the fuck are you talking about?"

"It's nothing to alarm yourself about just yet. Maybe in ten or twenty years, if I don't find him, it could get annoying. But, if strange things start happening around you, Nora with a zero, call me."

Kirsten reached for her personal NetMini, hesitated, and then offered the official department-issued PID. *Not giving a hacker my personal.*

"Weird? Like on the net?" asked N0ra.

"No, weird like something you can't explain. Hauntings, ghosts, that sort of thing."

Dorian, halfway across the room, forced himself into the world and waved at her. N0ra fell out of her chair.

Kirsten extended a hand to help her up. "You're trembling. What happened?"

"I just saw a man." She pointed. "He... had the same uniform as you."

"That's my partner." Kirsten patted the girl on the shoulder. "I think he was trying to give you an example of what I meant by 'weird.' Don't be afraid of him, he's harmless. Do you have any idea where Vikram hung out?"

N0ra shook her head. "Sorry, he never stuck around long after a job. Just sent me the address to this blown-to-shit place where I found the deck. Everyone thought he was a bit of a snob. I mean he was a decent jockey and he walked the walk, but he didn't live the life, ya know? They said he had a *real* job somewhere and only ran nabs for the jollies."

Kirsten leaned back and stared past multiple layers of hanging faraday plastic at the exit. "I'm starting to wonder how much I *don't* know about Vikram."

3 2

THE NAME OF DARKNESS

K irsten rested her head on her folded arms, staring at metallic starbursts floating in a sea of dark grey gloss. The scents of various foods mingled in the air. All around her, the din of a few hundred people going about their day filled in the gaps between snips of conversation nearby in the food court. She wanted to grab an hour-long nap on her 'lunch break,' but feared what she'd see waiting for her on the other side.

"Something's wrong." Dorian's voice pierced the swirling miasma of fatigue, fear, and nausea gripping her. "You haven't touched your food."

She lifted her head. Increased light made the shimmering pattern on the table flash bright silver. A plate of chicken salad sat beside her—the expensive stuff with vat-grown meat. Kirsten frowned at it, not having much appetite.

"You should eat something. You *did* skip breakfast."

"Yeah I guess." She stuck her transparent plastic fork into a strip of genetically perfect chicken and several layers of lettuce. Kirsten held it up, moving the utensil in a slow spin as she appraised its contents. She risked taking a bite, and her nausea exploded into hunger.

"Didn't sleep well, and running around all morning with nothing to show for it isn't helping."

Dorian let her take a few bites, her interest in the salad increasing with each one. Once half her meal had vanished, she took a break to poke at the table console and order an iced coffee, hydroponic—fifty-eight credits. *Screw Kinkaid and his fleas.*

"Please don't tell me your mother came back?" asked Dorian, concern wafting from him.

"No." She rested her elbows on the table, her head in both hands. "Something new: Shani killing me, me killing Shani. It happened a dozen times and I kept waking up each time. It's like my brain is trying to sort out which scenario sucks the most."

"Is that why you wore Evan like a backpack when you dropped him off this morning?"

Kirsten sat up, letting her arms fall into her lap. "I'm so worried something will go wrong, or something will happen to him. Maybe I should leave him at the dorm so *they* can't get to him."

"They who?"

"I dunno wha"—her NetMini started beeping; she fumbled it to her ear—"Wren. Hello?"

The holographic bust of Konstantin Dobrynin appeared, the shoulders of a shiny blue suit with a bright teal ascot underlining his image. He bowed his head in greeting. "Good afternoon, Agent Wren. I hope the day finds you well. That dark highlight truly brings out the sapphire in your eyes. A siren should be so beautiful."

"He's trying too hard," grumbled Dorian.

Her gaze hardened for an instant before she looked at Konstantin's floating bust. "I appreciate the compliment, but it's not makeup. I had a rough night."

Konstantin's lips pursed into an expression of sympathy. "Perhaps I can brighten it for you this evening? Would you care to join me for dinner at the Toko Lounge? Charming little place I recently became aware of."

"Charming little place." Dorian rolled his eyes. "It's only about three thousand credits a person to eat there."

She peered through Konstantin at Dorian, registering what he said. "I… I'm flattered, really. That place is so expensive, I would feel guilty."

"Think nothing of it." He smiled. "I have some more information for you about the inscription you found."

"The silver circle?"

Konstantin nodded.

"Okay. What is it?"

"I'll pick you up at seven?"

Kirsten bit her lip, head moving up and down as if in slow motion. "Oh. Umm. All right."

"Excellent. I will see you then." He bowed his head again before hanging up.

As soon as his hologram vanished, she scrunched her nose at the way Dorian looked at her. "That's not jealousy is it?"

"Feeling protective is a better way to put it. Men like him are not used to being denied what they want. To him, you're nothing more than a conquest. He's expecting you will trip all over yourself if he shows the slightest bit of interest."

"You don't know that for sure. Besides, he might have some useful information. I bet he's one of less than a dozen men in this entire city I could talk to about ghosts or abyssals and not send him screaming for the door."

Dorian laughed. "You might want to tell him you're psionic *before* you sit down at Toko. It would be an expensive tab to get stuck holding."

She glared. "He already knows."

THE WIND SEEMED TO FIND EVERY LITTLE SPOT THE EMERALD-COLORED gown left accessible to air. Shivering, she tugged at the too-short right side. Not wanting a repeat of the last time she wore this, she had ordered a more conservative pair of shoes, heel wise, which she found much easier to walk in. Of course, the thin black cord holding her toes to the sole did nothing at all to stop cold air. Her mind wandered away from the regret of not adding green polish to her toenails as a gust slipped under her small white jacket and chilled the bare skin of her back.

Why couldn't he have invited me to the steakhouse or something? I feel like a damned half-naked peacock.

"Kirsten..."

She faced toward the voice as her father stepped out of the wall of the apartment building. A few seconds of concentration aligned her body with the astral realm, and she hugged him. Alas, he was neither cold nor warm, and did nothing to lessen the chill in the breeze.

"Dad." She squeezed her arms tighter around him. "It's so good to see you."

"You look amazing, honey." He rubbed a hand up and down her back.

"Oh, my. You don't have a bra on, do you? Go back inside this instant and—"

"Dad. I'm not a kid anymore and this dress is backless. It will look ridiculous to wear a bra with it."

He sputtered. "The thing is almost *frontless*, too. If you bend forward too far you'll pop out. Do you at least have—?"

"Dad!" she screamed, blushing.

"—your weapon?"

She slouched, forehead thudding into his shoulder. *Weird that ghosts shake when they laugh.* Grumbling, she pushed herself up and waved her silver handbag at him. "Of course. Umm, Dad, you haven't seen Vikram anywhere around here have you?"

"No, sweetie. I just wanted to make sure you're all right. Don't try so hard to force yourself to be with a man—or a woman if that's your thing. Let nature take its course."

That's why he's lingering. Doesn't want to leave me unprotected. A single tear squeezed out from between the collision of guilt and gratitude.

"I have a bad feeling about this Russian playboy."

"You and Dorian both. What's wrong with you two? Someone finally doesn't run screaming for the hills when they learn I'm psionic, and suddenly he's dangerous?"

"It's not that, I simply have a bad feeling is all."

"What, like he's going to sell me overseas as a concubine or something? Slip me some chem in my drink and I'll wake up on a yacht off the coast of Russia?"

"No, not that kind of bad feeling." He stopped mid train of thought and blinked. "Does that really happen?"

Kirsten shrugged. "I dunno. It depends on who you talk to. Urban legend and all. I'm not in the department that investigates those kinds of cases. Besides, if anyone ever kidnaps me, I'd just go astral, come back here, and tell someone who could see me exactly where to send help."

"*If* you could find someone capable of seeing you. That's—" He stared at a black limousine settling in for a landing a block away. "Something doesn't feel right about him. Too much money, too good looking, too interested in a cute, girl-next-door blonde who happens to be a cop and psionic on top if it all."

She fell quiet, measuring him with an even glance. "I'm not sure if you insulted me or not."

He pulled her close and kissed her on the forehead. "Hon, you're very pretty, but guys like him go for a different kind of pretty." Her father grimaced. "Bigger umm." He cupped his hands over his chest as if holding something large and bulbous. "Lots of cosmetic work."

"You're making generalizations. Not all rich men favor airheads with built-in floatation devices." She looked down at herself, cheeks reddening. "My boobs aren't *that* small. They're *athletic." I can't believe I'm talking about my bust size with my father.*

Dad blushed. "Look, hon. All I'm saying is I want you to keep your guard up and not do anything you'll regret."

"Did whatever thing that gives ghosts information out of thin air tell you anything specific, or are you merely hoping I don't put my legs in the air on the first date?"

He blushed harder, no longer able to look her in the eye. "Kirsten... I don't know how to explain it beyond saying it's a bad feeling."

"I'll keep alert, but he might have valuable information. I have to find Vikram before they kill him, umm, again."

The limo glided to a silent stop beside her. A holographic driver shimmered into view on the curb, acting as though it pulled open the motorized door.

"Miss Kirsten Wren?"

"Yes."

From the back seat, Konstantin held out an arm, offering a narrow glass of champagne. He had changed into a black velvety suit with a violet ascot. Interior lights gleamed over his shaved head. Kirsten suppressed the urge to bite her lip, staring at this too-handsome man. He looked as if he'd walked straight off the title page of the sort of interactive holo-vid women tended to log into alone at home while wearing a senshelmet— and nothing else.

It might almost be worth it to wake up on a yacht.

"Be careful, hon." Her father patted her on the shoulder and dissipated.

She hiked the long left side of the dress up and slipped into the car before accepting the glass. The holographic driver pantomimed pushing the door closed. The effect would have worked better had the motors responsible for the door closing been silent.

"You're radiant." He held up a matching glass.

Clink.

"So is this where you tell me you're not really like twenty-whatever, but instead, you're some kind of thousand-year-old vampire from Siberia who's going to take me back there with you?"

He laughed, long and deep, both eyebrows up. "You have quite the imagination, Miss Wren."

He's moving closer. Miss now, instead of agent.

"Well, I've seen some things that make me wonder what might be out there."

Konstantin smiled. "I believe those creatures are still a thing of myth. Any vampires you see are ordinary people with spare credits and a fixation with cybernetics. However, I am familiar with one or two unusual beings that may have given rise to the legend."

"I'm psionic." She studied the half-drained glass in her hand, only now noticing she forgot nail polish. *Dammit.*

Again, he chuckled. "Working for Division 0, I sort of assumed you were. It is a requirement, yes?"

"It doesn't bother you?" Her defense crumbled as her head spun left.

"I find it fascinating. The world is full of too many closed-minded fools who hate everything they cannot understand." He lifted a few strands of hair from her eyes, tucked it behind her ear, and brushed his fingers across her head. "It angers me when the innocent suffer due to ignorance."

Her gaze slipped off him to the floor as a tremble ran down her body. Something about his touch unsettled her. Or maybe it only bothered her because her father had kept saying how he'd gotten a bad feeling. "I…"

Konstantin clasped her left wrist, drawing her arm toward him. He held her hand in both of his, stroking the back with one thumb. "Someone hurt you, someone close."

Giant moths did backflips in her gut. Her unease *could* simply be due to his wealth. Ever since her days of living on the street as a child, she'd developed a strong contempt for anyone with money. All those people had more credits than they could spend in ten lifetimes, and not one of them did anything for the children starving in the Beneath or the alleys of West City. On some level, she knew her prejudice for what it was—simple jealousy. Though, she detested people who thought themselves better than others for no reason other than the size of their bank account. Could that be it? The idea of dating Konstantin made her a traitor to her values. Sleeping with the enemy, or something along those lines.

The interior of the limo blurred into a spiral as she tried to figure out how she should feel. His fingertips traced the soft skin along the underside of her left forearm, sending ripples of energy up into her chest.

"Mother." She swallowed the rest of the champagne. "Religious nut.

She tried to beat the Devil out of me." Kirsten thought back to being a grime-covered ten-year-old with only a nightgown to protect her from the Beneath. How she'd gone from being a starving ragamuffin crawling around the underbelly of the city to sitting in a limousine wearing a six-thousand-credit gown while sitting next to a billionaire mystified her.

He continued to caress her arm. The touch changed from strange to soothing. "I am thankful you are so resilient. I find it odd how often it is the people who claim to be holiest are usually the ones who cause the most suffering."

"Yeah. I know what you mean. They always say forgive and turn the other cheek. But they only want your other cheek so they can slap it."

Konstantin chuckled. "I think you have dwelled on misery long enough for one day. Come, let us enjoy ourselves."

Kirsten hadn't even noticed the car land. He let himself out and met her at the curb as her door opened. Konstantin took her by the hand, walking past a long waiting line in front of the Toko Lounge. Giant Japanese kanji traced themselves in the air above the door, as if painted by an unseen brush. They started to shimmer into English letters, but she lost sight of them as he led her beneath the archway.

Konstantin addressed the doorman in Japanese. They exchanged bows, and soon a kimono-clad woman escorted them to a quiet table in a small private room on the third floor. Pale wood and rice paper partitions sectioned off an area a little larger than the square table at its center. None of the tables downstairs had chairs, offering only cushions, though this room catered to those in search of a less authentic virtual visit to Japanese custom. Konstantin pulled a chair out for her. She surrendered her jacket to the attendant and took a seat.

The dark red cushion pressed icy against her exposed back. She tensed, sheer fabric pulling taut over her breasts as she arched in response to the chill. Fortunately, Konstantin appeared to be a gentleman, and didn't stare. Eventually, she adjusted to the temperature and eased her weight into the seat.

"I do hope you fancy sushi. It is rather good here. Of course, they have plenty of other things as well."

"I'm fond of it. I think I'll have the sashimi."

"Why don't we order the 'for-two' then. I was thinking the same."

"All right. Excuse me a moment, need to use the ladies' room."

The simulated rice-paper door slid open on its own at her approach. She found the restrooms at the end of a short hallway past another dozen private dining rooms. After setting her bag on the counter between sinks, she rummaged it in search of her Nanochroma wand. Squeezing the handle turned it on, and a plain white light at the narrow end flashed in a slow blink.

Kirsten held it to the side of the dress until it beeped, and then positioned the tip over her left thumbnail. A single drop of green liquid exuded from it, fell onto the nail, and spread into an even coating of the exact same shade of green as her dress. She repeated the process for every nail, finger and toe, and blew the powdery white remnants of spent nanobots away from the enamel.

By the time she returned to the table, salad and miso soup had arrived.

"I took the liberty of requesting a pot of green tea. I wasn't sure what manner of drink you fancied."

This is where I need to be careful and not... damn he's too handsome to believe. Well maybe I can have one.

"Umm. A SynVod and orange juice is fine."

His mouth gaped. "Oh, my."

"What?"

"I can't imagine referring to such a ghastly substance as vodka." He winked.

"Sorry, I'm on a police budget. I also don't drink often, maybe once every few months. Usually, I only drink when I need help falling asleep after seeing something really awful."

Konstantin gestured at her. "I think you should try the real stuff, at least tonight. So you know what you're missing."

"If I know what I'm missing, it will ruin me for the cheap stuff." She chuckled. "All right, but I shouldn't lose my wits in the presence of such a dashing rogue."

He cocked his head to the side and grinned.

"So, you said you found something out about the circle? Can we get that out of the way?" She battled her purse to remove her NetMini.

"Of course." He tugged his NetMini from his suit jacket, set it in the middle of the table, and prodded it. A hologram of the circle shimmered into existence, a gleaming silver wheel about the size of a dinner plate. He pinched at the transparent image, twisting and pulling to zoom in, then pointed at some of the symbols inside the border. "This part of the pictograph binds the ritual to an entity named Charazu."

"Charazu? Is that what he calls himself as a ghost?"

Konstantin swallowed a condescending chuckle. "I trust you have heard of the Abyss." He waited for her nod. "Mankind is still a baby in the eyes of the universe. Beings existed long before we did, some of which are native to that place. Charazu is one such being, ancient."

"A demon?" She set the empty soup bowl aside.

"He, or it, would better be served by that moniker than an escaped spirit. Things such as Charazu never took a mortal breath. Some of my colleagues refer to them as 'They Who Always Were.'"

"Okay, so the circle was what, dedicated to one of these things? By name?"

"I believe so. Mind you, this is merely an assumption based on old texts and a little instinct. If your mind is open to accepting that this sort of thing is real, a circle such as this could have provided the creature a gateway into our world."

She stared down at her wakame salad, strands of semi-transparent seaweed glistening in the light. "Is there any way to tell if anything came through or not?" She thought back to the burning scratches. Her fingers traced over her exposed back, icy against the undamaged skin. "Never mind."

"I found one reference to him. He is known for trickery and shadow; however, the texts claim his greatest ability is to recall the souls of the dead from the prison of Gehenna."

"That means Hell, right?"

"Well, I think of the Abyss as a place sectioned off by degrees. Gehenna is the place where the wicked are sent, those with little hope to change. Souls who are tainted yet seek redemption languish in Sheol, while the outermost realm of the Abyss overlaps our world. Those too impure to..." He made an upward patting gesture. "Go up, but not tainted enough to attract the Harbingers linger around the mortal world as ghosts."

"The astral world? You're saying the astral realm is purgatory or something?"

Konstantin leaned back while servers cleared away the salad and soup dishes and placed a large tray of sashimi between them. A small woman refilled their hot tea. After he assured the waiter that everything was in order, the serving staff left, sliding the rice paper door closed behind them.

"Hauntings are souls who didn't make the cut to get let in upstairs and weren't bad enough to be dragged down. It's a romantic notion of mine to consider the powers of fate giving them the opportunity to make up their mind where they want to go."

"I've met ghosts who 'didn't go up' because they decided not to. Some of them enjoy being here as ghosts. Others *can't* leave because things aren't settled for them... like murder victims where the killer is still out there. And I don't think of it as going 'up.' That conjures too much of an association between good and evil." She used her chopsticks to move a few pieces of sashimi to a smaller plate in front of her. "What do you think sits on the other side? Do you think there's a God?"

"I doubt an entity exists that matches anything humanity envisions as a supreme being. If there *is* something of that nature, it would be so vast as to operate at an entirely different level from us—a cosmic force incapable of interacting with human consciousness. Or, or it's simply cruel. Don't you think? Are you familiar with Epicurus?"

"No," muttered Kirsten, before stuffing a piece of unagi in her mouth.

Konstantin paused long enough to eat two pieces of salmon. "He was an extremely ancient philosopher who questioned the existence of 'god.' Something along the lines of: if God is willing to stop evil but unable to, he isn't omnipotent. If he is able to but refuses, he is evil. If god has the ability and desire to stop evil, why is there suffering? And, if he is neither able nor willing to prevent evil... why call him God?"

"Wow..." She stared at him. "Dorian said something once about life just being some kind of test for the soul, but it's different on the other side."

"I've heard similar theories bandied about as well." He popped a piece of tuna in his mouth and froze with a meditative calm to endure an overdose of wasabi. "I still think it unfair to force the weak to suffer for some metaphysical evaluation. Life should be enjoyed, not simply tolerated."

Easy to say with a starship full of credits. "I think this Charazu whatever he is escaped the Abyss, and he brought some spirits back with him."

"I'm sure you will be able to stop it"—a glint sparkled in his right eye—"now that you know its name."

An uneasy smile spread across her face. Much to her surprise, the dinner conversation did not damage her appetite. The sushi, and real vodka, proved to be quite good, though she didn't expect she'd ever return to this place, both because she didn't expect to see Konstantin again and she'd never come here under her own budget. No sushi was worth three thousand credits, even if an army of shirtless, stone-sculpted men hand-fed it to her.

"MAY I INVITE YOU IN FOR COFFEE?" KONSTANTIN HELD HER HANDS AS THEY waited for the limo to come around.

The shifting azure-to-red of the Toko Lounge sign changed the color of his face, lending an otherworldly glow that made him hard to resist.

"I'm in the process of adopting a gifted boy with a similar talent. I left him with a babysitter who's expecting me—"

Konstantin leaned toward her, dark eyes sparkling. She turned away with demure reluctance. His kiss fell on the side of her neck rather than her lips. The warmth of his breath plunged into her body like droplets of blood striking water. Strength in her legs faltered. She twisted into him, achingly aware that only a thin drape of cloth prevented her breasts from touching him. Craning her neck, she let go of his hands and held on to his body to keep from falling. His lips traced from her jawline to the nape of her neck.

Fire swirled within her heart. Despite the cold, she felt at the verge of sweating. He slipped a hand under her jacket, warm fingers at her back. Helpless in his arms, her breaths came in deep rushes that sent waves of warmth down her body. She waited for the imaginary fangs to pierce her neck, for an instant not caring what he did to her. Wanting him, needing him, she edged to the precipice of surrender, ready to plunge headlong into to the delight of his desire for her, to her body's response to his touch. This man, wealthy enough to have any woman in the world, wanted *her*.

Kirsten toyed with the idea of making love to him, and didn't care how many ghosts would crowd around the bed to watch. She leaned into him, savoring the warmth radiating from his body. He had to stoop to kiss her. Blushing, she rose up on her toes as he walked a series of short kisses across her shoulder and up her neck. Burning threads of longing paralyzed her. Every ounce of her body cried out for him. Nila could watch Evan a little longer. He wouldn't mind a sleep-over.

Evan.

The boy's face floated in her thoughts, grinning, hazel eyes gleaming with innocent love.

Kirsten lifted her head. Why would she think of Evan now?

Konstantin kissed her on the cheek, then on the lips, a scoundrel's grin on his face as he brushed the back of his hand up her cheek. "Have you reconsidered?"

She shifted to meet his gaze, sinking until her heels touched the ground. As though his speech startled her out of a daydream, she blinked.

"I…" *What am I doing?* She shivered, though not from the cold. "I'd love to, but…" *In the limo? Gah, no!* "I only have someone to watch Evan 'til ten. He's the worrying type." Her heart tried to beat its way past her ribs. *Konstantin's going to get mad.*

Drawing her hand up for a kiss along the back of her knuckles, he winked. "I admire a woman who understands things worth having are things worth waiting for. Instant gratification is the purview of weak minds."

Oh, I wouldn't mind some instant gratification right now. Her body protested the abrupt roundabout her brain pulled. *Why did I think about Evan? Oh, shit, maybe he's in trouble…*

"Shall I make reservations for next Friday?" He helped her into the limo.

"Okay." The answer came autonomic. Body overruled brain.

If she could stop worrying about the abyssals running around, perhaps she might allow herself to stop suffering. Her desperate stare at Konstantin's chest lasted a few seconds before she turned away. He opened the door and got in. If she looked at him, if he asked one more time, she might not be able to resist.

"Kirsten?" asked Konstantin from the car. "Why are you standing out there? At least allow me to offer you a ride home."

She blinked and stared down at her silver handbag. *Duh. What's wrong with me. I was really about to just stand here and watch him drive away.* "Oh, right. Sorry." She got in. "I have a lot on my mind now with this case."

BEHIND THE FIREWALL

After ditching her one-inch heels, Kirsten sprinted barefoot from the parking deck to the elevator. She shook with worry the entire way to the thirty-ninth floor. The instant the doors opened, she bolted down the hall to Nila's apartment and waved at the sensor pad to ring the doorbell. At the sound of two happy sounding children shouting "I got it" at the same time, she finally relaxed.

The door squeaked as it slid open to the left, revealing Evan and Shani squished into each other in a race to be the first to push the button. Shani looked down at the floor, a quiver of fear rattling her tiny body.

Kirsten stumbled into the apartment, half dragged by the enthusiastic grip of a nine-year-old boy thrilled to see her. Nila wandered in from the back, investigating the ruckus. Patches of blue, pink, and white light painted the ceiling of the dim living room, cast off from a large holo-bar projecting the image of a paused video game. Whatever it was, it exuded girlishness and involved cartoon rabbits—though Evan had apparently tolerated it, since it appeared to be in two-player mode.

"I'm sorry." Shani ground her toes into the rug.

Kirsten let her black bag slide from her shoulder, then took a knee in front of the girl. "Shani, it wasn't your fault. A bad man did something to your head."

Shani stared down, fidgeting with her dress. "I have bad dreams. Do you still want to shoot me?"

Her brought tears. Kirsten looked at Nila, as if for permission, and after receiving a nod, pulled the girl into a hug. "I never wanted to shoot you, Shani. I..." She closed her eyes, knowing she would've simply stood there and let the girl kill her. "...could never do it."

Evan gasped in horror. "Why would Mom shoot you? You're not a bad ghost."

Kirsten pulled him into the hug as well. "Not everyone who has psionic powers is nice. A man forced her to point a gun at me."

Shani sniffled and wiped her eyes. "Thank you for not killing me."

Nila shivered. "Commander Ashford said you got it all. He couldn't find any latent triggers... in either one of us."

"Great." Kirsten sighed with relief and stared Shani in the eye. "Please don't be afraid of me. I'm not upset with you. The man who hurt you is gone."

The girl nodded, grinding her toes into the rug. "Okay."

"Can I borrow your bathroom or bedroom to change real quick?" asked Kirsten.

"Of course." Nila gestured at the rear hall. "Coffee?"

The kids ran around the couch and dove into the cushions before putting on their senshelmets and resuming the game.

"Sounds good."

In the back bedroom, Kirsten unpacked a plain, blue long-sleeve shirt, black pants, and a pair of Nomz from her bag. After changing, she pushed the small metal cat face on the tip of the sneakers, and they adjusted themselves to a perfect fit.

She paused at the entrance to the living room, watching the children control cartoon bunnies navigating a three-dimensional maze in search of candy-like fruits, vegetables, and stars. When the smell of coffee reached her, she dropped the bag behind the couch and went into the kitchen. At the sight of her pink-and-white cat sneakers, Nila laughed.

"Aren't you a little old for those?" She poured them each a cup. "I didn't know they made them in adult sizes."

"They're huge in Japan. It's a cult thing, I guess." Kirsten fell into a tall stool-seat by the island counter. "I thought they were cute."

"I thought you were tired of people teasing you about looking young. They don't help."

"Bah." She sipped her coffee black. "I guess I'm trying to sneak in a few moments of a lost childhood here and there."

Nila gave her that patronizing, sympathetic look people always tended to do once they found out about her life, the kind of look only someone with parents who accepted their kid's talents could give someone like her. For Dorian's sake, she didn't take it as condescending.

"How are your parents doing?"

"Oh, they're okay." Nila squeezed an inordinate amount of Glucosim to her mug, adding so much of the clear gel sweetener that Kirsten expected the spoon would stand up in the coffee like pudding. "I called them once Ashford finished scrubbing my brain. I don't even remember if I'd spoken to them since Dorian was killed. They're doing well, considering going to Cairo on vacation next month."

"Cairo? What, actual Egypt?" Kirsten blinked.

"Don't look so shocked, it's not ACC. Most of the region is independent still, though not for lack of the Corporates trying. I don't think anyone will ever take it over." She winked.

"Thanks for watching Evan tonight."

"How'd it go? I want all the juicy details."

Kirsten regaled her with the ever-so-boring recap, leaving out the finer details of demons—a topic she still hadn't quite committed to accepting herself yet.

"Oh, hard to get? That's evil of you. Well don't push it too far; millionaire playboys like him don't come along every day."

"No." She furrowed her brow. "They don't. And that's the problem. Something doesn't feel right."

"Did you check his thoughts?" Nila slurped at her coffee.

"I didn't. Not sure why. Never even thought about it the whole time. He didn't creep me out in a way that made me look."

Nila raised an eyebrow. "Yet something bothered you?"

"It's his money." After a sigh, she rambled on and on about her contempt for the rich.

KIRSTEN GUIDED THE PATROL CRAFT INTO THE AIR, AWAY FROM NILA'S building, and hung twenty feet below the stream of hover traffic, waiting for an opening. She barely resisted the urge to hit the bar lights when the flow offered no quick opportunity to enter.

As tired as she felt, Kirsten found it amazing Evan's endless ramble on the drive home about the game he and Shani spent most of the day playing didn't bother her. Nothing odd happened to him. He didn't feel threatened or watched, though he did admit to a sudden pang of worry about her. She found it disconcerting that a random thought of him would be such a powerful distraction from Konstantin's tongue on the side of her neck.

"Why are you red again?"

"I'm worrying."

"Oh. Job stuff?"

"Yeah."

"Shani said she had a bad thing in her head that made her shoot her mom." Evan's expression hardened into a determined glare. "Don't worry. No one is powerful enough to make me shoot you."

She reached over and held his hand, flashing a smile. An opening in the lane came up. Kirsten rammed the left stick forward. Fortunately, the patrol craft had a significant advantage in power over civilian hovercars, and she cut off the guy trying to edge her out with ease.

The vid-comm in her forearm guard rang, muffled. She'd left it bundled with the uniform in the bag, which sat in the back. Evan scrambled between the gap in the front seats and rummaged for the source of the noise. It stopped ringing right as he held it up. With a shrug, he carried it with him back into the passenger seat and studied his reflection in the shiny black surface.

It rang again. This time he answered. N0ra appeared, eyeliner smeared down her cheeks, her voice wavering.

"Kid? Sorry, I guess I misdial—"

"Nora?" Kirsten shouted. "I'm here, just driving. That's Evan. What's wrong?"

The teen's holographic head rotated to face Kirsten. "You told me to call you if something weird happened."

"Did you see Vikram's ghost?"

"I dunno what I saw, but it was weird." She sniffled, threatening to explode into tears at any moment. "Something black came out of the walls. The Promacor guys went crazy. They started shooting at everything. I'm so damn scared I can't stop shaking. I ran like a mother... This, umm... This black thing followed me out of the building. The guys at the front gate were all dead. I had to climb the friggin fence 'cause the power was out." N0ra held a bloody, shredded sleeve up into the holographic image. "I really hate barbed wire." She shivered, hands against her mouth for a moment, then turned toward someone behind her. "I'm, okay… I've got the police on the phone." She faced back to Kirsten. "It felt so evil, it wanted to kill me."

"Where are you?"

N0ra's holographic head blurred and faded, though the sound of crying came over the connection loud and clear. An olive-skinned man in his middle forties appeared, wobbling and blurring as the phone attempted to compensate for moving.

"Who is this? Are you this girl's mo—no, sister?"

"Agent Kirsten Wren, Division 0 police. You are?"

His suspicious stare relaxed. "I am Father Carlos Villera. We're at the Five Hundredth Street Sanctuary."

The expected instant dislike of anyone associated with religion surprised her with its absence. "I'll be right there."

"Can I turn on the police stuff?" Evan bounced in his seat.

"Go ahead, but put your belt on."

Evan readily secured himself in the seat. "Yaaaaay! Are we gonna go shoot bad guys?" he yelled, louder than the siren.

"I have no idea what's waiting for us. Stay in the car, please."

He nodded, smirking. "Aww. Okay."

Dorian leaned in from the back seat, yawning as if coming out of a deep nap. "I'll keep an eye on him."

"Did you sleep well?" she asked.

"Yes. Like the dead."

Evan rolled his eyes.

THE FIVE HUNDREDTH STREET SANCTUARY OCCUPIED THE HUSK OF AN OLD hardware store in an abandoned strip mall. In a merchant-zoned section of the city, it sat at about the midpoint of City Road 500, an east-west conduit running through a poor manufacturing section. Churches, per se, had not much survived the Corporate War and subsequent relocation of society to the coastal regions. Increasing secularization combined with the need to cram so many millions of people into one city had all but eliminated the plausibility of monolithic cathedrals, temples, mosques, or the like—a fact Kirsten didn't mind. However, as the faithful are wont to do, pockets of them continued in improvised locations. Most of the religious buildings she knew about existed down underneath the plates. Some of the truly dedicated would even make the trek down there, believing the original places to be sacred. Some, like Father Carlos Villera, made do with more easily accessed locations.

"I didn't even realize they put a church here," Kirsten said, eyeing a line of vagrants stacked up at the door as she landed in the parking lot. She set down nearer the street so as not to disturb them with the ionic downblast.

Other shops in the strip mall had closed at this hour, save for an all-night liquor store at the far left end.

"Well, that's convenient... free meal and booze in one stop." Dorian chuckled. "I think it's less of a 'church' and more an outreach to the homeless." He slipped into the driver's seat as Kirsten got out. "There *are* still a few religious people left in the world." He winked.

"I know, but the majority aren't in this country." Kirsten leaned back into the patrol craft to ruffle Evan's hair. "Okay. Dorian's here with you. I—" She froze, sensing something dark approaching. *Harbingers?*

The boy spun to stare out the false window. "I'm scared."

"I feel it, too." Dorian pointed. "Something's in the alley."

"Stay in the car, Ev." Kirsten grabbed her E-90 from the back seat and eased the door down to close.

After stuffing it in the back of her belt, she hurried across the parking lot to the 'church.'

N0ra appeared the doorway, clinging to the doorjamb to edge past the line of people waiting for food. She started to step out onto the sidewalk, but recoiled as if she'd put her foot into lava. The look in her eyes said she wanted to rush over, but terror kept her from leaving the building.

The teen's odd behavior worried Kirsten up to a jog.

Some of the men on line looked her over, a few whistled and winked. Being out of uniform, her presence didn't have the usual repelling effect on citizens, so none of them moved out of her way. She squeezed past two guys, one of whom grabbed her arm.

"Hey, no cuttin'. Even if you are pretty."

"I'm not here for food." She stared at him, then pointed at the patrol craft. "I'm a cop. Off duty at the moment, but there's an emergency."

The vagrants glanced at the car, and a note of unease came over them. *Ahh. Back to normal.* She slipped into the building.

N0ra reached grabbed her. "That thing is still out there. I saw this place and ran inside. It didn't come in after me." The teen sniveled, as if ten years had been scared out of her. "Is Kincaid still alive? I didn't see him in the chaos. Everyone was shooting. Please, don't let it get me."

282 | LEX DE MORTUIS

Kirsten held the young woman, patting her on the back until her sobs petered out. "I won't."

N0ra gasped. Her face paled, eyes focused over Kirsten's shoulder.

Kirsten reached behind her for the E-90, and whirled—locking stares with Seneschal standing at the middle of the parking lot, arms wide to either side.

"Well, Agent Wren. You seem to be out of uniform."

She narrowed her eyes. "Still here, I see. Guess you got away from them."

"Indeed. They are rather single minded and a bit dim. Like cops."

"Why are you after the girl?" called Kirsten. "She has nothing to do with this."

The vagrants shuffled around, glancing back and forth between Kirsten and Senesschal. A few appeared to sense something odd in the air and fled for the safety of the nearest alley, putting a solid building between them and whatever would happen.

Seneschal paced to the left, hands folded behind him. "The same reason you dragged our buddy around with you for a few days. Bait. He knows what she did to him. It is Vikram who wishes to harm her, not us. My team is simply following her waiting for him. That girl *helped* us. If not for her, Lyris would never have known who compromised the production facility. Vikram cost us billions, by the way."

"Why do you care? You're dead." She waved the E-90 at him. "You're beyond dead! You're dead and returned."

Someone tapped her shoulder from behind. The scent of vomit mixed with piss choked the air from her throat. "Hey, you got any left?" asked a dangerously thin man clad in grimy, tattered clothes. He shook with constant trembles—a human chihuahua offering a hopeful smile.

"Any what left?"

"Whatever you're on dat yer talkin ta no one."

She blinked. The vagrants hadn't been looking at Seneschal... they'd been looking at the 'empty parking lot' she'd been yelling at. A flash of white energy shone in her eyes. "*Go inside, eat something.*"

He spun on his heel and went into the building with the rigid walk of an automaton.

"It's a question of oaths." Seneschal stopped pacing. "He will come for her, and then we can finish what we need to finish."

"I won't let you destroy him."

"You still think he's innocent, don't you? Even after the girl told you what he did. He has the blood of thousands on his hands. At 3:08 a.m., valves opened. Pumps kicked on, triggered by a spark that formed across a synapse in his brain and traveled over the GlobeNet. He may have been thousands of miles away, but he still killed people. Tens of thousands."

"Neither you nor I are fit to judge anyone." She advanced two more steps toward him. "You don't belong here."

"Your friend Vikram is one of us, *girl*." He snarled the last word. "The Eternal One called all four of us. My team had instructions to take Vikram alive. He cost the company a great deal of money and caused irreparable damage to their reputation. Lyris management wanted him to work it off. Dead men cannot pay debts. We trapped him in his lair. Once he realized he had no way out, he blew us all to hell. Your innocent Vikram killed all three of us, and himself, and twenty thousand people halfway across the world. Those little wispy horrors of yours dragged us all down."

"Innocent people are being caught up in your idiocy." Kirsten traded the E-90 to her left hand, and lowered it. The laser wouldn't do much to an abyssal. Like some kind of ancient gunslinger, she flexed the fingers of her right hand, but didn't yet call the lash. "You don't have to be consigned to your fate, Desmond. Destroying Vikram won't make you any less dead. Let go of your anger and help me with the real problem. Help me deal with Charazu."

Seneschal flinched at the spoken name. His stare intensified as if he couldn't believe she knew it.

Silence, but for a vortex of wind pushing a cloud of plastic cartons along, hung between them. Seneschal's eyes narrowed, deepening crows' feet. A distant cat picked that moment to yowl. Amid the thrum of an ion thruster, a single oblong advert droid rounded the corner of the strip mall. The battered thing crept closer to her like a child afraid to be hit. Its holo-panel displayed recruitment propaganda intended to attract the local poor into the flock of Reverend B.G. Wallis, a middle-aged black man in a plum suit wearing the smile of a salesman.

Kirsten ignored the bot.

"That would be something, wouldn't it?" asked Seneschal. "Turn around and bite the hand of the entity responsible for my power?" A polyphonic laugh, deeper than any human could create, leaked from his throat as his eyes flared with crimson light. "You are living a delusion. There is no redemption, only varying degrees of suffering."

With those words, a cloud of black vapor fell out of the folds of his

long black coat, settling over his arm into the shape of an assault rifle—
that he aimed at Evan's face in the open driver side window.

Evan let out a yell and ducked down; the armor panel slid upward out
of the door. Kirsten screamed and lunged into a sprint, calling the lash.
Seneschal's confusion at the boy seeing him distracted him enough for
Kirsten to find an opening. She raked the energy whip across his body,
the tendril snagging midway in his chest. He let out an agonized wail and
staggered from the hit, nearly falling to his knees. Shuddering in pain, he
looked down at the line of white light tracing from his body to her hand.

The sight of the blinding-bright psionic weapon sent the last holdouts
in the food line dispersing in a screaming panic.

Seneschal gurgled, shuddering as he forced himself to walk closer to
her, impaling himself deeper and deeper on the stream of energy bathing
him in harsh shadows. "You are too easy to manipulate." Another step and
agony cracked his attempt to remain stoic, with a cough and a tremble.
"N-Now I k-know who to kill once Vikram is destroyed. It won't be
quick. The boy will suffer long."

Kirsten gathered her rage, but before she could send it down the lash,
he blurred. Metal crashed into the side of her head. The butt of
Seneschal's rifle swatted her to the ground, ending her concentration on
the whip, which remained only as a latent image in her eyes from its
brightness. Pain throbbed over the side of her skull.

Wheezing, he clutched his chest where the whip had left an inch-wide
hole gushing with thick, black ichor. Anger flared in his eyes. He raised
his hand, tar-like blood seeping between the fingers of his shuddering fist.
Kirsten braced her head in both arms, trying to make the world stop
spinning.

"I'm getting really rather bored of you." Seneschal held his arms as if
pointing a rifle at her, and it appeared from thin air in a flash of dull red
light.

At a thought, she made herself tangible to spirits, and spun into a kick
that took his left leg out from under him. Her cat-themed sneaker
meowed with the impact. The rifle went off; spectral bullets clicked on
the traction-coated plastisteel behind her, gouging shiny stripes in the
grainy black surface. Seneschal flailed, staggering backward, but didn't
fall. Kirsten spun out of the kick in a maneuver that brought her upright.
Calling on her power, she thrust her arm out, projecting the lash straight
at him. Seneschal aborted his shot and dove to the side.

She stepped in with a sideways swing that he ducked. A trio of implanted cybernetic blades sprang out between the knuckles of his left hand a second before black pulsating veins raced down to cover. He jabbed the demonic claws at her face. She whipped the lash up, parrying. A brilliant flash accompanied a concussive *bang* that sent shards of plastisteel and burning black veins flying everywhere. He staggered back, staring in horrified shock at his destroyed claws.

"Heh." She smiled. "I guess adding 'from hell' to a weapon isn't always an advantage."

Incoherent anger roared out of him on a scream. He hurled himself into an overly telegraphed right hook. She pivoted to the side and controlled his arm as Silva showed her, then swung her body into him with an attempt at a ju-jitsu throw. Her back tucked against his chest, she tried to pull him around and over her shoulder. One shove with her hips should've sent him airborne; however, her feet found no ground beneath them.

Her mind stalled at the unexpected sensation of floating. She realized Seneschal had lifted her one-handed. Nubs of broken claws scratched at her stomach as he groped at her belt for a better grip, hefting her up over his head like a barbell. Kirsten shot a pleading stare at the patrol craft as he carried across the parking lot toward it. He reared back as if to slam her into the hood. She screamed with a mixture of fear and fury, struggling to break free of his grip.

Dorian leapt out through the armored windscreen, tackling Seneschal. Kirsten fell in place, feet on the ground, chest on the hood.

EVAN STARED AT KIRSTEN'S FACE, ONLY A FEW FEET FROM THE 'WINDSHIELD,' but unable to see him. He did *not* like the man trying to hurt her, and not only because he wanted to hurt his mother. Something about the fiend scared him in a way that Theodore could never hope to. True malice hung in those deadly crimson eyes. He crawled down and curled in a ball on the floor in front of the driver's seat, plenty of armor around him to stop a conventional attack, though a *conventional* attack would likely be the last thing to happen here.

Seneschal grabbed Dorian with both hands. The men rolled over each other several times, grunting. Kirsten shoved away from the patrol craft and summoned the lash, searching for an opening while refusing to move out from in front of Evan. *This is my fault; I should have taken him back to the dorm first.*

The men popped apart, though Seneschal lit off a flurry of precision hand-to-hand strikes any one of which likely to have crippled a living man in one hit. Dorian grunted, barely impressed, and lost himself to a moment of rage. He tackled Seneschal to the ground again before grabbing the man's face in both hands and pounding the back of his head repeatedly into the ground.

A vagrant darted out from behind the only other parked car there, running in a panic toward Kirsten as if on his way out of the lot. *Nice try. You might look human, but I can feel you.* Kirsten frowned, and snapped the lash at the homeless man. A blast of shadow exploded out of the man's back, gliding away from the lash as the rest of the human visage disintegrated to smoke. A curtain of darkness fell to the ground, rematerializing as Mariko a few feet away. Her face, the most distorted of the trio, became even less human. Her too-wide mouth opened revealing zig-zag teeth.

She snarled in a demonically low voice.

"Ninja sminja. You're still a damn paranormal entity. I can feel you coming." Kirsten fast-stepped closer and whipped the energy tendril out again.

Mariko evaded, still hissing. She scurried left in a circle, moving low to the ground in an inhuman creep. With the lion's share of her worry in front of her, Kirsten risked moving a little farther away from the car. She swiped twice more, hitting only the ground as Mariko leapt flea-like into the air to avoid her.

Dorian came sliding past her, startling her attention over to Seneschal's rifle. She dropped focus on the lash and channeled her power directly at him, fixing her mind onto the coalescence of his energy. His entire figure shuddered, forced down and to the left. Her attention concentrated on his gun arm, pushing it away and down. She growled, tapping into her need to protect Evan.

Seneschal howled in rage, but dropped to one knee under the weight of her power. Dorian lunged and walloped him across the face with a stunrod, knocking him flat. Mariko came out of nowhere; her sword cut a path of ice through Kirsten's left calf. No blood sprayed. No wound appeared, though pain like the leg had been cut off paralyzed her mind.

Concentration shot, Kirsten fell forward. A hasty look to the rear found no trace of Mariko. Seneschal, enraged, drove his fist into Dorian's gut with such force it threw him ten feet in the air. The rifle formed in his grip.

"Seneschal!" Kirsten screamed, forcing herself up on her one working leg. She used her fear at losing track of Mariko to call the lash. Her rage at his threatening Evan empowered it.

Her attack blasted Seneschal's body apart into a vee from the stomach upward, two halves scarcely connected at the crotch with a few traces of inky black strands threaded between them. Mariko leapt again out of the dark. In one smooth motion, she grabbed, twisted, and broke Kirsten's right arm at the elbow. Shrieking, Kirsten rolled onto her back, projecting the lash up at the demonic ninja out from her forehead.

The energy whip swiped across Mariko's chest, knocking her back a step.

"Oww, you bitch." Kirsten winced. "I don't need to aim it with my damn arm."

Kirsten swiped again, but Mariko leaned over backward at an inhuman angle, allowing the sideways strike to pass clean over her.

She kept bending over backward until her face poked out between her knees with a cute toothy grin and a tilted head. Pointed teeth gleamed from a mouth twice as wide as it should be.

Gah. That bitch is so damn creepy. Kirsten scurried away, waving the lash back and forth, parrying the death sprite's continued attempts to dart in and stab her. At least the woman appeared afraid of the white energy. As fast as the demonic ninja could move, she couldn't beat the speed of Kirsten's thoughts.

The mangled Seneschal flailed his arms, emitting odd groaning grunts while futilely trying to pull his split self back together. Ignoring him for the moment, Dorian charged. Mariko avoided him with the grace of a matador.

Her breath in short gasps, Kirsten reached for her belt to grab a stimpak, losing control of herself and screaming 'shit' about a dozen times when she remembered her civilian clothes didn't include a utility belt—or a panic button. Seneschal's right half waved an arm about, trying to get a grip on the left side of his body. Mariko pounced at Kirsten, catching her too-slow roll to the side. The semisolid blade pierced her other thigh, sending a burning chill along the bone.

Neither one of Kirsten's legs wanted to obey, both dragging limp and useless as she clawed at the traction coating to pull herself toward the car. Bits of rubber caked like coffee grinds under her nails.

Mariko went to swing for Kirsten's head, but lurched off to the side, when Dorian shot her with his ghostly version of a sidearm. The ninja whirled on him, throwing a transparent Nano-shuriken into his face.

Dorian smirked. "That works better on live targets, hon."

Screeching, Mariko flung herself to the ground, scampering on all fours, a human-headed shadow spider. Dorian rotated, following her circuitous approach. Mariko closed in and sprang upward, flying in an arc behind her sword. Dorian barely got his stun rod in the way of the first strike. Ninjato struck stunrod with a sharp *clang*. Alas, her next four swings, so fast they blurred, slashed into his chest before he could pull his arm back from the first block. Mariko's body had split into four pairs of arms wielding four swords. Kirsten cringed away from the sight.

Dorian wheezed, staggering away. He sent a longing look at the car, but fixed her with a determined stare as he swooned to the ground.

Mariko grinned, her eyes flickering red as she pushed Dorian's head away with her foot. "You watch girl die now."

A wave of flame spread over the woman, tinting the air with a hint of sulphur. Thick, dark smoke wafted from the edges of her silhouette. Mariko stepped past the boundary, manifesting herself solid into the world. The twisted, demonic smile shrank to a more human-sized mouth, somehow cute and terrifying at the same time. Her skin faded grey and lifeless. She raised her sword and pointed it at Kirsten. A line of gleam slid down the blade.

The blade could cut flesh.

Kirsten grabbed her thigh with her one working hand, trying to rub warmth into it, to get her dead limbs to respond. She pushed at the ground, sliding back a few inches. Mariko stalked closer, taking her sweet time.

Seneschal's fingers caught some hair, pulling the two halves closer.

Dorian groaned and forced himself up to stand. He staggered into a run at Mariko from behind. She froze in place, smiling at Kirsten with the sort of mournful look a little girl might give to a favored doll that had broken. When Dorian's came within two paces of her, she thrust herself backward. The now-solid Mariko passed through Dorian's ghostly essence, leaving him stumbling over Kirsten.

Kirsten flung a lash upward from her left hand the same instant Mariko stabbed at Dorian's back. Her flinching blade nicked his side rather than impaled him, but he still fell to the ground and melted into a cloud of fog. The energy whip slid past her head, missing by inches as she twisted herself into an impossible contortionist dodge.

Mariko stepped up on Kirsten, raising her blade. Such mania shone in her eyes, she seemed likely to willingly walk straight into a lash to get a clean kill shot. The tip of her sword pointed at Kirsten's heart, Mariko leaned forward, palm on the end of the handle. Kirsten wrapped her power around the woman's spiritual essence her weary mind struggling.

The sword slid back and forth, locked in an opposition of strength between the two women.

Growling, Mariko forced the tip down an inch at a time, lost an inch, gained two, lost three. Kirsten's nose leaked hot blood, flooding her mouth with the taste of copper. Exertion beyond her limit taxed her body to the point of self-harm. If she slipped, even a little, a solid metal blade would impale her in her chest.

Kirsten searched for any last trace of extra power. *Please... I can't leave him helpless.*

The dark shape hovering over her washed out with a sudden blinding light. Mariko crossed her arms over her face to shield her eyes, hissing. Kirsten let off a mental gasp, having no idea what she just did.

Hot ionic downblast buffeted her as the patrol craft thundered overhead, two feet off the ground. Kirsten's mouth filled with ozone. Crackling sparks covered her body. She sat up once it passed, and stared in disbelief as it crashed into the front wall of the Five Hundredth Street Sanctuary, Mariko wrapped over the front end. The armored hovercar slammed to a halt, flinging Mariko into a group of folding chairs set up in front of a pulpit.

Smoke and light filled the building. Mariko arched her back, emitting a tremendous roar that should've come from a 400 pound monstrosity, not a four-foot-eleven Asian woman. All the electric lights in the place flickered, went dark, and exploded.

Mariko shuddered and wailed. Patches of crimson radiance shone from cracks spreading over her augmented bodysuit. White smoke billowed off her, crackling with embers. She flung herself over forward, clawing at the floor, feebly attempting to drag herself to the exit. Her legs collapsed first. What had once been Mariko Moriyama melted into a puddle of black ooze. The disintegration raced up her body. Her face receded into the liquid with a belabored final wail that faded off to silence. The last part of her to remain solid, her fingers, clawed at the floor for two seconds as she fought in vein not to sink out of sight, before all traces of her vanished.

Absent the spectral glow from an abyssal's destruction, the interior of the church went dark.

Kirsten pounded a fist into her thigh, but it didn't help—she didn't even feel it. Evan emerged from the patrol craft door, dragging her utility belt behind him. His face, red and tear-streaked, brightened when he noticed her moving despite trickles of blood leaking from his nostrils.

"Mommy!" He cried out as he ran to her, leaping into a hug.

Hearing *that* word come out of him for the first time brought tears to her eyes. She forgot about her numb leg and squeezed him. When the embrace relaxed enough to notice his fat lip and bloody nose, she almost panicked.

She fussed at his injury. "What happened?"

"Uhh. I just drove your car into a building." He wiped his mouth with the back of his arm. "I kinda kissed the console."

Kirsten took a stimpak from the belt and pressed it to his shoulder.

"You need it more," he said, grabbing another and stabbing her in the thigh.

The return of sensation to the leg was less pleasant than numbness. A billion icy needles exploded deep within her thigh. Kirsten clamped her arms around him and howled from freezing agony.

"I'm sorry." He cried again. "I wanted to hel—"

"It's fine." She didn't let go. "Gimme another one."

He did, making a noise like a stepped-on goose as she clenched her grip under the wave of agony. A moment later, she flopped flat to the ground, paralyzed by the absence of pain. "Oh, yeah. I'll feel that in my dreams for a few months." Kirsten lifted her head, but the smile she wanted to give Evan fell away at seeing all the color absent from his face and his mouth open in fear.

She whirled around, pushing the boy behind her. Her heart skipped two beats at the sight of an intact Seneschal seething at them as if their happiness offended him. He glared at Evan as if attempting to stare into the depths of his soul. Kirsten wobbled to her feet, keeping the boy behind her. Her legs faltered before she stood fully upright, dumping her on her ass. Evan stepped protectively in front of her. She bit back a scream when she tried to grab him, forgetting her right arm had been broken in multiple places. Seeing stars from pain, she forced past it and snagged his shirt collar with her left hand, trying to pull him back.

He glared up at the former corporate soldier. "Leave my mommy alone."

Kirsten tugged him back, glaring doom at the abyssal. "No. You will not touch him." Another trickle of blood left her nose as she forced a lash into existence.

With a final promising glare at the child, Seneschal dissipated into a mass of black fog that sank into the ground.

"Damn him…" She rested her chin over his shoulder. "I won't let him hurt you."

"Mom?"

Tears leaked from her eyes. She adored hearing him call her that. "Yes, Evan?"

He pointed at a foggy mass clinging to the ground. "Do stimpaks work on Dorian? I think he needs one."

HOLY GROUND

Evan clung to Kirsten's side, helping her stumble across the parking lot to the door of the Five Hundredth Street Sanctuary. Despite his small size, he made the difference between walking and crawling.

The reek of bad eggs and wood smoke blanketed the interior along with a cloud of off-yellow haze. Glass crunched under their feet, scattered about from the crash. None of the local poor remained anywhere in sight. Tilted nose-down, the patrol craft had lurched to a stop with its rear end propped up on the windowsill and the nose on the floor. Fog leaked out from the seams around the armored doors still closed over the ground wheels.

Evan guided her along by the belt, helping her stumble over to a row of still-intact chairs. A sudden crunch from the left made her whirl and Evan gasp. Her instinct to raise her E-90 resulted in a twitch of her broken right arm, and a stifled scream as she clutched it to her side, staring at the spot that moved.

A slab of crumbled drywall rose up and fell off to the side, exposing N0ra. She crawled out from the debris and dusted herself off. Kirsten let all the air out of her lungs, creating whorls in the fog. The teen dragged herself free of the collapse and leaned against the wall, then proceeded to gnaw her anxiety out of her fingernails.

"What the fuck just happened?" asked N0ra, abandoning her nail biting after making a sour face and spitting.

Kirsten let gravity plant her in the seat and pulled Evan into her lap. "My best guess is Vikram has been following me and overheard your confession. I bet what happened at the wharf was him trying to take revenge on you. There are other entities in play, the ones who showed up here. They're trying to destroy him, and their distraction let you slip away."

N0ra slid down with her back against the wall until her butt hit the floor. "That shit is real?" She trembled hard enough that her voice quivered. "B... But it's not fair. He was doing evil shit and I just turned him in. I didn't do anything bad." For a few seconds, the girl seemed about to sob, but her expression became inexplicably placid.

Oh, shit. That's not a good sign; she's not handling it well. "It doesn't always work this way. Vikram should not have been able to leave where he wound up."

"He's going to keep coming after me, isn't he?"

Evan looked at N0ra, lifting his face out of Kirsten's shirt. "My mom will get him."

Kirsten kissed him on top of the head. Despite logic saying she should be worried sick, she felt proud and loved. Father Carlos Villera emerged from a rear hallway, waving his arms at the lingering smoke and trying to clear his throat. He seemed equally stunned by the patrol craft in the main room and the utter lack of vagrants waiting for food.

Noticing the blood on everyone, he ran over. "God save us, are you all right?"

"I've had better days, but I think so." Kirsten coughed from the dust.

Evan gave her a thumbs-up.

N0ra stared into space.

Dorian stumbled through the wall, his body transparent, his expression exhausted.

"Father, would you please grab the bag in the back seat of the car?" Kirsten winced. "I don't really feel up to standing right now."

He nodded.

"What the..." The priest froze, aghast at the ground in front of the car.

The alarm in his voice worried Kirsten enough to attempt standing. Evan squirmed off her lap and pulled her up by her unbroken arm. He held on, a living crutch supporting her as she ambled over to stand next to the priest. A black scorch mark stained the cheap orange and white tiles in front of the patrol craft. Fragments of glowing embers remained, having settled to the ground in a pattern resembling some form of writing. From the center of the spot, a dark green wisp of sulfur-scented smoke wavered.

Despite the ominous appearance, Kirsten sensed no lingering presence. "Whatever it was, it's gone now. At least this one didn't scratch me."

Father Villera shifted toward her, muttering something in Latin before asking in English, "Scratches?"

Kirsten sighed. "Yeah, three lines down my back. Hurt more than it should."

He put a hand on her shoulder, closed his eyes, and muttered Latin again for a moment. "That is the sign of a dark creature. Why it has marked you, I cannot say. Perhaps it watches, perhaps it weakens you against itself... I shall pray for you."

Yeah, go ahead and do that. She softened the bile in her stare. "Thanks..." *S'pose I'll take any help I can get at this point.*

Father Villera helped her back to the seat and retrieved her bag, then fetched some stew for N0ra. She remained sitting on the floor against the front wall, staring at the steaming bowl as though she had no idea what it was. Kirsten took a stimpak from the bag, bit the safety cap off, and tried to press it to Evan's shoulder.

"No, mom. You're way more messed up than me. I'm fine, just banged my nose on the car." He grabbed her hand and redirected the autoinjector into her leg. After, he fished her armguard out of the bag, which she used to call for backup.

Dorian limped over to the stain on the ground, and the matching smear on the hood. "Well, you were wondering if the choice of location did anything for Ritchie. If this is any indication, I'd say it might help."

Kirsten surveyed the room, sighing in her mind at the religious proverb posters, paintings of Jesus, and crosses. She frowned at Dorian. "I think Evan did it."

Evan looked at her, then at Dorian, then back at Kirsten. "What?"

"Sent Mariko back where she belongs."

"Demon ninjas are bad," he said, one nod as a period.

Father Villera wandered out of sight into the hallway, returning in a moment with a broom.

Dorian glided closer and sat in the next chair. "You've got ratings in Mind Blast as well as Astral Sense, and somehow found a way to mix them into the lash. They say you're one of the strongest astral sensitives discovered, and you've never been able to make a *ghost* spontaneously explode, never mind an abyssal."

Distant sirens grew louder.

"You know as well as I do that emotions can amplify psionic output, sometimes far beyond anything we can do consciously." Her face reddened. "She was kicking my ass."

"Well, the NSK trained her how to kill since she was probably younger than him." Dorian nudged Evan's hair. "Her sanity was most likely a matter of debate even before she died."

The front windows glimmered with arriving patrol cars, and a MedVan.

N0ra ran and hid behind Kirsten. "I hate cops. They always give me a hard time."

"You stick your virtual nose in places it shouldn't go?" She cringed; pain shot down her broken limb.

"Sometimes." N0ra sank into a chair in a row behind her, sniffing at the food.

"Well, stop doing that and they won't give you a hard time." Kirsten shot a pleading look at the two women in white coming through the door. "I don't know if these things got to Vikram before they came after me. Considering they wanted to use you as bait, I think he's still out there. I'm going to take you into protective custody for a little while until this gets sorted out."

"What? No..." N0ra recoiled. "That's like being arrested just without any charges."

"I'm not standard police." Kirsten winked, waving one of the Zero Tactical officers over. "This girl here is being targeted by a paranormal entity. Please take her into protective custody. Set her up in one of the glass rooms. She's an innocent victim, so treat her like a guest."

The officer saluted. "Yes, Agent."

Kirsten frowned at her broken right arm and twitching legs. Evan reached around her head and saluted for her.

"They have ghost-proof rooms." He rubbed his nose. "Magic-body-proof, too."

N0ra gave Evan a confused smirk. "Umm. Okay."

"Go with them, the creatures coming after you can't get through the walls of a special room where you can stay. If you want to talk to a psych, just ask."

N0ra stood and followed the officer out, staring around at the room as though she had forgotten who she was.

"Poor kid." Dorian sighed. "She's going to need a lot of therapy. She saw too much too fast."

"Oh, like I didn't. I saw"—Kirsten winced as the medtechs peeled the shirt off her arm—"ouch, ow, dammit, frack."

While another medic checked out his facial bruises, Evan rolled his eyes and gestured at her twisted and bruised arm. "That's worth at least a fuck or two. Maybe even a moth—"

She covered his mouth with her left hand. "You're going to wait 'til you're old enough to shave before using *those* words."

He pulled her arm down. "Mom, it's 2418, it's not like—"

"I don't care. You're nine, and too cute to drop F-bombs."

The medtechs smiled at him.

Evan blushed.

Beep, chirp, tweep.

Kirsten stared at the silver box in the tech's hand as it glided up and down over her arm.

"Agent, your arm is broken in three places and there are bone fragments invading some of the ligaments. We'll need to get you back to a treatment room."

"Yay. Naked time." She made a flag-waving gesture with her left index finger. "Fine, let's get it over with. What the hell happened to my legs?"

The dark-skinned man in a white jumpsuit scratched his head while staring at his handheld. "Best I can tell is an unexplainable cause deadened all the nerves below a precise plane. There's no reason I can find for it, but your body is behaving as if it stops existing past that point."

"Let me guess, the deadening kind of looks like a sword cut?"

He stared at her.

"Thought so. Can you fix it?"

"It's fixing itself already, just taking a while. But... the tank will help. There's some ice crystal damage in the muscles, which we'll take care of."

The medtechs helped her stand and guided her onto a hovering stretcher. She rolled her head to the side, smiling at Evan. A ring of symbols seemed to hover like a halo around his spherical mop of hair. He blurred as her focus shifted to a half dozen religious icons for various faiths mounted on the far wall. *A trick of the eyes.* Evan held her good hand, walking alongside the stretcher on the way to the door. Every few seconds, a twinge of ice ran down one of her legs.

Kirsten searched the sagging, stained tiles of the drop ceiling for answers as the medics pushed her out into the cool night air. She couldn't explain what destroyed Mariko, nor could she wrap her brain around meeting a religious man who didn't trigger an immediate sense of repulsion.

She sighed, less certain than ever about anything. Too exhausted to think, she stared up at ad-bots cruising overhead until the ceiling of the MedVan blocked off the sky.

DEMONS

K irsten sat on the edge of her Comforgel pad, adoring the soft warmth of her pajamas. She idly grabbed at the carpet with her toes, fighting to stay conscious while she waited for Evan to finish getting ready for bed. Her hand ran up and down her arm, massaging the memory of the injury away. Evan stumbled out of the bathroom wearing a beard of toothpaste foam and pajamas.

"You forgot to wipe your face," she said with a tired giggle.

He stopped, blinked at her, then turned around and walked into the wall. "Ow," he grumbled, then wiped his face on his sleeve.

"Close enough. You should have napped at the medical facility; you're up too late."

Evan plodded over. She pulled him into a hug, patting him on the back. "Night, kiddo."

He muttered a few incoherent words and turned to face his sleeping bag.

A pang of worry came out of nowhere. Kirsten stood, snagging him by the shirt and keeping him on his feet.

"What?" he asked, yawning.

"I want to teach you something." She put a hand at his back and whisked him over to the front door. "You remember the glass rooms?"

"Yeah."

"I'm going to show you how to do something similar to our

apartment." She put her hand on the door. "The astral world is like a shadow of the physical world. Almost everything in our world casts a spiritual echo, except for little stuff like trash rolling along. We can temporarily cause an object or a wall to merge with its astral copy. That makes it solid to spirits so they can't get through. Even if you're asleep, if something tries hard enough to break down the blockade, you will feel it."

Interest dispelled some of his fatigue. He nodded and put both hands on the metal door.

"Think about wanting to pull a little bit of the astral world into this one. You should feel energy shifting, like a wall of jelly."

"What flavor?" He grinned.

"Here, look in my head while I do it. It's a lot easier to understand if you take in my surface thoughts—it's hard to explain what it tast... uhh, feels like."

When she sensed his telepathic peek, she channeled a Blockade into the walls. A sense of the apartment's three-dimensional form spread open in her thoughts as energy seeped around and drew the physical and astral realms close. Walling off the entire apartment drained her more than only doing the bathroom, but making herself even more tired didn't matter since she planned to be asleep in minutes anyway. When she'd finished about three quarters of the way, the exertion lessened and the glowing seep picked up speed around the room. Evan started helping. Soon, the line of glowing light met up with its start point and the entire space glimmered in sublime golden radiance.

They stepped away from the wall, Evan's eyes wide at the spectacle of phantasmal light shimmering across the surface and sinking into the material.

"That's awesome." He beamed up at her once the light had absorbed into the wall. "How long does it last? Does everyone see that light?"

"No, it's like ghosts. Only we can see it. The effect remains until we break the integrity—umm, until we open a door or window, though it will falter after a day or so, even if we don't."

He nodded, scampered around the Comforgel pad to his sleeping bag, and crawled in, burrowing into it until all she could see of him was a little face staring at her from a bundle of blue cloth.

If they approve permanent custody, I'll get a bigger place. He needs a real bed.

She flopped on the squishy, gelatinous mattress. As soon as her head hit the pillow, the ability to sleep grew distant. She whined to herself, unable to comprehend how she could still be wide-awake while being so worn out? Kirsten sighed at the ceiling tiles. Worry ranked high on the list of suspects, as well as latent adrenaline from almost dying *again.*

Kirsten shifted onto her side in a fetal position with an arm tucked under her head, and smiled at Evan. For a few minutes, the memory of his calling her 'mommy' brought back a sense of placid calm. In the short time he had been staying here, he'd never quite gotten to that point. In fact, she couldn't remember him ever using any term to address her directly. He always walked into view before speaking so he never had to call her anything at all. The more she thought about it, the more it seemed likely the boy did that on purpose. Watching him sleep, she didn't feel so alone anymore. Even though she didn't bring him into the world, she couldn't deny her feelings of motherly protectiveness toward him. She'd do anything for him. That thought made her feel utterly worthless for a few seconds—how awful must she have been for her mother to have not felt the same way?

No. It's not my fault. That woman was insane.

A few quiet tears slipped from her eyes, tracing her nose and cheek into the pillow. The first few came from sorrow, but the last from joy at watching him so quiet and peaceful. Her momentary peace splintered as her mind veered off at random to her other near-death experience this week: almost shot dead by a seven-year-old. Kirsten sat up with a hand on her gut, trying to push the same kind of sleepless nausea out of her stomach that plagued her the night after the Saguaro Asylum.

She bent forward, easing the nightstand door open to retrieve the bottle of SynVod. A delivery droid had brought it well over a year ago the night she dealt with the Wharf Stalker. It had been her first time touching 'hard' liquor, and she'd put the bottle away half-gone the next morning. Sleep after the soul collector from the asylum required another quarter bottle.

Her right eye gazed back at her from a thin strip of reflection on the glass. She flicked her thumb back and forth over the label. *I wonder how mother got started.* Mother always had something on her breath whenever she screamed to Jesus about her Devil-touched daughter. *Did she have to numb herself so she could do such things to her own child?* Kirsten's lip quivered. *If the woman hadn't been an alcoholic, would things have been different?* Her gaze focused past the bottle to Evan. *Did Mother ever tell herself it was only so she could sleep? Only say it was once or twice a year?*

Evan's eyes popped open. The beginnings of a smile faded to a worried stare. He sat bolt upright.

"What's that?"

The fearful look in his eyes hurt. Mick, his former stepfather, was drunk more than sober. Kirsten thought back to the wash of vodka breath on the back of her head when he tried to kill her.

"Something I"—she stood, walking to the kitchenette—"wanted to get rid of." She slipped the bottle into the disintegrator chute and hit the button. Yellow light flickered from the hatch seams as the mechanism disassembled the bottle's molecules into inert matter. A brief gasp of blue fire and the stink of burning vodka puffed past her.

When she returned to her Comforgel bed, Evan climbed up beside her. "Mick drinks, too."

"So did my mom." Kirsten ran a hand over his hair. "I'm not going to have any more. I only used it to help me sleep after a *bad* night, but I guess that's how it starts."

Evan relaxed. "Can I sleep with you tonight? I'm..." He fidgeted.

Kirsten held the blanket up so he could crawl in. "It's okay, they can't get through the blockade."

He cuddled up, back against her chest. "Mom? I don't like the way he looked at me. Is he mad 'cause I blew up his ninja?"

She held him tight. "I..." *Aww, he's shivering. Don't bullshit the kid.* "Yeah, he's probably mad. I'll get him."

"He's a weird ghost."

"He's not quite a ghost anymore, hon."

He squirmed around so he could look at her face. "What is he?"

"A bad person who wound up where bad souls go, but he escaped somehow. I need to make sure he goes back where he belongs."

"Oh." He snuggled into the pillow. "Why did you talk to him?"

"I don't think violence is ever the first or best answer to a problem. There are still pieces of who they were in there, and if I can reach one of those pieces, maybe I can help him, too."

"Mom? He's a demon, right?"

"That's what some people call it." Kirsten closed her eyes, too tired to split hairs with a nine-year-old. Technically, a returned soul, an Abyssal, wasn't the same as They Who Always Were—assuming she even believed Konstantin's scary stories.

He held on to the arm she put across his chest. "They're lying. Don't talk. Just smack them. They're not people anymore."

Kirsten clung to him like a teddy bear, wondering if he really feared that ghosts would come after him in the night or if he wanted to cuddle for her benefit. She lay still for a few minutes, thinking about the sight of Mariko melting away.

"Ev?"

"Mmm?" He asked, voice hazy from his rapid journey to sleep.

"What *did* you do to Mariko?"

Evan whispered. "Ran her over."

36

MISSING

C old brushed at Kirsten face and leaked in the button gaps in her pajama top. Her eyes fluttered open, though her body refused to move, more tired than when she had first tried to pass out. The blanket, folded away, exposed her to the chill of the room. She pulled it back up to her chin, seeking warmth. *He probably had to pee.*

"Mom!" A distant tiny yell echoed in the dark. "Mom, help!"

She flew upright, gazing at the dark and empty bathroom. Her head whirled left; the front door hung ajar.

"Mom!" The cry grew distant.

Kirsten bolted from the bed, scrambling in a crawl as she disentangled herself from the blankets and ran out into the pitch dark hallway. Icy tile froze her bare feet; cold air swam up inside her thigh-length shirt, making her teeth chatter. She gazed up at the ceiling, unable to even see it five feet above her head. Not even one light remained on. The corridor lights should always be on. *Something drew the power out of the entire building.* Worry rattled her to the point where even simple Darksight became a chore to activate, but in seconds, the hallway shimmered into visibility. Blurry sepia-toned walls wavered back and forth shimmering on top of the real world she couldn't see.

"Evan?" she yelled, her voice echoing into silence. "Dorian?"

A distant metal door slammed so hard, the entire building trembled.

"Mom!" called Evan, his voice sounding as though it emanated from the bank of elevators.

Kirsten sprinted down the hall. She took the corner fast, yelping as she smashed her toes into the metal pot of a large fake plant that had been recently moved, and didn't appear in her astral vision. Flailing, she fell into a mass of plastic leaves and landed on thin carpeting. Beyond the last elevator, a small flickering glow caught her eye: a vaporous handprint on the knob, recent contact from a spirit. She scrambled up to a limping run and burst past the door, shoving it with both hands as she pivoted to follow the railing.

"Evan?" she shouted.

"Mom!" he yelled, a few stories down.

Kirsten barely noticed her toes going numb from the cold concrete steps. She raced down the stairs teetering at the edge of falling over from going too fast. "I'm coming!"

His cries led her down the shifting blur of the stairwell; Darksight made the walls weave and dip in a nauseating undulation, the superimposed images of real and astral wobbling in a futile effort to align. Faces leaned out of the dark every so often, curious when they saw her bright white eyes go past. She knew one or two nice, elderly spirits who'd died here, resident haunts of the building.

"He's going for the basement," a feeble old man voice called out behind her.

Landing after landing passed as she chased the sound of a pleading boy down sixty stories until she reached the litter-covered basement level. Two steps onto the landing, sharp pains lanced into her sole. Kirsten screamed and fell against the wall—broken glass in her foot.

Shivering, she looked at her bloody foot, and then at the debris all over the ground. Shattered autoinjectors, bottles, and anything else some idiot dropped down the stairway from who-knows-how high. The heavy basement door shimmered, paranormal energy fluttering from the knob. Kirsten plucked a sliver of brown glass from her skin, and gently eased her toes into the trash.

"Mommy!" wailed Evan in a teary scream. "Help!"

"Evan!" she sobbed. Disregarding the glass, she bolted forward, gasping each time her foot came down on pain.

It hurt so much her body wanted to collapse. She forced her shaking body to walk over razor-sharp agony, bracing herself hand-over-hand along the grey cinderblocks to keep her balance. She took faltering steps, screaming, and staggered to the door on trembling legs.

Locked.

The code panel on the wall defied her with its dead display. Police override codes didn't do much good without electricity. Evan screamed on the other side, shrieking as if stabbed. In her mind, Seneschal's claws raked down his belly. She flung herself at the door, pounding on it, screaming.

"No!" She screamed, banging her fist again. "Please don't do this to him!"

Evan shrieked again.

More glass pierced her foot. So much of it remained embedded in her soles that even stepping on clean floor felt as though she walked on needles. She sobbed, forcing the pain out of her awareness, no longer feeling crystalline shards grind with each step. Evan needed her. Nothing else mattered. She thrashed at the unmoving knob, a hundred pound willow attempting to tear down an armored door.

"Evan! No!"

Moving shadows above her head caught her eye. She struggled to stand up taller on tiptoe, peering through a tiny window. Deep in the boiler room, small legs kicked in the air, hovering within a vast cloud of living inky darkness. He screeched, calling out for his mommy between sobs.

Kirsten smashed her fist into the glass again and again alternating between shouted threats and wailed pleas until she broke her hand. Evan's little foot clipped a tool cart and sent it rolling.

The echo of small metal objects clattering to the floor from high and right slapped her like an open hand. She stared at a ventilation duct. Not even bothering to tiptoe around the junk, she rushed over and climbed a shelf. Hanging from a rack of dusty tools, she grabbed an old wrench and bashed at the grating until it failed. Rats scurried out of her way as she crawled down a metal tunnel untouched for decades.

A moment later, the screaming and pleading ceased; replaced with the sound of a man's sinister chuckle. Kirsten, eyes blurred with tears, let out a yell as the ductwork gave out under her weight and sent her sliding into the air. She bounced off the top of a boiler, rammed her knee into a pipe, and spilled out onto the ground hard on her chest. The windblast from her landing lofted a cloud of soot around her. Her subsequent involuntary breath sucked a good portion of it into her lungs.

Gagging and coughing, she grabbed the frame of a giant heating unit. Her grip faltered as the pain of shattered fingers overruled her desire to hold on. Seneschal grinned at her when she she dragged herself along the floor into view, trailing blood from both feet.

"My, my, my. Enter the valiant hero."

She snarled, pushing herself up to kneel. Her shuddering body protested the idea of putting weight on her feet, toes curling. Evan squirmed in Seneschal's grasp, held aloft by a fistful of his shirt, his hands and feet bound with wire. Beyond terrified, Evan sniffled and whimpered. Seneschal caressed the boy's face. The child cringed away. Black fingernails lengthened into claws, teasing at the tender skin of Evan's neck.

"No… Please…" Kirsten struggled to stand. An unconscious moan of pain slipped out as her weight drove hundreds of glass shards deeper into her soles. "Don't hurt him…"

"I promised him I'd let you watch." Seneschal's arm tensed.

"No!" Kirsten screamed, fear and worry rolled into wrath that exploded out of her hand in the form of her Astral Lash.

It only hurt the dead; Evan wouldn't be a human shield. She let out a war scream and swung the tendril downward, tapping her love for Evan and all the agony in her body. The whip wrapped over Seneschal's face, stalling like a wet noodle—useless. Kirsten's broken hand throbbed as if she punched a brick wall. The lash slipped off him, limp to the ground.

Seneschal leaned back with a great bellowing laugh, claws poised but drawing no blood. Evan wriggled in a futile struggle against the wires binding him.

"You can't hurt me here," said Seneschal. "I've cursed the whole basement. After I bleed this little lamb out, I'm going to make you call out for *your* mommy. She was an amateur, but if you beg for her enough, I'll set up a reunion."

"Let him go!" Kirsten lashed out; again, the whip bounced away from him without effect. Shock reverberated in her hand as though she had punched stone.

She staggered closer; bloody feet peeled away from the ground with an audible sucking noise accented in scratching glass. Two more strikes left her hand bleeding as well, as if every bone inside had splintered to mush. Seneschal laughed at her useless attack.

"No…" Kirsten sagged to her knees, unable to look away from the claws at Evan's throat, overwhelmed at the sense of imminent loss.

Unable to stop it.

A lone droplet of blood appeared at the tip of Seneschal's middle finger claw. It dribbled downward, tracing a thin red line before pooling in the hollow at the base of the boy's neck. That blood became the only scrap of color in the sepia-toned world. Undulating boilers and blurry walls closed in. Grief mounted atop claustrophobia.

Evan stopped moving, stopped fighting the cords binding him. The fear faded from his face. *He knows he's about to die.* Kirsten's arm refused to rise for another lash. Nothing mattered anymore.

She couldn't save him. She wasn't good enough. She failed.

The room blurred as she cried. Battered, broken, she fell to her knees.

Evan locked eyes with her. "Mom, stop. You're hurting yourself."

A droplet of blood from the index claw joined the pool. Kirsten convulsed, shoulders shaking, unable to stop, unable to look away from this demon gradually slitting the throat of this child she had come to love as her own.

"I'm going to take away the only thing you love." Seneschal grinned as his ring finger claw birthed another droplet.

The pool at the base of his neck overflowed down the center of his chest.

Her convulsions increased as she tried to lash again.

"Mom. Stop! You're hurting yourself," yelled Evan.

Kirsten wheezed, a leaden weight settled into her chest, making it impossible to breathe.

"Foolish woman." Seneschal chuckled. "No one wants you. How dare you try to love anything. You deserve to be alone. This boy deserves far better than a basket case like you."

The voice started as Seneschal's, but morphed into that of a fortyish dark-skinned woman in a neat but inexpensive skirt suit. She appeared normal in every way except for her glowing red eyes. The cord binding Evan turned into red tape. Serpentine heads hissed as it unraveled from his wrists and ankles, spreading and mummifying his entire body except for his eyes.

"I'm sorry, Agent Wren, you can't keep him." Danita Reed, demonic caseworker, laughed with dark glee. The mass of red tendrils sprouted right out of her gut, drawing Evan into her. "We're taking him."

"Mom!"

Kirsten's convulsions turned into thrashing.

"Mom, mom, mom." Evan's voice grew desperate.

Astral walls spun into a vortex. She wanted to throw up.

"...determination that you are unfit to act as guardian..." Danita's voice faded into the same swirl consuming the basement.

"Mom." Evan sounded so close his breath touched her face.

Kirsten's eyes opened.

Evan knelt on her chest, shaking her by a two-fisted grip of her shirt. Her right hand throbbed, bleeding from a tiny cut. The icy hardness of a filthy basement floor had gone, replaced with carpeting.

"Ev?" croaked Kirsten.

He collapsed on top of her, hugging as best he could while she lay flat on her back. She sat up, clinging to the hard-breathing child clamped onto her, and rubbed her hand up and down his back. She stared at her feet, aglow in a slanted rectangle of moonlight upon the rug. No glass. No blood. The nightstand lay on its side, its contents scattered on the floor. A little blood had dribbled down the side where she had punched it in her sleep.

"I thought the demon got you. You freaked and started screaming and yelling my name."

Kirsten held him tight. "It was just a bad dream... just a bad dream."

Who am I trying to comfort?

"Mom?"

She didn't let go. "Hmm?"

"Did you have another bad day? You're all squeezy again."

Kirsten burst into tears while laughing and carried him back to bed, refusing to let go of him. Evan didn't seem to mind, and snuggled tight. She lay on her side, clinging to him like one of the stuffed animals she always hoped would protect her from Mother.

37

THE GATE

Regardless of how long she stared at the terminal, the Citycam system refused to commit to spontaneous generation of another sweeping power anomaly. As if the dream had not been bad enough, her feelings of impending doom grew with an exponential leap when she received a vid mail from Danita Reed confirming an evaluation meeting with Evan as well as a staff psychiatrist. Her panic spiked, then faded once she remembered Danita had scheduled it two weeks ago.

Kirsten couldn't focus on the map and let her head fall atop her arms upon the desk. *It's just procedure... They have to let me keep him. I'm the only one on the West Coast who can teach him. I'm not nuts. Okay, I am a little young to be a mother, but...*

"Hey."

With a shriek, Kirsten whirled to the left, raising her arms in a defensive posture. Her elbow clipped a cup of coffee. The beverage sailed into space, slowed, and hung in place. A stream of brown liquid glistened in midair as if in zero gravity. Hand over her chest, Kirsten's sat there gasping for a second before firing an annoyed glare at Nicole for sneaking up on her yet again.

The redhead's eyebrows wiggled about, evidence of the massive amount of concentration necessary to use telekinesis on a formless liquid. Mesmerized by the undulating ribbon of wakefulness, Kirsten remained quiet until Nicole managed to put most of the coffee back inside the cup and set it on her desk.

"You okay?" Nicole flopped into her seat. "What's wrong, you look like your cat died again."

"I don't have a cat. How was Mars?"

Nicole smiled, kicking her boot off the floor to set her chair spinning. "The shuttle food sucked so much. It makes the café here look like... uhh simply bad instead of atrocious."

"I'm worried about losing Evan."

Squeak. Nicole put her boot down to stop the spin. "Why would you be? You two are so cute together."

"I'm probably just—"

"Oh! The hotel had these amazing little bath—"

"—being paranoid. Demons might influence—"

"—beads. I wouldn't worry too much, you were perfectly justified—"

"—the caseworker." Kirsten sighed, and leaned her head in her hand to wait for Nicole's energy to fade out.

"—in taking him out of that home. They locked him in a room. That asshole you lobotomized beat him. Oh, I hope you're okay with hazelnut. It's all the corner place had left. So dusty up there, ya know? Like nothing but red rocks and dirt and mines. The virtual beach in the hotel was lame, could do that here. Why would they even put something like that on Mars? The lighter gravity was kinda cool, though. Hey wait, did you say demon?"

Nicole stopped with a dumfounded look and wide eyes.

Wow, not one word about what's-his-name. Either things must've gone south, or she's trying to be nice. Kirsten gave her the short version, leaving out the neurotic nightmare.

"I heard three marks means it's a demon." Nicole scratched the air as if using claws.

A weak laugh drowned in a long sip of coffee. "Hazelnut's fine. Coffee is coffee as long as it isn't decaf. That's a crime against nature. So yeah, once again, I feel as if all I can do is just sit here and wait for someone else to get hurt. Dorian doesn't think attachments persist after a spirit turns into whatever they are now."

Boots lifted, Nicole gave her chair a telekinetic shove. After rolling close enough, she patted Kirsten on the back. "Hey, cheer up. You'll find a way to—hey, I heard you put the car through the wall of a church? I know you're not a big fan of priests, but isn't that a bit much?"

Kirsten clutched the coffee with both hands, elbows resting on her desk. "I didn't drive into the wall. That was Evan, saving my life. I already told you the reason everyone else had problems with the car was Dorian possessing it. He had some anger issues to work out."

"Oh. Was it damaged much? Hey, check out these little Mars earrings." Nicole turned, showing off marble-sized Mars replicas hanging on either side of her head.

I'm surprised they're not being blown out to either side. "No, the little bugger hit the window pretty clean; armor made up for the error. Cute, they go with your hair. Nice and big for a perp to get a hold of and tear out."

"Is Dorian here? I don't feel the usual creepy vibe from his desk." Nicole squealed, clamping her hands over them. "I'm not gonna wear them on duty."

"He's resting, and you already are on" —the desk terminal beeped— "duty. Sec."

Samuel Chang appeared in hologram as Kirsten poked the button. His expression of confused determination melted away to a silly grin. The holographic version of her in front of him tinted his face faintly blue.

"Hi, Sam…"

Nicole flashed a coy smile.

He's just a tech, Kirsten projected the words into Nicole's head.

Sorry, I thought you might've found some—who's Konstantin?

Kirsten flushed crimson. *Not now. Please, just not now.* "What's up, Sam?"

Nicole shrugged and kicked off from the side of Kirsten's desk, rolling back to her workspace.

"I kept looking around for a better triangulation of the IPv12 you gave me," said Sam. "I got another active hit. Your boy seems to be logged in right now. I'm picking up a signal trace coming from Sector 848."

She almost sprayed coffee. "Sector 848? Tell me it's not #1998 City Road 130?"

"Wow, you really are psychic."

Kirsten leapt to her feet. "Thanks, Sam. I owe you one."

"Maybe lunch sometime?" Hope seeped from his smile.

"Yeah, sure."

Sam blinked. "Really? Where do you—?"

"Gotta run, Sam." Kirsten shut down the terminal and rounded the desk.

"Need a hand?" Nicole glanced up. A red light wailed behind her. "Never mind." She hurriedly removed her earrings and dropped them in a desk drawer.

"No, Nikki. Not sure you'll help much here and… you'll see stuff you don't wanna see." *They'll probably wind up making you turn on me.*

Driving alone felt wrong. Kirsten kept peeking at the empty passenger seat. Dorian had taken quite a beating in front of the church, sure to the point of being vulnerable to Harbingers—but none came for him. That calmed her somewhat, bringing up the question of justifiable homicide all over again. However, she didn't have the time or the inclination to ponder such things.

N0ra had lost Vikram's cyberspace deck, leaving it behind at the warehouse while fleeing in total panic. According to the reports, six of the security detail died in the chaos. Lorelei, the drug-boosted goth faerie, had taken a bullet in the gut and didn't even notice. Probably would've died if not for N0ra running and Kirsten calling it in.

Since the deck, as far as she new, currently sat in the Division 0 evidence room. If Vikram's digital fingerprint emanated from the blasted out building, it meant one of two things: either Vikram attempted to influence cyberspace directly, or Seneschal tried to lure Kirsten. The second option seemed the more likely, and all the more terrifying because she went there anyway. She pushed the patrol craft to the limit of her skill to control it, teasing at 400 MPH, and approached Sector 848 within a few minutes of leaving the PAC.

Silvery glass gleamed up ahead, except for where the bomb had scarred a ring of black around the high-rise. The story devoid of windows had darkened as though the sun couldn't breach it. Kirsten added a vertical drop to the patrol craft's forward motion. After levelling off at the thirteenth floor, she circled about once to survey the interior. Deep shadows concealed most of the interior, though she didn't spot anything alarming enough to scare her away. Upon locating a wide, clearing, she eased the vehicle in past dangling strips of aluminum window framing.

She ignored the scratching of metal and set the car down on its wheels. After shutting the car down, she pushed at the handle at her left. Nerves kept her in the seat despite the motorized door opening to full extension with a deep *clunk*. Kirsten ran a hand over the sheer fabric of her I-Ops uniform, staring into the dark ruin in front of her. *I miss the armor.*

Headlights chased away the shadows. Inside the building, it felt like the middle of night, despite it being barely ten in the morning. Nothing leapt out at her or even moved in the distance. Steeling herself, she grabbed the frame of the window and pulled herself up to her feet.

Her boots crunched on bits of charred debris as she navigated the shredded remains of a former apartment level. Charred furniture, the twisted frame of a file cabinet, computer pieces, trash, the occasional lightpen embedded like an arrow in a plasticrete column, all lay wherever the detonation dropped them. A glint caught her eye in a pile of ashes. She approached and squatted beside it, picking at a fragment of gold. She unearthed a jade earring, a flat square carved with a Japanese character. The image of Mariko's demonic face came to mind. Kirsten tried to imagine what she'd looked like in life. She brushed ash from the grooves in the kanji with her thumb.

"What a rotten end to a miserable life. For what it's worth, Mariko, I'm sorry. You didn't deserve what they did to you."

She tucked the earring into her pocket, not sure what to do with it. Dropping it felt wrong, keeping it felt wrong, and as far as Kirsten knew, the woman had no known relatives. *Maybe David Ling will know what to do with it.* Standing, she took her E-90 out and prowled.

Aside from the oddity of it appearing to be midnight in here, nothing seemed out of place. When she neared the silver ritual circle, the faint cries of a child wafted in the air. The second time she heard it, recognizing the voice stole her breath.

Shani.

Kirsten sprinted around the column and vaulted a mangled steel desk. The circle glittered as if in moonlight, despite solid plasticrete ceiling above it. Kirsten spun in place, turning amid the graveyard silence, but no crying child reached her ears.

Oh, no! They couldn't get to Evan past the blockade. How did they know about her?

"Shani?"

Another distant, muffled sob.

She ran toward the weeping, climbing over a thick debris pile by a bank of elevator shafts that had weathered the explosion with only minor denting. Behind them, a tangle of drywall, Epoxil planks, and other debris collected like sand against the pilings of a dock. She found no trace of a girl, a ghost, or anything but the unnatural dark. Kirsten leaned on an exposed metal stud in what used to be a wall to catch her breath, unnerved at how the city outside appeared to be in the throes of midnight.

A few minutes later, she paced around the circle. When she neared it, a sense of energy shifted within her body. The faint sensation reminded her of someone's hands passing millimeters over her skin without touching. *There's something here. I feel it. A breach? I don't see anything.* Memories of her flight to the Intera tower came back, those strange dark spots in the landscape below. She put the laser away and walked backward to the only intact desk on the entire floor. After taking a seat on the ground with her back against the metal, she closed her eyes and tried to calm down.

She focused on the sense of her spiritual energy within her flesh, isolating it, empowering it, and willing it out into the world. Like leaving a warm bed on a cold morning, the chill of the astral realm embraced the figure of amber light rising out of her body. Vague lines hinted at her curves, her form seemingly nude yet without explicit detail, a being of pure light. No sooner had she departed from her flesh than the great rushing sound of a waterfall overwhelmed her.

At the center of the silver circle, hung a gaping oval rimmed with ebon flames. Violent swirls of silver energy roiled around it, the center black. The deafening roar emanated from it, deep and thunderous. Against her better judgement, she floated closer.

The portal neither drew her in nor pushed her away. Despite the violent roiling energy about it, she had a feeling the portal had closed. White flames licked at the writing on the ground, evidence of infused power of some form she had never seen. She drifted sideways, following the circle but too afraid to cross it.

"This is how they got in... This must be a gate." Kirsten raised a glowing arm, fingers splayed. "I wonder if I can close it."

She hovered in an angel's pose, hands folded to her chest, feet together, head tilted forward, and reached out with her mind. It didn't take her long to connect with the energy permeating the distortion in space. The portal reminded her somewhat of the fused door in the asylum, only far more potent and much darker. Kirsten wrapped her power around it and strained. A chill washed down her body as if she had embraced a slab of onyx while naked. She grunted, twisting and struggling while attempting to move an object she had the strength to lift but found too cumbersome to handle alone. Evil rippled into her senses.

Every fiber of her being wanted to stop touching it, but she gathered her will and pressed on.

She pulled, twisted, pushed; a soft moan issued from her abandoned body a short distance behind her as if lost in a nightmare, the sound a pale echo of the determined scream coming from her astral self. The more she struggled, the heavier it became. Kirsten stopped, opened her eyes, and glared. A sheen of white glimmered over the glassy surface.

Of course. I'm trying to crush stone; I need to shatter it!

Blackness billowed up from the floor around the portal, flooding the inside of the circle with a column of standing smoke. Seconds later, a creature emerged. Nine feet tall, an elongated body of overlapping chitinous plates balanced on six long spindly legs. Six red eyes at the front end glowed, dying embers in a pit of ash. Four insectoid arms, two man-sized and two vestigial, reached for her. Kirsten shrieked and zoomed backward. A dark tendril lanced from its mouth, wrapping her astral form about the throat with the sickening feeling of a tongue so hot it burned.

The slimy tendril reeled her in close. Its larger arms had pincers which clamped around her by forearms while its tiny limbs ripped and clawed at her chest, filling her lungs with fire. Kirsten shifted her gaze up at the silver thread tracing in the air back to her body from between her eyes. *It knows.* The creature forced her arms apart, holding her so she could not reach the safety of her flesh.

She screamed from the pain in her chest and the searing tendril around her neck. Somehow, she managed not to panic at the idea a giant flea wanted to eat her. She kicked at it, her spongy foot thudding against its shell, as effective as it would have been kicking a car trying to run her over. The tongue squeezed her throat; she flailed, terrified at the gurgle emanating from her physical body.

The demon lurched forward all of a sudden, its six eyes snapping open wide in shock. Dorian crashed into its back, sliding up and over its curved shell. He reached past its eyes to grab its tongue in both hands as he fell down in front of it, swinging to use his weight, grinding the fleshy tendril into the creature's own transparent teeth.

Roaring with anguish, it hurled Kirsten through the floor. She tumbled in a disorienting blur as a number of furnished-yet-abandoned apartment spaces blurred past. When she stopped, she righted herself in the middle of a cluttered living room piled high with months of unwashed laundry. Six stray cats fluffed up and ran, knocking things over in their haste to get away from her.

Kirsten glanced at the ceiling, gasped for breath, and grabbed the cord at her forehead. Reality disintegrated into a smear of color. Her astral form lurched upward, colliding a split second later into her skin from below with enough force to knock her standing. Stumbling from the rapid shift from astral to mortal, she grabbed the column for balance.

Dorian whirled about on top of the gargantuan flea-like creature, a rodeo clown come to save the contestant. He smashed it in the side with his stunrod, the loud *click, click, click* of his simulated weapon striking its shell echoed in the cavernous space.

The monster twisted with a sharp jerk that sent it stumbling to the left, spear-like legs poking gouges in the plasticrete slab floor. Dorian lost his grip on its shell and flew forward into the creature's waiting pincers. Holding him by the legs, the beast swung him high overhead, then pounded him into the concrete floor.

"Oof!" barked Dorian.

It picked him up and did it again. Back and forth, it slapped him between the same two spots of ground six times. Ectoplasmic smears slid across the dust with each strike; Dorian rag-dolled in its grip.

Horror at what she witnessed paralyzed Kirsten for the better part of several seconds. This monstrosity towered over her, the top of its back all but scraping the ceiling when it extended its legs. Its shell glistened as if wet, traces of crimson tinted the material away from pure black around joints and seams.

Pure malice exuded from this monstrosity of hatred, filtering into her deepest consciousness that harkened back to childhood nightmares. Kirsten found herself tempted to find a Comforgel pad to hide under and scream for her Dad… but she managed to stand her ground.

The demonic beast leaned to the right, all three of its left legs lifting off the ground to add power to a swing intended to bash Dorian into the portal she could no longer see. Kirsten snapped out of her stupor, calling the lash as she ran in.

She whipped at its legs, wrapping the energy cord around them and pulling the demon off its footing. Dorian flew out of its pincers, the creature flailing its four arms wildly while emitting a shrill scream like plates of glass grating against each other. It careened over sideways. Hundreds of pounds of shell and hatred smashed to the ground. The creature loosed a gurgling polyphonic roar that sounded as if it came from eight mouths at once. Kirsten spun with the motion of her first swing and brought the lash straight down on top of its prone body. Once mild red light in its eyes flared orange. The astral whip didn't penetrate the shell, but slammed into it with great force, blasting a cloud of dust into the air around the creature. A loud *whump* from the hit sounded as though a two-ton object had fallen on the giant flea. Luminous orange liquid leaked from a crack in its shell. Flowing, watery lava broke into a shower of sparks, hissing and skittering over the cold concrete.

It flailed its legs, jabbing them at her. Kirsten yelped, dodging back from razor-tipped spears as thick as her thighs, studded with backward barbs. The monster flailed, scrabbling for purchase while emitting a roar so loud it shattered some windows on facing buildings.

Kirsten backpedaled to a safe distance and tried to catch a second wind. All the terror she'd poured into two lash strikes had drained her.

"Kirsten, help! It hurts!" Shani's tiny voice pierced the darkness from the left, breaking into sobs.

She whirled toward the sound. "I'm here. Where are you?"

No answer came.

Rage in her eyes, Kirsten raised the lash once more and faced at the ground where the demon had been, but it had disappeared. Halfway across the vastness of the gutted building, a cloud of inky smoke receded along the floor.

Dorian melted down from the ceiling and fell flat on his back next to her. "Well, that was certainly unique."

"Are you okay?"

"Oh, I'm fine." He folded his hands over his chest, not bothering to get up. "I'm not sure what it thought it would accomplish by smashing a ghost into the floor, plus I had a wonderful nap last night." He shifted his gaze to her. "Aren't you going to chase it?"

"No. I know how to destroy it." Kirsten pointed at the gate. "It'll return when I attack the portal it made. I have to find Shani first."

"What?" Dorian sat up. "Shani is here?"

Kirsten shivered. "I... think so. Seneschal, it has to be. Demons know what hurts you, and he couldn't get to Evan."

Dorian floated to his feet and put a hand on her shoulder, staring at her. "Don't let your emotions run away. Stay professional. You go right, I'll go left. Yell if you find her."

"Would you tell a man to control his emotions?" She smirked.

He didn't break eye contact. "Yes. Anyone who doesn't freak out at the sight of that thing isn't alive."

Shani's face floated over an aimed gun in her mind, her expression a mixture of amusement and horror. A simple suggestion would have ended the situation, but Kirsten had let the shock of a little girl pointing a gun at her cloud her mind. Demons would certainly exploit her weaknesses. The first time she found Evan in astral form, she'd wondered if he was a child ghost or a demon trying to trick her. *I knew I'd fall for that someday.* She took a breath of confidence, trying to convince herself she could distance her heart from her mind until the danger abated.

Kirsten readied her E-90. "Okay. Let's find her."

CHAOS

E phemeral pleas echoed around Kirsten in the voice of a child, always seeming just around the next column or pile of debris. She edged past a pile of junk, aiming her E-90 at empty ground.

"It has to be a trick. She can't be here. There's not enough places left to hide."

Dorian, on the other side of the building, yelled. "It's an entire level of an apartment building; we haven't been everywhere. Check floor vents."

Sudden motion came from her left. Kirsten whirled on it, weapon raised. Seneschal winked, and fired.

Kirsten flung herself to the ground, her cheek scuffing over grit-covered concrete. Crumbles of smashed plasticrete stuck to her face as she crawled behind a damaged conduit containing bundles of wire running between floors. Icarus rose straight up from the floor ten feet away behind her. He aimed a massive handgun, but hesitated.

Their gazes locked for a split second before Seneschal's bullets kicked up dust around her boots and sent her shrieking into a ball.

"What the hell are you waiting for?"

Icarus glanced at Seneschal. "This woman is not our objective."

"Did you forget her brat destroyed Mariko?"

Destroyed? Kirsten blinked.

Anger rippled over Icarus, white teeth stark against his face as he snarled. "Mariko... changed." He twisted his head about as if cracking tension out of his neck. "And the boy is not her blood. We should be focusing on Medhi."

"You've gone soft, Michael." Seneschal's boots echoed as he circled. "Did you forget she wants to send us *all* back?"

"Do we not deserve to go?"

Dorian whipped around the bank of elevator shafts, and fired a ghostly simulacrum of a laser pistol at Seneschal. Icarus ducked for cover behind a crumbling column and returned fire. Dorian twisted himself to the side at an inhuman angle, avoiding the shot. Seneschal dove into a forward roll, bounded back to his feet, and slid out of sight behind a huge stack of junk.

Kirsten sighted over the E-90, sweeping her aim back and forth over chair arms, table fragments, broken appliances, and chunks of plasticrete. *Which side are you gonna come out?* "It's not too late for any of you." She favored the left side.

"Oh, but it is." Seneschal emerged right under her gunsights.

As soon as he appeared, she put a blast of azure light through is face. He retreated, but she corrected aim and fired again into the junk. Judging by the angry roar, the laser had penetrated the debris and nailed him. She kept shooting, attempting to guess the route of his evasion. Alas, he didn't cry out again.

Behind her, Dorian and Icarus traded shots.

"Dorian, focus on the other asshole. Icarus, I don't think you're a lost cause like the others. There's good in you still."

"Nauseating." Seneschal sprang up from the floor beside Kirsten, and grabbed her right ankle.

She swung her arm to aim, the shot fouled as he twisted her boot with such force it rolled her onto her stomach. Dorian stopped shooting at Icarus, trading wary stares with him instead. Kirsten scrabbled at the ground, flinging dust and fragments of building material to the rear as she tried to crawl forward.

Seneschal dragged her backward by the leg, then pounced on top of her back. She pounded him in the crotch, an attack he ignored while yanking her head back by a fistful of hair to expose her throat.

"Don't have those anymore, blondie."

The scrape of a knife sliding from a belt sheath pissed her off more than scared her. She lit off a blast of psionic energy and blasted him with repelling force that launched him into a graceful arc. He crashed to the ground sliding on his back, and came to a halt belt-deep in a column.

"I am so fricking *done* with having knives at my throat," she roared, and stood.

Her indignant fury turned on a dime to fear when he floated up to stand, rifle appearing from thin air. She leapt over a broken wall, landing in a somersault behind a column amid a hail of deafening automatic weapon fire. She huddled down, arms over her face to shield it from a rain of plasticrete fragments.

The shooting paused, then resumed, but the debris no longer fell on her.

"Look who showed up to the party." Seneschal laughed. "You got your wish, Ic."

Kirsten risked a peek. Seneschal pivoted to the right, chasing Vikram with an unending stream of bullets as he sprinted between columns and junk piles. Icarus pursued Vikram on foot, while Dorian fired at Seneschal, who dissipated into a cloud of grey fog to avoid the shot. He rematerialized twenty feet away by a fragmentary wall, firing at Dorian from an unexpected angle.

A blast of white spectral energy erupted from Dorian's shoulder and chest. He howled, grabbed the spot, and fell out of sight. Kirsten reached for an empty holster, and then spotted her E-90 lying on the ground out in the open, near the handprints her somersault had left on the floor.

Icarus fired somewhere in the dark, the report of his enormous pistol knocked dust off the ceiling. An uneasy wail came from Vikram as he vanished behind a mangled interior wall. Kirsten jumped up, running at Seneschal while unfurling the lash from her outstretched arm. He saw her coming, but lacked the time to bring his weapon around at her. He ducked, backpedaling as she swiped at him. The seething tendril passed inches over his head.

His rifle vanished in a puff of greasy black smoke as his body billowed with silvery flame. Seneschal stepped through the veil into the physical world, catching her arm on the next downstroke. He spun her around and smacked her chest-first into a concrete post.

"Delicate little arm you've got, girlie." He twisted it higher. "Mariko broke it like a twig. What shall I do to it?"

Her cheek squished against the hard plasticrete, she struggled to get air back in her lungs.

Seneschal hauled her backward, swung her around, and tried to mash her face-first into a still-standing wall. Kirsten got a foot up in time. She ran up the crumbling surface, spun over his shoulder, and slipped out of his hold to land behind him. In the second it took him to process where she went, she swiped the lash across his back, burning a gash into his body as he whirled about to face her. Icarus appeared at her side, grabbing her with one hand at the throat, the other on her right wrist. Everything about his body said rage, except his eyes, which held regret.

He tore her away from Seneschal and flung her to the ground. She slid, spinning, over several small painful things before she came to rest on the edge of a debris mound that had to be made entirely out of sharp corners.

Yep. I miss the armor.

Seneschal slumped to the ground, clutching his gaping wound. Icarus stomped over to her. Conflict glimmered in his eyes, regret clashed with inflated rage. Vikram dashed between columns. The sight of him pulled Seneschal to his feet. His rifle appeared, and he fired a long, chattering burst that chewed up the column.

Vikram laughed. "Missed me again."

A thick mass of shadow gathered in the distance, eight dim red eyes focused on Icarus. Dorian fired at Seneschal, driving him to cover. Kirsten looked at Icarus, trying to make contact with the man he used to be. Momentary hesitation gave way to an emotionless expression. The eight glowing eyes grew brighter. Icarus stormed toward her. She scampered away, trying to get to her feet. Icarus lunged in and grabbed her around the throat, hauling her into the air one-armed. She clawed at his wrist, gasping for air. Sound plunged into blurriness, as if underwater. Her world became total silence except for the chittering whisper of the massive flea.

"Kill, kill, kill."

Icarus' hand squeezed tighter around her neck. A blackout approached, surely to mean death.

I'm sorry. She had no choice. Evan needed her to stay alive. Kirsten hastily gathered a lash and plowed it into him. The blast of psionic energy launched Icarus sliding away. She landed on her feet, stumbled, and fell to her knees gagging for air and trying not to vomit. Her mind ached; empowered by her fear of imminent death, the attack caused the same painful mental recoil she suffered from mind blasting the living. Icarus rolled into a heap, motionless on the ground, his flesh and clothing melting into a puddle.

"One down," Vikram cheered. "You are next, Desmond."

Kirsten dragged herself against a post, rubbing her throat and trying to get the dancing specks out of her vision. Hazy shouts and the constant rattle of gunfire echoed around her. She ducked down, gasping for a second wind. Dorian's surprised yell pitch-shifted as he flew past her like a missile. Kirsten groaned and forced herself upright, hiding behind a column. Vikram sprinted through it, and stood beside her.

"Bad man is coming," he whispered.

Kirsten edged two steps back. Vikram whirled to face his pursuer. He looked around as if searching for a hiding place. Seneschal appeared seconds later, raising his rifle with a dark grin.

"You're out of ammo. I counted. All 1,493 shots." Vikram pointed while backing away.

Seneschal chuckled, stalking after him. "Doesn't use ammo anymore."

Kirsten kept herself tight to the column, allowing Vikram to lure the mercenary past her. As soon as she had a clear shot at his back, she leapt from the shadows and raked the energy whip in a hard, downward swipe. The tip struck between his shoulder blades with a tangible *thump* that released a blast of whitish energy. Seneschal howled, back arched, up on tiptoe. Large chunks of his body disrupted into black flakes that floated away like ash on the breeze. She growled, remembering the dream, remembering the claws taking blood from Evan's defenseless throat. Dorian jogged out from behind a section of solid wall. The intensity of the lash made him pause, raising an arm to shield his eyes.

Kirsten swing again, the tendril fluttering in the air with a sound like roaring flames. Like a ten-foot-long energy sword, the lash sliced deep into Seneschal, entering at the shoulder and snagging on something at the center of his being. Kirsten pulled it taut, starling at this monster who would hurt Evan.

He clawed at the thread of light protruding from his chest, howling at racing cracks spreading across his armored vest.

All sound sucked into a vortex of silence. Kirsten's eyes leaked white fog as she thought of the look on Evan's face, the blood on his throat. Anger and grief mixed, flowing down her arm into the lash, which flared to a dazzling glow.

Seneschal detonated in a flash of white light and black smoke. Scraps of ash lingered on the breeze, some fluttering to the ground. A racing wave of energy spread out in a ring, shattering windows on the adjacent high-rises at the same story. The force of his obliteration knocked Kirsten off her feet, sending her sliding into a pile of collected metal scraps. The sound of glass shards raining to the ground outside continued for several seconds over the silence. Somewhere, far away, car alarms went off.

She lowered her arm to expose her face, no longer worried about debris. Icarus, still a puddle, moaned. Dorian surveyed the spot of floor where Seneschal had last been, shaking his head with disbelief.

Vikram peeled himself out of a mound of junk and grinned. "You did it! You got him." He approached, offering a hand.

Kirsten stood without his help. "Yeah, I did. You're forgetting something else. I found out about you. You're not a ghost, Vikram. You are the same as they were."

The out-of-his-element affect of a hacker in a warzone darkened to menace.

"Thousands of people died horrible, lingering deaths because of what you did for money. You played both sides, wearing a white hat by day and a black one at night." She circled him. "You know I have to send you back, too. I'm not going to let you hurt that girl. Desmond and Mariko already refused to accept their fate. Now, neither one of them exist in any sense of the concept. Don't make the same mistake, Vikram."

"Backstabbing whores, both of you." He leapt, clawing at her throat.

Kirsten leaned out from under it, recovering her balance. "She did what's right. The stain is on *your* soul for murdering the innocent. She may have been responsible for Lyris coming after you, but *you* pushed the button yourself. Seneschal's team didn't go in there to kill. You made this afterlife, and entered it by killing yourself."

"She violated the code." He leapt again, raking with claws.

A quick sideways dodge spared a deep wound, but he still scratched a tear down her uniform.

"Like you wouldn't turn on a fellow deck cowboy if someone offered enough money." Kirsten shifted her stance from retreating to ready, lash raised. "I guess you're not planning to go back where you belong without a fight."

"I belong right h—"

Dorian sacked him from behind, driving him into the ground and riding him like a surfboard for several feet. "I've been looking forward to this."

Vikram growled and whipped around with claws, but Dorian wrenched him over, struggling to contain him. Kirsten shifted, searching for an opening to sneak a lash in without hitting Dorian. Their grapple came apart; Dorian ducked a claw swipe and punched Vikram square in the side of the cheek, knocking him back several paces. The former shifted his gaze to the glimmering lash as Kirsten closed in, distracting him from Dorian's fist. The downward punch across the face knocked Vikram to all fours.

Kirsten feigned a swing to the right, and then whipped it back the other way, catching Vikram in the head and chest when he tried to dodge the fake-out. The hit knocked him on his back, his form faded translucent. He gasped, raking his fingers at the air, moaning.

"Either avarice and greed make weaker demons than hatred, or the crew got a piece of you when I wasn't watching." Kirsten stalked after him. "Last chance, Vikram. Do you accept the consequences of your life? Will go you back where you belong?"

He held a hand up in surrender, nodding. She relaxed.

His fearful stare went dark. He leapt. Kirsten yelped, startled. Vikram's mouth spread to inhuman width, packed with pointed teeth. She spilled over backward as they collided; warm drool and a lick of a tongue touched her throat before a prick of painful fang found skin.

Dorian's face rose up over Vikram's shoulder, brows jammed together in an angry glare. He'd seized Vikram by the shoulders, halting his dive. Kirsten shoved Vikram back with a quick mental nudge, and rolled out from under him. Dorian stepped into a spin, hauling Vikram around and throwing aside. Still lying on the ground, Kirsten swung her arm around and brought the lash down. The energy tendril split Vikram in half through the abdomen with a dazzling flash of blue-white light.

A demonic wail rose into the air as his severed lower half sank into an expanding black miasma. She shifted up to her knees and slapped the whip down once more, splattering what remained of his upper body into a detonation of hot, black ectoplasm. The energy wave from Vikram's obliteration fluttered her hair and washed over her on the breath of an icy wind. His destruction passed like a pleasant winter breeze. Either Seneschal had been far stronger or no windows remained anywhere in the area to break.

Kirsten relaxed her mind. The lash flickered and went out. She sat back on her heels, staring at the spot, tracing fingertips over a bloody scratch on her shoulder.

"Are you upset you had to do that, or upset you were wrong about him being savable?"

"Everyone's savable," she whispered. "They only have to want it."

He reached for her, valiant in his effort not to appear weakened again.

"Thanks." Kirsten stood, accepting his hand. "I'm not sure I have enough left for the gate."

"Help!" Shani's yell warped into a shriek of primal terror.

"I heard her that time." Dorian shot her a look.

Kirsten held up a fistful of three stimpaks, stuck between her fingers like tiny claws. She pulled the safety caps off one by one before stabbing herself in the thigh. A triple dose of synthetic adrenaline hit her with the force of a full night's rest. Almost.

"Yeah. I did, too."

SACRIFICE

A child's wail emanated from the far reaches of the blown-out thirteenth floor. At the corner of the building, a still-intact enclosure contained the stairwell. Kirsten sprinted up to it, frantically clearing debris away from the door. Expecting it to be stuck, she yanked hard on the handle, but leapt back with a squeal of alarm as the entire door fell toward her, free from its hinges. She kicked it to the floor, pulled her E-90, and stomped over the metal slab.

On the landing in front of the steps, a circle of black spray paint surrounded a small altar, the perfect size to hold a sacrificial seven-year-old. Lengths of blood-red rope dangled from metal eyebolts at each corner, waiting for a victim. Pictographs similar to the ones drawn around the silver circle etched the entire surface. Fortunately, the altar held only an ancient knife that gleamed in the feeble light of a solitary LED bulb dangling from a naked wire overhead.

Shani cowered against the innermost corner of the room, under the stairs. Smears of dirt stained her nightgown. She struggled, hands tied behind her back and ankles bound. A scrap of cloth hung loose around her neck, soaked wet where it had been used as a gag.

"Shani," whispered Kirsten.

The girl's shivering lessened. Her tear-streaked face lit up with recognition.

"Shani." Kirsten rushed over. "Are you hurt?"

"I don't think Seneschal did this." Dorian shook his head at the altar. "There's someone or something else we haven't seen yet. Maybe even a living person."

"I'm scared," Shani whined.

Kirsten picked her up, balancing the girl on one arm as she reached for the decorative knife to cut the rope. She stopped, hand two inches away.

"I... no, that just seems like a bad idea to touch that knife. I don't want that thing anywhere near you."

After carrying the girl out to where the patrol craft headlights created a bright spot in the unnatural night, Kirsten set her down, took a small utility cutter off her belt, and got to work on the rope binding the child's twig-thin legs.

"Who brought you here?"

"A man." Shani sniffled. "He put something over my head, I didn't see him."

Icarus gurgled. His puddle-self changed shape as if trying to drift closer.

"I'll call them in a moment." Kirsten stopped cutting for a second to look at him, cringing at the ghastly sight. She pushed down on the cutter, digging black cord into Shani's skin. "Damn. What the hell did they use? This thing has a Nano edge and it's not cutting."

"What?" Dorian leaned over.

"I don't see a knot in here, and this cord is laughing at my uti knife."

Dorian folded his arms. "I've never seen anything ignore those blades... except another Nano blade."

"Son of a bitch. There's a ton of paranormal energy in this cord." Kirsten pulled at it.

"I'm scared," whispered Shani, shivering. Her eyes widened, huge and brown. The sight of her stabbed Kirsten right in the heart.

Icarus's arm slurped out of the muck, dark flesh sliding off the bones in pink clumpy glops. "Aaaahhhhzzz..."

"Damn." Dorian looked away. "If there was only a way to take a picture of her face, we could get rid of violent crime for good."

"Damn it all. I'm not making a scratch. Let me check your hands." Kirsten leaned over Shani, tugging at pink sleeves to expose the cord binding her wrists. "Crap. The same stuff."

Impact struck Kirsten broadside from the left. She flew a short distance, falling into a painful elbow-to-knee roll across the concrete. As if time paused, Icarus hung in mid leap where she had just been, somehow having found the energy to reintegrate. Shani's head had enlarged into that of the flea-shaped demon, biting down where Kirsten's neck had been a second before.

The great demon burst forth from the diminutive shape it had assumed, standing with the screaming Icarus in its mouth. Great pincer arms seized him and rent him in half. Roaring, the monster hurled the upper body in one direction and legs another. Both remnants of Icarus splattered on the ground, little substance to them beyond puddles of black goo. The creature rotated to face her, emitting a growl, deep and inhuman, from its throat in both the world of man and the one beyond. Furnace heat billowed past its teeth, making her scoot back.

"He looks upset," said Dorian.

"Ya think?" Kirsten scrambled to her feet.

"I think I'm gonna sit this one out, too weak." Dorian looked at her, winked, and blurred into the car.

"Oh, nice, leave me alone with this thing…"

The demon's growl morphed into laughter.

A WICKED CASE OF FLEA

Concrete pylons slid from right to left in Kirsten's vision as she and the demon circled. Dust rolled by in glimmering clouds where it caught in the headlights. Long, thin projections from its chitinous back scraped the ceiling, making a grating scrape that rattled down her spine. In some bizarre way, this creature scared her less than a mortal with a gun.

Kirsten would feel no guilt for destroying this thing.

"So, you're an actual demon, huh?" She called the lash. "I was expecting something a little more... fiery. Maybe, you know, wings? Nice pecs or something. Not a six-ton flea."

I wonder if this is what Kincaid was talking about.

The demon's roar rose up to a screech, fell to a low frequency rumble, then to a lingering popping noise in the back of its throat. It stomped toward her, swinging a giant pincer arm in a sideways arc. She ducked. The enormous limb passed over her head and bashed one of the pylons, lofting a cloud of powdered plasticrete and leaving a trench of mangled rebar. It swung its massive body around and rushed at her, both arms grasping. Kirsten dove to the floor, spinning around on her hip while slashing down its side with the lash as it barreled by. The energy cord left a smoldering trail down its shell.

Unable to stop, the demon careened into a column headfirst, cracking it and causing the ceiling to buckle in that spot. She scrambled to her feet as the monster whirled around and charged again, swinging both of its big arms together in a downward whomp. She again dove to the floor, narrowly avoiding a crushing death. The demon snagged her by the boot in one claw when she tried to scramble away. Her hands scraped over debris as it hauled her into the air, swinging her around by one leg.

At the memory of how it pounded Dorian back and forth into the floor, she screamed, "Shit!"

Demolished apartment blurred into a haze around the demon's face as it swung her high into the air. She raised her left hand, focusing on the claw holding her boot. The instant it started to swing her down at the floor, she forced the claw open—and went flying. She came down hard on top of an old desk, a hollow *boom* echoing from her impact. The demon roared, waving its claw around as if it had grabbed a hot pan.

Kirsten slid off the desk as the demon came for her again. A panic-induced swipe of the lash missed high. The monster skidded into her, its body colliding with the force of a cargo truck. She bounced away and landed flat on her back. Before she could even moan in pain, it grabbed her ankle in one claw again, holding her upside down like an asshole uncle at a family gathering.

"You're really starting to piss me off," muttered Kirsten.

The demon spun, swinging her around and around, building up speed. Kirsten yowled in pain, her hip close to dislocating. Her clenched jaw cut off her scream. Again she seized on a sense of the demon's presence, a battle of wills. The demon shuffled to the side and slapped her into a column.

"Oof!" she gasped, momentarily unable to breathe.

It held her against the plasticrete and drew its other large arm back. The sight of the huge claw about to impale her broke her concentration. The pincer tightened around her boot; that foot went numb.

"Gah!" she yelled, swiping the lash at the huge flea's nose in a hasty attack meant more as a distraction. It roared again, shaking from side to side. Ignoring the confusion of dangling upside down and bouncing against the column, Kirsten flicked the whip again and again. The demon staggered backward, wailing in protest, trying to put a hand in the way to guard its face. She got the feeling her feeble strikes did little in the way of damage, but if the noises the creature made meant anything, she caused a great deal of pain.

Kirsten kept swiping again and again. Due to close range and its huge size, she couldn't possibly miss. Eventually, it spun and hurled her aside, emitting an enraged howl. She hit the ground on her chest, sliding over numerous painful bits of debris. Her spinning slide came to a halt against a pile of drywall slabs, which collapsed, burying her.

"Shit!" She shoved at the junk, trying to dig her way out.

Growling, the demon swayed in place like a cat about to sneeze. Its two tiny arms raked at its nose. She pushed at the debris trapping her, tossing hunks of ruined furniture aside. The great creature shifted and came stomping toward her. She screamed at its approach, struggling harder to free her lower body from the mountain of junk trapping her.

The creature set its six legs in a wider stance, face hovering low to the ground. Its mouth opened with a roar, exposing an orange furnace glow deep inside its body. Waves of scalding air blasted over her, rife with the choking rot of sulfurous decay. Flames winked into being on the drier bits of junk around her. Kirsten crossed her arms in front of her face to shield it from the burning gale.

After a few seconds, the roar—and searing wind—stopped.

"Damn," she said, coughing. "I don't think there's enough breath mints in the world."

The demon's six eyes narrowed.

Kirsten kept chucking debris aside, digging herself out. The demon lurched into a charge that shook the floor. More junk slid from the top of the pile. A slab of drywall cracked her over the head, shattering. She ignored it, flailing at the collapsing heap.

Sudden bright light flooded over the demon's right side. For a brief second, crimson flecks glowed from deep within its smoky transparent onyx shell—and the beast vanished with a tremendous crash. Demonic screeching warped to the right, the sound bending in the manner of a passing train.

Wham.

Flakes of concrete clattered as the floor, indeed the entire building, shuddered. More debris fell on top of her. Grumbling—more annoyed than scared—Kirsten continued shoving broken furniture and explosion-twisted appliances away. Eventually, she dragged herself free and stumbled back to her feet.

Favoring her right leg, she limped toward a rolling cloud of dust. The patrol craft's taillights resembled the eyes of an even larger demon in the mist, until she approached close enough to see. The enormous flea lay on its side, pinned between the front end of the armored hovercar and the metal-reinforced elevator enclosure. A spatter of luminous orange liquid streaked the wall above the creature, seeping out from cracks in its chitinous plates. Arcs of azure lightning leapt from wires at the ceiling to the hood. Glowing flecks spat in intermittent bursts from a power box between two shafts.

Dorian appeared out of thin air beside her, holding up a thumb. "Worked for the kid. Figured I'd give it a shot. One moment. I need this." He walked over to the electrical discharge and basked in it. Some of the sparks dimmed and stopped.

"Wow. I guess there *are* stimpaks for ghosts after all," said Kirsten.

He chuckled. "This much power leaking into the air isn't common. Surprised they haven't shut this place off."

"The one guy said they were going to film a holovid here."

Dorian shrugged and blurred back into the patrol craft. Plasticrete groaned and shifted as he backed up. The armored hood had a small dent from where the demon's arm smacked it.

"Holy crap. That thing dented the PC."

"Shit," muttered Dorian. "Now I'm mad."

The demon exhaled a deep labored moan, somewhere between agony and exasperation.

She gave her partner a worried look. "Are you feeling all right?" *He risked his security blanket, his home...*

He blurred from the driver's seat to stand at her side. "The old girl's tough... and it's just an armor panel. They'll replace it."

Scraping; stone on stone. The demon shifted, twisting to bring all its eyes to bear on Kirsten.

Dozens of middle-aged women appeared in a horseshoe around her, holding drinks and nicohalers. Her uniform vanished, leaving her naked, ass bright red and sore. The women pointed at her, laughing at her shame.

Kirsten frowned. "Mother only had six friends, not eighteen, and you forgot to shrink me into a kid. These old biddies aren't too scary at eye level." Anger filtered down her arm, making the lash glimmer. "I'm also not afraid of this anymore."

The illusion shattered. She lunged at the demon, the ribbon of energy coiling after her, aiming for its face. The gargantuan flea scrabbled at the ground, sliding away from her, forcing itself up onto its legs. She struck the whip at it the closest thing it had to a head, drawing forth an agonized roar that knocked more silt from the ceiling. Dorian took the sidearm from his belt and took a stance directly beneath the panel of snapping electrical arcs. Spectral energy focused, he projected attacks in the shape of laser blasts. The demon cringed from the strikes, though seemed to regard them as a nuisance.

"Damn. This thing is tough. Feels like I'm using a handgun on an A3V," muttered Dorian.

Kirsten raked the lash across its shell twice more. The demon stopped reacting with agony to her strikes. It turned toward her, lowering its head, and drifted closer on its long, spindly legs—oblivious to her attacks.

"Umm. Dorian… It's either really damn tough, or I'm not hurting it."

He gave up shooting it. "I can feel it doing something. It's got some kind of protection. Maybe we need to draw it away from the gate."

Kirsten backed up, stepping with care over hunks of mangled furniture. Her spine involuntarily clenched at the delicate crunch of glass under her boot. Dropping the lash, she held both hands up and focused her power at the massive insectoid horror. The demon shuddered, clawed leg-tips gouging the floor as it strained to force past her resistance. She closed her eyes, digging deeper for strength. The great demon shuddered to a halt, snarling and seething foul-smelling fumes.

They stalemated.

Konstantin seemed confident in my ability to stop this thing, but it's so damn strong.

"Dorian," she gasped. "What else can I do?"

"How should I know? Try some priesty shit?" Two more of Dorian's blasts bounced away.

Priesty shit? What does that even mean? Kirsten grunted. Fear of what this thing would do to Evan gave her a second wind. She pushed it back one inch, its six spiked legs engraving wavy trails in the plasticrete.

Its jet-black tongue lanced out, wrapping around and crushing her wrists together. Despite the searing-hot flesh at her skin, she widened her stance and pulled back. Her boots slipped in the dust, unable to stop her from sliding toward it.

"Back!" she screamed. "Back to the pits of hell with you! Get y—" Her voice became a wail of agony as the boiling-hot tentacle coiled up her arm and encircled her neck.

Her panic caused a surge in her power that pushed the demon back, though it merely dragged her along.

Dorian leapt in and grabbed the slimy tendril close to her wrists. A combat knife flickered into existence in his hand. "Put more feeling into it. Like, 'in the name of God I command you.' You know, something of that nature. Maybe demons only know Latin?"

I can't say that... I don't believe it. She scowled. *I'd feel so stupid.* The scent of her burning skin distracted her. The demon's tongue pulled her lean into a forward tilt.

A cry of exertion erupted from Dorian. He sawed at the tentacle with his knife. Of course, he didn't have an actual knife, merely focused his ghostly power into a cutting attack. Dorian's eyes glowed white. He let off a war shout like a barbarian from the Monwyn world, and ripped his blade downward. The slimy appendage broke apart, snapping in two directions like an enormous rubber band. One end whipped her in the face, the other shot back down the demon's throat.

The sudden absence of tension threw her over backward. Gagging on its own tongue, the demon fell into the closest its shape could approximate to sitting. Its shell-covered pointy ass punctured a two-foot hole in the floor.

"Hope no one lives in that apartment..." Dorian blinked at the damage, before running to Kirsten's side. "Oh, right. This whole building is abandoned. Damn. Demons are awful for property values."

Whimpering, Kirsten struggled to unbind her wrists from the still-boiling tongue. Severed from its owner, it took on a life of its own. The several-foot-long section dangling from her hands whipped at her head and face while the other end coiled ever tighter around her throat. Dorian grabbed the loose end and held it still. Kirsten braced one boot between her wrists and pulled her hands out of the rubbery cord, screaming in agony as layers of skin peeled off. Having lost its grip on her arms, the tendril squeezed as if to pop her head off. Kirsten held her breath, swatting at the abomination with a lash. It burst into a spray of black slime. Dorian jumped back, cringing in disgust.

The demon's four arms scrabbled at the floor, howling in rage. Great claws shredded long gouges in the plasticrete floor from its efforts to pull itself out of the hole its rear end made.

Blisters covered the back of her hands and red oozed around each wrist where the skin had melted. Kirsten clawed at her belt, dosing two stimpaks before shock wore off and she had to feel *all* the pain such a burn should cause. Her skin bubbled, blisters fading. She howled, as though her hands had been cut off and the stumps sealed with the same cauterizing fire that wreathed her neck. Dorian whirled at her shout, cringing at the realization of what she had done.

I'm a fucking idiot. Don't use stimpaks on burns. Day one of the training manual.

She shrieked herself hoarse, drifting into a delirium of endorphins. An army of microscopic machines destroyed scars, replacing melted skin with new tissue; she felt every single tiny biting mouth. *What did Konstantin say?*

His voice drifted amid the misery. "I'm sure you will be able to stop it, now that you know its name."

Its name. Her legs gave out from the pain and she swooned to the floor.

"Kirsten!" Dorian shouted. "It's loose."

Tremors in the ground, rumbling as it stomped at her. So much pain. *I don't want to move.* She thought about getting up, but couldn't.

"Mommy!" Evan's voice screamed in her imagination. It didn't matter that the voice came from her subconscious rather than the real boy—it motivated her all the same.

She sat up, once more focusing her psionic energy at the demon. Its charge became a forward stumble, her effort to halt the monster only slowing it. *Oh, he's pissed.*

"*Charazu!*" she screamed. "Your name is Charazu, and by that name, I command you back to the Abyss."

The demon faltered. In an instant, the battle of opposing forces went completely in her favor. Six legs swept out from under it like noodles in a hurricane. The massive body crashed straight down. Kirsten stepped toward it, pushing it back with her mind. Charazu burst into silver flames and slid twenty meters before crashing against the elevator bank. The resonant *boom* of crushed sheet metal echoed back from nearby buildings.

Kirsten forced herself to stand and staggered after it. "Charazu, you have no power in this world. I cannot allow you to remain here."

She whirled the lash around once above her before slicing it straight down. This time, the scintillating energy cord split the shell wide open, cracking it like brittle onyx. Charazu wailed. Its formerly menacing growl had an air of pleading. Legs and arms flailed, a remnant of its tongue lolled out past jagged teeth, spraying black gunk.

"Charazu, I consign you back to the Abyss."

Kirsten put her hands together, gripping the lash like a two-handed sword. She whipped it around and swung it sidelong into the giant flea. The whip burrowed deep into the massive body, melting a trench in its shell like a mining laser chewing up stone. Power welled out of her mind with an unsettling feeling like an impaled knife withdrawing from a head wound. Her power spike rode down the lash as a small swell of energy that disappeared into the demon. Seconds later, what remained of Charazu detonated in an explosion of gore and shell fragments.

"Back to the Abyss!" shouted Kirsten

Only a black splat mark remained where the demon had been. She sagged to her knees. Piece by piece, fragments of shell liquefied into puddles of tar. Before long, they became watery and appeared to soak into the concrete. Faint wisps of energy exuded up from the splatter, curving in midair before hurtling into the portal she couldn't see. Blood dribbled over her upper lip, the worst nosebleed she ever had. One hand to her face, she sat back, too tired to breathe.

Dorian approached. "Kirsten... look."

She turned. The portal flickered into view, silent roiling energy at its edges.

Her trembling hand wobbled before her eyes. The effort to use her power came on with the sensation of needles in the brain. More blood seeped between her fingers. *I couldn't bash it... it looks so much like glass.*

"Dorian..." Kirsten crawled over the dusty debris-strewn mess until she found a length of rebar. Clasping it with her bloody hand, she smeared her blood on it while drawing the metal and its astral echo together. It hurt to use even that minor power, but far less than a lash. Her blood soaked into the steel, leaving the bar clean.

"Got it." Dorian took the bar and approached the gate.

Kirsten put both hands over her nose to stem the tide of blood. *Damn stimpak case is empty.* A great shattering rumble broke the stillness. The delicate twinkling of glass combined with the blast of a bomb going off. Spectral winds ripped past, whipping her hair. She lacked even the strength to raise her arms over her face. Dorian slid to a halt on his back next to her, a surprised expression on his face. The rebar in his hand had bent into a curve.

"Well... it broke." He tilted his head to smile at her, not bothering to sit up.

The unnatural darkness lifted from the shattered space, allowing early afternoon daylight to wash over them.

She stared up at the ceiling, with little desire to move. *The sun is so warm.*

41

ACCEPTANCE

Kirsten lay still for some minutes, chest on fire, wrists sore, neck burning, and a rod of pain impaled in her mind. Dorian grunted and managed a slight manifestation—enough to rub her shoulder. She sniffled.

"Why are you crying?" He squeezed.

"I…" She looked at him. "I'm having those silly thoughts again."

Dorian chuckled. "Partners often have a close bond, but it's different than lovers. You deserve a live person. I will never be there for you in the way a living person can be. I'll always be at your side, but I can't be what you need."

Kirsten shrank into herself, offering a reluctant nod. "Yeah… I know. I still love you though, even if it isn't *that* kind of love."

"I'm ready," said a deep voice.

She rolled her head to the left, and peered up at Icarus. He'd somehow managed to scrape himself back together, though he appeared weak. He swayed as if standing took all his concentration. She asked Dorian for help with a look and he pulled her to her feet by her grip on the bound rebar.

"Thank you for saving my ass. I'm sorry it's this way for you, Icarus."

He chuckled. "Michael. Please, call me Michael. I can't argue I did a bunch of awful shit in life. I wound up where I belonged. No sense bemoaning it. I just don't have the stomach for it anymore. Honor and valor and all that... Damn corporations don't have any of it. Go ahead and call me a taxi, eh?" He closed his eyes.

"Admitting it is a start. I don't know how it works down there but... there's hope."

She beckoned.

Dorian squeezed her hand as the mood changed. Within a moment, the area filled with whispering darkness. Michael nodded at the sound of myriad whispering. He held his arms out.

"Come, I am ready to go."

One large Harbinger exuded from the mass, gliding up to him. It matched his arms-wide gesture and leaned its vaporous head back. Kirsten, still clinging to Dorian to stay on her feet, bowed at it as much as her pain allowed.

Michael took a step closer to it, but the Harbinger lowered its gaze before sliding backward and rejoining the rolling wall of darkness, leaving Icarus to stare at Kirsten with a quizzical look. She shared his confusion, more so when a shimmering cloud of silver unfolded in the air. The light spread outward from a point, causing the mass of Harbingers to recede further.

Ribbons of silver energy emerged from the center, spreading up and to the sides in a shape semblant to wings. Between them, the body of a woman faded into focus. Alabaster skin glowed with blinding purity; long white hair streamed behind her, lofted by an intangible wind. She wore nothing aside from light, strands of it wrapped about her body like the robes of a Greek statue.

"Michael Coley, twice you have accepted your proscribed fate, and you chanced oblivion to spare the life of one who you once considered enemy." The woman gestured, and a silver-rimmed doorway opened.

Beyond it waited a man, similar in appearance to the floating woman, only his wings resembled feathers made from fire rather than strips of glowing white energy. He bowed in a welcoming way as more people, perhaps Michael's ancestors, faded in around him.

Michael took a step back. "There are more deserving souls than I."

"A determination you have not been tasked with making." The floating woman smiled.

He bowed, his body bolstered. No longer appearing hurt or weak, he vanished into the doorway, which collapsed around him.

Kirsten stood stock still, making no sound other than a mild squeak when the strange woman faced her.

"...Angels?" Kirsten whispered.

"You must have questions, though my time here is short. Know that I am a being of energy. I am mercy. Your kind once called us Seraphim, but such a word only brings to mind a concept not fully understood to the minds of mortals. Such ideas can be tainted by belief, twisted by men for their own ends."

She remembered a wispy tendril of light appearing behind her seconds before she smashed into the advert droid. "Thank you."

The woman floated higher, energy ribbons spread to the sides. "We are guardians of another world who stand against the ancients who dwell within the Abyss. Our kind are not necessary in the realm of humanity. My presence here is an after-shadow, permitted by Charazu's trespass. Kirsten Wren, we have chosen you as our instrument in this place, a warden between worlds."

I guess that's why you keep saving my dumb ass.

The Seraphim smiled as if hearing her thought, and reached a hand to rest atop Kirsten's head. "Indeed, but we have limits, and you have more to do. Darkness comes, be ready."

———

HEAD SPINNING, KIRSTEN FOUND HERSELF FLAT ON HER BACK, PAIN AND fatigue gone. When a bright light jabbed her in the eye, she flung her arm up and squinted past it at a blue helmet around a silver visor.

"She's alive." A man's voice crackled from a speaker on the helmet.

Division 1 officers milled around the area, as well as a small number of forensic techs. Captain Eze emerged from another all-black patrol craft and jogged over. Kirsten looked down at herself, finding no trace of injury aside from the dried blood on her hands.

"Kirsten..." Eze came to a halt at her side, helping her up. "Your bio monitor sent a distress call... we all thought..."

She stretched, examining herself. "Yeah, I got my ass kicked again but... Nothing ten stimpaks couldn't handle." Kirsten picked at the empty belt case.

"What happened?"

"Let's just say I'm probably going to wind up in Burckhardt's office the morning after you send my report up the ladder—assuming I didn't just dream all this."

"That bad?" He raised an eyebrow.

"No, that *weird*." She glanced at the runic circle.

The immutable silver lines had become trails of powder eroding away on the wind.

42

NEW FRIENDS

Kirsten fidgeted, seated on a bench at Sanctuary Park. She couldn't remember the last time she'd worn a skirt, and the thigh-length grey fabric let an awful lot of cold air in where she didn't much like it. Nila sat to her left, picking at a salad, enjoying the bright Saturday morning. Evan and Shani ran in giggling circles on the grass in front of them, weaving among bio-engineered trees and piles of leaves. Somewhere, a dog barked.

"Cross your legs." Nila laughed, then demonstrated. "You're not supposed to sit like a man when wearing a skirt."

"This was your idea." Kirsten crossed her legs. "I hate these things. I feel as if I'm walking around pants-less."

"You got panties on, don't you?"

Kirsten blushed. "Of course. What kind of question is that?"

Nila munched away, the scent of ranch dressing on her breath. "I adore the freedom. I'm stuck in that damn armor all day long, rides up."

Kirsten giggled—which got Nila laughing.

"So…" Nila lowered her voice. "How did it go with the hearing?"

Kirsten folded her arms, gazing at her lap.

"Oh, no."

"It's not bad news." Kirsten straightened. "The hearing hasn't happened yet. I'm worried sick. The caseworker interviewed Evan a few days ago. He said it went fine, but I can't help but expect everything's going to go wrong. I don't want to lose him."

"They cleared me for duty again."

Kirsten clung to Nila's arm. "That's great."

They both glanced over at Evan's cry of glee. He flew about in the pose of a superhero, lofted by Shani's telekinesis. The girl turned in a slow rotation, her face dour with concentration.

"Having a telekinetic daughter must be... interesting." Kirsten finally took a bite of her turkey wrap. "At least they seem to like each other."

"I almost fainted the first time her toys put themselves away. You know, it's kind of funny," Nila said, sounding more sad than amused. "We both wound up with kids we never expected."

Kirsten squeezed her shoulder. "I'm so sorry Nila; the way Dorian made it sound, I thought you were..." She cringed.

Nila's eyes widened. "Oh, I can imagine how bad he made it sound. I was dating this guy and he was... well." Nila sighed. "He started off nice but turned into a controlling ass. So, I left him. He made threatening calls, kept following me. I never told him I was pregnant. He almost beat me to death when I wouldn't take him back." She scowled. "My own damn fault for not wanting to burn him."

"Oh..." *Dammit, Dorian, you made it sound like some guy raped her and made her pregnant.* "Dorian said he killed him for it."

Nila stared into the grass for a long few minutes, the distant giggles of children a surreal backdrop to the current topic. "I see. Well, that explains why he stopped bothering me. He would have eventually killed me, or Shani. I don't feel sorry for him. Attempted murder on police personnel is usually a death sentence anyway. Besides, I probably would have done it myself eventually. Pyrokinesis gets scary in moments of primal fear."

Kirsten shifted, picking at her skirt.

"I know you're squishy about killing and all. Not everyone is as sweet and innocent as you are. I won't feel guilt over killing someone who's trying to kill me or hurt Shani."

"Mmm." Kirsten couldn't help but stare at Evan, grinning as he flew in circles. "You heard they got Rene?"

"Yeah, it was foolish of you to go in there after him, but I appreciate it." Nila grinned, returning Shani's wave as she darted about. "So, I hear you're dating some millionaire playboy?"

"Konstantin isn't hurting for credits." Kirsten giggled, a trace of blush in her cheeks. "Or looks. And I'm not so sure we're 'dating' really."

"Did you or did you not go on a date with him last night?"

Kirsten held out her right arm, showing off a glittering gold bracelet shaped like a serpentine dragon with ruby eyes. It closed by eating its own tail.

Nila held her friend's arm, tilting the jewelry in the light. "Wow. He's either loaded or really interested."

"He's showing off. The place we went to cost like two grand per plate." She fidgeted, a guilty look evident. "It doesn't feel right."

"Something wrong with him?"

She cradled the bracelet to her chest, staring at her lap. "Oh, no! He's perfect. It's just that… There's so many people in the city who can't afford to eat. I can't not feel like a horrible person for wasting so much money on food."

"You look like you're smitten, that glint in your eyes. Besides, it's not your money."

Kirsten waved at her. "Oh, come on. You know what I mean."

The boy flew over a tree, waving at them.

"Evan!" yelled Kirsten. "Sorry. Shani, not so high please."

"So, how did you meet this perfect man?" asked Nila.

"Would you believe there are only three people in the entire world who have an understanding of ancient Sumerian pictographs?"

"What's that?" asked Nila.

"A form of writing."

Evan shouted in the distance. "Race ya!"

"No fair!" wailed Shani. "You got a head start."

Giggling, Kirsten idly twisted the gold serpent around her arm. "He helped me kick a demon back to the Abyss."

Nila's eyebrows went up. "He's okay with all the weird stuff?"

"Oh, yeah." Kirsten gazed into the sky, an adoring smile on her lips. "He's quite comfortable with all that stuff. For a non-psionic, he has a surprising amount of knowledge of spirits and such. Guess it's a hobby."

Evan's gleeful run slowed to a stumble, then to a halt. Shani collided with him, knocking him forward a step. He froze in place, staring into the thick cluster of trees and bushes bordering the grassy area where they played.

She tugged at his arm. "What's wrong?" She peered at the same spot, then scrunched her face at him. "What is it?"

The boy stared into the woods for a few seconds more before grabbing Shani's hand and running toward the bench, pulling her along.

"Mom!" He skidded to a stop in front of her, face pale and eyes wide, his arm curled protectively around his confused playmate. "There's something watching us!"

---

fin

Kirsten's story continues in book 3 - Thrall.

Agent Kirsten Wren has her fair share of demons to deal with—and some are literal.

Despite discovering the world beyond death is more complicated than simple ghosts, she's almost got her life in order. Her effort to adopt Evan appears to be on track, no one's tried to kill her for a whole week, and most unbelievable of all, a billionaire is in love with her.

Kirsten's bleak childhood has left her with great contempt for the wealthy and a deep mental scar that makes intimacy terrifying. Konstantin's high-society world is not for her, but thoughts of leaving him make her physically ill.

A series of murders with ritualistic overtones leads her to suspect someone's using paranormal means to destabilize the nation. Stuck between her tortured past, an even scarier future, and a government doubting her stories of the Abyss, she has a mere week to find the killer before all hell breaks loose.

However, the demons are far closer than she expects.

ACKNOWLEDGMENTS

Thank you for reading Lex De Mortuis, book two in the Division Zero series!

Additional thanks to Brandy Yassa for her help proofreading the revised edition.

ABOUT THE AUTHOR

Originally from South Amboy NJ, Matthew has been creating science fiction and fantasy worlds for most of his reasoning life. Since 1996, he has developed the "Divergent Fates" world, in which *Division Zero, Virtual Immortality, The Awakened Series, The Harmony Paradox, and the Daughter of Mars series* take place. Along with being an editor at Curiosity Quills press, he has worked in IT and technical support.

Matthew is an avid gamer, a recovered WoW addict, Gamemaster for two custom RPG systems, and a fan of anime, British humour, and intellectual science fiction that questions the nature of reality, life, and what happens after it.

He is also fond of cats.

Visit me online at:
  Facebook: https://www.facebook.com/MatthewSCoxAuthor
  Amazon: https://www.amazon.com/author/mscox
  Pinterest: https://www.pinterest.com/matthewcox10420/
  Goodreads: https://www.goodreads.com/author/show/7712730.
Matthew_S_Cox
  Email: mcox2112@gmail.com

OTHER BOOKS BY MATTHEW S. COX

Divergent Fates Universe Novels

Division Zero series

- Division Zero
- Lex De Mortuis
- Thrall
- Guardian
- Harbinger
- The Shadow Fixer
- Neuroshock

The Awakened series

- Prophet of the Badlands
- Archon's Queen
- Grey Ronin
- Daughter of Ash
- Zero Rogue
- Angel Descended

Daughter of Mars series

- The Hand of Raziel
- Araphel
- Ghost Black

Virtual Immortality series

- Virtual Immortality
- The Harmony Paradox

Prophet of the Badlands Series

- Prophet's Journey

- Prophet's Mercy

Divergent Fates Anthology

(Fiction Novels - Adult)

The Roadhouse Chronicles Series

- One More Run
- The Redeemed
- Dead Man's Number

Faded Skies series

- Heir Ascendant
- Ascendant Unrest
- Ascendant Revolution

Temporal Armistice Series

- Nascent Shadow
- The Shadow Collector
- The Gate to Oblivion
- The Queen of Discord
- The Burning Alchemist

Vampire Innocent series

- A Nighttime of Forever
- A Beginner's Guide to Fangs
- The Artist of Ruin
- The Last Family Road Trip
- The Phantom Oracle
- How Not to Summon Demons
- Ordinary Problems of a College Vampire
- A Vampire's Guide to Surviving Holidays
- An Introduction to Paranormal Diplomacy
- A Vampire's Guide to Adulting

- How to Stop a Vampire War in Six Easy Steps
- Ancient Vampire Death Cults and Other Annoyances
- Hunting Vampires for Fun and Profit
- A String of Seriously Unlucky Events
- The Summer of Completely Usual Strangeness
- Demonic Crisis Management for the Modern Vampire

Standalones

- Wayfarer: AV494
- Axillon99
- Chiaroscuro: The Mouse and the Candle
- The Spirits of Six Minstrel Run
- Sophie's Light
- The Far Side of Promise anthology
- Operation: Chimera (with Tony Healey)
- The Dysfunctional Conspiracy (with Christopher Veltmann)
- Of Myth and Shadow
- The Girl Who Found the Sun

Winter Solstice series (with J.R. Rain)

- Convergence
- Containment
- Catalyst
- Catacombs

Alexis Silver series (with J.R. Rain)

- Silver Light
- Deep Silver
- Silver Quarrel
- Silver Crucible
- Silver Heart

Samantha Moon Origins series (with J.R. Rain)

- New Moon Rising
- Moon Mourning

- Haunted Moon

Vampire For Hire series (with J.R. Rain)

- Moon Master
- Dead Moon
- Lost Moon
- Vampire Destiny
- Infinite Moon
- Vampire Empress
- Moon Elder
- Wicked Moon
- Moon Blade

Maddy Wimsey series (with J.R. Rain)

- The Devil's Eye
- The Drifting Gloom
- Dark Mercy
- Primal Wrath

Samantha Moon Case Files series (with J.R. Rain)

- Blood Moon

Immortal Operative (with J.R. Rain)

- Broken Ice
- Broken Wing

Four Elements series (with J.R. Rain)

- The Elementalist
- The Black Rose
- The Wakefield Curse

Witches series (with J.R. Rain)

- The Witch and the Hangman

Zeb Clemens series (with J.R. Rain)

- The Beast of Devil's Creek
- Wanted: Undead or Alive

Young Adult Novels

The Eldritch Heart Series

- The Eldritch Heart
- The Cursed Crown
- The Sapphire Soul

Evergreen Series

- Evergreen
- The World That Remains
- The Lucky Ones
- Nuclear Summer
- The Nuclear Frontier
- The World We Make
- The Threat Unseen

Progenitor Series

- Out of Sight
- Out of Mind

Diary of a Teenage Fey

(Short story series)

- Elder Horror
- The Hag of Barrow Falls
- Babysitter's Nightmare
- Lharakki
- Bauble for a Soul
- Simulacrum

- Amorphous
- Manticore

Middle Grade Novels

www.ingramcontent.com/pod-product-compliance
Lightning Source LLC
Chambersburg PA
CBHW051944240626
47153CB00005B/1625

* 9 7 8 1 9 4 9 1 7 4 1 7 5 *